SMOKEPIT
FAIRYTALES

Tripp

This book is dedicated to the men and woman of the First Marine Division, service members everywhere, and the Veterans of Iraq and Afghanistan.

CONTENTS

ACKNOWLEDGMENTS

Thank you to Parker Chlovechok, Erin Shaw, Christopher O'Quin, and to all the regulars at smoke pits and smoke decks, bars, and Sailors, Marines, Soldiers, and Airmen around the globe for inspiring the nonsense put together in this story.

1 THE PURPLE CHURCH

How damn long is this patrol going to be? I thought as the sand crunched under my boot. *Fuck Now Zad, fuck Sangin, and fuck Afghanistan.*

The sun melted my platoon as we walked along the wadi. My legs ached from carrying about a hundred pounds of ammunition over the last week. I didn't even bother looking at the ground anymore. *If I step on an IED, at least I'll be done carrying this bullshit. How fucking long have I been here?*

The further away from the FOB we walked, the more the sand transitioned to a fine powder. Moon dust is what we called it. A cloud of dirt trailed the patrol bathing us in a golden light as day soon gave way to twilight and the sun set over the mountains. The sight was beautiful, but the call to prayer made things eerily quiet.

We circled Sangin's outskirts. The moon rose. The mud huts seemed to grow into towers of steel. The Afghans watched us from a distance. Their skin was rotten. They treated us in the same regard as they would a wild animal in their fields. A hint of fear, but mostly indifference.

Sergeant Fowler stopped the patrol and we bedded down for the night. I dropped my pack and pulled out my poncho. It was still too hot for a sleeping bag. I left my boots on and curled up with my rifle. I tried to think of Satin and her beautiful eyes. It would help me sleep. I dreamed of the beach and the day we met. As I dozed into the realm between sleep and awake I felt something under the poncho with me. I ripped the blanket away. A demon was on top of me! His beard was long and dark covering a feral gaze, his skin tighter than wet leather, and his eyes pierced my soul. The monster released an evil screech from his dragon-like mouth.

I screamed myself awake. Wearing only a thin layer of sweat and my tattoos, I scanned the room. I was in my girlfriend's bed in Oceanside.

"Baby, are you alright?" Kennedy grogged, turning to face me in bed.

"Yeah…" I panted. "I just had a nightmare." I put my head back on the pillow.

"Back in Afghanistan?" she asked.

"Something like that."

I waited for Kennedy to fall back asleep. When I was sure she was off in her Persian dreamland I put on my patch jacket and jeans and slipped outside. I lit a Lucky's and texted Doc to come get me for breakfast.

Doc's blue 1972 Mustang pulled around the corner of Wisconsin Avenue a few minutes after the sun broke the mountains' crests. I fell into the passenger seat. "Sup Doc."

"Not much, man," he said as he reached to open the passenger door. The engine roared and we shot down the street.

I tried to shake the memory of the nightmares, Satin, and demons.

"What do you think would happen if we were invaded by aliens?" I asked, looking at the trees passing us through the window.

"You mean like that one?" Doc pointed to a grotesquely overweight Latina in spandex pants, which clung for dear life around her flabs.

"No, like green and from Mars or something, the truth is out there kind of alien. That fat bitch right there needs to be eaten by wolves."

Doc laughed. "Yeah, how do you let yourself go like that?"

"She probably got that way eating extra food from the seventy-six cats she keeps in her house, and laying around reading *Twilight* instead of doing something productive, like killing herself," I replied.

"You ever pinned a hog like that before?"

"Listen, I'll jump on a grenade for a friend now and again, but that doesn't mean I go trolling the circus."

"Is that why you like the Purple Church so much?"

"Hey now, Kennedy's fucking hot," I defended my girlfriend. "Just because they have to ask you for tips doesn't mean it's not a classy establishment."

Doc looked over at me. "Dude, the dress code allows for sweat pants."

"Eh."

Doc continued, "And hey, our girlfriends work there. And they're hot."

"Only on the outside, Doc. Those bitches have twisted souls."

"Hey now, Reagan's not that bad."

"Doc, you couldn't even say that with a straight face because you knew you were fucking lying!"

We laughed for a bit before Doc brought up, "We should go see them tonight."

"Why the hell wouldn't we?"

Reagan and Kennedy were part of the "Presidential Entourage" at the local strip joint. Kennedy, Nixon, Reagan, and Bush's ensemble had a patriotic show they put on Sunday nights—you know, for the troops. The Purple Church was the trashiest strip club I'd ever seen, at least in the States. When the girls were done dancing they'd walk around the room and come up to your table and ask you if you watched them dance and stand there until you gave them money to leave. I'm not saying that the girls there weren't attractive, but I had seen more class in a Thailand whorehouse.

I looked over at Doc. "You know what time they go on?"

"No man, ask them."

I sent Kennedy a text and put the phone back in my patch jacket.

We cruised down Highway 101 through Oceanside. The town was a palace built out of 1950s nightlife and surf riding that the citizens neglected to care for over the last sixty years. The movie theatre had stickier floors than a Hong Kong porno shop and the bars were dusty and run down. The civilians were either burnouts or punks sporting their *swag*, and everywhere you went there were roaming packs of Marines still in infantry school with their overly motivated backpacks and high and tights. The restaurants were all right.

Doc pulled the Mustang into the 101 Café's parking lot. The white building had a bright red roof and big bay windows. The tabletops and counters were stainless steel, all with red trim. It was a true old-fashioned burger and shake place. Oceanside's history hung in black and white photos on the walls. Some were of the restaurant from as far back as the thirties.

We sat at a booth by the window.

"Hey trouble." The waitress put down a coffee for me.

"Hey what's going on, Rachelle?" I asked.

"Oh you know, livin the life," she said as she pulled out her notepad. "Know what you want yet? Maybe start you off with a drink?" she asked Doc.

"Wait. Why'd you bring him coffee and not me?" Doc asked.

"Because he comes in here five times a week and always orders the same thing."

I grinned like an asshole at Doc.

Doc gave me an unamused glance.

"What?" I shrugged.

"Nothing." Doc put down the menu and looked up at Rachelle. "So you have to put up with his shit as much as I do?"

"Yeah, but he tips well."

"Just the tip?"

"Ha ha very funny. You gonna order anything?"

"Yeah…" Doc scanned the menu. "Gimmie a Denver omelet."

"Coffee?"

"Please."

Rachelle disappeared behind the counter.

I stirred cream into my coffee, blurting the first random thought that came into my head. "I want an M16 that shoots burning cigarettes at people."

"How would that work?" asked Doc.

"I dunno. Some mechanism that lets me jam a pack of Lucky's into the well instead of a magazine and a lighter inside of the receiver."

"And that would work how?"

"Fucking science dude!" I exclaimed.

Rachelle placed Doc's coffee on the table. "You two need anything else?"

"No thank you." I smiled.

"Speaking of that, I think I should quit smoking."

"Really Doc?" I threw my spoon on the table. "That's a *fucking* terrible idea."

"How is quitting smoking a terrible idea?"

"That's how you end up homeless!"

"Hank, what in the *fuck* are you talking about?"

"Think about it man." I pointed at Doc. "First you quit smoking, but you don't *just* quit smoking, you wean yourself down. You don't buy any smokes, you just bum them off people so you have this illusion of quitting because you're not buying any. Then you do the same thing with beer, then your rent. Then you're sleeping on someone's couch smoking re-burns and licking drops of High Life out of bottles in an alleyway. Next thing you know you're under a bridge giving out blowjobs to hobos for sandwiches so you don't starve to death. All because you tried to quit smoking."

Doc shook his head. "That better be a damn good sandwich."

"Suck the right dick and you can get a double bacon with cheese."

"Maybe that wouldn't be too bad then." We both laughed.

Rachelle walked up with our food. "Call me if you need anything else."

I opened a packet of jelly and smeared it on my toast.

"I think she wants your dick."

"Doc," I leaned in closer to him, "They *all* want my dick."

"*All* of them?"

"Oh yeah. They just don't all know it yet."

"Yeah, that's definitely not something a serial rapist would say."

"Just because I banged a chick that looked like the leprechaun from the Lucky Charms box doesn't mean I'm a cereal rapist."

"What?" Doc started laughing.

"It's not rape if she's on top!"

"Why do I take you into public?"

"Because you need mobile entertainment." I poured the grits over my eggs. "Did I ever tell you about the time I dressed up like a pirate and Dick

10

dressed up like a ninja and we got foam swords and had a duel at the barracks?"

"No, how'd that go."

"We ended up accidently pushing the A-duty down the stairs and got free barbeque from some dudes on third deck."

"Cool story bro," Doc huffed. "Now shut up." Doc started to chew his food. "Do you think leprechaun shit is rainbow colored?"

I replied, "No, but it tastes like Skittles."

"How do you know that?"

"Well, you see…"

He stopped me, "Wait, I don't want to know."

"No, you remember that redhead though, right?"

"Midget with the short hair."

"She wasn't a midget."

"She was like four foot ten," Doc insisted.

"*Anyway*, she took me to her parents' place while I was on leave one time. Her mom needed her for something so she stepped out of the room, leaving me with her dad. *This guy* has the audacity to ask me this stupid ass question. Keep in mind his daughter is like twenty-five at the time. He says, 'So, have you been playing hide the salami with my daughter?' Now, I don't have much tolerance for dumb people and I give stupid answers to stupid questions. I leaned in and said, 'No sir, it's more like a Vienna sausage. It's only two inches long but I have eight of them.'"

Doc chuckled. "Yeah, that's funny. Hey, I thought of something."

"Thinking is dangerous, Doc."

Doc sighed, "Well, you know how both of us are half-Indian?"

"Yup."

"That means between us we're a whole Native American."

"Yeah, but that also means that between us we're a whole white guy."

"Ugh," Doc winced. "Yeah never mind."

"It's whatever, but it proves we're racists. I mean if you're black and proud, you're a proud black man; if you're proud you're Mexican, you're a proud Mexican; and if you're proud you're white, you're in the fucking Klan."

"That is kind of fucked up."

We stacked our dishes and napkins on the table. I tossed Doc a twenty and told him I was going to go smoke. I walked outside, flipped open my lighter and led it to the end of my cigarette. I loved the first cigarette after breakfast. It always was the best one of the day, especially in the cool California mornings. It's the small things that make life livable.

Doc came out, lit his smoke, and leaned on the car. "Whatcha wanna do now?"

"I got a text from Kennedy saying they go on stage at eight. Then some bitching about me leaving before she woke up. Whatever."

"Then we have the whole day to kill."

"Yep."

"Wanna just drive for a bit?"

We loaded into the Mustang and hit the 101 going south. That was the best road to just cruise. Heading south after Encinitas, the highway lies just off the beach. You can watch the surfers ride the waves in and look at the women bouncing around in their sexy little Cali bikinis from the road. Through the other small towns the bars and buildings are decorated with a mild extravagance that says, 'Yes, this is So-Cal. I hope you came to party.'

We drove down to where the 101 started to narrow out towards San

Diego and turned around.

"You know what would be a great movie?" I asked.

"If they remade *Lord of the Rings* but a Predator stalked the fellowship?"

"Dude that would be good! But it wasn't what I was thinking. Okay, check this out." I turned in my seat to face Doc. "There's a Marine in Afghanistan, and he's always in these really bloody firefights and everyone around him gets hurt but he always gets away unscratched. And uh…" I snapped my fingers in an effort to remember. "Do you remember those dogs back in Afghanistan?"

"The fucking Lykens?"

"Yeah those. Anyway, at the end of the deployment he gets mauled by one of those fucking things."

"Would you get a Purple Heart for that?" Doc asked.

"I wouldn't think so unless the dog had on a suicide vest. But anyway, the Marine's battalion goes home and they have the ball right before post deployment leave. Then it turns out the night of the ball is the first full moon since they got home and the guy turns into a werewolf and attacks the first sergeant and gets busted to private."

Doc laughed, "Man, *No one* would go see that."

"I would!"

"Yeah, but you're a deranged fuck."

"And you're not?"

"I'm not saying I'm not. But no one would see that movie. Unless Keanu Reeves was in it."

"Keanu Reeves can eat my dick."

Doc screamed back at me, "No man. Keanu Reeves is immortal!"

"That doesn't mean he can't eat a dick!"

Doc glared at me.

"He'd like it too!"

Doc looked back at the road. "Negative devil dog…"

"Don't you fucking devil dog me, squid!"

"Keanu is phenomenal, spiritual, visceral… unstoppable! He's an amazing immortal demi-god of acting! Keanu can surf, man."

"Whatever, Doc. Brad Pitt would own him. Hands down. Pitt would scalp that fucker."

"No, Pitt has never jumped sideways whilst firing a pistol at bad guys."

"Mr. and Mrs. Smith! How about that jackass?"

"Regardless, no. Reeves wins."

"No, Brad Pitt would take him into a basement and burn Reeves' skin with bath soap and carve a swastika into his face then tell Keanu, 'There is no Brad Pitt.' Then disappears into nothing."

"They're not the same person, fucker!"

"No, Brad Pitt is the real life Highlander!"

"Whatever, man," Doc grunted.

I put the cherry of my cigarette into the skin on my forearm all the while staring Doc down as the smell of burning flesh filled the cab.

Doc pulled out the cigarette lighter under the radio and put it to his wrist. He took turns between staring at me and looking at the road. We burnt daggers into each other's eyes until Doc swore and threw the lighter out of the window.

"Fine fucker, you win!"

We drove the wild streets of San Diego County until the sun fell from the red sky into the Pacific.

Doc killed the engine in Purple Church's parking lot. We walked in and sat in the dark violet electric sex lights of the strip joint. Doc and I had ordered stouts. The girls were on the stage, shaking their asses in front of the mirrors, charming the dirty old men in the crowd.

"Hey Doc, have you had the Black Lager?"

"Na man." Doc leaned back into his seat. "I want it so bad but I can't find it anywhere."

"It's good."

"I've heard. Oh, but a few weekends ago, I was at the liquor store and I saw this big old black guy, and he was dressed head to toe in this full Carhartt getup—boots, coveralls, sweatshirt, gloves, and beanie. I was like 'WTF'. He walked over to the beer cooler and grabbed a six-pack of the stout draft. Then when he talked he had this huge cartoon smile and a thick Jamaican accent."

"Doc, what the fuck racist bullshit are you talking about?"

"I wonder if he was just fucking around."

"So what you're saying is black people can't drink stout?"

"That's not what I'm saying."

"You're a fucking racist," I joked.

"Fuck off."

"Well, you know what I think is funny, Doc?" I calmly drank my beer, staring at Kennedy's breasts on the stage.

"What's that?" Doc asked, not taking his eyes away from the stage either.

"That all of these presidents were dirty old white guys and none of these chicks are even a quarter fucking white."

"Yeah?" Doc nodded his head. "Yeah!" Doc half-pointed at the girls. "They don't even look like people that whatever president they're pretending to be messed with."

"Right? I mean, I could understand if there was a fat white chick named Clinton, or if Kennedy looked like Marilyn Monroe."

"Or if Bush was Arabic or even had a giant, unkempt hairy snatch."

"Well who's to say she doesn't? They don't let them take off their panties," I said.

"Reagan told me that most of the girls keep pretty clean down there."

"That's another one!" I exclaimed. "Reagan? What does a short Filipino stripper have to do with Star Wars, the fall of the Soviet Union, *or* fucking Reaganomics?"

"What does a big-tittied Persian have to do with the Bay of Pigs, getting shot in the fucking back of the head, or assassination conspiracies?"

"Well, I call her pig when I'm choke-fucking her."

We both laughed.

"So what is Nixon?" Doc inquired.

"I dunno." I squinted my eyes to get a better look at her. "Maybe she's…"

"…Unfuckable?" Doc shrugged.

"Not without a hell of a lot more beer anyway!" I finished my drink. "Did George Bush ever do anything to Mongolians? I think that's what this Bush is."

"I don't think so man."

"Hmm."

Doc and I had a few more beers through the show. The girls rubbed on each other and shimmied about the stage.

When the routine was over the girls sauntered around the club asking the other patrons if they liked their dances and solicited tips.

The gratuity patrol came to completion and Bush and Nixon went back behind the doors. Kennedy and Reagan came and sat at our table.

"You enjoy the show?" Kennedy asked.

"Not really." I took a drink.

"You're such an asshole." Kennedy pushed me.

"Well, I mean you've got stiff competition. Right?" I looked over to Doc for testimony.

"Yeah," Doc said, "Like in Hong Kong."

"What happens in Hong Kong?" Reagan inquired.

"Well, they have banana shows there," Doc stated.

"What's that?" Kennedy asked.

I motioned peeling a banana and spread my legs.

"Gross!" Kennedy shouted, "I don't want details."

"OH!" I exclaimed. "Doc, you remember the bird show?"

"The bird show?" both girls said in unison.

"Yeah." Doc made a bird with his hands.

"This woman took a fucking blue jay and stuck the whole bird in her snatch…"

The girls had an abhorrent look on their faces.

"…Then she shoots the bird out and it flies around the room!" Doc blurted out. "Oh, then there's another girl with pool balls. She'd put five balls in her pussy, each one has a number on it, and she would ask what number you wanted and she'd pop it out."

"That shit was awesome," I confirmed Doc's story.

"There's no way I'd ever do that," Kennedy said.

Reagan asked, "Well how much money do they make?"

"*Real!*" Kennedy slapped Reagan on the leg. "There's *no* amount of money…"

Says the stripper. Is what I wanted to say, but I also wanted to have sex that night so I kept my mouth closed. "Speaking of pay for lust, shouldn't people be shoving cash into your knickers instead of you having to go around asking for it?" I smiled at Kennedy.

"Well…" She grabbed my beer and took a swig. "If California wasn't run by a bunch of left wing socialist faggots, maybe I wouldn't have that problem!"

Kennedy was born a few years after her parents emigrated from Iran. She was a tall, dark, beautiful lynx. Long, dark hair with black holes that not even gravity could escape for eyes. Her skin was the perfect shade of caramel.

"Well, I've got something I'd like to stash in your undergarments," I chuckled.

Kennedy smiled and shook her head. "So, what are you two trouble makers getting yourselves into tonight?"

"I don't know, I was thinking maybe robbing a bank and using that money to buy cocaine. Then snort'n the blow off of a stripper's ass, maybe kill a few hookers."

"Well that sounds like a solid plan," Reagan sneered.

Doc put his hand on Reagan's thigh and said, "Well you're both invited if you wanna join."

"Or how about El Taco instead?" Kennedy suggested.

"If we can do a cigarette first." I used my teeth to pull a Lucky's out of the pack.

The girls stood up. "We'll meet you up front," Kennedy said. "Let's go get dressed Rea."

"Awe, you're not going dressed like that?" Doc asked.

"Sorry hun." Reagan rubbed Doc's balding head.

The girls walked into the back, Doc and I went out front and lit up. "It's just as well they won't go out dressed like that," Doc muttered.

"What?"

"Well, I mean do you really want them walking around like that, having other assholes ogle them?"

"Dude, they're fucking strippers."

"Yeah, but…"

"But what?" I interrupted. "Their job is to be ogled by creepy, dirty old men, who can't get laid, and have money shoved into their thongs."

"It's not just guys who can't get laid. What about people who just want to look at some titties?"

"Doc, you're an idiot. Who wants to watch tits shake around when they could get their dicks wet? If prostitution were legal *no one* would go to strip clubs. Just be happy that your little Filipino girl isn't an actual Filipino stripper."

"Right." Doc took another drag. "Because of the whole banana thing… and five-dollar blow jobs."

"That and she's not a twelve-year-old boy in a dress."

"Oh God that'd be terrible." Doc shuttered.

"Oh shut up Doc. You're so head over heals over that bitch you'd suck her dick if she had one!" I laughed at Doc.

"Fuck *you* man!" Doc punched me in the chest.

I jumped on Doc and wrestled one of his arms away from him. "Tell me you love Brad Pitt!"

"Fuck you, Brad Pitt sucks!" Doc screamed trying to wiggle away.

I shoved the hot end of my cigarette into his skin. "SAY IT!"

"Never!" Doc howled. I ground the cigarette in harder. "All right!" Doc confessed. "I love Brad Pitt." I got off of Doc and helped him stand back up. "You're a dick."

"Yeah, but I'm the best friend you're ever going to have."

"It's nice you're so fucking modest." Doc rubbed his burn.

We patted ourselves off and lit more cigarettes. The girls came out and we all loaded into Doc's Mustang and blazed down to El Taco.

We walked into the dingy grease hole of an eatery that was El Taco. The floors looked like at one time they were white, but now were a dark yellowish-brown and the windows were in serious need of a cleaning. The place was empty except for a crazy homeless-looking woman sitting in the corner folding paper bags and talking to herself. We ordered our food and sat down.

Reagan took a bite out of her burrito and a hunk of beef-greased bean paste fell onto her shirt.

Doc tried to say something but couldn't manage more than a mumble because of the food he had stuffed in his mouth.

Reagan grabbed a napkin and started wiping the goo off her blouse.

"Dude, English," Reagan told him.

"Ar rermmsh mere err a ory."

Kennedy bowed towards Doc. "EN-UN-CI-ATE."

Doc swallowed his food. "Fuck both you. I was trying to say that reminds me of a story."

"'Trying' is the key word there," Reagan said still working on her top. Her efforts were spreading the stain more than they were cleaning it up.

"When I was sixteen I was dating this chick named Allison."

I interrupted with, "Oh yeah Doc that was a great story!"

Doc glared at me. "She was eighteen and I met her at a party. After we had been dating for a bit she said she wanted to use anal beads."

Reagan gave him a dirty look. "On you?"

"No." Doc gave Reagan a disgusted look. "*Hell* no! She wanted me to use them on her."

"Yeah, okay sure," I said to Doc. "Go on with your sorry *ass* story."

"Anyway, she goes to a sex-shop and buys these anal beads. She brings them to her house and we take them to her room. She takes off her clothes and sits up on the bed with her legs spread. I start popping them in one by one." Doc made a gesture with his hands to illustrate. "Then when they were all in there, being the sexual boot that I was…" Doc jerked his fist downward. "… I pulled them all out like I was trying to start a lawnmower. And shit flew all over the place!"

Reagan dropped her burrito on the table. "Yeah, I'm done."

2 BARRACKS DUTY, BLOOD, VOMIT, AND NINJA PUNCHES

I hadn't done anything besides drink since I'd gotten back from Afghanistan. I'd go through the motions at work then drink at the barracks with Doc until I felt like I could sleep, More often than not just a few hours before morning formation.

"Why the fuck can't we have alcohol in the barracks, Doc?" I asked.

"I don't know. It's fucking stupid, man." Doc took a swig of his whiskey.

"I mean, we're allowed to have a six-pack, and that's it. That's encouraging drinking and driving, like I'm going to drink six beers then drive to the PX for more? Fucking stupid," I started to rant.

"Yeah, like why do they trust us to go ten thousand miles away from home and kill people with millions of dollars worth of equipment, but don't let us have bourbon in the barracks?"

"Because they're fucking with us." I flicked my cigarette off the balcony. "I'm going to bed, dude. My staff sergeant's got us doing a fucking death run tomorrow."

"Have fun with that shit, man." Doc said goodnight.

I fell into my chair with a bottle of spiced rum and opened my computer. I did what I normally did when I was that drunk. I opened up my picture folders and looked through my old photos. I found myself looking at pictures of my old girlfriend, Satin. I wanted to blame her for the breakup, but I knew everything that happened was my fault. I hated myself for causing us to split. I took a swig of rum and stared at the light illuminating her face. My heart had a chunk of iron weighing it down. Things were so long ago to me. Being in the Corps and twenty-three wasn't much different than being nineteen, except I had two deployments to Afghanistan under my belt, and felt like a dumbass.

I looked up my deployment photos. I fucking hated the way our unit worked. I was a Combat Cameraman in the First Marine Division. We would attach to the infantry to deploy then return to our home unit when we got back. I was assigned to Second Battalion Seventh Marines and they were up in Twentynine Palms, three hours away. No one ever has friends like they make at war; I'd venture to say that's the strongest bond you could ever build with another human being. All my war buddies were hours away.

Doc was in the same boat with me in Pendleton. He was one of the corpsmen that got slung all over the place. We just happened to deploy together. He lived a few floors up from me at the barracks on Camp Margarita. He also went on 2/7's deployments. The Marine Corps wasn't a good model for logistical efficiency.

With all of the shit going through my head I needed someone to talk to, and a cigarette. *Fuck it, I'll stay up and just die on the run tomorrow.* I looked out the window, Doc was still downstairs smoking. I figured I'd go smoke and bullshit with him a bit more. In my half-drunken stupor I didn't think to put the bottle of rum away before I left the room, I kept it in my hand.

When I opened the door, the officer of the day just so happened to be walking right in front of me. He stopped, eye balled me from head to toe, and saw the cocoa colored liquid swishing around the glass bottle. He turned his body to face mine.

"Devil dog! What the fuck is that?" The short Mexican gunnery sergeant knife-handed me.

Fucking great, I thought to myself. I was about to get the full extent of the big green digital weenie, and there was going to be absolutely no lube. I presented the hooch to the gunny. "Spiced rum. Contraband material which is unauthorized in these barracks, Gunnery Sergeant."

The gunny snatched the bottle out of my hands. "If it's contraband *why* is it in your possession, Marine?"

I stood at parade rest, or the best I could manage at that point. "Because I'm a stupid ass lance corporal, Gunnery Sergeant."

He demanded my ID. He wrote my information down and stormed off. I went back into the room, closed my door, and fell face first onto my rack.

I stood in front of the company gunnery sergeant's office the next morning.

Standing there, all I could think was that I knew better than to do something stupid and get caught like that. In garrison the difference between a good Marine and a bad Marine was his ability to not get caught breaking the rules.

From the gunnery sergeant's office came a loud, "ALLENSWORTH! GET THE FUCK IN HERE!"

I marched into the room and centered myself in front of the gunny's desk at the position of attention.

"Good morning Gunnery Sergeant, Lance Corporal Allensworth reporting as ordered."

"You know why you're in here, Devil?" he barked.

"The officer of the day found my rum, Gunnery Sergeant."

"Yeah that's it." The gunnery sergeant produced the bottle and placed it on the desk. "Stand at ease."

I complied.

"You know that the commanding officer's policy is no hard liquor or glass bottles in the barracks, right?"

"Yes, Gunnery Sergeant."

"Then what the fuck, Marine?"

"Dumb lance corporal, Gunnery Sergeant."

"And you think that's an excuse?"

"No Gunnery Sergeant, it's not."

"Do you have anything to validate your blatant disregard for the rules and regulations? Or is it just that good order and discipline does not apply to you?"

"I'm not making any excuses, Gunnery Sergeant." *Don't dig the hole deeper Hank.*

"Drinking alone in the dark in the middle of the week. Do you have an alcohol problem?"

"No Gunnery Sergeant, I was just up there drinking for no reason."

Then the gunnery sergeant began to rant. His volume steadily rose as he spoke. "Oh, well that makes everything better! You obviously know the commander's policy and you're about to face the fucking consequences! I'm going to run you up the flagpole! Marines in this barracks have been getting away with this too long. I would just let you get away with it too, but you've probably been getting away with it for a while!" The gunnery sergeant stood up and started knife-handing me. "I'm going to make an example out of you, you're going to be a private before the end of the fucking week! Marine, how long have you been getting away with this shit anyway?"

"Since I got back from my second deployment to Afghanistan a few months ago."

The gunny gave me a confused look. "You've been overseas, Marine?"

"Twice to Afghanistan."

"Just how long have you been in?" Gunny demanded.

"A bit shy of three years."

"How long were your deployments?"

"Nine and seven months."

"Why are you still a lance corporal? You been in trouble before?"

"No Gunnery Sergeant, my op field just promotes slower than the infantry does."

The gunnery sergeant glared at me over a heavy breath.

"Get the fuck out of my office and don't let me fucking see you again unless it's at Company PT."

"Aye aye gunnery sergeant." I stood at attention. "Good morn…"

"GET THE FUCK OUT!"

I about-faced and scurried out of the company office down to the smoke deck on the other side of the building and lit a cigarette.

That Thursday I had barracks duty. The corporal on duty with me was a two-ribbon communications platoon boot. You learn a lot about a Marine just by looking at his uniform. It's like a visual resume, you can see where they've deployed to or whether they're water walkers or skaters. The corporal spent most of the day touring the barracks. I knew he was napping or playing video games, but I didn't really care, that was less time I had to sit there and listen to him run his suck about how cool he thought boot camp was.

I still hadn't heard anything from the company about non-judicial punishment, maybe I was in the clear.

Private First Class Kelly was sick in quarters. I didn't particularly like Kelly. He was a malingering piece of shit who had the choice to go to Afghanistan, but declined. It was between him and another guy. The other guy went instead.

Kelly came down to the duty hut mid-morning. "Lance Corporal I'm sick, I'm going to lay down."

"Okay." I didn't care enough to look at him. "You're SIQ right?"

"Yeah." He breathed out of his mouth.

"Then go lay down. That's what SIQ is for."

Kelly disappeared back up the stairs. I returned to reading the porno magazine on the desk, texting Kennedy, and listening to the news on the TV on the other side of the room. The local news network talked about political tensions between Iraq and Iran, North Korea pulling their usual jackassery, the mayor of Los Angeles' new crime program, and Russia's interests in the Baltic States. None of this was really new to me.

Some Marine had the day off and checked in a female visitor. *Someone's having a good day.* I smiled watching the short brunette walk up the stairs and went back to my money shot mag.

I looked up and saw Kelly standing at the head of the desk again, this time wrapped in a blanket.

"What Kelly?" I returned my attention to the tits in the magazine.

"I feel really sick."

"Do you need to go to the Naval Hospital?" My eyes were still glued to the alluring redhead displaying her irresistible sex.

"No."

I sighed and looked up. "Do you need some ginger ale for your stomach or to go to the PX for anything?"

"Not really."

"What about douche to get the sand out of your pussy?"

"No, I just wanted to keep you updated."

"Kelly," I pointed at the stairwell, "Go back to your fucking room and don't come back down unless you actually need something."

He went back to his room. I stared at my desk with my forehead in my hand. I zoned out staring at the fake grain on the particleboard table.

"Lance Corporal Allensworth," Kelly's voice scratched my ears again, not five minutes later.

"What Kelly?" I snapped my head back up. "What the *fuck* do you want?"

Kelly said in a calm tone, "I'm trying to kill myself."

"What?" I demanded, not completely registering what he said.

"I'm trying to kill myself. I just took a bunch of pills."

I wanted to scream at him to just go lay down in the corner and die, but as much as I hated being a lance corporal I would have hated to be a private again a whole hell of a lot more. "Go stand outside."

I dialed Corporal Scott's number.

"Sup?" Scott said over the line.

"Hey Corporal, fucking Kelly just took a bunch of pills trying to kill himself."

"What?"

"I'm on duty at the barracks and he's SIQ and he came down and told me he was trying to kill himself."

"Well don't call me! Call 911!"

I called an ambulance and walked outside. Kelly was standing facing away from me. I grabbed his back collar and kicked his legs from beneath, leaving him half on his knees with his face to the ground. I stuck the two middle fingers of my other hand down his throat. Vomit gushed to the pavement, but not before spilling over my Charlie uniform. I looked at the regurgitated mess on the sidewalk and I saw the 'pills' he had taken.

I got in his face, pointed to his mess, and screamed, "Kelly, are those mother fucking vitamin C tablets?"

He hacked out, "Yes, Lance Corporal."

I yanked him back up and sat him down against the wall. "Just sit there. Don't move or fucking say anything until the ambulance gets here." I wiped the puke off my arm and trousers. They were already ruined. I was going to smell like bile the rest of the day. "You're buying me a new pair of Chucks, Boot!"

The paramedics arrived and hauled Kelly away. I went to the head to try to wash the gunk off of myself. The water just smeared the puke making it worse. I gave up. When the corporal showed back up I explained the whole thing to him and he logged it in the duty binder.

The rest of the day dragged by. The Marine with the brunette from earlier came back down to check out of the visitor's log. The chick had a nice thick head of *I just got fucked* hair.

Around twenty-one hundred I saw Doc walk out of his room leaving his door open. I crept up. On his floor laid a box of tidbits of plastic from a model kit. A perfectly built model F-14 sat on the secretary. I picked it up and examined the details Doc put into it. He did a good job. I noticed the tube of glue sitting by where he had placed the model. I picked it up, applied a generous portion of adhesive onto the bottom of the landing gear, placed it back on the secretary, and left.

I found Doc in the smoke pit burning a cigarette.

"What's up man?" Doc cheered. He had a big smile on his face and glazed eyes.

"You drunk already?" I laughed.

"Yeah. What about it, *Duty?*"

"Nothing man, nothing at all."

"What happened to your Chucks, dude?"

"Some fucking boot puked on me."

"HA!"

"Fuck off."

I lit a cigarette and bullshitted with Doc for a bit. He was going on about someone he knew in high school back in Oklahoma. I intentionally egged him on about whatever drunken ramblings he was speaking for about half an hour, mostly to give the glue on the plane time to dry. When he said he had just built this awesome model airplane and jabbered about how badass of a job he did on it I asked, "That sounds cool Doc. Can I see it?"

"Yeah man!" Doc was excited to show off his new exhibit of plastic engineering. He waved at me to follow him upstairs. We got to his room and he swung to grab the model plane. His hand brought up the fuselage. The landing gear stuck firm to the desk, all the middle parts flew all over the room. "SON OF A BITCH!" Doc screamed.

I just laughed. "Looks like the MIGs got you, *Maverick!*"

"That ain't funny, man!" Doc looked around the room in the despair only a drunkard could have. "Oh well." He casually tossed the model out the door.

"So what's going on tomorrow, man?" I asked.

"Awe man, I got this stupid class I have to teach."

"On what?" I stepped out onto the catwalk and put a Lucky's in my mouth.

"It's some bullshit class on operational stress."

"Huh?"

"It's cool though man. The class will be boring, but…" Doc half hiccupped and half burped. "…But I'm teaching it with this hot ass lieutenant."

"Doc, last week you were giving me shit about fucking girls that ain't my girlfriend."

Doc gave me an indignant look. "Girlfriends aren't wives, man."

"Doc, one day I'm going to write a book about the Marines I know and everyone in the book I talk about is going to have their wife or girlfriend dump them before they're half done with it."

Doc laughed and stumbled back against the wall. "Whatever man. Anyway, Lieutenant Chu…"

"Like a choo-choo train?"

"Yeah man!" Doc exclaimed realizing the correlation. "Dude, she's so hot. Tiny little body, short, silky black hair, I just wanna… UGH!" Doc pretended to fuck an invisible woman.

"Well, alrighty then." I took a deep drag.

"Imma call her."

"You do that!" I smiled at the idea of a petty officer drunk dialing a lieutenant in the Navy. He whipped out his phone and put it to his ear. "Ch… Lieutenant Chu? Hey what's goin on, it's Doc Evans… How you doin? Nothing, just drunk-dialing people." Doc laughed and pointed at his phone. "Because it's Thursday night. Do I need a holiday? Huh? Well yea, it's… it's a…" Doc looked at me. "What day is tomorrow?"

"Big Indian Day in Georgia," I promptly replied.

Doc gave his attention back to the phone. "It's Big Indian Day in Georgia tomorrow, and… *and* it's my two-year anniversary with a stupid chick that left… I live in the… of course I'll be safe… I live in the barracks… they put *all* people who are mature adults in the barracks…" Doc began to laugh at whatever Chu was saying on the other end of the phone. "I think I was told to be there at seven… Do you like, do you, do ya like Jim Beam?" Doc waited a few seconds to speak and with a merry tone said, "Awe, well good for you!" Then he gave a sad, "Awe… whadda ya mean you're older, how old are you? You're like twenty-five ri… really?

You're the first lieutenant who's older than me… usually they're like half my age." Chu began a long monologue. I couldn't hear anything she was saying but Doc took the liberty of drinking more while she spoke. "Okay, well… Well I have half a bottle to finish before I can go to bed… Well I can't drink before, I mean I can't drink at work so I *can't* save the bottle for tomorrow…"

I decided to butt in to his conversation. "Chugga chugga chugga…" I moved my arms to imitate a train. "Chugga chugga chugga, *CHU CHU!*"

Doc started laughing. "Shut up, dude!" He fell on the ground, managing to keep the phone to his head. "What's wrong with you?" he said still laughing. "Yes ma'am…I'll be safe." Doc put his phone away.

"So how's she doin?" I chuckled.

"She's good, man. But hey, I gotta get to bed, man."

"All right, Doc." I waved and walked back to the duty hut.

All was quiet in the California night when I sat down. The news was telling more about unrest in the Middle East and North Korea being a renegade state. I checked my phone, Kennedy texted me that she had tomorrow night off and wanted to know if I was coming over. I sat there for a while and counted the stucco bumps in the ceiling. I still stank like vomit. Then I stared at the wall. There was nothing special about the wall, but there wasn't anything better to do than to stare at it, so why not? I flipped through the duty log book for entertainment. Some female Marine was on duty a few days before. I had no idea who she was, but judging from her eloquent handwriting, she probably wore skin-tone satin panties and fucked like a tiger shark.

A little bit before midnight, Soito, one of the Marines from battalion headquarters, came running into the duty hut. "Allensworth!"

I looked at him with half-unconscious eyes. "What?"

"Need you out back." Soito gestured his thumb backwards.

I followed him to the far side of the barracks where Doc was sitting half limp on the grass with an empty bottle of whiskey. "YOU FUCKING POGS MISSED THE WAR! WHY DID YOU EVEN FUCKING JOIN? WHAT THE FUCK!"

He was just screaming at the building, no one specific. No one was outside with him and no one was watching him, at first. But Canada probably heard him yelling. A few Marines began to open their doors to see what moron was doing what this night of the week.

"DOC!" I grabbed his attention. "Who are you talking to?"

"All these fucking headquarters faggot POGs!" he cried. "They *missed* the fucking war, man! They missed the fucking war…" Doc dropped his head and began to sob.

I kneeled down next to him and put my arm around him. With a sympathetic voice I said, "I know buddy." I looked him over to make sure he wasn't hurt. "Let's get you back to your room, okay?"

Doc looked up at me with tears in his eyes. "NO!" He jerked back. "How are they supposed to know that they weren't there, man?"

I stood there for a few minutes trying to reason with Doc. If you've ever tried to reason with a drunken sailor, I don't need to tell you about the futility of my efforts.

One of the corporals in the barracks opened his door. "Allensworth!"

"Yes, Corporal?" *NCO involvement is the last thing I need.*

"That's your boy, right?"

"Yep."

"Take care of that trash, people are trying to sleep."

"Aye Corporal." I looked up at Soito and said, "Help me carry him to his room." Doc protested, but I didn't pay any attention to what he was saying. I grabbed Doc's shoulders and Soito got his feet. The whole way upstairs Doc rambled about how the rest of the Marines in the barracks were useless because they never went to Iraq or Afghanistan.

When we got Doc outside of his room, which was on the fifth deck, I fished his keys out of his pocket. While I was unlocking his door Doc managed to stand up and pull the fire alarm. As soon as the sirens started to blare I screamed, "GODDAMNIT DOC!" and knocked him out with a punch to the face.

"Soito, drag him into his room. I gotta go call the OOD and deal with this shit."

I called the officer of the day. The phone rang long enough for the fire department to show up. I hung up the phone when they walked into the duty hut.

"Hey guys. There's no fire, some asshole just pulled the fire alarm and ran off. I didn't see who did it."

The firemen rolled their eyes. "Where's the alarm?"

"Fifth deck."

They opened an electrical box outside and silenced the alarms.

I tried to call the OOD again—nothing. I posted a sign that read 'DUTY ON TOUR' and walked to the Command Shack. I could see the top of the back of the OOD's head over the partition on the desk. *Oh great, he's sleeping on post.* I went to go shake him, but when I looked down he wasn't sleeping. He had a gun in his hand. His brains were splattered across the opposite side of the desk. The last entry in his log book was 'OOD BANG!"

"FUCK!"

I called the MPs.

3 WALAIKUM ASSALAM

I got exactly zero sleep that night, I spent it with PMO and NCIS.

When I got off duty I threw my uniform in the trash, took a shower, and slept until the early afternoon.

When I woke up I didn't get out of bed. I laid there enjoying the warmth. I checked my phone. Kennedy had sent me texts about going to town that night with Reagan and Doc. It didn't seem like too terrible of an idea. Staring at the ceiling I wondered if I really needed to blow off steam or chill. I decided that if I went out drinking it would get to the point where my mind would be honest with itself and I'd either go hog wild or find a nice quiet place to relax. I forced myself out of bed, brushed my teeth, and combed my hair. It always took an extra minute to do the hair. Marine Corps regulations state that hair shall be no longer than three inches long, mine was seven, so I had to be careful fixing it so no one would call me out. I know it's hard to understand, but imagine a forward combed over faux hawk with no hair at all below the temples. In spite of my best efforts, it still smelled vaguely of vomit.

I got the rest of myself together and drove to Kennedy's apartment. She rented the second floor of a house about two blocks away from the beach in Oceanside. It was cozy. There was a little kitchen that she shared with the people downstairs. Her living room and bedroom weren't segregated by anything except a loveseat that rested a few feet away from the foot of her bed. The walls were decorated with posters of pin-up girls and wooden masks from Central Asia. There was a beautiful view of the beach from the patio.

Kennedy and I stood on the patio smoking and drinking pomegranate martinis she mixed. An Aerosmith vinyl played from inside the apartment.

"LA wasn't bad growing up in." Kennedy sucked on her menthol.

"Is that how you ended up being a stripper?" I joked.

She smiled and said, "Fuck off joker. My sister didn't like it and moved to Chicago."

"What's she doing out there?"

"Going to school. She's studying some kind of engineering, but I really couldn't tell you what."

"Eh," I shrugged.

"What about you?"

"What about me what?"

"Tell me about Afghanistan, Hank."

I grimaced. "Yeah, I don't really want to talk about that."

"Okay," Kennedy said solemnly. "Well what about the horns on the front of your Jeep?"

"What is this an interrogation? Doc and I were off-roading through an impact range a while back and we found this buffalo that had been blown in half before the coyotes had their way with it. I tried to strap the head to the back of my jeep, but when I picked it up the horns fell off. So I put those on the grill instead."

"Did you wash your hands after that?" Kennedy laughed and bit her bottom lip.

"No. We went straight to the 101 Café and got breakfast."

We had a few more drinks and spouted off nonsense about how life seemed futile and incoherent. Lance corporals in the Marine Corps and strippers are the pinnacles of philosophy, and as we all know, if you give anyone just a few drinks they can solve all of the world's problems.

The sun bounced its golden beams off the Pacific's waves making white diamonds in the blue.

Kennedy opened the top of her white caftan dress revealing a scarlet and cream-colored laced mess of a brassiere. She moved closer to me with her martini in one hand as she embraced my body and kissed me on the neck.

My hands caressed her shoulders, making their way to the small of her back. Her sweet lips met mine, her tongue danced in my mouth better than she did on the pole. She ran her hands through my hair, caressing my scalp as I slid my hands under her skimpy black panties. My hands grabbed her shapely ass and I pulled her hips to mine.

Our lips broke contact so she could pour the rest of her martini into my mouth. She put the martini glass on her end table without looking away from me.

I caressed my way to the small of her back. I slid my hands into the sides of her skimpy black panties. I groped her caboose and pulled her hips into mine. I downed her drink. She stood on her toes and her lips made their way to the back of my ear. Kennedy's breath grew heavy. I ran my tit-grabbing hand to her shoulder blade and my other to the back of her upper thigh. I leaned her back, picked her up, and carried her to the bed.

The next couple hours felt like heaven, her my angel.

Her clothes looked amazing carelessly disregarded on the floor. We laid on the bed in the still of the night. She hugged the arm I wrapped around her shoulders.

"Hank…"

"Kennedy…"

"Why won't you tell me about Afghanistan?"

"Why do you want to know so badly?" I ask in an annoyed tone.

"My dad doesn't talk to me much because he doesn't approve of my lifestyle. His job takes him back to that part of the world a lot. He spends most of his time abroad," she confesses.

Kennedy reached over to her nightstand and showed me a photo of her parents, siblings, and herself in front of the pyramids at Giza.

"He took us to Egypt when I was a kid. My mom told me that he's been in Afghanistan for the last few months. I figured that maybe your insight might let me in on what's going on in his life."

I took a deep breath and thought, *Afghanistan was like the remnants of a beautiful paradise that an unspeakably grim war burnt to the ground; a place where the survivors fought tooth and nail for a thousand different things of which only they knew the importance. Then we showed up and tried to rebuild what the Soviets decimated. But the people there were too busy fighting each other over trivial bullshit instead of working together for a better future. So we stood with the side that didn't kill women and children… as much; and started mercilessly hunting down and stamping the life out of the Taliban, but not without shedding our fair share of blood into the sand. I decide to let her down easy.* "Afghanistan was beautiful, and the people were very nice when they weren't trying to kill you."

"Hmm." Kennedy squeezed my arm a bit tighter. "I've also been thinking, what if we go to war with Iran?"

"What about it?"

"Well, would you go fight?"

"Yeah. I joined the Marine Corps to go kill people, not sit around state side with my thumb up my ass. Personally I'd rather get my hands on those ISIS fucks, but Iran wouldn't be a bad fight. Terrorist-supporting bastards, they're probably funding ISIS."

"Iran isn't just a bunch of terrorists, Hank."

"No, but the government is. A war with Iran would be just like the war with Iraq. Half the Iranian army would surrender and the US would spend half of a decade killing insurgents from third-party countries. Iran wouldn't really be a problem, but it would turn into another war with Al Qaeda, or ISIS, or a fucking proxy war with the Russians or Chinese."

"So you'd have no problem going straight over there and fighting?"

"Not really. I mean all that bullshit you hear in the movies where the main character says something stupid like 'a real warrior prays for peace and only goes to war when it's absolutely needed' is straight bullshit. If you want peace go be a politician and make peace happen by not letting things get to where a war has to happen at all. I can't speak for the Army or the Air force, but Marines pray to God for war before we go to sleep at night. What would we do without it? There'd be no point to exist. There are people out there with problems and people who need to be killed. All that coexist bullshit is a fantasy. You can't coexist with people that want to kill you. I want to put all the people who think pacifism and peace can be achieved by just putting down our guns, smoking weed, and hugging on a plane and drop them off in the Helmand province of Afghanistan and let them see first-hand how that works. They'd get raped a few times and then have their heads cut off, if they were lucky."

"Yeah..." Kennedy sighed with frustration.

"I mean, I don't know everything about how the world works, but I do know that there are a lot of people who need fifty-caliber aspirin for their head. Especially those ISIS cunts; I'd go kill those fuckers tonight! It's not that people are out there just killing people just to kill them. They have an ideology, however fucked up it may be. I mean, do you think that the assholes out there who cut a woman's face off because she was trying to learn how to read would stop being the fucking pieces of shit they were if some pot smoking hippie just gave him a hug?"

"Okay Hank, I get it..."

"And another thing. All these Woodstock-going, free love, fucking pussies that want to live in harmony. Why do they want to live in harmony with these goat fucking cock suckers that spend their…"

"Hank!" Kennedy cut me off. "I get it!"

I think I pissed her off, but she asked for it. I looked at the clock. "Weren't we supposed to go see Reagan and Doc tonight?"

"Yeah, I'll call Reagan," she irked. Kennedy stood out of bed and walked to the bathroom.

I put on my jeans and my denim patch jacket and walked to the patio. I leaned on the rails and looked into the western sky.

Kennedy came outside clothed in a tight leopard-print top and dark blue jeans.

"They're going to come pick us up in about ten minutes." She didn't look too happy. "Go put your shirt on."

She started to walk past me. I stopped her and planted my lips on hers. Then wordlessly retrieved my Slayer shirt. I saw her smile at me from the corner of my eye. I knew she wasn't really that mad at me, but she wanted to act indignant anyway. *Fucking women.*

Once Doc and Reagan showed up, Kennedy and I loaded into the Mustang. I looked into the rearview mirror at Doc's face.

"Hey Doc, what happened to your face?" I pretended not to know.

"I don't know, man. I woke up with it. I don't remember much from last night."

I smiled at Doc. "Okay, man. Where we going tonight?"

"The Kraken," Doc replied.

Reagan turned around to face Kennedy. "Yeah, it's got a good atmosphere."

"Oh I know." I pointed at Kennedy. "You two have gone there before together?"

Kennedy looked over at me. "Yeah, we used to go all the time."

The Kraken was already packed. There was a real shit band butchering an old Styx song. I was probably the only Marine there, Doc the only sailor. We were definitely the only people under thirty. We ordered some drinks and proceeded to the smoking area in the back. We bullshitted for a while, smoked a few cigarettes, and even danced for a bit, although I only dance when the booze convinces me that just because I can't dance doesn't mean I shouldn't. The combination of the martinis at Kennedy's place and the rum and Cokes here began to take its toll on me. That's when my phone started buzzing.

Normally I didn't pick up the phone while I was out, but the caller ID said it was Corporal Scott. I answered the phone with a cocky "Good evening, Corporal!"

"Hey, Allensworth. What are you doing right now?" Corporal Scott said over the phone.

"I'm in the process of getting so drunk I forget how to speak English."

"Well I have good news and bad news. Which do you want first?"

"The good news, Corporal."

"You're getting promoted tomorrow."

I turned away from my phone to Doc and screamed, "Hey Doc!" over the blaring music of the trash band. "I'm getting promoted tomorrow!"

"Tomorrow's Saturday, man!" Doc screamed back at me with a beer raised.

I redirected my attention to the phone. "Corporal, don't you mean Monday?"

"No, it's tomorrow. Ready for the bad news?"

"What's that?" I sighed.

"There's a battalion formation at midnight."

"What the *fuck* for?"

"I don't fucking know, Allensworth; just be there. I got a bunch more brokedicks to call tonight and I don't have the time to hold your hand." The phone went silent.

I stared dumbfounded at the phone. "Motherfucker." I looked over to Doc. "Hey man, I just got a call that said battalion formation at midnight."

"What?" Doc looked at his watch. "That's in an hour and a half."

"Yeah, we gotta leave now." I looked around the room. "Where are the girls?"

"In the head."

"Okay, I'll get them. Go start the car."

Doc left and I hunted Kennedy and Reagan down and explained to them what was happening. By the time we exited the building the Mustang was already idling in the street. We sped the whole way to Camp Pendleton. The traffic was terrible for tonight. It was usually people fleeing base for the weekend, not the other way around. The gate guards weren't even checking IDs, they were just waving everyone onto the base.

"Yeah Doc, I don't think this is just our battalion."

"No, something big had to happen. At least they're not checking people though, I'm *way* too drunk to be driving."

We set down the long, dark winding road to our part of Pendleton. Doc got a call similar to the one I did about the formation. We got to our barracks in Margarita and changed into uniform. We told the girls to stay in my room and headed to the battalion's parade deck. Doc found the aid station sailors and I found Combat Camera.

We assembled into formation and were called to attention. The battalion commander stood in front of us and instructed us to stand at ease.

"Good evening gentlemen. Unless you've been living under a rock, you know the situation with ISIS in Iraq."

I cracked a smile. *We're finally going to go after those pieces of shit.*

"Apparently the Islamic Republic of Iran…"

Wait what?

"…Has also gotten tired of the Islamic State. Nine hours ago Iran sent ground forces into the Republic of Iraq. Currently the Pentagon is deciding on what course of action is to be taken in the event of Congress or the President ordering us into action. Seeing as how the United States currently still has about ten thousand troops in Iraq, I don't think the decision will be too hard to make. The Eleventh Marine Expeditionary Unit is making its way up the Persian Gulf and standing by for orders. Meanwhile, the First Marine Division will prepare for deployment. I know for a fact that we are ready to leave tonight if we get the tasking. That being said, be prepared to draw your weapon and wait for the busses within an hour's notice of getting the call. If you live in the barracks don't stray too far off base. Get all of your gear together, have your sea bags packed, and have it sitting by the door. We live in uncertain times gentlemen. Good night."

The Battalion commander walked off with the other officers and we fell out of formation. The Combat Camera Marines stood in a circle around Gunnery Sergeant Cantut.

"Alright fuckers, I know it's weekend and half of you are drunk, but I need you all in here tomorrow at eight."

The platoon groaned about the thought of coming in on a Sunday bright and early.

"Don't give me that shit!" Cantut barked. "Come in with your gear. I'm going to issue you out your camera kits, so if things do pop off we can get you out of here quickly. The faster you work tomorrow the faster you'll get off and be able to go spend time with your families."

When we were dismissed I went and found Doc.

"What the fuck is this shit about?" I asked.

"If I had to guess I would say that Iran thinks we're too tired of war and unwilling to invade a country we just pulled out of to go back and fight them, so they're taking advantage of the 'Fuck ISIS' bandwagon and pissing on us all in the same sweep," Doc replied.

"Yeah, but we were in Afghanistan when we invaded Iraq in '03. That makes no fucking sense," I replied as I lit a cigarette. "Shit, we just got back less than a year ago and half of the ComCam guys are still over there. Not to mention the Marines that are already in Iraq fighting those goat fucking Islamic State fucks."

"Yeah, I don't know man," Doc said puzzled.

"Yeah, well in the words of Lewis Burwell Puller, 'As long as we have the First Marine Division, we'll be all right.'"

"Hank, shut up. You get too motivated when you drink."

"Oorah!" I smiled and gave him the thumbs up.

When we got back to the barracks Doc took Reagan to his room. I told Kennedy what happened at the formation. She didn't say anything for a while. I don't think she knew what to say if she wanted to. I just held her until she fell asleep.

That night I dreamt I was driving an old Pontiac GTO down a desert highway. There was an accident on the side of the road and I stopped to help. As soon as I got out of my car a fuel truck exploded as it passed me on the freeway. The fire melted the green paint off of the GTO but the rest of the car remained intact. From the fire a giant red face rose through the flames. It had three glaring eyes and the mouth of a demonic, great white shark under which a long black beard grew. It laughed at me. When I turned away I saw Satin, my ex, pulling a totem pole out of the wrecked car on the side of the road.

I didn't know what to think of that when I woke up. I got out of bed, showered, and shaved. I woke up Kennedy and gave her the keys to my Jeep so she didn't have to stay on base all day. She told me she was going to sleep in for a while. I walked to the shop.

Work wasn't nearly as exciting as I thought it would be. We held a quick promotion ceremony. Corporals Meowry and Scott pinned the new two stripes of a corporal on my collar. We then divvied up camera equipment and prearranged teams for deployment. The teams were set up by battalion, two or four Marines were assigned to the infantry battalions that weren't currently deployed. Then if whichever battalion were sent down range the respective combat cameramen would attach to them. My team was Lance Corporal Staz, Lance Corporal Éclair, Sergeant Hunter, and me. If called we were going back to Second Battalion, Seventh Marines.

Staz had been on my first deployment with me, and Hunter was the team leader on my second. Éclair had only been in the fleet for a few months and had no combat experience. It was pretty close-knit with the team, except Éclair, who was a fucking boot.

For the next few weeks no one left base unless they were married and lived in town. Veterans spun up the boots on how to operate in the field.

I helped Éclair put the attachments on his flack.

"Put your grenade pouch here and put your drop pouch on your belt."

The drop pouch was essentially a gallon-sized pocket used for quick storage.

"Take the strap on your camera and clip it into your grenade pouch so its dummy corded to you in case you accidently drop it. When you're not using your camera keep it in your drop pouch."

I picked up his flack jacket. "Put your med pack on this side and your magazine pouches on the other so you can get to them easily."

"What if I want them up front, Corporal?" Éclair asked.

"Then boot, you'll be a teeter totter and you'll be four inches higher off the ground when you're down on your belly. Do you really want to be any higher than you have to be when Ali Baba is shooting shit at you?"

"No, Corporal."

"Then don't put anything on the front of your flack if you can help it. You want to be able to get as flat as possible."

"Aye, Corporal."

After I showed him how everything was set up I completely disassembled all of his gear. Éclair gave his gear a pathetic look.

"All right boot put it back together." I lit a cigarette and watched him reassemble his flack jacket and pack.

"Corporal…"

"What?"

"You deployed with Two Seven to Afghan, right?"

"Yup."

"What is it like? What's the battalion like?"

"Well," I paused to French inhale the thick smoke from the Luck's. "Don't be embarrassed if you piss your pants in your first fire fight, just keep pushing and don't pussy out. At first, combat is nothing short of sheer terror, but after a while you just get pissed off and want to kill shit. Trust me, my first fire fight, I was scared as shit, but eventually I got used to it."

Éclair looked at me confused.

"Keep putting your shit together, boot."

He went back to working on assembling his pack.

"Now the Seventh Marine Regiment is the greatest group of warriors that have ever treaded the earth. You'll be in good hands there," I explained.

"Corporal, if Seventh Marines is so great why does everyone always talk about Fifth Marines?" Éclair asked

"Because when Fifth Marines went to World War One, Seventh Marines were too busy fighting guerillas in South America to care about what Europe was doing. Either way though, as long as you're in the Blue Diamond you'll be okay."

The First Marine Division's logo was a red number one inside of a blue diamond encircled by five stars.

"You know when they talk about every clime and place?"

"Yes."

"They're really talking about the First Marine Division."

Éclair smiled to that. "Aye, Corporal."

During the day we'd listen to the news on the radio about the escalating situation in the Middle East. Kennedy would drive on base to see me after work. At night we stayed drunk at the barracks. Most Marines loitered on the catwalks, smoking cigarettes and playing guitar.

During a game of beer pong in the smoke pit one of the Marines came outside screaming that the Iranian Navy sank an American warship in the Persian Gulf. Everyone started asking questions and pulled out their phones to find any news on the situation. All anyone could find out was that an Iranian naval vessel had fired upon a US Navy ship. I couldn't find anything about anything sinking on either side.

Kennedy sat on the gravel and nervously lit a cigarette. She panted and shook as she tried to smoke. I sat wrapping my arm around her shoulders in an effort to calm her down.

"It'll be all right, Kennedy."

"I don't want you to go over there."

"I haven't gotten word that it's a for sure thing yet babe."

"How could you not know?" Kennedy's eyes watered and tears started to flow from her eyes.

"Well, even if we do go, you don't have to worry about me."

"But I *am* worried about you," she whimpered, eyes becoming more bloodshot by the minute.

"Babe…" I pause and took a hit from my cigarette. "When Iran and Iraq fought in the '80s they were pretty equally matched, then we kicked Iraq's ass." I exhaled. "Twice. Adding some insurgents to the mix just makes it a target rich environment."

Kennedy went from a whimper to panting wails. She clutched my jacket and buried her face into my chest. She screamed, "People still died! I don't want to deal with that shit!" I picked her up and took her to my room to let her cry it out.

The next day at our morning formation we were told the Second and Third Battalions from the Seventh Marine Regiment, Second Battalion Fourth Marines, First Battalion First Marines, along with First Tank Battalion, and elements of the Third Marine Air Wing were deploying to combat the Iranian aggression in Iraq. We also got the full report from the naval incident in the Gulf.

Gunnery Sgt. Cantut told us, "Yesterday the USS Pearl Harbor, currently deployed with the Makin Island Amphibious Ready Group carrying the Eleventh Marine Expeditionary Unit, hit an Iranian sea mine and lost control of their well deck, which shortly thereafter flooded. This wasn't a catastrophic hit because the ship's well deck was designed to be flooded to deploy amphibious vehicles. After the Pearl Harbor put her fires out an Iranian frigate fired several missiles at her. Most of the missiles either missed or were shot down. One, however, hit the Pearl Harbor and disabled her power leaving her dead in the water. The crew managed to put out the fires and keep her afloat. Shortly after, two F18 Super Hornets, from the USS Harry Truman, carrying anti-ship missiles located and fired upon the Iranian frigate. The frigate was critically damaged and leaned to port. She burned for several hours until the fire reached her ammunition magazines and detonated, thus sinking the ship. The Iranian survivors were rescued and are currently being held on the USS Makin Island and the USS Truman. The Pearl Harbor is currently being towed to Bahrain."

"Holy shit," Éclair whispered.

"Yeah, holy shit," Cantut spouted. "This morning Three-One landed in the Iraqi port city of Al Faw to secure a beachhead."

"How'd they get there so soon?" Éclair asked.

"They're the MEU's landing team," Corporal Scott answered.

Cantut continued, "Here's the meat gentlemen, the battalions I listed earlier are set to deploy. If you're going with Seventh Marines, what's going to happen is tomorrow at zero five you're mustering here and you'll be driven to Twentynine Palms. Everyone deploying with anyone else is to stand by for further orders. You guys have the rest of the day to get your shit together. Make sure you have all your gear here tomorrow morning at zero five. You'll draw your weapons and busses will take you up to the Stumps."

That night the barracks Marines partied like coked-out, eighties rock stars on the eve of the apocalypse. The ground was littered with broken beer bottles, crushed cans, and cigarette butts. Every genre of music blared from the rooms, the moans of girlfriends and female Marines could be heard, and since it was Iran, every fucking Marine who owned a copy of *300* with Gerard Butler, watched it at the maximum volume cranked to eleven.

I sat on my rack. The room's only light came from flood lights through the half-open blinds. I had a bottle of rum in my hand. Kennedy emerged from the bathroom wearing only a forced smile. She didn't come to me. She danced. She didn't give me the normal whorish frolicking of an Oceanside stripper; it was the seductive gyration of a Mediterranean belly dancer. Her torso melodically flowed like a brook tumbling over stones. Her thighs quivered and her feet danced her across the room. I could only see every other inch of her, the blinds cast their shadows on her body leaving black stripes. The California sunset subtly beaming between the shades painted her orange and red. Kennedy moved her hips in a figure-eight pattern. She slid her fingers between the lips between her legs and dipped them in her mouth. She danced like the fire of a candle in a thunderstorm struggling to keep aflame.

I sipped my rum and clutched the headrest. She shimmied and twirled. Her arms were fighting serpents. Kennedy appeared as a golden goddess engaged in a sword fight against invisible demons. Her hair was black waves of a sea in turmoil. She finished her dance by dragging off my jeans.

Neither of us got more than an hour or two of sleep that night. Nothing beats 'Please don't die' sex.

In the dark California morning the Marines who were to go to the desert stood with their loved ones by the parade deck waiting for the busses. We had drawn our weapons from the armory about an hour before. The air was cool and the wind blew gently. Everyone's sea bags and packs were neatly lined in rows. The area was filled with wives and girlfriends embracing their Marines.

Éclair smoked by the road with his M16 slung across his body with his muzzle towards the sky.

"Hey boot, what are you doing?" I barked.

"I'm going over to my packs, Corporal," he said confused.

"Why the fuck is your weapon slung like that?"

Éclair looked at me wide eyed.

"Look at everyone else. All their muzzles are facing to the dirt, right?"

Éclair glanced at the crowd of Marines. "Yes, Corporal."

"Fucking fix yourself. How are you going to fit in with the grunts if you look fucked up when you're compared to the POGs?"

"Aye Corporal." he said almost scared.

"Who taught you to carry it like that anyway?"

"My combat instructors."

"Well they were fucking idiots, and so were your fucking drill instructors. Go find Sergeant Hunter."

"Aye, Corporal." Éclair paced away.

Doc, Reagan, Kennedy, and I stood smoking cigarettes until the busses came. Kennedy nor I spoke; we just held each other.

I didn't know what to think about Kennedy. We hadn't been together for all that long, and I didn't think I was in love with her. But only God knew how long I was going to be gone and it would be nice to have someone waiting at home. I thought about telling her I loved her, but only because it would make her feel better. I ultimately decided against it.

The white busses resembled the yellow ones I rode to school when I was a kid. They sat idling as senior Marines called names and assigned us to the vehicles. Before I loaded onto the bus, I held Kennedy and gave her one last kiss.

Kennedy's eyes, red with the subtle hint of tears, pierced my soul. "As-salamu alaykum," or 'Peace be upon you' in Arabic.

My last words to her were, "No promises."

4 OPERATION CERBERUS

I slept most of the ride through the desert. I woke up in time to see the endless fields of windmills along the highway. They were surreal as if I was in a science fiction movie. The giant white beams towered out of an otherwise desolate landscape. I passed back out and didn't wake again until we were in Twentynine Palms. The sun beat down on the sand. We were drenched with sweat before we even started unloading our gear from the trucks.

We were quickly checked in and assigned to companies. Hunter, being the team leader, stayed with Headquarters and Services Company. Staz went to Golf, Éclair to Fox, and I went to Weapons. It was about the same set up as our last deployment, except Éclair who was our boot that time.

The four of us were stashed away into the same barracks room while we waited to deploy. I had a good reunion with my platoon when I found them. They were already half drunk. Everyone across the battalion was already set to deploy, all there was to do was wait. The rumor going around was that we were heading out in four days. Marine Corps rumors usually carry the accuracy of middle-school cheerleader gossip. We had a battalion formation the next morning and we'd more than likely get better word about pushing out.

Combined Anti-Armor Team 1, CAAT 1, was the platoon in Weapons Company with which I had deployed before. We had a different way of going about things. The Second Battalion of the Seventh Marine Regiment already had a reputation of being cowboys, but CAAT 1 was a ragged group of straight-up pirates. We flew the Jolly Roger on our trucks, we even had our own slogan, 'Cock-Strong Warrior Man-Gods.' Go ahead and think we were vain, you're just jealous. Our mission was to roll up in armored vehicles with heavy machine guns and missiles and provide fire support to the guys on foot. In Afghanistan we never got to use our weapons on tanks, it was always against Taliban with AK47s and RPGs. We joked about maybe actually getting to use the TOW missiles to fight armor in Iran.

The next morning the battalion cramped into the base theater so the colonel could speak to us about the deployment.

"Good morning Marines. As you know we are about to depart for Iraq to combat the Islamic Republic of Iran's aggression in the region. When Iran assaulted into Iraq they pushed over the Tigris River all the way to the Euphrates. Our coalition and the Iraqi military have halted the Iranian advances along the river, but they're feeble and won't hold forever. Personally I don't understand how they can hold Iranians over a river but can't keep ISIS in Syria, but that's neither here nor there.

"The course of action for our initial mission, Operation Cerberus, will be to occupy the line along the Euphrates River to deny Iran any further movement west. US and other NATO forces will hold up against the river to secure the coast against Iranian aggression. When I know what will be happening to the west in Al Anbar, I will be the first to let you know. Hopefully, the Russians will stay in Syria.

"Now gentlemen, it is my intention to bring you men home alive, but seeing as how things are and looking and the history of conflicts, I know that there will be those of us who will not live to see the end of this conflict. When it happens though, and we medevac the fallen, there will be no time for remorse. We will still have a mission to accomplish.

"The Iranians should have no doubt that we are their enemy and we will bring them their ultimate destruction; show no mercy or pity to them or ISIS if we're to fight them.

"Be ferocious in combat but if someone surrenders to you remember that the laws of war dictate that they must be treated with dignity. The ones who fight us, give them two in the chest and one in the head.

"We will bring shame to neither our God, our country, nor Corps. Do not stain this battalion with dishonor.

"What is going to happen with the units defending the Euphrates? Units are flying into Turkey and Kuwait and are going to be convoyed to the locations they're holding down. The units will receive their vehicles and heavier weapons as they become available. I'm not counting on anything for a while.

"Now Marines, here comes the bad news. Two-Seven is departing tonight. Your company commanders will pass further word to you."

We were called to attention and dismissed. Everyone bitched about the short notice of the deployment. It would be a magic trick for everyone to bang their wives one more time before we left.

The battalion left the theater and consolidated into companies, except for Weapons who broke into platoons. Weapons companies don't normally act as a company. Instead, the individual platoons break away and support the line companies with mortars, missiles, rockets, heavy machine guns, hate, and other miscellaneous death-dealing.

The Marines of CAAT 1 formed a circle around the platoon commander, 1st Lt. Brzescer. Brzescer was a tall, lean, mean, sonofabitch with a sharp nose and crystal eyes. He put enough Copenhagen in his mouth to form a horseshoe around the teeth in his lower jaw. In his commanding voice he admitted, "Nothing the BC said gave me a hard on. I haven't gotten any goosebumps yet. Are you motivated about this?"

The Marines screamed, "OORAH!"

"Here's a secret about the Marine Corps that you have more than likely already figured out. We hide things from you and play games with your mind. Fuck, I knew we were leaving tonight weeks ago! We didn't tell you because we want you guys to be pissed the fuck off." The lieutenant spit Copenhagen into the sand by his feet. "Well, I'm going to motivate you guys a bit. Iran… Fuck that! I'm not going to quote *300* like I've heard the lance corporals do around the barracks. Who knows who John Glenn is?"

Fonzie, one of the machine gunners, spouted out, "He was an astronaut, Sir."

"That's right," Brzescer growled. "John Glenn was the first American in space. He was also the oldest man to go back into space, but before all of that he was a fucking Marine! He was an air winger…" Brzescer spit again. "But we're not going to hold that against him right now. In 1974 he ran for senate. He ran against a man named Howard Metzenbaum. Metzenbaum was a cock-sucking son of a bitch!" He put his thumbs in his pockets and started to walk around the circle. "This ass hammock was having a debate with Glenn and asked him, 'How can you run for senate if you've never held a job?' Now, how the fuck would you feel if someone said that shit to you? I would have jumped across the podium and fucking stuck my thumbs in his eyeballs. However, John Glenn was a little tamer than I am."

"ERRR!" shouted the Marines.

"Anyway, John Glenn looked at that piece of shit mother fucker and said, and I'm paraphrasing here…" Brzescer's voice became loud enough to shake down a mountain. Hell's anger was in his tone. "'I served twenty-three years in the United States Marine Corps. I served through two wars. I flew one hundred forty-nine missions. My plane was hit by antiaircraft fire on twelve different occasions. I was in the space program. It wasn't my checkbook; it was my fucking life on the line. It was not a nine-to-five job where I took time off to take the daily cash receipts to the bank. I ask you to go with me, as I went the other day, to a Veterans hospital and look at those men, with their mangled bodies, in the eye and tell them they didn't hold a job. You go with me to the space program and go, as I have gone, to the widows and orphans of Ed White, Gus Grissom, and Roger Chaffee, and you look those kids in the eye and tell them that their dad didn't hold a job. You go with me on Memorial Day, coming up, and you stand in Arlington National Cemetery, where I have more friends than I'd like to remember, and you watch those waving flags. You stand there, and you think about this nation, and you tell me that those people didn't have a job. I'll tell you, Howard Metzenbaum, you should be on your knees every day of your life thanking God that there were some men, *some men*, who held a job. And they required a dedication to purpose, a love of country, and a dedication to duty that was more important than life itself. And their self-sacrifice is what made this country possible… *I have held a job, Howard! What about you?*"

"FUCK!" The lieutenant spit again. "ISN'T THAT BADASS?"

"OORAH!"

"Hey, roger that Marines." Brzescer pointed to Fonzie. "Fonzie, you motivated?"

"Fuck yeah, I am, Sir!"

"Good. Hey Marines, when we get there, fuck that 'let the training take over' bullshit. Do what you need to do out there for the Marines to the left and right of you. God Country Corps, that don't matter at that point. Do what you need to do to bring you and your brothers home. When we push ISIS and Iran's ass out of Iraq the Iraqi people will be on their knees every day thanking Allah that *angry,* pissed-off Marines had been cut loose to save them.

"We're going to go in there with tremendous capability with weapons systems, combat power, and motivation. And I'll tell you right now the very reason you joined the Corps, regardless of where you've been or you past experiences… Except Sangin and Now Zad…"

The platoon gave the officer another "OORAH!"

"…You're going to get everything you've been hungry for. It's going to be in your face and personal and you're going to give the enemy what he's asking for. A good American ass kicking! With that being said, I don't want to see any of you again until zero two tomorrow. Have all your shit and be ready to go on the grinder."

We scattered to the winds. Doc found me, he too got put in CAAT

1 because their old corpsman had broken his leg and couldn't deploy.

"Hank!"

"What's up, Doc?"

"Dude, that lieutenant was a badass."

"I know, right?" We stopped at the smoke deck and lit up. "Now, about him, no one can prove it, but the rumor about him from last deployment was that he's a dip-powered robot from the future sent back to save mankind."

Doc laughed. "That awesome, huh?"

"Yeah man. You know how when you watch a movie the officer is either a moron or the god of fucking death?"

"Yeah."

"Brzescer kicked the god of death in the dick. We call him the SirBot."

The next day we flew from March Air Force Base in California to Maine, to Germany, and finally to Kuwait. When we got to Kuwait we were loaded onto trucks and convoyed to the city of Al Najaf. Najaf didn't have too much going for it. There was a huge cemetery, a giant golden mosque, an airport, and the rest of the city was the typical beige brick of Middle Eastern cities. The only tactical aspects of the city were that it was on the Euphrates so we could stop any further Iranian aggression.

The battalion was spread through the city. Fox Company, CAAT 1, and a mortar section were put in the airport. At one time the facility was an air base for Saddam's Air Force. There wasn't anything military left in the place, but since the war started the airport was closed for business. Iranians had shot down any civilian aircraft that had tried to fly out.

Marines slept together as squads. If there was an artillery attack or an air strike they didn't want more than a handful of Marines to get killed with just one bomb. The Bravo section of CAAT 1 slept in a hangar on the floor. Our territory was marked by a few Jolly Rogers and a wooden sign that read, 'Abandon All Hope Ye Who Enter: CAAT 1B Cock-Strong Warrior Man-Gods!'

We had three parts to our days at the airport in Al Najaf. We spent eight hours a day standing guard, eight hours filling sandbags and laying down barbed wire to fortify the area, and we had eight hours to sleep. We only had MREs to eat, until care packages started coming in from loved ones. There weren't set meal times; we'd just eat whenever we had a minute.

We wore our boonie covers and always had to have our weapon and at least one magazine on us at all times. When we washed our clothes we had to do it with water bottles and soap, if we could get our hands on it. I wasn't trying to impress anyone. I never cleaned my uniform, it was painted with dirt and sweat stains. My trousers were stiff enough from salt to stand on their own.

The designated smoking area was next to the air terminal. It read 'Al-Najaf Al-Ashraf International Airport' in English. I assume the Arabic writing above it said the same. There were camouflage nets draped from the side of the building to dilute the sun. A wooden bench and a table made by some engineers rested in the shade.

It was a little more than a hundred degrees outside; the heat radiating from the tarmac did us no favors. I sat under the netting on a bench smoking a cigarette with a few other Marines. Sergeant Fields, CAAT Bravo's section leader, asked if he could bum a smoke.

"Thanks, man," said Fields as he drew the cylinder out of the pack.

"No problem," I quipped as I looked over the airstrip. A mirage of invisible fire burned over the asphalt.

"Hey sergeant?"

"What's up?" Fields said with his deep southern accent.

"When are we getting vehicles? I mean, what's a CAAT section without trucks?"

"Hell if I know. Shit, we don't even have missiles."

"Yeah, just the .50s and mark nineteens, right?"

"Yup. I hope the Iranians don't decide to start anything before we get set up. I really don't want to walk the whole way," he laughed.

"Do you know if we're getting MRAPS or hummers?"

"Now, I don't know for sure." Fields blew smoke out of his nose. "But I heard we're getting MATVs."

"That would be cool. Those things are badass."

"Yeah. My chief concern though is I hope this shit doesn't play out like Desert Storm did. I don't want to cross the river and have them all surrender before we can kill any of them." Fields ashed.

Everyone in the smoke pit laughed.

Doc showed up from around the corner and sat down next to me.

"So what's all this shit about anyway?" Doc said as he lit a cigarette.

Fields said, "They probably think we're too tired of war to do anything about them starting shit. Apparently they haven't read a history book and didn't see what we fucking did to Japan. There's all kinds of political bullshit about what's happening. I'm just here to fight; point me towards the enemy."

"There are other reasons to be here, Sergeant," McBland said. "I want to see some hot-ass Hajji chicks."

"Yeah," I added. "Persian chicks are hot."

Fields shot back, "Yeah, when they don't have their faces cut off because they live in some shit-hole country. I mean seriously, your chick wants to show some skin? Here's militant Muslim rationale, I can see my woman's ankles. *Let's burn off her face!* Fuck that shit!" Fields spat on the concrete.

"I will go and fight these fuckers anytime anywhere in any country. What's wrong with these assholes is that they don't live in America. Let the women walk around *ass* naked, I'd bet you money that even super-militant-feminists would rather let women be viewed as sexual objects than a piece of property whose face I get to burn off because I'm bored tonight. I mean, how fucking fucked in the fucking head do you have to be to take a smoking hot woman and beat her face in with a rock just because I can?" Fields added

"Well…" Doc interrupted Fields. "I've never hit a woman, but there are reasons to do it, if you want equality any reason to hit a man is also a reason to hit a woman, you know, if a person is a person." We all stared at Doc.

"Just say'n."

Fields gave Doc a blank look. "Dude, for me to cut off a chicks face, that bitch would have to be the person lighting the ovens at Auschwitz."

I laughed out, "So what you're saying is that even in the midst of a Holocaustic nightmare the women are still stuck working ovens."

Doc added, "Yeah, and these jihadists hate Jews too. Maybe the SS were all Persians. I mean, Iran means 'Land of the Aryans.'"

Fields laughed. "Well, fuck all of them. Fucking damn Nazis. Nazis and jihadists are the same kind of assholes. Shit, they should get together with the ancient Egyptians and build a base on the moon and try to ethnically cleanse that. You know what the problem is? Israel is *packed* with smoking hot women who strut around in jeans and skimpy t-shirts. All these dickless, faggot, cocksuckers are jealous. That's all that it is. That's why they hate the Jews."

"Yeah, well I was just going to say that I want to put my dick under a burka, but I guess that would work too," Doc said.

I looked at Doc and inhaled my cigarette. "Doc, have you ever fucked anything that wasn't from the Philippines?"

"Uh…"

"What about your pocket pussy?" Fields jabbed.

Doc threw his hands up. "You guys are assholes! And no, I think my pocket pussy is from there too."

We laughed at Doc.

Fields flicked his cigarette into the ammo can we used as an ashtray. "Stay motivated, gentlemen."

I said, "Cock-strong warrior man-gods," as Fields walked off. He raised his hand to make the metal horns as he walked away.

After we had been in Al Najaf for about a month and a half doing little more than cleaning weapons, filling sand bags, and smoking cigarettes we stopped fortifying. We hadn't received any word about movement or actually kicking off the war, we had just built up enough to where it wasn't necessary any more.

We got our first mail call around that time too. Most of us had been writing letters and sending them home, but this was the first time anyone got anything back. I got a letter from Kennedy. It read:

Babe,

I hope you're enjoying Iraq. You know what I think of the situation, so I won't go into that. Nothing much is going on here except for the weather's been unusually cold. I've been having some issues with the people at the Purple Church so I don't think I'll be working there much longer. I just about have enough money to go back to school.

What do they have you doing there? The news says you guys are just waiting there for something to happen. Everyone's asking for pictures of you in Iraq. When you can, please send one, if you can.

I miss you! I miss the feel of your hands on me… my hair, face, head, back, and chest, ANYWHERE! I miss that one-eyebrow raised thing you do, it's very sexy. I miss the feel of you inside of me. I miss your cute ass and gorgeous eyes.

If it was up to me, I would spend every day with you behind closed doors, whether you're just playing with my hair or we're having, as you put it, "freaky monkey sex" even though there's nothing freaky or monkey about it. Except for when you have been drinking tequila and you… well, you know what you do. I probably sound like a babbling idiot. I'm sorry but I miss you.

Yours,

Yasmina Gulbadan Kassandrazaden

"Kennedy"

She also enclosed a provocative photo of herself covering her breasts and vagina with her hands, the perfect amount of her body was left to the imagination. I put the picture in my wallet next to the one of Satin that I'd been carrying around since boot camp, even though we broke up right before my first deployment.

I re-read the letter a few times lying on the hangar floor propped up against my pack.

A voice from behind me spoke, "That chick's pretty hung up on you, huh?"

I looked up to see Fonzie. "What's up, dude?"

"Nothing much, man. Your girl's gotta interesting name."

"She's Persian." I pulled out her photo and showed it to him.

"Damn!" Fonzie exclaimed. "What are you doing about to kill a bunch of Iranians if you're banging one?"

"I'm doing it Genghis Kahn style. Kill the men; fuck the women."

"Nice." Fonzie said as he handed me back the photo. "I got a package, man, but I just got off watch so I haven't opened it yet."

"Well let's go open it," I added enthusiastically.

Fonzie and I walked to his area. He had one white US postage box sitting on his pack. He picked it up, pulled out a knife, and cut away the tape. "What'd ya get, man?"

Fonzie started pulling out the contents of the care package and displaying them on the ground. "Turkey bites, drink mix, wash cloth… hand warmers?"

"Oh yeah, you're definitely going to need those." I laughed.

"Yeah, it's not like we're in the desert or anything, right?"

"Who's that from?" I asked.

"This girl I know. We're not super serious or anything. I met her on the Internet when we were in Afghan last year."

"That's terrible, man."

"Naaaa, it's not bad."

"Never trust women from the Internet," said the Marine laying at our feet. The Marine, Corporal Becker, sat up. "I met this one chick on some dating site, and it was fucking terrible."

"Oh yea? Tell us about it," we asked.

"Okay, so I get on this dating website. I'm talking to chicks all over the place and I meet this one girl, Rebecca. We email each other for a while, then we start texting, then she says she wants to meet me. So before I go meet her we video chat first just to make sure she's the same girl in the pictures she sends me. We chat for a bit and she's fucking hot, long blonde hair, big fat tits—the whole nine yards. Anyways, we set up a date and I go to her house to pick her up. Her dad answers the door and I tell him I am there to meet Rebecca. He says okay and goes back into the house to get her. Two minutes later he pushes this bitch out in a wheelchair. I'm thinking 'Fuck.' Anyway, he helps load her into my car and we drive off. I'm trying to keep my eyes on the road and not make it look like I noticed that she doesn't have any fucking legs. I ask her what she wants to do that night. She tells me there's a baseball diamond just up the road. Now, this is back in Alaska, *nothing* is just up the road. The drive takes about an hour. We're chitchatting for a bit and she pulls her compact out of her purse and instead of makeup in it she's got fucking cocaine! She asks if I want some and I tell her I'm good. She snorts a bunch of it. I mean a fucking lot. Eventually we get to this field and I park and carry her to the dugout. She starts talking about how pretty the stars are and blah blah blah. Then she kisses me. I'm like whatever, I'm weirded out, but tits are tits. After a bit she starts taking my pants off. I'm like 'whoa girl' and she says 'What? You don't want this?' I let her go at it. She didn't have legs, like at all. Body ended at the hips. So she's holding onto the chain-link fence behind us to bob herself up and down like she's doing pull-ups. We get done and I carry her back to the car and drive back to her place without saying one fucking word. I bring her to the door and give her back to her dad. He tells me to wait a minute while he puts Rebecca to bed. I'm thinking, *'Great, this guy's going to kick my ass for fucking his daughter.'* A few minutes later he comes back and tells me thanks. He says 'Rebecca hasn't been out in a while and she seems like she had a good time with you. She doesn't date much and the last asshole that she went out with ditched her in a baseball field an hour away from here.'"

We laughed at Becker's story.

"So yeah," Becker said. "Don't meet girls on the Internet."

Fonzie shook his head. "Dude, you made that shit up."

"No man, that happened, I swear to God."

"Come on, Fonz." I slapped Fonzie on the arm. "Let's go smoke."

Éclair was in the smoke pit with a few grunts from Fox Company.

"Good afternoon, Corporal," Éclair acknowledged me.

I just gave him a "Hey" as I pulled out my cigarette.

"Corporal Allensworth, hey I have a question for you."

"What's that, boot?"

"In Afghanistan did the locals play ridiculous music at dawn every day?"

"Yeah. It's an Islamic thing. They play it from the mosques."

Fonzie added, "It always reminds me of the *Lion King* with the AASAAAAAAAAAAMBAABAAAAAAAMAAAAA!"

Everyone in the smoke pit chuckled.

"It's fucking annoying," Éclair said.

"Well get used to it, they're not going to stop," I answered him.

"Yuck. What else did they do in Afghanistan, Corporal?"

"Fuck, all kinds of shit. You can ask Fonzie here. We weren't allowed to just kill people we took prisoner. But when we were in Lashkar Gah we caught a few guys with IED-making material and we gave them to the Afghan National Police. Their headquarters prison was adjacent to our FOB. At night we'd hear the police just beating the shit out of the guys we caught laying bombs. Even with those guys' blood-curdling screams, the worst part of it was laying there at night listening to them scream while right outside donkeys were fucking."

"What?" Éclair said in disbelief.

Fonzie threw in.

"Yeah man, it was like something out of a horror movie. There'd be guys screaming and at the same time you'd hear HHHHAAAAAAWWWW HAAAAAAWWWWWW!" He thrusted his hips, fucking an imaginary donkey.

"Jesus H. Christ, dude," Éclair said with a disturbed look on his face.

"Yeah man," I added. "It was fucking weird."

With the defenses built up, things started to get boring. We all still stood post, but that became the biggest part of the day. Most of the time when we weren't staring into the desert watching for Iran we tried to work out, read books, smoke, and bullshit. We weren't getting complacent, but we were on that road.

As more troops started flooding into Iraq a few things got better.

We started getting hot chow for dinner, and since CAAT got our vehicles we got to drive across the city every evening to pick up food for the Marines at the airport. The chow came in these big green coolers. It kept the food warm. It wasn't necessarily good, but it was a hell of a lot better than MREs. We'd return the previous day's empty containers and load the trucks with that night's slop.

One night while the sun was falling out of the western sky I opened the mail I had gotten from Kennedy. She was doing fine, she didn't really have anything to say, but she did enclose another provocative photo of herself. I stood on the smoke deck next to Doc and Éclair. I showed Kennedy's photo to Doc.

"Nice, man," he said. "She's got some nice tits."

Éclair then asked curiously, "Who's that?"

"Naked photos of my girlfriend."

"You must not like her very much, Corporal."

"She's a stripper," Doc defended what honor an Oceanside stripper could have.

"Oh." Éclair nodded. "Can I see it?"

"No," I laughed.

"Why not, Corporal?"

"Because you're a fucking boot."

Doc and I laughed at him. "Doc, I'm glad that she tries to keep these kinda classy. Like she doesn't have a magic marker shoved in her ass or anything."

I handed the picture to Éclair. "Here ya go boot."

Éclair examined the photo. "Damn, Corporal, she's hot."

"Yeah, no shit."

Éclair handed the picture back to me. "My girlfriend Ginny won't do that."

"The tit photo thing?" Doc asked. "Or shove random writing utensils up her ass?"

"Neither," answered Éclair. "She kinda writes me kinky letters, but all I get picture-wise is bikinis, and they're pictures of her at the beach anyway, so I'm not getting anything more than what everyone else gets to see on the Internet."

"Dump her ass." I lit another cigarette.

"I don't think it's *that* bad," Éclair added.

"It is," said Doc.

"Yeah." I exhaled a thick plume of smoke. "Think of it like this. Naked photos are *essential* to a relationship. It says to you that she loves you and wants you to come back and it shows what she's got waiting for you when you come home."

Doc took over. "It's also physical proof that she has faith in your relationship. It also says that she trusts you and she thinks enough of you that you're not going to put the pictures of her tits on the Internet or anything."

"The thing about it though," I continued, "it's NOT cool that she won't send you sexy pics, but it's even more not cool for you to tell her that it's not cool. Don't even deal with chicks like that. Just dump her."

"Yeah," Doc agreed.

"I guess I never looked at it like that." Éclair was at the end of his cigarette.

"I mean, unless the chick's the great white buffalo," I went on.

"The Ted Nugent song?" Éclair asked.

"No, dude," Doc said. "You know the chick you used to date or almost dated or whatever and you think about her all the time but because of whatever it was that happened you two are *never* going to get back together. But if the opportunity would present itself then you would totally leave your girlfriend or wife in the drop of a hat."

"Okay," said Éclair. "I know who you're talking about."

"But there's a catch to that," I added. "You absolutely cannot actually be with *that* woman. If you never break up with her you'll get married and be fucking miserable and you'll end up just fucking hating the bitch because there would have been *so* much more that you could have done with your life that she held you back from, and you'll know it. You'll have three kids before you're twenty-five and you won't actually start having a real life until you're in your forties and halfway to death."

"And what you think of that chick now is different than it would actually be," Doc butted in. "Like, it's kind of the same situation. There's this chick named Alice, I've been in love with her since I was seventeen. She'd never give me the time of day; I'm firmly in the friend zone. It's fucked up because before every deployment I talk to her and ask her if it's cool if I could write to her and she says 'yes' all excited and shit, then I write her all deployment long and she doesn't write one word fucking back. It's a morale killer. But anyway, Alice is more like a fantasy for me because if we ever did get together what would actually happen would probably be completely different than what I worked up in my head. And, fuck, it's at the point now where if I did ever go for it with Alice I'd fuck it up and never talk to her again. Right now I'd rather have her as a friend and talk to her every once in a while than fuck it up and never talk to her again at all."

"It sounds to me like you're not talking to her now Doc." I laughed at him.

"Okay, well then maybe I'm just a pussy. But I guess it's good I'm not with her. I'm always gone fucking fighting wars and shit. I'd never actually be around for her and she'd probably end up leaving me anyway. It's probably better she's just happy somewhere. And you know I'd like to think that she was thinking of me too sometimes, but she's probably not."

"Yeah," I threw in. "She's more of a fantasy at this point anyway."

"You lost me on that." Éclair was slightly confused.

"Just write your girlfriend and tell her to show you her tits and if she doesn't, stop talking to her. Or if this war ever fucking happens you'll get too busy to want to talk to her and you'll ignore her and she'll fuck some guy at a party and leave you anyway."

"Corporal," Éclair said. "You seem like the kind of guy that's going to be a sergeant major one day, but still single and banging random chicks all of the time."

"I don't know about *that*. I actually almost got married one time."

"Really?" Éclair said in disbelief. "What happened to that?"

"Well, I went to Afghanistan and she started fucking one of the guys at her college. You know, that bit. Satin Sheats. Can you believe a stupid name like that?"

"Oh, shitty. You still ever talk to her? Is she *that* girl to you?"

"Fuck no. That bitch wouldn't piss on me if I was on fire to save her life, much less talk to me. And I don't know about the buffalo thing. I think there has to be a bridge that hasn't been burned into the ground to qualify for that one."

"Ah," nodded Éclair.

"And the whole thing pissed me off. I saw pictures of them together on the Internet and all, and the dude was uglier than a bulldog and fatter than a whale. I don't understand chicks, man."

"It could be worse, dude," Doc said. "At least you didn't find out she left you by way of seeing a video of her getting gang banged by a bunch of black dudes like Walters."

"I forgot about that!" I laughed.

"What happened?" Éclair asked.

"Well you see what happened was…" Doc started. "Walters' girlfriend decided that she wanted to do porno, and Walters is a weirdo anyway so he agrees to it. His only stipulations were she couldn't fuck more than one guy at a time or any black dudes."

"Okay," Éclair chuckled.

"So we're in Afghanistan for like three months," Doc continued. "And we find a video of his girlfriend, because we all knew she was a porn star. We bring him into the tent and make him watch this video. He sits down and we start to play the movie on someone's laptop and his girlfriend comes out and starts saying slutty things to the camera. Then five giant black dudes show up and start gang fucking her."

"Dude that *is* fucked up," Éclair laughed.

"Then Walters starts crying and trying to leave, and since no one liked him we made him sit there and watch the whole thing."

"It was awesome," I said. "It wasn't the most fucked up thing that ever happened, but it was up there."

"That sounds pretty fucked up to me, Corporal."

"Yeah, but about the old single sergeant major thing. The stars come out at night and diamonds are a girl's best friend, but bombs and rifles win wars."

The next afternoon I laid with my head propped up against my pack on the cool concrete floor of the hangar failing to fall asleep.

I heard Becker outside telling a story. I figured I'd go listen in. Becker was reading aloud from a book to several other Marines who were sitting on the ground listening.

"Claudia laid awake in bed. The early morning sun cut between the curtains of her bedroom window. The red satin sheets felt warm against her skin. They were soft to the touch. Claudia ran the material between her fingers. She hadn't opened her eyes for the first time that morning. She pretended the body pillow she cuddled was the tall tanned man from her work. She fondled the pillow's midsection and imagined the things the man

would say to her if it was him, in fact, lying beside her. Claudia's hand slowly made its way from the pillow to the side of her thigh. She caressed herself to the part between her legs that was growing increasingly moister. She rubbed her fingers over her sex through her lacy green boy-shorts. She imagined what the muscular man from work would do to her if he were there. Keeping one arm wrapped around the body pillow she stroked her kitten. She started to breathe heavily."

"This is starting to get good," Alvarado said through a mouth full of tobacco.

"Claudia felt a bit adventurous that morning. Using just her fingers to love herself wasn't going to cut it," Becker continued. *"She slowly removed the linen from over her perfect body and slid her feet to the floor. She was home all alone and there was a fire in her loins. She made her way to the kitchen. Claudia had heard stories of people using food to please themselves. Maybe she had something that would be her lover for the morning."*

"What in the fuck are you reading, Becker?" Doc interrupted.

Becker showed Doc the book's cover. *Fifty Shades of Dave.*

"Where did you get that?" I inquired.

"I stole it from the USO in Kuwait," Becker responded as if it was of no consequence.

"Alrighty then," Doc interjected. "Continue, please."

Becker looked back at the pages.

"Claudia opened the refrigerator door to find nothing she felt comfortable with. She decided that she'd eat breakfast while she thought of something to do to herself. Pulling out a cup of yogurt and a spoon she thought that maybe she'd visit one of those silly sex sites. She had never been to one; maybe while she was all worked up would be the best time to go."

"Who writes these?" Alvarado asked.

"Some fat bitch fulfilling her fantasies," Doc answered.

"Claudia walked into the living room and slid the cold moist yogurt into her

mouth. A drop of the white goo fell from the spoon and landed on her left nipple. She was, after all, only wearing her panties. She went to remove the splotch with her hand. When her palm made contact she found herself rubbing her breast instead of cleaning up. Claudia didn't know why but she enjoyed the feel of the cool semisolid gunk spread across her chest. She took another spoonful of the yogurt and plopped it between her breasts. Using both hands Claudia massaged her upper body with the yogurt. Her breathing became labored again."

"This bitch is a tease," Doc complained.

"She glanced up and through the window she saw Dave, the pool boy, toiling away at the water. He had no idea what she was doing, and Claudia didn't care that if Dave turned he would see her. In fact, it made Claudia's blood boil knowing that he could. Dave had his hands in the pool scrubbing away the gunk that had been growing. The pool looked as a swamp. Claudia imagined that her feminine parts were the water and Dave's hands were working away on her. Dave was tall and lean with short blonde hair."

"Now it's starting to get good!" Alvarado spat.

"Dave pulled his dripping wet hands out of the swamp-like ooze and pulled his shirt off. Claudia, in turn, slipped off her panties. Her sex was oozing wetness like honey from a comb. But she didn't lay a finger between her legs. She was getting all that she needed from the yogurt on her breasts. Dave grabbed a pole to scoop out the algae that was growing in the ill-kept water. Matching his movements, Claudia took her spoon and swirled it around her nipples. She closed her eyes and rolled her head back into the sofa, still using the spoon to pleasure herself."

"I wonder if the carpet matches the drapes," Doc chuckled.

I responded, "It does, but the upholstery doesn't."

"What does that even mean?"

"I don't know, Doc. Becker, please continue."

"When Claudia opened her eyes again she saw Dave standing in the window with a look of surprise on his face. His mouth was half open and a blunt rested on his lip. Claudia wasn't shocked. She wanted him. She scooped a spoonful of yogurt from the cup and splattered it where her legs met. Looking Dave straight in the eyes, she used the

spoon to play with the ooze melting on her pussy. She tapped her love button. The cold metal was surprisingly delightful. Claudia beckoned Dave to come."

"Okay, I'm out." Doc tapped my shoulder. "Let's go smoke before we have to go get chow."

I heard Becker continue the story as we walked away. *"Claudia stood from the couch and dropped to her knees, abusing the spoon with her tongue…"*

Fox Company, along with the attached CAAT platoon stayed at the airport. The battalion headquarters was ten minutes away on the west side of the city. I don't know why they didn't just send a cook or two out to each company. They kept them all up at HQ. We ate MREs for breakfast and lunch and every night CAAT would go get dinner for Fox. We loaded the previous day's food containers in the trucks and drove to the cooks. We traded our dirty green tote boxes for new ones, filled with what only qualifies as food because it doesn't kill you if you eat it. The food wasn't prepared anywhere special. It was just outside a tent. On the inside, there were wooden tables for the Marines who stayed in that area to eat. We pulled the trucks right up to the back of the tent. Chow wasn't ready yet.

Everyone in my truck got out to stretch our legs, except Fonzie, he stayed up in the turret; he had plenty of room to move his legs around. Kyle the driver, Fields our vehicle commander, Doc, and I stood behind the truck smoking cigarettes. We were sarcastically commenting on how nice it had to be to work around the battalion staff officers and get to eat hot food three times a day when we heard a whistling. Everyone's face grew stern.

"INCOMING!"

5 DEMONS AND DIRT IN THE LAND BETWEEEN THE RIVERS

Artillery rounds screamed through the air, screeches ripped the atmosphere, shells exploded in the dirt. Fields, Doc, Kyle, and I dove to the ground and hugged the sand. None of our platoon had been hit yet. Incoming fire was close enough that the earth blown to the sky rained down on us.

The four of us were not having a good time.

Kyle looked up at Sergeant Fields. "THIS SUCKS!" he shouted above the roar of explosions.

"It's not that bad!" Fields screamed back at Kyle.

An artillery round screamed to the earth and uprooted a large plot of soil. It was so close that it bumped us off the ground an inch or two.

"SEE!" Fields screamed. "Just missed!" Pantomiming the closeness with his thumb and index finger.

Doc flipped off Fields, while keeping his hands close to the ground.

Over the deafening sound of the shells I saw the SirBot walking around the trucks as if the rounds that were falling from the sky were but single drops of rain.

"What the fuck?" he shouted at the platoon. "Get the fuck in your trucks!" Lieutenant Brzescer pointed into the distance at what looked like a small village. "THEY'RE FUCKING LANDING TROOPS! GET IN YOUR GODDAMN VEHICLES, WE'VE GOT MOTHER FUCKING PEOPLE TO KILL!"

Doc, Kyle, Fields, and I nervously crawled out from under our truck and loaded up. Through the window I saw Iranian soldiers repelling from helicopters into the village. I saw the SirBot tread back to his truck, swearing the whole walk. Kyle started the engine and the platoon rolled towards the enemy landing.

The lieutenant ordered the platoon to line up so that everyone could fire at the enemy troops ahead without shooting each other. As soon as our line of fire was clear, Fonzie opened fire from the turret.

As we got closer it turned out that the village wasn't a village at all. It was a *massive* graveyard. It must have stretched out for miles. Graves over in Iraq though aren't like they are in the States. Instead of a plot of land and a gravestone, there's a small building just big enough to put a body in. They were made of beige bricks with headstones protruding from the top of the structures. They'd have a name inscribed and sometimes a picture of the person lying beneath.

Our trucks slowed down as we approached the edge of the cemetery. I heard four ear-splintering cracks. Kyle and Fields screamed from the front. Doc and I looked to make sure they were all right. They were okay, only startled from bullets turning the windshield into a glass spider web.

Fonzie kneeled down into the truck from his turret. "Allensworth!" He pointed at a box of ammunition behind me. "Hand me that ammo!"

I shoved him the olive colored box. Fifty-caliber ammunition is heavy, but the adrenaline canceled it out.

Fields barked orders to another truck via the radio. The sun was starting to set. Fonzie let loose the fifty caliber.

Doc nudged me. "Hey Hank!"

"What's up man?"

"We're getting a second Combat Action Ribbon!" he laughed amid the loudness of the machinegun fire.

"Yeah," I shouted back sarcastically. "Because we need another one."

Fields turned around and yelled, "Doc, Kodak, get your shit; we're heading in." He shoved open his door, sprinted to the nearest grave, and took cover. The Marines from the other trucks were doing the same. Doc and I followed suit.

Minus the drivers and turret gunners, the whole platoon huddled next to graves. It was dark enough to see the flames from the machine guns on the trucks and the tracer rounds flying into the yard. Enemy rounds split the air over our heads. Some hit the trucks but the Marines inside were protected by ballistic glass and an inch of steel.

Intermittently, Marines would swing around the graves and fire a few rounds of suppressing fire towards the Iranians. It was too dark to take photos. I leaned out from the tombstones enough to see where the Iranians were. I had the stock of my M4 against my cheek and the scope up to my eye. I squeezed the trigger two or three times. The weapon's butt beat back into my shoulder. There was hardly any kick. Not that I would've normally noticed, all the adrenaline made it feel like a tap.

Above the *pops* and the *pows* there was a screech and an explosion. Our truck's front end rose into the air in a gust of fire, throwing shards of metal in every direction. The vehicle breathed orange flames.

"FUCK!" Doc screamed. He started pulling at his medical bag. "Come on, Hank!"

We ran to the truck and opened up the driver side door. Kyle was knocked out. I grabbed his flak jacket and started to yank him out of the truck. I was startled and fell to the ground at the sound of machinegun fire coming from the turret. "I guess Fonzie's okay!" I shouted at Doc. I stood back up and helped get Kyle out.

We dragged Kyle to the tombstones where he'd be safe from enemy fire. Doc started looking over Kyle. Fields screamed at me to get Fonzie out of the truck before it blew.

I sprinted back to the vehicle. Fonzie was still spraying out fifty-caliber hate like it was the Fourth of July. I tried yelling to get his attention. He didn't respond. I crawled in the driver side door, flames were starting to sear through the windshield. I grabbed Fonzie's leg and pulled at his pants. The machine gun fire kept up for a few seconds before he leaned down into the cab. He was panting heavily. His forehead bled from just under his helmet.

"Come on man, you're on fire!"

Fonzie looked towards the windshield and nodded. "Yeah…"

I helped him out of the truck and took him by Doc. Kyle was starting to wake up. Doc looked at the Fonz. "Shit, man." Doc leaned Fonzie against the bricks and took off his helmet. Doc applied gauze to the wound that was destined to leave a gnarly scar just below Fonzie's hairline and wrapped his head with a green bandage.

The SirBot ran up to our position and kneeled by Fields. "How are your Marines?" he demanded with a stone face.

Fields didn't miss a beat. "Kyle's got a concussion, but he'll be okay. Fonzie's hit a little worse."

Doc looked up at the lieutenant. "He'll be okay, Sir! He doesn't quite need an emergency casevac."

"Alright," Brzescer said to Fields. "Our orders are to hold our position and deny the Iranians any advancement. We'll move when Fox Company arrives, they're already en route. This gravesite's gonna be close quarters. If you've got your bayonets, fix them." He slapped Fields on the shoulder. "Stay in the fight." The SirBot sprinted to the next group of Marines near another set of gravestones

I looked at Doc; we both started to laugh. "I guess we're fucked now huh!"

Doc grumbled.

Fields unsheathed his bayonet and fixed it to the end of his rifle while Kyle, Doc, and I did the same. Fonzie still needed a minute to recuperate.

An hour crept by as we waited behind the first line of graves. Silence was broken by sporadic artillery rounds that fell around us. Small arms fire chipped away at the tombstones. The irony of the dead protecting the living was not lost on us.

There was a fog of Iraqi dirt creating a haze and the ground shook below us.

It was dark now. All I could see were muzzle flashes from the guns. The stars and the large crescent moon hung above us. It felt surreal, like a dream. Like hell was slowly creeping upon us.

There was a sound of rolling thunder in the air; the enemy's bullets cracked the sky as they flew over my head.

BOOOOOMMM!!!

The ammo that was in our truck finally exploded amongst the flames. Random POPs and BANGS of 50 cal. Ammo shot out from the fire like the crackle of some demented burning log. My night vision goggles were in the burning vehicle, along with most of the rest of my gear, food and water.

It was all probably melted into a black puddle by now.

I took a look at my wounded brothers in arms.

Blood oozed from under the olive wrap around Fonzie's head. The streaks of black dried blood on his face gave him a ghoulish look. It was staining his uniform too, but he was ready to go. His rifle was in the burning truck, leaving him with his pistol and a couple dozen rounds

Fox Company arrived at our position and we got orders to flush the Iranians out of the cemetery, back over the Euphrates. It would have been suicide to stand up and charge them, even with night vision, which I didn't have. Weaving between the unevenly placed tombs at night didn't sound too appealing to me anyway.

Fields laid prone in the dirt and started crawling between the graves towards the enemy. Kyle, Fonzie, Doc, and I followed. The sand was hard with bits of rock; it mixed with my pouring sweat into mud and stuck to me. I put the buttstock of my M4 in my armpit so that it was facing forward and I crawled like a snake.

I was scared out of my fucking mind. We had only the darkness and haze to mask our movements. We had the advantage because they couldn't see us return fire.

The last time I saw enemy muzzle flash was about three hundred meters down range. It was either going to be a long ass crawl or it was going to be over real fucking quick. I wasn't able to put any words together in my head besides *fuck* and *shit*.

After we crawled for what seemed like fifty yards into the cemetery a POP and a HISS broke out from the gunfire, and the sky turned orange. Someone, either the Marine mortar team in the rear or the Iranians, must have started firing flares to illuminate the battleground. Everything was bathed in orange. The company froze in their tracks, not moving so much as an inch. The human eye notices movement more than anything. If they saw even an arm move we would be dead. But illumination goes both ways.

The flares died out, but not before ruining my eyes' adjustment to the night. I heard a rustle and barely made out the sight of Kyle in front of me starting to crawl again. After only a minute or two there was more hissing and another flare, again we laid still. I closed my eyes in an attempt to readjust to the darkness.

I heard the sand under Kyle crunch as he started to crawl again. I opened my eyes. My vision was still blurry. It was quiet besides the shifting of the sands and machinegun fire in the distance. There was another pop and hiss. The sky turned orange again. Only this time between the gravestones, about five yards in front of Kyle, were the silhouettes of men with AK47s walking toward us. Time slowed to a crawl.

Lead flew in all directions.

I couldn't see anything except for their outlines when the muzzles flashed. If I were to shoot from the prone I would have either hit Kyle or a gravestone. *Fuck it.* I rose to a kneel. Most of my body was still covered but I could see a bit better. I sighted in and placed my reticle on the muzzle fire from the enemy's guns. I pulled the trigger over and over again until there was a click. Kyle kept the chaos going as he sprinted toward the enemy just as I was about to get down and reload. His first order of business was smashing someone's face into a crater with his butt stock. He was pissed and it showed.

"Don't just look at him!" Fields screamed as he ran towards Kyle's position.

The rest of the Marines rushed.

Before long there was an all-out brawl. No gunfire existed in the immediate vicinity, just the screams and roars of warriors bludgeoning each other into the dirt tombs around us. Free-for-all melees in a cemetery that stretched to the horizons. Hundreds of men fighting tooth and nail amidst the crypts of millions of already fallen souls, mangled each other in an effort to survive getting chewed by the jaws of death and swallowed into the very mouth of Hell, a battle for the city of the dead. Each man trading blows to avoid joining the dead in their slumber.

I was lost in an emotion between terror and rage. I felt my mind resorting to its primal state. The enemy's faces were blurred into nightmarish ghouls. Doc had resorted to holding his weapon by the handrails, swinging it like a baseball bat. An Iranian soldier charged towards him from behind while Doc was beating one of their faces into meatloaf. Before the soldier could get to Doc, I drove my bayonet into his gut, right above his beltline, and ripped it through to the other side of his belly, spilling his intestines into the sand. He groaned and fell back onto a tomb. I put the blade in his neck. His blood soaked the earth.

I looked behind to Doc. "You owe me a beer, fucker!" I shouted amidst the chaos.

Then suddenly, a black mass slammed me to the ground. My helmet cushioning the shock. I looked up and found myself straddled by an Iranian with his rifle in the air preparing to swing it into my skull. He plunged the weapon down to kill. Fire in his eyes, the white of his teeth looked like fangs.

Mere moments before the weapon could hit my face. I saw his skull explode with bits of bone and brain splattering my face like some kind of fucked up bukkake. He fell on top of me, oozing viscera and brain matter.

Doc kicked the heap of meat off me and offered his hand. "I hope that fucker didn't have AIDS."

I wiped the warm red liquid off my face. My vision clearing; I could see our guys were literally beating back the fuckers who wanted to rumble.

It seemed the enemy in our neck of the woods didn't want to play anymore. The few that were left ran back into the darkness. That didn't save them though. Everyone who had ammunition emptied it into their backs.

It was an exhausting moment that only lasted minutes, but had felt like hours. I counted a dozen dead in our vicinity. Most of them looked like pulverized ground beef. Hell Field's mouth was bloodied, not from wounds, but from the chunk of neck he tore out from one of his victims.

Miraculously, with the exception of some bruises and cuts, we took no casualties.

The enemy was in retreat for now. We had to keep the momentum going.

Over the course of the next few hours we slowly cleared our way to the Euphrates River and halted. We looked behind every rock and in every house. Along the shore Doc and I found a large stone to prop ourselves onto. I pulled out two Lucky's and handed one to Doc.

"What was the deal with that graveyard?" Doc asked.

"Besides that it was scary as fuck?" I replied.

"Why is it so big?" he exhaled thick smoke.

"Your sister asked me the same thing one time," I laughed.

"Ha ha, very funny," Doc droned.

Neither of us said much for a while. We just smoked our cigarettes and gazed at the river as the sunlight rose over the horizon. What we didn't know then was that Wadi Al Salaam was the largest cemetery in the world. It was three square miles. Over five million souls were estimated to rest there. They didn't get too much sleep that night.

A squad from Fox Company came and sat next to us. Éclair was with them. I motioned him over to us. "You were in that, right?"

"Yes, Corporal. I pushed all the way through with Fox. It was fucking nuts!"

"Yeah." I looked up at Éclair, who was still standing. He looked a bit shaken, but then again I suppose we all did. "Where were you guys at?"

"We came up by the burnt-up truck on the way to the graveyard."

"That was our truck," Doc stated.

"Jesus Christ, dude!" Éclair cried.

"Yup." I pulled out my pack of Lucky's. I offered the open end of the pack to him. "Want one, Éclair?"

"Corporal, I don't think you've ever called me by my name

before." He pulled a smoke from the pack.

I lit another for myself. "Well, you're not a fucking boot anymore. You shit your pants?"

"No, but it was scary."

"Keep it up and that'll go away."

Doc chuckled at that.

"Well, congratulations Éclair, you're not a fucking boot anymore."

"Thanks."

"You get any good pictures?"

"You really care about that, Corporal?"

"No, but if I don't ask I'll get my ass chewed." We both laughed.

"The Marines here call me Peter Parker. So, you know, that's cool."

"Yeah, my platoon calls me Kodak."

A rapid thumping sound grew louder above us from along the river. Everyone lifted their heads to the sky and watched a pair of Cobra helicopters buzz past our position.

"I haven't seen Cobras in a while. Where the fuck were they six hours ago?" I grumbled.

"I think they call them 'Vipers' now. Cobras were the old ones," said Éclair.

"If it looks like a Cobra, I'm calling it a fucking Cobra," Doc said with his eyes following the serpents.

For the next hour the Marines on the bank of the Euphrates held tight. Word was passed down to start digging in. Fox Company made fighting holes, the mortar platoon dug pits, CAAT 1, on the other hand, was in vehicles and needed to be mobile. So we helped fill sand bags. There were a few extra seats in Sergeant Kumer's truck, and since ours was destroyed we jumped in his.

Kyle and Fonzie were taken to a field hospital in Kuwait to recover from their injuries. They weren't in too terrible of shape, but they weren't exactly up for another fight right now.

Doc and I helped one of the mortar teams build their pit. Instead of filling sand bags, we cut down cedar trees for the mortar men to use as a barricade. The sun was peeking over the eastern horizon. The skies began to turn from a deep purple to a blazing red.

We thought we heard the dull sound of thunder rolling in the distance. But as we paused from fortifying our positions and looked across the river we could see fires rising.

"Well, it's official," I said to Doc.

Doc looked up to the east. By the time the sun had shown half its face over the horizon we could start to make out the small dots in the sky that were raining down hell across the water. "How long until you think we cross it?"

"I don't know." I searched my pockets for a cigarette. "A day, a week, maybe we'll pull a Desert Storm and just bomb it for nine months before we cross the berm."

"I fucking hope not. I'd rather get over there and get it over with." Doc looked over at me. "Let me get one of those?"

I handed him the pack. "I just hope I don't fucking run out of cigarettes."

After gawking at the Navy jets like high-school girls for a few minutes we went back to work chopping. For the next few hours we could still see and hear faint explosions in the distance. Most of them just below where the sand met the sky to the northeast.

The rest of that day was fairly uneventful. Around dusk word came down that we would be on half-watch for the night. I stayed up with Doc for the first watch. It was only two hours, but after being awake since about six the previous morning, keeping my eyelids open wasn't exactly all that fun. I didn't think I could manage that much sleep anyway. When the time came for me to rest I didn't bother taking off my flak jacket or boots. All the soaked in sweat would keep me cool. I took off my helmet, rested my weapon in my lap, propped myself up against one of the tires of our new ride, and passed out sitting up.

That night I dreamt a terrible dream. I dreamt that I was in a valley, green and lush. Wild bulls danced and kicked around me. I saw a stream cutting through the land. When I laid my eyes upon it I became thirsty; I knelt down and drank. Then from nowhere the sky turned black, darker than any depths I've ever fathomed—a deep, hopeless, infinite black. Then suddenly, a phoenix ripped the sky with a thunderous screech, spitting fire from its mouth. The fire vaporized the water. Plants withered away. The bulls became skinny and emaciated before falling over dead. The phoenix flapped its wings so terribly that it leveled mountains into a crumbled flatland. The giant, blazing, avian beast landed in the inferno just before my feet. The sand melted into glass. It gazed at me, staring into my very soul with its black eyes. "Hank!" The booming wind from its voice shook me. "HANK!"

I woke with a startle. Doc was kicking my boot. "Hank, wake up, man."

I squinted, looking towards the sun rising over the river. I rubbed my forehead and put my hand on my rifle.

Doc threw an MRE on my lap and sat down next to me. "Gotta love this weather." He pulled out a small knife and opened the brown indestructible bag of food.

I looked down on mine. The brown rubbery plastic bag read, 'Chicken Tetrazzini.' It wasn't my favorite, but it was a hell of a lot better than half the other shit the government packed into bags they called MEALS READY TO EAT. The coffee-colored plastic stretched as I tore off the top. I pulled out the main meal and the spoon and shoved the rest of the contents into my cargo pockets for later.

I looked at my watch, it was zero six. The sun was already high in the sky and I had sweat like a pig in my sleep. I scooped myself a bite of the noodley chicken then took a swig of water from my camelback.

"Any word yet?"

"Na, man," Doc replied

I looked over the river to the north. "Are they still bombing it over there?"

"I haven't been hearing anything." He wiped his mouth with his sleeve. "But I slept like a rock, so who knows."

"You mean on a rock." We both chuckled.

"Yeah, on a rock down by the river." Doc picked up a small stone and flung it towards the Euphrates.

"Doc," I said as if I were narrating a children's book. "Here sleeps Doc! Doc on a rock! See Doc sleep like a rock on a rock in Iraq!"

"Hey, check it out," Doc interrupted and motioned his head towards Brzescer's truck. "The leadership's over there talking about something."

I looked at the congregation. "It looks like they got word on something." The senior NCOs had their maps in their hands and were taking notes as the lieutenant talked.

Doc and I watched with a mild sense of curiosity as we finished what we were calling breakfast. After twenty minutes they dispersed to their teams. Word was passed to us that everyone not on post was to meet by the command truck at zero-eight for a brief. I hoped we were rolling out instead of just sitting here on the banks of the river for another month with our dicks in our hands.

I got up, took a piss into the river, and went through my pack to see what I still had on me. I didn't shave. Hopefully Gunny would let it slide, you know, because of the 'I lost my hygiene kit because my truck got destroyed' excuse. It was an excuse, not a reason; I imagined he'd say. I should probably just will my stubble to grow back into my face.

I opened my Alice pack. Most people had newer gear than the Alice system, but the new gear sucked. Sure, the new stuff was lighter, but it also tore and broke more easily and I couldn't manage to fit half of what I needed into it. I still had my poncho, poncho liner, rifle cleaning kit, a skivvy shirt, three pairs of socks, two camera batteries, one camera lens, four packs of Lucky's, my lap top for editing and its charger, a few cords, some letters, my emergency canteen, two MREs, half of a container of orange Tang, half of a bottle of lighter fluid, and my camelback. The rest of my fifteen thousand dollars worth of equipment was melted into Iraqi earth on the other side of the graveyard. I was already cringing at the thought of filling out the paperwork for that. I stowed my gear back into my pack and headed to the brief.

Lieutenant Brzescer studied a map by his truck before asking all of us to take a seat, or in this case, a dirt plot. "Morning gents," bellowed his thunderous voice.

"Good morning, Sir," we all replied.

"I know we had a tough night."

We Oo-rahed back in a humorous and satisfied tone.

"Thankfully none of us got too hurt. A few Marines won't be coming back anytime soon, and sadly a few more won't be coming back at all. Fox Company wasn't quite as lucky, they lost a squad." The SirBot paused for a moment, the silence showed his humanity through the cracks in his wrinkled face. He then spit a wad tobacco into the dust. "God rest their souls. We, however, do not have time to mourn the dead," he continued. "I'm sure you've all noticed the hell we've been bringing down across the river. The town that's getting pounded into dust just over the horizon has a battalion of Iranian soldiers. What's left of that town is named Al Hillah. Tonight, 2/7 is going to take it away from those cocksuckers. At twenty-one hundred hours CAAT will roll out and stand fast one mile south of the city. The line companies will insert via helicopter. Fox Company will be with us. Echo and Gulf companies will be to our flanks. Barring shit hitting the fan prior to crossing the line, we'll hit the city around midnight. Intel claims the Iranian night vision systems are subpar, so we have the advantage in the darkness."

"I think we proved that last night," Gunny added.

The SirBot smiled. "Make sure your weapons are cleaned and you're stocked up on ammo. If there's anything you need that isn't in your trucks, well, supply ain't coming. Be ready for anything and count on nothing. Prepare yourselves, gentlemen."

The Marines stood and wandered back to their trucks. Sergeant Fields slapped my shoulder. "Cock-Strong Warrior Man-Gods."

"Semper Fi," I grunted back.

When we returned to the truck, Sergeant Kumer had laid out a few ammo cans and a box of MREs. "Take what you need, boys." I grabbed two MREs, cheese tortellini and chicken patty, and enough ammo to kill a feral pack of T-Rexes.

I looked at my body. My flak jacket and cammies were half-covered in blood and stained with sweat. I was going to have to deal with that for at least a month. I highly doubted that we were going to get any kind of supplies for quite a while. At least the kind that doesn't kill or help us kill anyway.

I laid down next to the truck and spent the time I could in an unrestful half sleep. I didn't dream. I waited for the time to come to leave. When the time came we checked our gear one last time and loaded into the trucks. CAAT rolled north through the gritty Iraqi dust and dirt to a bridge to take us across the Euphrates. Through the truck's rear windows I saw CH53 helicopters blow sand into the bright orange sunset painted across the horizon. The rest of 2/7 packed into the giant metal birds and ascended into the night sky, some to seize a dirty city, and some to a violent death.

The trucks snaked single file over the hills. The date trees and brush gave us some concealment but nothing special. I thought to myself about never before being in Mesopotamia. I couldn't see much out the windows because the sun had fallen. I imagined what it had to look like during the day. I figured it looked exactly the same as it did on the other side of the river, but there was just something about being between the Euphrates and the Tigris; Mesopotamia, *the* land between the rivers, the cradle of civilization. I was on ground over which was built the first civilizations, Acadia, Samaria, and Babylon. Hell, Genesis was in this very same dirt. I knew that I should probably have had my head in the game, but I didn't.

From what I could observe outside, it looked like we were starting to weave through fields and canals. The ride got rough. Driving through Middle Eastern irrigation systems is an absolute pain in the ass. The truck thumped and rattled savagely over every foot-tall berm.

Hofstadter, the driver, shouted something about beginning to see buildings. I didn't have my night vision on me; I couldn't see Jack *or* his brother Shit. I did hear the helicopters. We must have been close if they're landing the line companies close enough for the birds to be as loud as they were. The trucks stopped. The radio's electric voice sang, "Hitting the town tonight!"

Another anonymous radio personality spouted, "Five mikes."

Three choppers touched down a few hundred yards away from our position. The Marines aboard stormed out the back, encircled the birds and hugged the dirt in a prone position. The birds disappeared back into the sky.

I could make out their silhouettes as they stood up and took off for the town. We were still moving, albeit slowly. I could see the Marines taking cover behind rubble in the outskirts of the city. The rubble looked odd from where I gazed. Granted it was night, it still looked… off.

The next string of helicopters arrived to give birth to furious warfighters.

Then, just as the first CH53 touched the deck, it erupted in a fiery ball of death; spewing shrapnel in every direction. The force of the blast flipped one of the other helos over onto its right side, thank God that didn't also get engulfed. The third bird didn't even hit the ground; it took off back into the night. Mere moments later, heavy machinegun and rocket fire rained down on us from the city.

"CONTACT!" screamed a voice over the radio. Our truck only seemed able to disclose obscenities. Sandison, up in the turret, started sending the Iranians fifty caliber hate mail.

Flames spat hot lead from the other trucks, the bursts of orange white light, silhouetting them out of the darkness. I looked through the front window, Hajji had so many guns firing on us that the buildings looked like they had Christmas lights strung around them. CAAT spread the trucks. Everyone across the board gave Hajji hell. TOW missiles, 50 cals. MK19s, and M16s from the grunts ripped into the buildings. Cobras arrived on station and made their presence known with the rockets they sent from the sky. We pushed up the rubble to Fox Company and parked the trucks sideways to provide some cover for the linemen. Fields, Doc, and I dismounted and ducked down next to a few Marines from Fox.

I gazed at the rubble around us. It wasn't modern. It was ancient bricks literally worn down by the sands of time.

The Marines popped up from cover like groundhogs firing only a few rounds at a time. More Cobras and jets arrived with hellfire, knocking down the buildings the enemy fired from. Our lasers guided their missiles. If the explosions and gunfire didn't take them out, the crumbling buildings did.

The mulched up buildings and dust kicked up by the firefight began to reduce our visibility. But we could see just enough to operate.

The enemy's return fire weakened right before Choppers resumed bringing in Marines. "Hey F-Bomb!" I shouted at Sergeant Fields.

"What?"

"There's no way that all these guys are Two-Seven," I shouted over the sounds of gunfire.

"Hold on!" he barked back. Fields ran back to the truck and leaped into the back. A minute later he plopped back out and returned to us.

"Apparently there are more Iranians than intel thought there was!"

"NO SHIT!" Doc spat, as a round ricocheted off one of the trucks giving us cover.

"That's Three Seven coming in now!" Fields yelled over the noise of the helicopters rotor wash. "One-Seven and Three-Four are landing on the other side of the city."

"Awesome!" I screamed over the noise. "They're bringing in the whole fucking regiment!" I said with a laugh.

When Marines started piling up behind us, the first wave started weaving an intricate knot around the ruins towards Al Hillah. Kumer jumped out of the truck and ran over to us. The MRAP turned towards the city and slowly rolled on. A squad from Fox ranger filed behind us. The trucks moved with the Marines in the rubble. It wasn't as fast as a light trot.

We couldn't walk more than 50 feet without our vehicles taking and returning fire. The 50 cal. was good for blasting the older buildings. The TOWs helped deal with the more stubborn ones.

I peered around the side of the truck. Directly in front, there was a building several stories tall. Muzzle flashes came from almost every window. A deafening blast emanated half way up the side of the building as it collapsed; taking its occupants with it in a smoldering red burst. That must have been one of the stubborn ones.

We entered one of the main streets of the town. The Line Marines moved on top of the rubble, creeping down the sidewalks with their rifles pointed in all directions. The squad behind us lifted their weapons to cover the buildings to our left and right.

We approached the first building on the block that was still standing and stacked up outside the entrance. The trucks stopped outside. The first Marine in the file blasted the hinges of the sheet metal door with his semi-auto shotgun. The Marines poured into the building as the door fell onto the street. Gunfire, flashes and screaming followed.

Fields, Doc, and I were still behind the truck providing security and observation. I could hear firefights happening in the adjacent streets. Flares lit the sky with an ominous yellow glow.

Building by building, floor by floor and alleyway by alleyway we cleared out the infestation up to the intersection a click down the road. It took us hours to clear them out. They must have spent days reinforcing their position. All that work gone to waste.

It seemed Ali Baba was determined to not let us have the rest of the town. When we approached the intersecting street, we were greeted by RPGs which screamed at the trucks and gunfire forced the Marines into the structures we had turned into ruins. A rocket hit the front of our truck, but all it did was blow off the grill and piss off Sandison, who angrily fired back to the enemy from the turret. The truck in front of us wasn't so lucky. The enemy concentrated their fire on it in an effort to block the path and halt our movement with our own materials. We watched in horror as Cpl. Stockton's vehicle brunted rocket after rocket; Iranian bullets chipped away at it.

Sparks, blasts and ricochets rolled over the front like a wave. A rocket struck the street directly under Stockton's vic and knocked off the forward wheels. Lance Cpl. Cherkov, the turret gunner, fired mercilessly at the enemy positions. He fired so long; the barrel of his 50 cal. turned bright red and started to melt. The steel became slag as the rounds pierced through the collapsed barrel and flung wildly into the buildings across the street.

Fire began to consume the vehicle. The Marines in the front of the vehicle, Corporal Stockton, the vehicle commander, and Lance Corporal Starlite the driver, simultaneously kicked out of the MRAP and dashed towards cover. Both were gunned down before they took six steps. Cherkov saw their bodies as they laid there, face down sinking deeper and deeper into pools of their own blood. Cherkov shouted obscenities, reloaded and resumed firing. Eventually the flames reached the turret and engulfed him. Never though did he flinch away from his gun. We could hear his war cry over the gunfire, but he kept his thumbs down on the trigger and fired his weapon until the instant of his death.

Alvarado and Reyes, who were supposed to be in that truck, looked on in horror and rage as they came close to losing their minds. "FUCK YOU! YOU HAJJI COCKSUCKERS!" Alvarado screamed towards the buildings at the enemy. He fired his SAW, screaming obscenities and weeping.

Reyes was trying to run to the aid of the fallen Marines in the street. Doc and I held him back with all the strength we could muster.

"Let me go!" he screamed at us.

"You'll just get killed too!" Doc barked.

Reyes thrashed to get free. We held him back behind the truck.

The enemy had to know that the Marines in the charred truck were dead. They stopped rocketing it, but they kept up the gunfire. They shot at the bodies of the Marines lying in the street. They were just trying to piss us off and get us to do something stupid. They didn't want us to have anything to take back to their families.

The enemy occupied most of the buildings across from us. They knew they were wasting ammo, they knew their minutes were numbered. But they wanted us to pay dearly for every block.

Sergeant Kumer opened the back door of the truck and stuck his head out to shout, "Get into a building! We're pulling the vehicle back. There's a couple of F-18s on the way to level the whole block!"

Fields, Doc, Alvarado, and I pulled Reyes, who was still angrily trying to wrestle away from us, to the building to our left. A couple of Marines from Fox Company saw us and kneeled just outside the doorway and began to provide covering fire towards the intersection.

"COME ON!" they shouted.

We bolted into the doorway before disappearing into the dark of the house and sat Reyes down by a wall, it felt like a wall anyway. We could barely make out his face as he looked blankly at the floor. Alvarado sat down next to him and wrapped his arm around his comrade. They both sat silently.

The two Fox Marines came back in and stood guard over the door.

The gunfire outside was deafening, even after hours of the constant chaos. The platoon leader, from whatever Marines we were temporarily adopted, shouted, "STAND BY FOR IMPACT! THIRTY SECONDS!"

I looked outside; our truck reversed down the road about fifteen yards. Sandison's machinegun's muzzle flash illuminated the street.

Reyes began to slowly sift through the junk on the floor beside him. The building looked like it was an apartment complex, but it was hard to be sure. Reyes picked up a naked plastic doll. It looked like a Barbie, but it was obviously knockoff Arab crap plastic. The doll was missing her right arm and half her hair was singed off. He rubbed his thumb over her head and stuck her in his flak jacket by his shoulder. I didn't attempt to rationalize any of what happened. Every man comes to terms with himself in his own way.

BOOOOOOOOOOOOOOOOOOOOOOOOM!

A deafening roar of explosions from the bombs leveled the block ahead of us. Anyone who was on their feet fell to their ass, including me.

Doc was kneeling during the impact. "Ha! Pussy!"

"Shut the fuck up, Doc," I said getting back up.

Alvarado looked over to Reyes and shouted into his ear, "Hey man, we gotta go soon. You gonna be okay?"

Reyes nodded his head. Alvarado stood up extending his hand. Reyes grabbed it and Alvarado pulled him to his feet. Reyes shook his head slowly. "Fucking, fucks. I'm going to kill every last one of them."

"Yeah I know buddy, we'll get 'em," Alvarado grumbled back.

Fields talked into the radio while he stood by the door. He stuck his head out both ways and came back in. "Doc, Allensworth, we're going back to the truck. Alvarado and Reyes, you're coming with us."

We followed Fields out the door, sprinted to the back of our MRAP, and crammed into the back seats.

We rolled up to the intersection. Marines from Fox Company were already pulling Stockton and Starlite's bodies out of the street. The truck was still smoldering.

The buildings on the next block were nothing but concrete boulders and twisted steel rebar. Our vic advanced only as fast as the Marines on foot did. We provided the crunchies cover from gunfire and they protected us from foot soldiers.

Half of the CAAT platoon trailed behind us. Slowly we prowled up the avenue with no resistance. We halted at a town square. There was a small park with a few benches and a fountain. The architecture was different here than the rest of the city. It wasn't modern. It almost looked like an ancient castle wall.

We sat there for about an hour with no word and no action. I pulled the crackers from that morning's MRE out of my cargo pocket. They were crushed, but not too badly. I'm pretty sure they were made out of wheat and asphalt; it didn't matter, I hadn't eaten since right after I woke up.

"Hey, Sergeant Kumer." I leaned over.

"What's up, Kodak?"

"Are we fucking doing anything? Is there any word or are we just sitting here?"

"Hold on." Kumer leaned into the radio on his shoulder. "CAAT 1 Actual this is Vic Bravo 2."

The radio hissed and CAAT 1 Actual, Lieutenant Brzescer, said back, "Send your traffic."

"Uh, yeah CAAT 1, what's the situation? Over."

"Bravo 2, Battalion's orders are to standby while we wait for armor…"

I looked up at Doc and gave half a smile. "Dude, tanks."

"I know, right?"

"Bravo 2," the lieutenant continued, "It doesn't look like we're going anywhere any time soon. Go on half watch, standby for further word. Out."

"Roger, out," Kumer said into the radio. He turned back to us. "I need the man in the turret and the driver to be awake."

Sandison kneeled down out of the turret. "Sergeant, I'm good for a few hours. I'll stay up."

"Alright," Kumer acknowledged.

"I'm good too." Hofstadter kept his hands wrapped tightly around the wheel.

"No, you're hitting the rack," Kumer said to him with a fatigued voice. "I need an alert driver, I don't want you bobbing for cock when we roll out."

"I'll take it," Alvarado volunteered.

"Okay." Hofstadter climbed back over his seat to allow room for Alvarado to crawl forwards. "Sergeant Kumer, we pop'n tops?"

"Yeah, if you're not on watch," he replied.

We took off our Kevlar helmets and tried to get some sleep. I didn't doze well. I kept coming in and out. I was kind of worried about Reyes. He didn't sleep at all, or if he did he was having a fucked up dream. He kept mumbling to the doll he had in his flak jacket.

"What do you mean? … No it wasn't like that… Barbara you're starting to…" Reyes said to the doll. I thought I should ask him if he was okay or wanted to talk about his ailments, but I decided not to. "No… I've never been there… yeah, no they didn't pay me for that…cactuses don't need water, Barbara… shit… shut up… Iraq is nothing like… no… I didn't see that movie…" Then Reyes started to speak to the dirty plastic doll in Spanish. I stopped listening and tried to sleep.

When I did finally nod off I had a nightmare. In my dream I was pulled through the bottom of the truck and underground by a demon. The ghoul was an abhorrently ugly woman with eagle wings and a lizard's feet and hands. Her body was pale with death. We descended deep into the earth and emerged in a vast system of caves. I could see everything, even though it was dark and full of fog. And it was cold. There were others there, too. It looked like their clothes were made out of bird skin, but the feathers were still attached, like a vulture-suede. There were large hound demons with wasp wings forcing the bird people to the clay on the cave's floor with their whips, digging it ever deeper.

I woke to Sandison tapping my knee with his foot from above in the turret. I rubbed my eyes and looked up at him. "You wanna get up here, Kodak?"

"Yeah." I grabbed my helmet.

Sandison came down into the cab. "Thanks, dude." He patted my shoulder.

I climbed into the turret. It was still dark and I didn't have night vision. There was no power in the city, but the moon and fires lit the area enough to where if enemy troops were running around I could see them. I made sure the 50. Cal. was loaded. There was another can of ammunition up here in case I needed it.

I looked up at the stars. I could see every one of them, which was one of the good things about the desert. The sky was always dark enough to be bright with the jewels of the heavens.

I leaned back into the frame of the turret. *What a fucking couple of days*, I thought. I was dying for a cigarette. I had a pack on me, but lighting it could make me a target for snipers. I knew those fuckers were out there watching us. "Fucking Persians." *Fucking Persians?* I thought. *Hank, your girlfriend's a Persian. Yeah but she's crossed over to being a dirty American—she's a stripper for shit's sake. Oh great, now I'm talking to myself.* "Snap out of it, Hank," I whispered.

There was rustling around inside the vehicle. Alvarado and Hofstadter were switching places. I rubbed my face and looked down on myself. I had a good two days of beard crusted over with blood and sand. My uniform was stiff with white lines from the salt in my sweat and dark brown from the dried vital fluids of other men.

I again looked to the sky. There was something peaceful in its darkness. Maybe it was all the stars. Maybe it was that it was so dark that I could see the satellites soaring in the atmosphere. There was something else, too. Not as far as the space capsules, although they did look like them. I could see artillery rounds flying way over our heads. They looked like faint shooting stars. They weren't landing anywhere near us. *Someone's getting some a few miles from here*, I thought. Hell, I could still hear sporadic machinegun fire no more than a mile from where I was. I guess I was lucky for getting a few moments of peace.

After a few hours the sun began to smile over Al Hillah. It was peeking over the short, brown brick city with its orange aura. Sandison relieved me and took his place back in the turret.

6 MUL APIN, ARROWS, STATUES, AND CHESSBOARDS

The tanks finally showed up. Well, they showed up somewhere; I didn't see any of them. Fox Company and CAAT 1 started crawling across the small park to the buildings on the other side.

BOOM! BOOM! BOOM! BOOM!

"INCOMING!" Kumer grabbed the radio.

Mortar rounds hurled onto the pavement. The line company Marines hit the deck and crawled for cover.

Hofstadter put the truck in reverse and punched the gas. Something held the back tires. We couldn't move. Hofstadter barked, "COME ON GODDAMMIT!" at the vehicle.

Then we dropped a bit. It felt like the ground beneath the rear of the vehicle gave way. I looked out the back window and saw that it had. The road behind us started to crack and splinter. Every time Hof hit the gas we sunk a bit more. Mortars exploded around us. They had us zeroed in. The truck made another loud bang and we fell a few feet deeper. Everyone in the vehicle grabbed something to hold on to. The truck tilted backwards, the front end rose into the air.

We fell another foot, then another. Then the truck plummeted into the hole in the ground. We flipped, rolled, and smashed. The Marines on the inside were thrown into each other.

We were finally still. The vehicle was upside down with its nose in the air.

The Marines in the front seats were jammed into the front windows. Everyone in the back was pretzeled into a pile on the ceiling, which was now the floor. We all groaned.

"Everybody okay?" Fields wheezed as he made an attempt to free himself from the mound.

We only offered him only moans.

Alvarado shrugged free and said, "Mother *fucker* that hurt." He reached out, grabbed the back door's handle, and pulled himself to the window. He peered out. "I think there's an opening back here."

"Can you open the door?" Doc winced.

Alvarado turned the handle and pushed. The heavy doors swung open. "Yeah." He rolled out of the truck into the shadows and dust. He turned back, stuck his arms back in, and pulled out Reyes.

Reyes softly spoke, "Thanks bro."

Fields, Doc, and I followed them out. We fell somewhere dark. Fields flipped on the flashlight attached to his weapon and scanned the area. "Turn on your flashlights."

We were in a room about the size of a twenty-car garage. The walls were built of large marble stones. I took a few steps into the expanse, shining my light over the area. There were twelve columns bearing the weight of the ceiling, evenly spread in a circle. Each one of them was carved into some sort of nightmarish, half-man half-scorpion monster. There was one large door in the center of three of the walls. The place gave me the creeps. I felt a heavy presence upon me. My skin walked and ice filled my spine.

I looked back to where we entered. Doc had climbed back into the truck to pull out the other three Marines. First came Hofstadter, then

Kumer. Doc came back out with a sick look on his face.

"What's up, Doc?" Fields asked.

Doc walked over to one of the columns and sat down. "Sandison's fucking crushed, there isn't much of him left above his waist."

"What?" Kumer crawled back into the truck.

I pulled out a cigarette and handed it to Doc.

"Thanks bro." He brushed the dust off of his shoulders and arms. "You got a lighter?"

"Yeah." I extended my hand flicking my light open.

No one said anything until Kumer came back out of the truck. He had a grim look with Sandison's dog tags and kill cards in his hand. "Looking up through the window, it doesn't look like we'd be able to climb out unless we broke through the glass."

"And that's ballistic," Fields said back.

"Yeah," Kumer continued. "So we can either try to blow them out and risk burning ourselves to death or burying us further, or try to find another way through all this." He pointed at the door on the other side of the room.

"Sergeant, what about Sandison?" Hofstadter asked.

Doc interrupted before Kumer could answer. "The way he's wedged in there we'd have to rip him apart to get him out. He's hamburger above the belt."

"And if we leave him in there," Fields argued, "they'll recover his body when they come to dig up the truck. They're not just going to leave it down here."

"So," said Alvarado, "are we going to wait here for a rescue party or try to find another way out?"

Kumer looked over to Fields. "You're the senior, man."

"Alright. We're going to try to get through, well, wherever the hell we are. Everyone check your chow, water, and ammo." As we looked over our gear Fields shot his head up. "Oh yeah, no shit."

"What's up?" I looked at him confused.

Fields pressed the button down on his radio. "Any station, any station, this is CAAT 1 Bravo."

No shit, why not try using the radio? I thought.

"Any station, any station, this is CAAT 1 Bravo. Do you read?" There was nothing but a faint hiss. "Well, so fucking much for that idea," Fields said. He put his eyes on the room. "You all look around for a way out. I'm going to burn the sensitive gear from the truck."

Fields climbed back into the truck to yank out the other radios, maps, and anything else that shouldn't be left laying around for the wrong hands to find. Kumer, Alvarado, Reyes, Hofstadter, Doc, and I searched the room. I took a closer look at the statues with the light on my rifle. They were expertly carved out of a milky white marble. I thought to myself that if we got out of this place, and if I made it through this war and got home and somehow became a rock star, I was totally going to put this room on an album cover. It was scary, but it was fucking metal. Looking up at the heads of the statues I noticed that there was something in the middle of the ceiling. It was a carving of a moon. I walked the perimeter of the room. The walls were engraved floor to roof in cuneiform. The other Marines were inspecting the door. It had a golden frame and the door itself looked as if it were made from bronze. It simply pushed open, but no one went through.

We returned to the truck. Fields had pulled out everything he felt the need to, put it in a pile, and poured fuel over it. He pulled out our battle colors, the Jolly Roger, and he put that in his pack. "Gents, it's a bit chilly down here." He lit a cigarette. "Smoke 'em if you got 'em." He lit his empty cigarette box and threw it onto the pile of radios, maps, manuals, and such.

The Marines who smoked, did.

When the fire had burnt its way to a smoldering heap of melted plastic and metal, we spread the ashes and gunk that was left to form an arrow in the direction we were going and headed through the door.

As soon as the six of us entered, the door slammed shut! We all turned to the door and frantically tried to un-lodge it. It was no use, that door was staying closed.

"Okay everybody…" Sergeant Kumer said trying to keep himself calm. "Just stay chill and look around the room and see what else is in here, hopefully there's another way out."

We turned to the room. It was darker than the last room. It was a good thing we had our lights. At first glance it looked exactly like the first room. It was the same size and shape with the same twelve scorpion men holding the roof up. I walked through the pillars to the center of the room. There were grooves on the floor. Not grooves like scratches from sliding something heavy, but as if the architect put them there on purpose. There were also seven smaller scorpion men in the room. These ones were only six feet tall and placed with no pattern at all. And there was another door on the far end of the room, just like the last one, only it didn't open from this side.

"Hey guys…" a worried voice called from near the other side of the room. We came to find Alvarado standing over several skeletons. They were all dressed in ancient armor brandishing swords and shields. They were positioned as if they had very nonviolent deaths. Alvarado looked up. "This isn't good. This isn't good at all."

"Nobody freak out." Fields took his flashlight off the skeletons. "Just keep looking around for something."

A few hours went by. Doc looked at the walls trying to read the extinct language. He couldn't even begin to understand it, but maybe he thought there was something. Kumer and Fields inspected the statues, both big and small. Alvarado and Reyes tried to pry on the far door, the one we didn't enter. No luck.

I leaned over to Doc and said, "Hey."

"Yeah, man?"

"Those bones…"

"What about 'em?"

"They looked like they starved to death and just curled up and died."

"Don't remind me." Doc ran his fingers over the etches in the wall. "You got any chow on you?"

"Na, man, I don't."

"Great."

No one had yet given up, but Reyes and Alvarado took a break and rested on the small scorpion pillars. Reyes mumbled to his doll that was still in his flak jacket. "I know… yes I *did* think of that and no it did *not* work… not now… no… Barbara, leave me alone… if that's the way you feel about it than maybe you shouldn't have come along… Barbara… Bar… SHUT THE FUCK UP BARBARA!"

"Hey!" Alvarado leaned in on Reyes. "Dude, are you okay?"

"What do you think?" Reyes bit back.

"Dude, I know it's shitty, but we hang in there and keep our heads straight."

Alvarado continued to console Reyes. I looked over to Doc. "Dude, I have a question."

"Yeah."

"Why haven't we run out of oxygen yet?"

"I don't know," Doc said with heavy sarcasm. I think he thought I was trying to fuck with him.

"No seriously. This room's not *that* big." I turned my light to the corners of the ceiling trying to find vents or shafts or something else to bring in air. If it brought *in* air it could lead us *out*! That's when I saw it. There was a carving on this roof too! It was of seven identical women

109

holding hands, side by side.

"Hey look at this!" I shouted. Kumer, Fields, Doc, and Hofstadter all pointed their lights to the ceiling.

"It reminds me of Pleiades," Doc said as he studied the carving.

"And what's that, Doc?" Fields asked.

"It's a constellation. It's supposed to be of seven sister handmaidens or some shit. I'm into that kind of thing."

"Stars or seven naked women?" Kumer jabbed.

"Both," Doc half laughed.

"Alright, so what the hell does it mean?" asked Hofstadter.

No one answered. Alvarado and Reyes' conversation transformed into a fight. Alvarado lifted Reyes by his shoulder harnesses on his flak and pushed him into a scorpion statue yelling, "Snap out of it!"

When Reyes hit the statue it rolled a foot or two across the floor. Everyone went silent.

Kumer let out a deep sigh. "Are you assholes telling me that no one bothered to check the statues?"

Everyone avoided making eye contact with him out of shame.

Fields looked around. "Okay, so we have the seven sisters' stars and these statues. Doc, do you know what the constellation is supposed to look like?"

"Uh, yeah actually," Doc responded.

"Well, get to it!" Fields ordered.

Doc went to each of the statues, pushing them with relative ease along the grooves in the floor until they made the pattern that resembled the constellation.

Then, beside the door we didn't enter, a lever emerged on each side. The lever to the left was made of silver and a large red ruby sat on its top. The other lever was made of gold with a large round ball of jade.

Doc walked to the door and pulled the red lever. The statues all rumbled, the room shook, and the scorpion-man statues rolled back to their original positions and the levers disappeared back into the walls.

"Great job jack ass!" I yelled at Doc.

"Hey, fuck you dude!" he cut back.

"Stop it!" Kumer interjected. "Doc, put the statues back and pull the *other* lever."

Doc pushed them back and once again the levers dropped back out of the wall. This time, Doc pulled the green one. The door opened!

"Hold on a minute," Hofstadter said before anyone could go through the opening. "What if that door closes too?"

"Well, we won't be any better off than if it stays open," Alvarado replied.

"Yeah, but should a pair of us stay back in here?" Hofstadter said back.

"No," Fields said in his deep voice. "We're sticking together, all of us. If the door closes and there's something fucked up in that next room, it'll be better to have more Marines. Also, the buddy system and blah blah blah."

Doc turned and led the way through the threshold. The moment all of us were inside the back door slammed shut.

"Told ya," Hofstadter scoffed.

Fields just grunted. This room was just as dark as the last. It had the same twelve statues in the same twelve places and another door on the other end. This room however, didn't have the smaller statues in the middle. In the very center of it there was a pillar. It was about four feet tall with a flat top and what looked like a chessboard with nineteen little scorpion-man pieces.

We figured the puzzle had to be similar to the previous one. We looked to the ceiling and there was a bull—Taurus!

Doc arranged the pieces to form the constellation and just like the last room two levers popped out. When the green one was pulled the door opened. When we all passed through the door, it closed.

The next room again was just the same as the first. Hell, for half a second I thought it was the first. We saw the seven man-sized scorpion-men statues and looked up. This one was odd. It was a shepherd with a very sad, lost, and confused look on his face.

"Yeah, I don't know what this one is," Doc muttered.

"Well, there are seven scorpion dudes," I said lighting a cigarette.

"So a constellation with seven stars," Doc said. "The Big Dipper has seven stars."

"Yeah, fuck it, why not. If we're wrong we can try again."

Doc pushed the stone monsters into the positions of the Big Dipper and the levers popped out just as in the previous rooms. Doc walked over and pulled down on the green handle. There was a metallic *thwing* and an arrow shot into the back of Doc's left shoulder.

Doc screamed and fell. The rest of us ran to him. He was squirming on the ground trying to reach the arrow with his other hand.

"Be still, dammit!" Kumer shouted trying to get a better look at Doc. "Reyes, Alvarado, shine some light on him! Hof, Allensworth, hold him down!"

"Oh this ain't too bad," Kumer said while looking at Doc's wound. "Doc, calm down. Your flak stopped it from going all the way through. The arrow is only about an inch in." Kumer ripped the arrow out and Doc let out a howl. The flak jacket he was wearing, the one we were all wearing, was a thick vest with Kevlar inserts to stop bullets and shrapnel.

The arrow hit the part by the edge that the Kevlar plate didn't cover. It was still enough to keep the arrow from going through.

Doc laid panting.

"This is going to sting a bit, Doc." Kumer cut a hole in the shoulder of Doc's uniform. After he made a decent enough sized slit, Kumer poured quick clot into the dime-sized hole in Doc's back.

Doc screamed.

We leaned Doc on the wall and gave him some water.

"Doc," I said to get his attention.

"I'm alright man," he panted.

"It wasn't the Big Dipper."

Doc cracked a smile and laughed. "Yeah, no shit." He looked up to Fields and Kumer laughing. "Do I get another Purple Heart for this?"

"Uh…"

Doc rubbed his forehead. His hand ran into his helmet. "Why the fuck are we wearing these?"

"Yeah, if you want to," Fields said, "if you guys wanna pop your tops, put 'em in your packs."

We took off our helmets and stuffed them inside our bags or strapped them to the side.

After a few minutes of recovery, Doc stood back up and reexamined the statues on the floor. "Seven, and not the Big Dipper." He looked up to the shepherd on the ceiling. "That's stupid. What does that have to do with a shepherd?" He looked over to me. "Thanks for getting me shot, asshole."

"That's what I'm here for, man."

"Dick."

"I'll buy you a six-pack when we get back," I joked. At least, for some damned reason our spirits were a little up. I was just happy Doc was okay.

"Must be Orion." Doc went back to pushing the statues, this time into Orion. The door crept up. We entered the next room. Yet again, the same looking room with the chess table. When we got through, the back door again slammed. We looked to the mural of the ceiling first. There was a hunched over old man with a cane and a raggedy beard. "Mother fucker," murmured Doc. When he got to the pillar with the pieces he exclaimed, "Awe *fuck* me!"

"What?" we said worried.

"Dammit," Doc gritted. "Goddamn *it!*"

"What? Why?" Gathering around the table we counted nineteen little scorpion-man statues on the board and shared Doc's dread.

"Any ideas?" Kumer asked him.

"I…" Doc scratched his head. "It might be Perseus." He looked to the carving in the ceiling. "What the fuck does that have to do with an old man?"

"Well, Perseus is a Greek name, and this place is probably a hell of a lot older than Greece." Fields eyed the figures. "Try it and then pull the lever from the side in case it's not right."

Doc sighed and stared moving the little figures around. "I don't remember where this star goes."

"Okay," Kumer said in a calm voice. "Put it where you think it may go then pull the lever from the side like Sergeant Fields said, and if it's wrong try it again."

Doc put the last statuette in one of the places on the board and walked to the levers that came out from the wall. He stood by the green one and carefully from the side pulled it down. An arrow shot through the dark and stuck into the wall a foot away from Doc's head and the levers disappeared back into the walls. Doc cursed the room. He came back to the pillar and arranged the constellation again to his best guess. The levers came back down and again Doc stood to the side and pulled the green one.

Instead of the arrow or the door opening, about a quarter of the floor fell from beneath us!

Kumer fell down into the pit with the marble tiles. We ran to where he had been standing, cautiously avoiding the gaps in the floor and crying his name. We looked down and saw only black. We shined our lights to find him. There was nothing but the void. We called to him and there was no response. Not even the echoes talked.

Tears fell down the sides of Fields' face. He took an empty magazine from a pouch and tossed it in to see how far it led. There was no echo. "Arrows and pits. You gotta be fucking kidding me. Doc, you'd better goddamn get it right this time."

Doc went back to the table. He made another guess at the locations of the stars. When the levers appeared he grabbed the green one once more, fearing for what would happen next. He pulled it down, and the door opened. He let out a great sigh of relief.

Silently the rest of us walked into the next room. Once more the door locked and there were statues and cuts in the floor. We looked up to see a scimitar. "I don't know what that is," Doc said.

We just glared at him.

"I mean, I know it's a sword…" He looked around and counted the statues. "… and there are seven stars in the constellation… it can only be Aries or Auriga… and since it's a sword and not a goat I'm going with Auriga."

"What if you're wrong?" Alvarado growled.

"Well, do you want to do it?" Doc shot back.

"I don't know any of this shit!"

"Then shut the fuck up!"

Alvarado was angry, but stayed silent.

Auriga was right. Doc also guessed correctly in the next two rooms, Gemini and Cancer, although 'Cancer' was a crayfish. All of the rooms were still identical from the last, except the carving on the roof and the variation between statues and chessboards.

The next room had a lion on the ceiling and fifteen little scorpion-man chess pieces. "It's Leo," Doc said panting.

"Alright then, Doc. Let's go," Fields instructed him.

Doc looked pale and sweaty, his skin was clammy. "Yeah, just give me a minute."

"You alright?" I asked him.

"I don't know, man. I feel like shit. There might have been something on that arrow." We all looked at Doc. "I think I'll be okay for a bit." He swallowed a few pills from his med bag. He stood up and made the figurines into the shape of Leo, and the lever opened the door.

The following chamber had fifteen pieces on the board and a plow carving. Doc was stumped and starting to get sick. We proceeded with extreme caution. The first try didn't work, and the arrow missed Doc when it flew. Before the second try everyone held their arms around a column so if the floor fell from beneath us then maybe we wouldn't fall.

Doc pulled the lever again after rearranging the constellation. Tiles from the floor fell into infinity, but none of the Marines fell. The tiles below Fields and me fell, but since we had latched ourselves to the big scorpion-men, we could make our way to more stable ground.

Doc tried the whole ordeal again. Six of the big scorpion columns swung down their hands so fast that no one knew what happened until it was over. Fields started screaming. We made our way to him. His arm was caught crushed under one of the column statues.

"Shit! Whadda we do?" Reyes grabbed at his hair.

Hofstadter started pulling at the statues hand, trying to lift it off of

Field's arm. "Guys help me!"

Reyes, Doc, and I joined Hofstadter in trying to lift the giant stone hand. We pulled and yanked it with all our might. Our efforts were fruitless.

"Damn it!" Reyes punched the statue.

Fields screamed in pain. Doc knelt down next to him and gave him a shot of morphine. Fields' screams turned into a subtle growl. Doc sat there with a terrible look of hopelessness on his face.

We stood around Fields, silently brooding over our predicament. We were about at the breaking point. No one said anything for a long time, until Reyes, who had made his way to the foot of the statue and sat, started talking again to that fucking doll. "Yeah, it's shitty... you're not helping Barbara... what does that have to do with anything... yeah he's... he's... where is he... where is he?" Reyes looked up at us. "Where's Alvarado?" he demanded.

Hofstadter, Doc, and I looked at each other in confusion. "ALVARADO!" we called. "WHERE THE FUCK ARE YOU?"

He didn't answer. We looked for him, being careful not to fall into a pit. We found what was left, his arm laid palm up from under one of the statue's hands and a pool of his blood. Reyes curled up in a ball next to him and wept. He cried, "No, no bro. Goddamn it man, no!" His tears were bitter with curses.

Hofstadter, Doc, and I crept back to Fields to give Reyes a minute alone. Alvarado had been Reyes' best friend. Fields was unconscious.

"So what do we do?" I asked.

"Try the constellation again," Hofstadter whispered.

"But what if I miss? What'll happen?" Doc asked.

"What about him?" I pointed to Fields.

"Well, we have to do something," Hofstadter said. "Doc, try the puzzle again. If it works I'll stay with Fields..." he looked over to Reyes,

"…and probably Reyes, while you two go ahead. If you get out then bring engineers down here and blow away the walls until you find us."

"And what if I get it wrong again and something worse happens?"

"Then Doc, we'll be dead and won't have to deal with this shit."

"Hopefully," I added. "I wouldn't be surprised when if it's wrong again Medusas and demons come out."

Doc looked over to the chess table pillar. "I don't feel right about leaving anyone behind."

"Cut it off, Doc," Fields groaned from below. We looked down to him. "Cut the damn thing off and we'll be out of here."

Doc glared at fields, "I'm not cutting off your arm."

"Yeah," Fields hissed at Doc. "How about 'Aye fucking Sergeant!?'"

"I'll take my chances of standing in front of the CO later." Doc leaned down. "I'm *not* cutting off your arm."

Fields huffed at him.

Not knowing exactly what to do, Doc walked over to the table again and played with the pieces. When he had set them all the levers once again came down and he went to pull the green one. The door opened!

"What was it?" Hofstadter asked.

"Virgo."

The two of them stood in the doorway debating what course of action to take. I went to Reyes. "Hey man."

Reyes held Alvarado's hand. "Yeah?"

"I think Doc and I are going to keep going and come back with help. Hof is going to stay here with Fields. Do you want to come with us or stay with Hof?"

"I'm going to stay here with Alvarado," he whispered.

"Okay." I patted his shoulder and walked over to Doc and Hof. "So what's the deal?"

"We don't know," Doc said with a frown. "We're gonna flip a coin."

"Oh! Well, that's a fucking *great* idea!" I barked.

"Well what the fuck do you suggest?" Doc shouted.

"Not that!"

"You're not helping Kodak, shut up," Hofstadter growled.

"Do you even fucking have coins?" I clenched my fists.

Fields' voice interrupted us, "We can all go." The three of us turned to see him standing there. His KA-BAR was in one hand, and the other was ten feet behind him under that statue.

"Sit down!" ordered Doc. Fields complied. Doc started swearing through dressing Fields' self-inflicted injury.

When Doc was done, Fields opened his mouth to say something.

Doc cut him off, "I don't want to hear a damn word from you!" He turned to Hofstadter and said, "Go get Reyes."

I pulled Fields' good arm over my shoulder and helped him to his feet. The next room was Libra—easy, there were scales on the ceiling. Scorpio was next, then Sagittarius, Aquarius, and Pisces. Every room was set up near identically. The next room's constellation was unknown with seven stars, but Doc guessed it correctly the first time.

We entered the following room. Doc was breathing heavy and sweating profusely, despite how cold the air was down in the dark. There was probably poison on that arrow. He leaned against one of the columns in the room and vomited.

I ran to help him, with Fields still hobbling over my shoulder.

119

"Doc, you alright?"

"Yeah I'm good." He spit up more, and then took a small sip from a canteen. Doc staggered to the pillar in the middle of the room. He leaned over it with one hand on each side of the board. He stared at it blankly for a few moments then fell over.

I sat Fields down and ran to Doc with Hofstadter and Reyes. "Doc!"

"I'm alive," he whimpered.

"Are you *that* sick?" I knew that he was. I kneeled down to him and gave him some more water.

"No, I'm not *that* sick." He put his hands over his face. "But this is too much!" Doc started to sob.

I felt terrible. I hated seeing my friends in pain, but watching them cry, especially in already shit situations, made me feel weak and helpless. "Come on, Doc. I have faith in you." I wanted to cry too. He shook his head and wept. "It can't be that bad, we only have Aries left, right?" I looked up to the carving on the ceiling and there was a great stag dancing in a meadow. "That's not Aries, but a goat and a deer kinda look the same, they both have horns."

Then I saw what upset Doc so terribly, the chessboard with the scorpion-man pieces. Thirty-four. *Thirty-four! What constellation has thirty-four fucking stars?* "What the fucking fuck is this fucking horse shit!?" I couldn't help it any more either. I started to cry. I was sure that there was no way out. We were going to die down there. Just starve to death like those skeletons in the other room who hadn't made it past the first door or make an attempt at the unknown and be stabbed, crushed, or flattened to death. "Fuck my life." I started to envy Reyes, having a damn doll as an outlet for his foundering mind.

Hofstadter and Reyes weren't quite in as bad of shape as Doc and I were, but the sun was nowhere near them either.

"Will you bitches quit crying like pussies and get up?" Fields scolded us. He walked past us almost in a trance and started playing with the chess pieces, those demons on the pillar. "Doc, if you don't have a hint and insist on being a vagina about this then fuck it. I'll guess." He finished arranging the constellation as he pleased and walked over to the levers. Remembering the arrows he stood to the side. When he pulled the lever the arrow struck beside him and the levers disappeared, and Fields again walked to the pillar to try again. "Everyone grab something in case this doesn't work." It didn't work. Half the floor fell out from beneath us. "Okay, I'll try it again!" he said frustrated. "Get behind the statues along the outer wall so that you don't get smashed if I'm wrong again." He was. The statues' arms swung down and would have killed people in half the places in the middle of the room. Fields swore and returned to the pillar.

"Doc, I don't think whoever built this thought about people being along the walls," I said to him.

Doc, looking pale and sickly, managed to hack up, "ehhhhh… yeah…" He looked down the boundaries of the room. None of the floor had fallen out and nothing was smashed.

"I don't know what's next gents!" Fields shouted. When he pulled the lever six of the stone columns crumbled into boulders and fell to the ground. Some of the boulders were big enough to cover the pits in the floor. One of the columns mangled Hofstadter's body leaving him lifeless. Another one pinned Reyes' leg to the floor.

Reyes yelped. We climbed to him through the new terrain the rubble had built and over the pits in the floor that were left. I'm sure they led all the way to Hell. "You're not cutting off my fucking leg, Doc!"

"*I* didn't cut off his arm!" Doc snapped back.

Fields went back to the table, rearranged the pieces, and pulled the lever again. There was a loud bang and the sound of grinding rocks. I looked up with my light. The roof was sliding down on us!

"You've got to be fucking kidding me!" Fields shouted. He tried again at the scorpion chess. "We don't have time for all of this! Doc, go over there and pull the lever when I tell you to!" He tried another combination and Doc pulled the lever.

Nothing happened.

"What's going on?" Doc shouted.

"I don't know, but I hear something," I shouted.

"Was that a free one?" Fields asked.

I shined my light around the room. "Fuck!"

"What?" Fields demanded of me.

"There's water coming down the walls!"

Everyone started to panic. The water was running down fast. A decent amount of it was falling into the pits, but the wreckage of the statues covered enough of them to let water build up.

Another try...

Long metal spikes extended themselves from the ceiling.

Water rose around my ankles. The spikes were still thirty feet away. They were slow, but coming.

Reyes couldn't get up, the crumbled statue pinned him to the floor. The murky, sand-ridden liquid covered his face.

The stones didn't budge when I kicked or pushed them. I tried to pull him up so he could get air. "No, no, no..."

Reyes stared at me from under the water. He was too panicked to hold his breath. Bubbles escaped his mouth as he tried to scream.

"I'M SORRY!" I started to cry again. I pulled, yanked, shoved, and pushed Reyes and the rocks. Nothing would budge. "I'm sorry."

Reyes laid crushed under demonic ruins. The last of his air had left him.

I wiped my eyes with my sleeve. "FUCK!"

Fields reorganized the pieces. "Doc!"

Doc pulled the lever and twelve spears shot out from the floor around the pillar in the center of the room impaling Fields. He was propped up dead where he stood. I climbed and swam over to the chessboard and stuck my hand through the spears and moved a piece. I called to Doc and when he pulled the lever the roof engulfed in flame. *Fuck.* "Fuck! Fuck! Fuck!" I moved another piece around. I called to Doc, the spikes were ten feet away and the water was up to my chest. Doc pulled the lever and the door opened.

The water rushed out of the room from the door, but still poured from the walls. The roof was still burning and falling. I waded as quickly as I could to the door. Doc and I left the room.

Then it slammed shut.

"Jesus, God… Fuck…" I caught my breath.

When we got to the middle of the room, there were more statues. Doc keeled over and vomited. I rested him on one of the twelve pillars. I looked up. This room was a man working a field. I didn't know what the modern constellation translation was. But there were nine statues on the ground and we hadn't done Aries yet, so I decided to try it. I only knew four constellations, the Big Dipper, Orion, the Southern Cross, and Aries. I pushed the statues to the right places and when the levers appeared, I pulled the green one.

The door opened and light shined out of the room! It was very dim light, but it was light dammit! I ran over to Doc, he was in a poor state. He couldn't hold his head up and was pale. I grabbed him by the shoulder straps of his flak jacket and dragged him across the floor into the other room. The door stayed open when we went through.

This room was a great hall. We stood on a platform made of the same marble as the rest of the dungeon, or temple, or wherever the fuck we were. Before us there was a long pool filled with mercury. There was a forest in the room. It stretched from the back wall on the platform with us and across the mercury lake all the way to the other end. It looked as if that was shorter than a hundred yards away. There was a giant stone statue of a warrior holding an axe at the position of attention as if he were guarding the room. The dim light that illuminated the room came from an opening in the wall on the far side. I didn't know how deep the mercury was, but if it were more than half an inch I wasn't going to walk through it. I took the axe out of the statue's hands and pushed it into the lake. The mercury didn't splash up, but that stone sank. There was no telling how deep that was. Doc was lying on the deck by the back wall. He was still breathing, but it was faint. He was destroyed. I looked at the axe I took from the statue and then at the trees.

I started as close to the edge of the platform as I could and cut down the trees. After the first tree fell I placed it horizontally in the lake. I hacked down more of the trees and shoved them into the lake. I tried to be quick. Most of them weren't too thick and only required three or four swings to topple. I didn't count how many I took down, but it had to be at least a hundred twenty before there was enough of a bridge to where I felt comfortable taking Doc across. First I tested it by walking halfway across the lake on the timbers. They were a bit wobbly, but they held. I went back and grabbed Doc. I put his arm over my shoulder and half-walked, half-drug him across the bridge to the light on the other side.

There was a platform on the other side too, and another statue with an axe and a door, which bright light shined through. When we came through the doorless threshold I cried for joy. The ceiling was as brilliantly blinding as the sun. The hall was great, it was easily larger than a department store. It was warm and there were trees, bushes, flowers, and grass bordering the walls. The floor was all one giant crystal that was so clear that I could see through it until the light faded away. There were two streams of running water on the edge of the plant life, and there were riches! Rich jewels, gems, and treasure! Piles and piles of gold and silver and rubies everywhere. No wonder it had been so damn difficult to get here.

I laid Doc by one of the streams and cupped him some water. He was only strong enough to drink in little bits. I went to explore the room for a way out or anything that may have bettered Doc's ailments. On the walls above the trees were murals of what looked to be Noah's ark. Lines of animals and the beasts of the earth lined up two by two following a bearded man with a staff onto a ship. At the far end of the room was a giant cobalt gate. There were golden reliefs of dragons and lions. On top of the gate were two large silver-winged bulls with human heads and long beards. In the middle of the gateway was a golden statue of a man with a square beard. He stood on top of a ship that looked like the ark from the flood myths. The streams in the room came in as one from the mouth of the gate and split at this statue. In his right hand he held a rod with two snakes wrapped around it. His left hand was pointing into the stream to that side of him. I followed his hand. In the water there was a large plant growing out of the floor. The plant was green and lush; there were purple flowers on it with five petals. It was covered in long thorns. I got down on my hands and knees to see it a bit more clearly. I wasn't a botanist, but I was pretty sure flowers weren't supposed to grow under water. That's when I saw the berries. Big red berries. They were just a little larger than the big lights my grandma used to have on her Christmas tree.

I didn't at the time know exactly what the statue of Noah meant by holding the caduceus and pointing to that bush with the red fleshy berries on it. But if I had known, I wouldn't have gotten into it. I would have just stayed there and died, but that story's for later, much, much later.

However, at the time a statue was holding the caduceus and pointing to something edible and Doc was sick; I took it as a blatant sign. I took my gear, clothes, and boots off and jumped in. I swam down, but I couldn't hold my breath long enough to get all the way down and back up. I tried it a few times, failing each one. I climbed out of the water and searched the room for something to help me. I found a heavy red ruby, about the size of a basketball, and took it to the stream. I stuck my KA-BAR, it its sheath, under my armpit to hold on to it, grabbed the ruby, and jumped into the water. I sank like a rock. When I got to where I thought I needed to be I let go the precious stone and cut off the branch with the most berries on it. Ascending water is a lot easier than going down.

I put my trousers back on and took the branch to Doc. He looked like death. I picked his head up and fed him one of the large, fleshy, red berries. He managed to get it down. After he had eaten two or three I put him back on his back. Then I ate one for myself. They tasted better than anything I had ever eaten. Their flavor was like a cool raspberry and a pomegranate mixed with a sunny afternoon. They had some seeds in them, but they were small.

I sat there for about half an hour admiring the hall in all of its beauty. *What is this place? Who built it and why?* It made me think of what would have happened if Ali Baba hid his treasures in the Garden of Eden.

I grabbed my gear and clothes and brought them over to where Doc was laying. There were still almost fifty berries on the branch I brought up. I ate a few more. I sat on the ledge and put my feet in the water and looked at the images on the wall of the animals loading onto the ark. Out of the corner of my eye I saw something move. I snapped around to see a snake curling around the branch. I picked up my M4 and smashed its head with the butt stock. "How the fuck did that get down here?"

"Huh?" Doc said waking up.

"How ya feeling, buddy?"

Doc sat up and rubbed his face. "I'm actually feeling pretty good," he said slowly.

"Not sick or anything? I'm kinda surprised. You looked like death."

"Yeah…" Doc looked around the room. "Where the fuck are we?" he said with a bit of awe. "I don't remember anything after the room where the statues fell down."

"There were a few more rooms, man."

He looked at me stone faced.

"But they ended up being the easy ones," I said with a smile.

Doc stood up and dropped his pack and flak jacket. "Huh." He walked around the room, just as I had, astonished at the marvel of the room. "Look at all this gold! No wonder it was fucking guarded like that!"

I stood up and walked with him. He saw the golden statue at the mouth of the rivers under the great gate in the room.

"Is that *Noah?*"

"The best I can guess," I shrugged.

"He's got caduceus! That's totally badass." Doc looked into the water where the statue was gesturing. "Is that where you got the sweets?"

"Yeah."

We spent a good amount of time investigating the hall with all its great treasure. We grabbed the berry branch and sat down in front of the golden statue and ate the rest of the Christmas-light-looking little red fruits. "Dude, I feel great!" Doc said. "I don't know if that poison was just short term, or if it's the berries, or if it's just that I'm not in the dark anymore, or what."

"Yeah, I don't know, man. I actually feel pretty good too… at least physically."

Doc frowned. "God rest their souls."

We didn't talk for a while.

I finally broke the silence, "So, how about we try to get the hell out of here?"

"I'm on board with that. What about all the loot?" Doc pointed to the gold and gems.

"I don't know about all that, man. It's down here for a reason."

"But there's so damn much of it." Doc eyed the treasures. "And after what we paid to get into here."

"Yeah but that's the thing, man. What if it's cursed or booby trapped or some other shit like the rest of this God-forsaken place?"

"This room seems pretty alright to me."

"Yeah, I killed a snake in here if you didn't see that."

"Gross."

"And besides that, don't you remember like *every* mummy or pirate or treasure movie ever made? This shit's bad juju. I'm telling you man, it's down here and guarded like that for a reason."

"But we made it past the tests and traps!"

"Doc, listen to me. You ever read up on Norse mythology?"

"Not really."

"In all of their old stories there's treasure, and nothing *ever* good happens to the people who have it. You know what, as a matter of fact, I think it was all the same treasure that was cursed and made all that bad shit happen. It may have just been an analogy, but the greed of the gold turned Loki from a trickster to a devil; it made brothers kill their fathers and then each other; it made the gods go to war with the dwarfs; and it made Sleeping Beauty kill the guy who saved her from her castle."

"Sleeping Beauty was a Viking?"

"Yeah, but that's not the point. I don't know if that gold's evil or not, but I don't want to risk it. And I don't want to take the wrong pieces and have mummies burst out of the walls and eat me! After all that other bullshit today, I'm more than willing to believe that that kind of fucked up shit could happen. Mummies or hydras or flying fucking monkeys! They're just going to pop out of the walls and cut our balls off with dull, rusty daggers and stuff them in our mouths and fist fuck us while they stab us in the eyes with forks!"

A worried look grew on Doc's face. "Yeah, you're probably right about that."

"Think about it. When has anyone ever taken treasure out of a hoard and had a happy ending?"

"None that I can think of, man."

"So we're going to leave it?"

"Yeah."

"Good." I stood up. "Lets get our shit together and try to get back the fuck out of this place."

We gathered what we brought in and absolutely nothing more,

except the berries in our guts, and headed out the door. We walked over the mercury lake and into the Aries room. When we got to the door at the back of the room, now the front, it slid open by itself.

"Why the fuck didn't it do that before?" Doc yelled.

"Probably because we're coming from the other side."

The next room was depressing and frightening. The ceiling was so low and the rubble was so high that we had to crawl through. The water was drained, but everything was scorched and black. We crossed by Fields. He was hard to look at. He wasn't much more than a skeleton. It put a sick feeling in my gut. I shined my light forward. I didn't look at him anymore than I had to.

After that room Doc and I walked through the rest of the dungeon. The doors opened for us and we cut through the darkness and the cold. We did, of course, keep our eyes out for holes in the ground.

When we got back to the room through which we first entered, that dreary pit of death, the truck was gone and there was a tunnel leading up through where it had fallen. Then there was a thunderous boom. The scorpion-man columns collapsed and everything came crashing to the ground.

Doc and I scrambled up the tunnel into the light above.

7 POKK; BACK FROM THE FLAMES, INTO THE CAULDRON

We exhaustedly climbed the rocky surface towards the light. The walls weren't slick, but it wasn't easy to get fingers and feet to hold onto anything. Not to mention that we were both hauling about sixty pounds of gear. Still, we managed. The hardest part ascending the pit was the very top. The rocks turned to loose sand and every step of the climb had to be taken carefully.

We didn't bother to take a peek around to see if it was safe emerging from the pit. I would have rather taken a bullet to the face the moment I surfaced than take any risk of falling back down into that dreary hole. We pulled ourselves to the street.

The sun was falling behind the horizon. There were sharp gouges in the street, probably from pulling the truck out. The buildings across the square were demolished, the fountain was leveled, and shell casings littered the ground. Blood stained the pavement. Doc and I were alone.

"Doc, we should get out of here before the wrong people show up," I panted.

"Yeah," Doc said as he looked around. "There's no telling how far they got."

I looked around the square. "You think we should get up on a building and look around?"

"No. I can hear something mechanical down there." Doc pointed in the opposite direction from which we came when we assaulted. "I say we head that way."

We went in the direction we were heading before the truck sank into the pit. We kept close to the walls, trying to be quiet and unheard, just in case the wrong people were around; hands on our weapons, ready to shoot at a second's notice. The sun set and darkness engulfed the city. Neither of us had night vision and the power was out.

Creeping along the streets, I whispered, "So, do you think they pushed through? I mean, if they pushed out the Persians then someone would still be around here somewhere. They're not going to move an entire regiment out that quickly."

"Dude, someone's gotta be around here somewhere. Why aren't there civilians around?"

"I don't remember seeing any on the way in." I kicked something on accident and it went jingling down the road. We both froze in out tracks. I looked down to the dark street trying to make anything out of the darkness.

"Shell casing," Doc whispered. "We're going in the right direction."

"I'm trying to see if it was ours or an AK round."

"Well, either way someone was firing here, so Marines must have made it this far."

We moved forward. Most of the buildings weren't more than a couple of stories tall. A few of them were painted a dull yellow, pink, or blue, but most of them were a sandy beige. The roads were somewhat modern. There were bullet holes in everything. Every single window had been shot out and large chunks of the walls had been blown away. We made sure to look inside the holes, doorways, and windows, just in case something was there. It was too dark to see much of anything.

After an hour of creeping through the streets we heard a voice scream from the dark. "HALT! WHO GOES THERE!?"

"Sweet merciful Jesus we found someone. Doc Evans and Corporal Allensworth!" Doc shouted back. We stuck out our arms to make our bodies into the shapes of crosses so the sentry didn't shoot us.

The voice in the darkness ordered, "Advance to be recognized!" Slowly Doc and I walked towards the voice. A shadowed figure stepped out from a hole in the wall of a building that had seen better days. "Who are you?" the figure demanded.

I told him, "CAAT 1, Second Battalion Sev…"

"Yeah okay, I'm Sergeant Duval with Fox." He motioned us to head into the building. "Get out of the open."

The inside of the building was dim but I could tell there was at least a squad in the dusty darkness. "What are you guys doing out here?" Duval demanded.

"We got separated," Doc responded.

"How long?" Duval asked.

"I don't know. This afternoon?" Doc fumbled with his words. "I think it was this afternoon. Whenever we came through, our truck got hit and we fell into a…" Doc didn't know what to call our ordeal.

"That was you guys?" Duval said in shock.

"Yeah," I responded. "And we've been wandering around trying to find Marines since we climbed out."

"That was two fucking days ago," Duval revealed to us.

"What?"

"They sent engineers down there to pull you guys out, but they only found the turret gunner in the truck. From what I heard there was a cave or a room down there with no way out and they didn't know where y'all went off to." Duval turned on a small red flashlight and shined it on us. "Where's the rest of the guys in your vic?"

"They didn't make it," I said solemnly.

"I'm sorry." Duval pulled out a notebook and took down our names. "I'm going to radio this in to battalion. You guys chill out."

Doc and I sat down next to a few of the other Marines and took off our helmets. We didn't talk. I didn't know what emotion I was feeling. I didn't know if I should be scared or excited, depressed or jubilant. One of the Marines from Fox Company sat beside me. "Corporal?"

I looked over, but it was too dark to make out a face. "Who's that?"

"Éclair."

"Shit, man, how are you?"

"I've been better."

"I'd bet."

After a few minutes Sergeant Duval came over. "Hey guys. I talked to the company. Your platoon's gonna send a section to come grab you guys in the morning. They're in a blocking position at the edge of the city."

"Thanks, man," Doc said. He turned to me and said, "Two days..."

"I don't know, man. I don't really want to talk about it." I pulled off my Alice pack.

"What's there to talk about?"

"I don't know." I pulled out an MRE. "Want some of my omelet?"

"No."

"Me either." I tossed the brown plastic package on the ground. I laid back on my pack and tried to sleep, but I couldn't. I didn't remember falling asleep but I must have. A mosque, somewhere near there, awakened me by blaring their morning prayer. I looked around the room, now illuminated by the sun. By every hole in sand-colored walls was a Marine pointing out his rifle. I hated the sound of morning prayer.

I stood up and through a rather large breach in the wall I started screaming, "SHUT THE FUCK UP! NO ONE WANTS TO HEAR THAT SHITTY FUCKING LION KING COVER YOU SONOFABITCH GOAT FUCKING FAGGOT MOTHER FUCKER!"

One of the Fox Company Marines jerked me back by my flak jacket. "Hey Marine, shut the fuck up! Hajji's crawling all over this fucking place."

I clenched my fists and gritted, "I'm sorry, man. I'm just fucking… damned…" I took a couple of deep breaths and rubbed my forehead, I hadn't even taken off my gloves from the night before. "I'm just…"

"Hey man, it's alright," the Marine said. "We're all a little on edge, just chill out."

"Yeah… I…" I didn't know what to say or do. "We're here trying to keep these goat fuckers safe from the fucking Persians and they want to keep us up playing that bullshit."

"I know," the Marine said back. "I wish the guy would take some singing lessons and get speakers that didn't crack when he hollers into the mic." The Marine produced a pack of smokes and handed them to me. "Sometimes you've just got to chain smoke your problems away."

I took the cigarettes. "Thanks," I said miserably and sat back down.

Doc looked at me and said, "You alright?"

"No." I pulled out a cigarette with my teeth and dug through my pockets for my lighter. Lighting the smoke, I offered the pack to Doc.

"Thanks." Doc pulled one out.

The floor was tiled and littered with debris from the walls, glass, shell casings, and cigarette butts. I peered outside and there were aluminum tables and chairs twisted, burnt, and bent in the street. I guessed the place was a small restaurant and the Marines tossed out anything that could become shrapnel when they came in. I burnt through another five or six cigarettes in silence.

"Hey Marines," Duval said and stood over us.

"I'm a sailor," Doc mumbled.

Duval looked at him slightly annoyed. "You've gotta truck coming in about fifteen."

"Awesome." I looked up at the sergeant. "Where's the rest of Fox at? They in the buildings around?"

"No, it's just this platoon," he responded. "Most of us are on this block, then Gulf's down the road a bit and Echo beyond that. And like I said before, your platoon's in a blocking position for something, but I'm not sure where."

"Killer." Doc and I waited by the blown-out doorway for our ride. When it pulled up I waved farewell to Éclair and headed out. From the inside of the MRAP Sergeant Flores opened the rear hatch and we climbed aboard. He welcomed us back. Flores looked dog-tired. He had about three days of beard growing.

At least we weren't the only ones that got rode hard and hung up wet.

All was silent for the first few minutes until Doc spoke up. "How far did you guys make it?"

"We pushed to the outskirts of the city," Flores said. "The city hasn't been completely cleared. We pulled up to our position last night and we've been checking fleeing civilians for weapons."

"There been that many people running out?" Doc asked.

"Not really, maybe a family every couple of hours." Flores looked us over. "What happened to you guys?"

"We fell in hole, man." I was dreading linking back up with the platoon, I *knew* everyone was going to shake us down wondering what happened. I didn't want to fucking talk to anyone about anything, and Doc felt the same way.

The truck stopped with the rest of the platoon. The sun burned down on us through the dust in the air. Doc and I found the platoon sergeant and the SirBot looking over some maps between a MRAP and a brick wall that had seen better days.

"Morning, Sir," I said downtrodden.

The SirBot looked a little bit less irate that he usually did. I guess he was happy to see us. "Just you two?"

"Yes, Sir," Doc responded.

"What happened to the other Marines?"

Knowing that if we told him, or anyone for that matter, what actually happened down there we'd spend a decent amount of time in the loony bin talking to the wizard, I decided not to lie, but not to tell the truth either. "They fell into a cave sir, and they were too far down to even see or hear, much less pull out."

"Fuck." The SirBot was silent for a moment. He spat a huge chunk of tobacco into the sand. "Well, are you two good to fight?"

Doc and I nodded, "Yes, Sir."

"Okay, if you guys need anything, let us know. Have one of the other corpsmen look you over, then talk to Gunny about what truck you should be in."

We sat in that blocking position for days. Scuttlebutt was that something big was supposed to happen soon. I laughed at that; I thought something big was already happening. But what did I know? I was just a corporal.

The platoon had taken a few other casualties while Doc and I were… underground. Gunny rearranged who was in what vehicles a bit. Fonzie and Kyle returned from the field hospital. Fonz had a gnarly scar on his forehead that was bound to scare little kids around Halloween. Kyle, Fonzie, Doc, and I were assigned to the same truck with Sergeant Char as the vehicle commander. Kyle drove, the Fonz was in the turret, and Doc and I sat in the back as dismounts.

We sat in the burning sun, beaten by the stick of fatigue. The heat over there is the worst on the fucking planet. You can't escape it and while you acclimate you never really get used to it. Right before we would go to sleep we would all drink a full canteen. It felt like drinking liquid fucking magma. At some point in the night, fire watch would wake us up again and we'd drink another canteen and go back to sleep. Thirst still taunted us when we awoke. I would maybe piss twice a day. Even after drinking a gallon plus of water, my urine was still brown. Everyone was that way. Our uniforms were so soaked with sweat that if we were to take them off our trousers could stand up on their own with the help of the salt deposits.

A logistics convoy came our way an hour after dusk one night. They brought us more chow, boiling hot, sunbaked water, a couple cases of Rip Its, and mail. To hell with water and chow, a Marine could live off of Rip Its, tobacco, and mail.

The convoy's Marines also brought their share of rumors. The Marine Corps' rumor mill was worse than the tabloids. While unloading our new supplies we heard all kinds of bullshit. 'General Mattis was brought back and is going to be the new Commandant.' 'The Division Sergeant Major is going to authorize us to wear shorts.' 'Ron Jeremy got a sex change.' 'Aliens landed and they love California.' No one ever put much credence into that shit, but it was fun to think about.

I sat down, propped up against the rear wheel of our truck, and looked into the desert. I didn't want to look at Al Hillah. Or what I thought was Al Hillah, hell I didn't know. Maybe it was a suburb or even the next town we made it to. It's not like I could read the road signs. I lit up a Lucky's and opened a letter that came that day from Kennedy.

Hank,

Please get this letter. I haven't heard from you in God knows how long. I know things are difficult, but please send me a letter or give me a phone call if you can. I'm worried about you. I heard that the fighting started over there. I'm so worried about you it's making me sick. Reagan hasn't heard anything from Wilson either. We figure that it's because you're busy, but that makes me think you're in danger. What happens if you get hurt? How am I going to find out? I don't want you to die then me never knowing what happened to you. I miss you Hank, and I'm so fucking worried about you. At least send me a letter, let me know you're okay.

Yours,

Yasmina Gulbadan Kassandrazaden

"Kennedy"

The paper looked like Kennedy was crying when she wrote it. Small stains smeared the ink. I couldn't handle that. I bottled up my feelings and burnt them away with a cigarette. Sometimes you have to chain smoke your problems away. I knew things were going to be bad when I got home, if I got home. Ever since my first deployment it was like that. Shit goes to hell while you're out there, but you can't deal with it then. If you do it'll kill you. If you have to shed a tear and talk to your friends that helps, but when you're *there* you can't really deal with it. If it doesn't kill you, it'll get other Marine's killed. I knew as soon as I got back to California I'd buy a bottle of rum, lock myself away, and drink until I puked and fell asleep. But that wasn't here or now, that was in the future, back in the real world. That's why sometimes I secretly hoped I came home in a box. I would never check myself out early, but a glorious death in battle seemed romantic sometimes. Hell, maybe if that happened I'd have lucked out and picked the wrong religion and instead of reporting to Saint Peter for guard duty on Heaven's scenes, Odin would welcome me into Valhalla. Wishful thinking. *God has a sense of humor, right?*

I decided I'd write Kennedy back and send it to her via the next log train out of here, but I didn't know what to write.

Dear Kennedy, I'm okay. I haven't been writing because...

Because why, Hank? Because I've been eating dirt and crawling on my stomach trying not to get my ass blown off? Because I'd been killing people the last few days? Because I literally lost a truckload of friends? Because I almost drowned in the River Styx on my way through the gates of Hell?

"Fuck it, she can wait," I grumbled. *I'll write her a letter back before the next supply truck comes.* I stuffed her letter into my pocket. I looked back out to the desert trying to see something, anything. It was dark and there was nothing. I looked for the lights of another city until I realized this city's power was out, and so probably were any others around here.

One good side effect of no power is the stars. When you go deep into the desert, with no lights anywhere around you for miles besides the occasional red flashlight and lighters, you can see every star with your naked eye. I wanted to go to space and leave the world behind. To be alone in the cosmic void, traveling the galaxy in search for new wonders. What's out there? If we ever got to the point where humanity left Earth in masses and traveled the sky like it was the ocean in the age of sail, would we call areas in space 'seas?' I went on daydreaming until Kyle kicked my boot.

"What's up, man?" I looked up at him.

"SirBot wants to talk to us."

"What about?"

"I dunno."

I walked with Kyle, Doc, and Sergeant Char to where the lieutenant was. The turret gunners stayed in the trucks keeping watch, the rest of the platoon formed a circle around the SirBot behind a battered wall.

The SirBot spit. "Alright gents." He opened a map of the area. "Tomorrow morning at zero five hundred we're moving out. The whole Goddamned division is starting its push to the Tigris. It's about a hundred klicks to the battalion's next objective, An Numaniyah. Enemy situation in the city is unknown, however, there is a base formerly controlled by the Iraqi Army. Intel doesn't know if it's being utilized by the Iranians. It doesn't seem as if there's anything between here and there besides sand. The line companies are loading up in seven tons and we're leading the battalion. We'll have a couple of tanks with us and CAAT 2 will provide security on the flanks. Make sure you have ammo and you have water and chow in your vics."

The next morning we were off. We had driven for an hour, there were no words except for radio chatter. I hated convoying. Anywhere else in the world a hundred kilometers, sixty something miles, takes about an hour to travel. Not on a convoy, especially one that's hauling an entire battalion. I don't think any one vehicle moved faster than fifteen miles an hour.

I was still pissed off; the whole truck was except for Kyle apparently. He was singing, "I wanna rock and rooooo oh oh, awe nigh! An' party every dayayay!"

Before he got to the second verse the rest of us chipped in. When it was over we sang Whitesnake and Motley Crue. I started to feel a little better.

We were singing for a good half hour, creeping across the Iraqi sands, before we started seeing the tanks.

We pulled closer to them. Iranian tanks, transport trucks, and ground soldiers—all lying burnt, twisted, and destroyed. Smoke and flames rose from the wreckage. Vehicles lay on their sides with their operators stuck frozen in the poses of their final moment, trying to claw away. Hundreds of bodies, burnt black from fire, sprawled across the sand like toys haphazardly tossed into a sand box.

"Looks like the Navy got to these guys first." Char leaned his face as close to the glass as he could to get a better view.

"Yeah," Doc replied. "It's not like the Air Force could ever shoot that good."

I said, "C130s maybe. They can lay down some hate."

"But not A10s or F sixfuckingteens," Char said without looking back to us. "Hey," he looked over at Kyle. "Whose truck got flipped back in Now Zad last deployment?"

"You mean when those fucking F16s dropped the ordinance on us instead of the Taliban?" Kyle replied.

"Yeah, that."

"I think it was Trujillo, but it might have been Lindman."

"No, Lindman's was the A10s," Doc interjected.

"It was Trujillo," Fonzie shouted down from the turret.

"What's the deal with that anyway?" I asked. "I mean, Fly Navy, that's cool. Marine Air, that's sweet too. Fuck, even the Royal Air Force pushed Hajji's shit in. Why can't the Air Force drop a fucking bomb in the right place?"

"It's not the whole Air Force, Kodak," Char said. "It's just the fuckers that don't know what they're doing. They're not good at being accurate. Hell, I'm all about that fucking AC130 Death Machine, but I wouldn't call it in to kill anything within a mile of my position."

"Eh, I guess." I tugged on Fonzie's leg. "Hey, man! Trade me places for a minute!" I shouted.

"What for?" he shouted back.

"I want to get some pictures of this shit!"

Fonzie and I switched places and I pulled out my zoom lens. I took pictures of everything I could for about five minutes, before it got monotonous. Then I crawled back down into the truck.

"That shit is fucking grizzly," I said in almost the same manner I'd compliment the engine of a muscle car.

"Yeah, you can't ever tell your girlfriend about this," Doc said with a smile.

"Why not?" Char inquired.

"Because she's Persian." I put my camera back in my drop pouch.

"What? Where'd you meet her?"

"Strip club."

"The Purple Church?"

142

"Yeah…"

Char laughed. "You fucking boot! She got nice tits?"

"Tig ol' bitties!"

We were quiet for a minute before Char led us back to, "IRAQ ROCK CITY!"

We continued our spiel until about a mile outside An Numaniyah. The line company Marines dismounted their vehicles and formed a marching order. When the battalion started its slow creep into the city Char declared, "Game time."

The Marines in the companies lined up dispersed between the trucks and tanks. We moved at walking speed with them into the city. Another dirty, shot-up shit show. It didn't look like there were many, if any civilians around. That was bad news. It meant that the Persians were here and the people fled. Unless you just got done killing everyone, silence was *never* golden. If there are kids playing in the street and the markets are open then you were nowhere near as likely to get shot up.

Kyle stopped the truck at the first intersection inside city lines. The Line Marines started clearing out the buildings. There was no gunfire.

"I don't like this," Doc muttered.

"Me either, man," I said back.

"No one's shooting. The buildings aren't completely destroyed, and there's no civilians. No one's here. Those dirty fucking Persians are here somewhere."

Kyle chimed in, "Maybe they came in and all the people jumped ship, then when Hajji left the city to come after us the air wing smoked 'em and that's why nobody's home."

Char kept his eyes on the windows in the buildings across the street. "The Japanese did this kind of shit in the Pacific. They'd let us take half the fucking island then *pow*, they'd have us surrounded and start turning the lever on the meat grinder."

"Somehow I doubt that Iranians are that smart." Kyle tightened his grip on the wheel.

"There is no greater danger than underestimating your opponent," Char added.

The Marines cleared the first block of buildings, then the next, and the next. There was no one and nothing there. By the time the sun started to set the battalion had cleared the city with no shots fired and no souls seen.

The battalion dug in for the night. A Marine from a passing platoon said that the bridge over the Tigris had been blown.

"So they *were* here," Char said as he lit a cigarette. He, Kyle, Doc, and I stood outside our truck bullshitting. Fonzie manned the turret. "I think it's cute they think that'll stop us from crossing."

"Who knows, man?" Doc said back. "Maybe they populated the river with sea monsters or giant killer crocodiles so that when we swim across it the animals will kill us."

"That's not really funny," I said almost laughing. "I knew a guy who was here in oh three that fell into the Euphrates. Dude's sterile now."

"Yeah, but it's probably not from that," Char said.

Doc scratched his face. "I don't know, man. Maybe he had insurgent plankton crawl up his p-hole and suicide bomb his nut sack."

We all chuckled.

"Well hey," I said, "at least now we know we've got 'em on the run."

"Dude, we're America. We've got everyone on the run," Kyle exclaimed.

"Except the Russians," Char said.

The battalion spent the night in An Numaniyah at quarter watch.

With the civilian populace spread to the winds it was a nice following morning. No Morning Prayer blasting in my ears, a decent MRE, as decent as they can be, and no one actively trying to kill me.

Word eventually was passed down that there was an Iranian division about fifty kilometers away in some place called Al Kut. It was on the other side of the river, but the Tigris wrapped around most of the city effectively making it a peninsula. Third Battalion Seventh Marines was already on the outskirts of the city making contact. First Battalion was on their way to reinforce Third. The Magnificent Second Battalion of the Seventh Marine Regiment was to wait in Numaniyah for the engineers to construct some inflatable bridge, cross the river, and flank those bastards.

The engineers were already working on their balloon bridge. While the sun fell to the west we could see helicopters in the distance picking up the One Seven Marines and flying them towards Al Kut.

We loaded into our vehicles and crossed the Tigris. When our truck started on the bridge Char said, "You know, I always thought it would be harder getting over rivers. Isn't there a ferryman we're supposed to pay?"

"That river's in Greece, man," Doc corrected.

"So if we go to war in Greece keep a couple of coins in my pocket for the fare?"

"No, dude. Just kick the ferryman in the nads and jack his ship. That's what Marines are for, right?"

"Eh, I think that's more like pirates."

"That's all Marines are supposed to be, man. Pirates with a certificate from the Department of Defense that says, 'License to plunder.'"

We rode into the night. Our lights all blacked out to make it harder to see us coming. We made good time. Hauling ass on the assault we made it most of the way to Al Kut within an hour and a half. As we approached we could see the city burning in the distance. The rest of the regiment was getting some.

Apparently though two Marine regiments weren't enough to keep the enemy satisfied. As soon as we were in range of the city they opened up on us.

Fonzie punched in the butterfly on the fifty caliber. PUPUPUPUPUPUPUP!

The radios erupted. Orders and interrogatives spewed through the speakers. Sergeant Char was doing the best he could to keep up with it all.

"GET SOME, FONZIE!" I shouted up at the Fonz.

Doc joined in, "HATE AND DISCONTENT!"

I could hear the Fonz up there swearing but I couldn't distinguish it. Knowing him it was probably something extremely racist that conveyed his wishes for the Iranians to sodomize themselves while they watched him force their sisters to perform analingus on him, more than likely in Spanish.

Artillery shells started blasting the earth around us. "PUNCH IT!" Char yelled. Kyle stomped on the gas and launched towards the city. The rest of the battalion followed suit getting out of the kill zone.

The buildings grew larger. Muzzle flashes shined from every window. That old familiar feeling of dread took my mind and did the only thought it ever had with that: "FUCK FUCK FUCK FUCK *FUCK!*" I squeezed my rifle. There was a bright flash, a loud bang, then darkness and silence.

Smokepit Fairytales

Tripp

148

8 BETWEEN IRAQ AND A HARD PLACE; COCK-STRONG WARRIOR MAN-GODS

I faded back into consciousness. My head pounded and my vision was blurry. My whole body ached. The muffled sounds of fire and Marines screaming orders thumped my ears. It was dark. The orange glow of flames illuminated the sand. I raised my hands to rub my face and felt a painful tug on my arm. I had an IV.

I was propped up behind our truck. Doc was tying a tourniquet on Char's arm. When Doc saw that I was awake, he patted my shoulder. "You're gonna be alright Hank. You're not hit bad." He went back to work on Char.

I closed my eyes hard enough to touch my cheeks with my eyebrows. *What the fuck happened?* I looked down at my arms. My uniform was singed and ripped. I had a bunch of shrapnel in my flak jacket. *Did we get hit with an artillery round? Where's Kyle and the Fonz? How far into the city are we? How close was that damn fifty caliber firing? Where's my rifle?* I felt my heart flat line. "DOC!"

"What, man?" Doc shot me a concerned look.

"WHERE THE FUCK IS MY RIFLE?"

"It's in the truck."

"Fuck me." I patted myself down and yanked the IV out of my

149

arm. My sleeve was sliced open up to my elbow.

"Ha." Doc grinned.

I looked up, Fonzie was firing the fifty caliber like a demon from the turret.

"Where's Kyle?"

"Calling in a nine-line for Char."

I came up to kneel from being sprawled out on the ground in a half-sitting prop. "He alright?"

"Yeah, he's going to be okay." Doc wrote the time he applied the tourniquet on Char's face with a sharpie. "He's just concussed and needs blood. He's probably not even going to go home for this. He'll just be out of the fight for a week or two."

"Lucky fuck."

"Yeah, and you need to lose weight. I had to drag your fat ass out of the truck," Doc said.

"Shut up, it's the flak jacket," I defended myself.

"Yeah, okay." Doc half smiled. "All three hundred pounds of it, right?"

There was another truck pulled next to us for additional security. It looked like McBland was in the turret, but I couldn't tell. The passenger side door opened. Sergeant Fowler jumped to the deck and ran to us. "How's it going, fuckers?"

"Char's out, but he'll be okay," Doc told him.

Kyle came back from the front of the truck. "I just called in the nine-line. Bird's five makes out. Sergeant Fowler, you got any chemlights?"

Fowler reached into his pocket and produced five glow sticks.

"Thanks." Kyle took two and cracked the sticks to make them

glow, shook them up, and tied them to a length of cord.

"Hank," Doc called. "You got your poncho?"

"Yeah." I scrambled to my seat in the truck and pulled out my Alice pack and my rifle.

Fonzie stopped shooting, loaded another can of ammunition, and sent another hundred little presents to the enemy. I don't think there was a second the entire time he was up there that he wasn't swearing.

Kyle took his lights and ran about fifty meters to our rear. He took one end of the cord and spun it so the glow sticks drew a circle in the night. The helicopter descended to the earth, sending a wave of sand and soot in all directions.

We wrapped Char in my poncho and as soon as the bird landed, Doc, Fowler, and I ran him to the chopper. When we passed Kyle he grabbed an edge of the poncho and assisted our labor. We put Char on the floor and Doc screamed something at the crew chief. The crew chief nodded and gave Doc a thumbs up. We ran back into the night.

"Get all the shit out of your truck and load it up in mine," Fowler ordered.

Frantically we grabbed anything worth taking out of our vehicle and threw it into Fowlers; water, ammo, chow, our gear. Fonzie finished off a belt of ammo and started taking down the weapon. Our truck looked like an aluminum can that caught the wrong end of a lawn mower. I don't know how the fuck we got away as luckily as we did.

Fowler tossed an incendiary grenade in our truck and we loaded up in his. The rest of the platoon was only about a hundred meters in front of us. I know you're thinking, 'Wow, dicks just left you there.' But when you're under that kind of fire your main objective is getting out of the kill zone, they wouldn't have been much good to us if they were dead too.

Fowler's MRAP was packed. There were seats for eight Marines in the back, but the designer's idea of a Marine is about eighty pounds and gearless. It was about as tight as a virgin dolphin's snatch.

The line companies had already started into the first line of buildings, kicking in doors and teeth.

Another shit city. Beige buildings no taller than five stories; holes and fire in the walls; glass, blood, and shell casings littered the streets. Muzzle flashes lit up the insides of the buildings around us. We didn't fire into them, we couldn't tell just from the flashes if the fire was theirs or ours.

The radio came back to life with orders from the SirBot, "Vehicle Commanders, leave your radios with your drivers and tell your gunners to provide covering fire. Everyone else follow me."

Another voice inquired, "Say again."

The SirBot came back screaming, "YOU'RE NEVER GOING TO GET THAT PURPLE HEART JUST SITTING IN A TRUCK! NOW COME ON YOU SONSABITCHES!"

We poured out of the vehicle and ran to the wall to try to catch up to the lieutenant. We started taking fire, everyone dove to cover, except for the SirBot. He raised his weapon and fired back alone in the open. The rest of us fired from behind cover. The lieutenant radioed back to the trucks, directing their fire. The face of the building in front of us fell apart like mud on a tire at a car wash.

The SirBot kept firing, closing the distance between himself and the building.

"Goddamned crazy-ass mother fucker," Kyle mumbled.

"I'm telling you, man," Fonzie said, "the SirBot's a dip powered robot from the future sent back to save mankind!"

When the lieutenant started getting further away from the platoon we all stood up and ran after him. Enemy fire erupted from the buildings around us. And we, CAAT 1, 2/7, The Cock-Strong Warrior Man-Gods, charged full force into the jaws of death.

We hit the building full force. We lined up and slammed our

shoulders to the wall. The Marine at the front of the line threw in a grenade. Not even a full second after the explosion we poured in through the door.

Marines shouted, "LEFT SIDE CLEAR!" "RIGHT SIDE CLEAR!" and we split up in teams of four to six into the adjacent rooms.

I followed Fowler and the Fonz to the next doorway, Kyle and Doc fell in behind us.

As soon as Fonzie and Fowler stepped in the doorway, bullets flew within inches of their faces. They already had their weapons up squeezing the triggers sending those Persian fucks to meet their virgins.

"Left side clear!"

"Right side clear!"

We continued this pattern up the floors, alternating who the first man into the next room was.

When my turn came I had Fowler behind me. We lined up facing the door from the wall. Fowler kicked my foot to let me know the team was ready. I stepped through the doorway and immediately took two bullets to my chest.

Fowler, who had been holding onto the back of my flak jacket, violently jerked me back to cover.

He whipped out a grenade. "THROWING A FRAG!"

"ROGER!" the other Marines shouted back.

He pulled the pin, let the spoon disengage for three seconds, and chucked it into the room.

BOOM!

Dust rained from the trembling walls.

I moaned. Flak jackets would stop bullets, but they don't stop the force. I looked up at Doc and gave him a thumbs up. I coughed, "May have broken a rib there."

"You'll be alright, pussy. Get up," Doc said with a smirk.

Kyle, Fowler, and the Fonz rushed into the room.

Doc helped me to my feet. I groaned, "Goddamn it."

"LEFT SIDE CLEAR!"

"RIGHT SIDE CLEAR!"

"Any trouble breathing?" Doc kept his hand on my shoulder.

"A little." I bit my lip to try to take my mind off of my chest.

"Sharp pain?"

"It's dull."

"It probably just knocked the wind out of you. You'll be alright. Try not to over exert yourself."

"HA!" There was a pain in my chest. "Ouch… hurts to laugh," I panted. "Don't say anything funny." I punched the wall. "Mother fuckers."

Doc helped me limp into the next room. There wasn't another doorway. There was shredded office furniture and dead Iranians. We jabbed them in the eyes to make sure they were dead. We pulled everything out of their pockets and put it in a bag to give to intel later. I took pictures of all their faces. It hurt to stand.

The platoon was scattered about the building. The Marines on the south side were exchanging fire with the building next door.

The SirBot and the gunny came down from the roof. "I need twelve Marines and an axe!"

Twelve of us followed him to the roof. The SirBot ordered Fowler, Kyle, Fonzie, Doc, and me to hold security on the south side of the roof but not to fire unless we were seen. We planted ourselves by the ledge and pointed our weapons toward the next building. There was some kind of radio tower antenna on the roof. The SirBot took the axe and chopped at the base. The other Marines held it so it wouldn't tip. When the tower was severed completely the SirBot ordered it placed between the two buildings.

Besides the Marines firing through the south side of the building, the rest of the platoon was brought to the roof. "Ranger file across the tower," the lieutenant demanded. "Follow me." The SirBot went first. When the platoon was positioned on the next roof Kyle and Fonzie grabbed the Marines from inside the building; we crossed over.

I hate heights, I always have. It would have been easier to crawl across it, but time wouldn't allow it, and that would have killed my aching chest. I just hoped that I wouldn't get shot, again, and fall five stories and splat on the street below.

When we were all across we staged by the doorway leading downstairs. The SirBot looked us over and said, "If you haven't already, fix your fucking bayonets. You get close enough to anyone stick it right up in 'em and turn."

The SirBot nodded at Fowler who kicked down the door, McBland simultaneously lobbed in three grenades. The SirBot screamed, "I AM BECOME DEATH! DESTROYER OF WORLDS!" and ran muzzle first down the hall, his whole platoon behind him.

We quickly cleared the top floor. The grenades McBland threw killed the few Persian occupants. The enemies in the floors below us fired up the ladder wells.

"Sometimes 'fuck you' ain't enough," the SirBot grumbled putting an entire can of Copenhagen in his mouth. "Who still has frags?"

A few of the Marines produced grenades. "Send'n 'em some love letters, Sir?"

"Yeah, standby." The SirBot grabbed his radio. "All stations this is CAAT 1 Actual; prepare to fire at the first floor of the building I'm currently occupying with fifty caliber and seven six two." He nodded at the Marines with the grenades then back into the radio he ordered, "FIRE!"

POP POP POP BOOM!

The building shook. The fire was so loud we had to use hand and arm signals to communicate. We charged down the stairs firing at anything we even thought was moving. We quickly cleared the fourth floor and moved down to the third.

Fowler, Kyle, Doc, the Fonze, and I cleared a room with nothing in it. When Fowler turned to step out a Persian we somehow missed lunged at him. But before he could reach him Fowler threw his rifle, bayonet first, toward the enemy, sticking him right in the chest. The soldier grasped the weapon sticking out of his body, desperately trying to pull it out. Fowler grabbed his M4, put his boot on the Iranian's chest, yanked out the weapon, and then shot him in the face.

Our group was the first down the next stairway. I had gone past the feelings of fear and dread to pure rage; I forgot about the pain in my ribs. The moment we hit the bottom of the stairs, half an Iranian platoon emerged from the adjacent rooms and charged us.

"FUCK!"

We started blasting. Bullets ripped the air. When they got too close we jabbed our bayonets into their guts, twisting and slicing out. The Marines behind and above us fired onto the Persians.

Fonzie dug his shoulder into one soldier's gut and flipped him down the ladder well. When he hit the first floor, rounds from the trucks shredded his body.

Kyle emptied his magazine into a soldier. Another one came after. Kyle dropped his weapon. He grabbed the Persian by the neck and slammed his head into the wall. Then he beat the enemy's face into a crater with his bare fist.

Doc punched a soldier in the throat. When he staggered back gasping for air Doc grabbed the enemy's rifle and beat him to death with his own weapon.

Fowler uppercut another one with his buttstock, and when the soldier hit the ground, Fowler stomped on his neck.

I was tackled. When I hit the ground I had the wind knocked back out of me. The soldier had his hands around my neck and was going for broke. He had his fingers all the way around my trachea and was trying to punch me in the face. I couldn't breathe, and I could start to feel my eyes bulge out of their sockets. I turned my head down so that his fist made contact with my helmet. He only did that twice.

He was too strong. I couldn't pull his hands off my throat. I reached down to my flak and grabbed my KA-BAR. I stuck the blade in his gut and looked up at him. His grip loosened but he still had some fight left. I drug the knife around his gut and felt his intestines fall on me. He tried to stand up but only faltered back. I stood up over him. He had a look of absolute anguish; I could only see despair and pain in his eyes. He grabbed at his entrails and tried to shove them back into his belly.

I grabbed him by the hair and leaned down into his face. "LOOK AT ME!" His eyes met mine. He looked at me as if he recognized me. Then he set his gaze on my dagger. "Oh this?" I taunted him. "I don't see any of you with these. You know why we have knives? So that we may get close to the enemy."

"Yasmina…"

"What?" I yanked his head closer. "What the *fuck* did you just say?"

He could see the look of confusion in my eyes. He grinned then spat a mouth full of blood in my face.

"YOU FUCK!" I stuck my blade in his windpipe and reciprocated in and out until his lifeless skull was severed. Then I kept stabbing his chest until Doc and Fowler pulled me off.

Fowler shook me. "Dude, Kodak, calm down."

"It's okay, man." Doc wrapped his arms around me. "We're all on edge. Don't let it get to you, man, don't let it get to you."

I stuck my KA-BAR into the wall and kneeled before the headless soldier. I started digging through his pockets, pulling out anything I could find. Old watch, cell phone… WALLET! I opened it looking for something

I hoped wasn't there.

I found it.

I was still breathing hard, and it was still hard to breathe.

"What's up, man?" Doc inquired.

I handed him what I found.

"Fuuuuuuuuck…" Doc's eyes grew wide.

"What are you two barking about?" Fowler demanded.

Doc showed him what was in his hands. Two photographs. One was the exact same photo Kennedy had in her room of her family, the other was of Kennedy and me at Laguna Beach.

"I just slaughtered my girlfriend's father." My hands fell to my sides. "I just cut off my girlfriend's father's fucking head."

Fowler was visibly shocked. Other Marines gathered around and looked at the photos and the man's severed head.

Fowler called the lieutenant, "Sir, you might want to take a look at this."

"Yeah, hold on a minute." The SirBot told the trucks to cease fire and radioed company that the building was clear. "Okay what's up?"

Fowler handed the SirBot the photos. "Allensworth just killed his girlfriend's old man."

The SirBot squinted with confusion. "What the fuck?" He examined the pictures. "What in the *actual* fuck?" He looked over his hands at me. "Kodak, what the fuck is this fucking shit?"

"She said her dad was always gone."

"Huh?" the SirBot barked.

"My girlfriend… Kennedy. She has those same pictures on her wall in her room back in Oceanside." I ripped my Kevlar off, gripped my hair, and stared at the floor, my mind blank.

The SirBot kneeled down beside me. "Listen Marine…" he looked down at the soldier's headless corpse. "How the fuck did you end up dating an enemy officer's daughter?"

"I don't know, Sir."

"Okay. I'm going to send you to the chaplain and you and he can sort this out."

"No, Sir!" I looked up at him. "I don't want to leave the fight!"

"You sure?"

"Well fuck, Sir, if that happens I'm going to lose my fucking mind."

"Are you positive you'll be able to keep your head in the game?"

"Yes, Sir."

"Okay, well either way, when we're done with Al Kut I need you to take this to the intel section."

"I can do that, Sir."

"Okay good." The SirBot stood up and ordered everyone back to the trucks. He pulled Fowler aside. "Keep an eye on Kodak."

I stood there with Kennedy's father's head in my hands.

Fowler brought me my helmet and knife. "We gotta go, dude."

"FUCK!" I threw the head out the window full force, snatched my gear, and followed the platoon back outside.

When we got back to the truck I pulled the Kevlar plates out of my flak jacket. The front one was shattered and wouldn't take another bullet so I put it in the back and put the back one in the front. I had a reasonably higher chance of getting shot in the chest than from behind.

"What'd you do now, Fonz?" I heard Kyle ask.

I looked up to see Doc putting a bandage around Fonzie's head.

"I got clipped in the ear," Fonzie mumbled. "No big deal."

"With that on top of what you've got going on up on your forehead you're going to be one ugly motherfucker," Kyle taunted.

Fonzie chuckled, "Yeah, but I'll still be going ass to mouth on your sister."

"And your sunglasses will still fit. You'll be alright, Fonz." Doc finished his mending. "Did anyone else get hit?"

"A couple guys in the other section got scraped. I don't know if they're getting medevac'd or if it's not that bad." Kyle checked his magazines.

"One of 'em got a bullet in the leg and the other shrapnel in the face," Fowler chimed in. "Hopefully he was wearing eye protection. I really don't want to hear First Sergeant bitch about that."

"That and keeping his eyes," Doc said.

"Yeah, that too." Fowler kept his eyes on the street. "You know, these Iranian dudes are tough, but they're not as hard as Tommy Taliban. And the damn Taliban was harder than the fucking Mahdi Army."

"That's because the Taliban was living in mud huts and caves and were fucking roughing it." I took a long swig from my canteen. "These fucks are posh in comparison. They've got food, water, equipment, and uniforms; the whole nine yards."

"I got nine yards for 'em," Fonzie said pulling out a belt of fifty caliber ammo. "Hey McBland, trade places with me." McBland climbed down and the Fonz settled into the turret.

"How y'all doin?" McBland said through a mouth of chewing tobacco.

"Oh you know," Kyle started. "Livin the fucking dream."

"I'd hate to see your nightmares."

CAAT 1 pulled through the city blocks providing heavy machinegun fire for the line companies. Us dismounts walked behind the vehicles and provided security for the Marines clearing the buildings.

The Iranians weren't in every building, but they were crawling the streets. Every time a Russian-looking firearm would protrude through a wall or a muzzle flash through a window Fonzie would blow holes in the building until it crumbled. The Fonz produced about fifteen swear words per round, and the Ma Deuce fired about five hundred rounds a minute. I'll let you do the math.

One night in Al Kut, during a lull in the fighting we taunted him about that. "Fonze, you're from Mexico, right?"

"El Salvador, you fucking racist." Fonzie laughed.

"Yeah but that's like the same place, right?" I lit a cigarette.

The Fonze smiled and gave me the finger.

"But you *are* catholic?" Doc asked.

"Yeah, so?"

"Well what about all the killing and swearing you do?" Doc inquired.

"What about it?"

"That's not very Christ-like." Doc French inhaled his smoke.

"That argument's bullshit, man. Christians think that the point of getting to heaven is to be moral, and it's not. It's to be close to God. And they don't translate it right. In the original context of Paul's letters, he swore all the damn time. And you know what Jesus would do? Be covered in blood and shoot a fiery sword out of his mouth and kill everyone in fucking sight or hearing. And think about this, remember when God led the

Hebrews out of Egypt and into the promised land and told them to kill all the Canaanites and kill their stock and burn their farms to the ground and offer no quarter or they would forever be a thorn in the Hebrew side?"

"Yeah."

"Well, Arabs are the descendants of those people the Israelis didn't kill. Killing them is God's work and if the fucking Jews would have done what God told them to do we wouldn't be here right now!" The Fonz reached into his cargo pocket. "That's why I have this."

I don't know what I was expecting Fonzie to pull out, a cross, a star of David, maybe a necklace of severed Persian ears, but it wasn't any of that.

The Fonze held up a plastic bag full of penises. Mine and Doc's smiles dropped to a mouth breather's facial expression.

"Saul told David that if he wanted to marry his daughter he had to bring back a bunch of Philistine foreskins."

"How many of tho…" I shook my head. "Wait, if this is about foreskins why do you have the whole schlongs?"

"Better question," Doc interrupted. "When have you been getting the time to do this?"

"Just whenever I can," the Fonze shrugged.

"And Saul isn't your CO and you're not banging his daughter. Are you going to propose with these?" Doc smiled.

"I don't know." Fonzie tossed the bag to Doc.

Doc caught it and in the same movement dropped it to the ground. The bag spilled its contents into the street. "Gross, dude!"

"Awe, you spilled my stash!"

"You'll be alright." I nudged the lifeless flaccid penises with my boot. "Dude, when you grabbed these things you weren't thinking about giving up eating MREs were you?"

"Fuck you."

Doc reached down and grabbed one of them. "This dude was hung like a fucking horse!" He started swinging it around the air like a sword. Doc raised the dick over his shoulder, brandishing it like a knight from the middle ages. "I challenge you to a duel!"

"Get that thing the fuck away from me!" I jumped back.

Doc swung the meat sword, hitting it on our truck and the walls of the building we were parked beside. "BEHOLD!" he declared in a terrible English accent. "I Sir Arthur have pulled the cock from the stone! Kneel before me as I am the predestined king of all of the Britains!"

While Doc continued his theatrics, I said to Fonzie, "So, David and you got a bunch of cocks to prove your worth in marriage."

"Well that's not why *I'm* doing it."

"Instead of going to Jarrod's are you just going to fashion jewelry out of dicks?"

"Don't go there, man."

"One might even say you proposed with a cock ring!"

The Fonz laughed. "You're fucked up, man."

"You're the one with a bag of cocks, dick skinner!"

"Yeah, well..." The Fonz pointed his thumb at Doc who was still slaying imaginary dragons. "At least I'm not playing with the things. He'll probably be sucking on it in a few minutes."

"Hey man," Doc smiled. "Anything's a dildo if you're brave enough!"

"Doc, quit acting like a fucking queer!" Sergeant Fowler appeared out of nowhere. He stood beside Fonzie and me, staring at the pile of dicks on the ground. "What the fuck is this horse shit?"

"War trophies." Fonzie didn't miss a beat.

Fowler gave the Fonz a look of confusion and disgust then shook his head. "You fuckers have problems."

"Hey, so Sergeant, do we know anything new?" asked the Fonz.

"Well, we know why we haven't been seeing any civilians running around. First Marines found a bunch of mass graves on the north east side of the city."

Doc stopped playing with his dick. Fonzie and I were silent.

"Looks like the Iranians didn't even bother shooting them. They just threw them in, buried them, and shot anyone who tried to climb out."

"That's fucked up." I tried to think of what Combat Camera Marines were in that unit. He would have to document that. "I'm really happy that wasn't us that found that."

"Me too," Fowler said. "Who's got a smoke?"

I offered him my pack. "Do you know what our situation is?"

Fowler lit the cigarette. "First and Third battalions pushed across the river and are pushing in Hajji's shit. We're supposed to hang out here and not let them get through. The Army PsyOps guys dropped a bunch of leaflets on them last night telling them if they surrender they'll get food and water and all that good shit, so if they come with a white flag don't shoot them."

"You do realize the irony of that statement with a Jolly Roger flying on your truck, right?"

"I don't call the shots, man. If I did I would have burned this place to the ground in 2006 and there wouldn't be anything here for Iran to invade besides sand and brass." Fowler looked at Doc. "How long have you had that thing?"

Doc still had the severed penis in his hand. "This?" He tossed it to Fowler.

Fowler leaned out of the cock's path. "The fuck, dude?" He gave Doc a dirty look. "Anyway, the crunchies are all dug into buildings waiting for the other regiments to push Hajji to us. We're doing support by fire."

"So pretty much chill out and wait for a call to go kick ass?" I asked.

"More or less."

"Well something better happen soon," I said with a smirk. "I don't think the Fonz has killed anyone in about two days. I don't want him getting that itch."

The Fonz shrugged. "Meh."

The next few days were relatively quiet. There were a few firefights, but none of them lasted for more than a few minutes.

Doc and I were on watch. It was about two in the morning and we were on the roof of a building near our trucks. I looked into the city. The power wasn't out in Al Kut, but half of everything had been destroyed. The Marines have a pretty solid policy on leveling things that aren't easy to access. There was one bridge that I could see. The lights shined a golden reflection off the Tigris.

I stood there thinking about how many ways Iraq was nothing like Afghanistan. For instance, the battalion that relieved us on my second deployment got chewed up pretty bad. When they showed up they didn't listen to us when we tried to tell them the wars were different. They said, 'We're good, we just got back from Iraq, we know what we're doing.' They paid for it. But that battalion went looking for the fight, those magnificent bastards. I digress, like Afghanistan, Iraq was actually a very beautiful place. I didn't get to know any Iraqis, but the Afghans were the most polite and hospitable people on the planet, when they weren't trying to kill you.

"Hey Doc…"

"What's up, man?"

"Remember that chick in Lashkar Gah?" I asked.

"The one with the tits?"

"Yeah. That was cool." I smiled.

Doc laughed and said, "Yeah, I thought it was awesome that she kept coming back for Pop-Tarts."

I replied, "And she was old enough to be smoking hot but not too old that she had to wear that burka shit."

"Yeah. You know, man, I miss Afghanistan."

"Yeah?"

"Yeah, man. I mean I'm glad I'm here instead of sitting around with my thumb up my ass Stateside, but I actually miss Afghanistan."

"What do you mean?"

"The landscape was prettier, the food was good when we got it, and the people there actually seemed to appreciate what we were doing for them."

"Yeah, man. The people piss me off. Not the Afghans, but the liberals back home always talking about how all we did was 'kill women and children.' I'm all like, 'Listen cock sucker! We were helping those people! What the fuck have you done with your life? Oh cool, you let your parents pay for your college and banged a bunch of sluts and drank a bunch beer and partied and got a minuscule job pushing a pen around and sucking your boss's cock and now you live a boring ass monotonous life and you've never actually done anything that matters and you never fucking lived!' Fucking pussy ass no lifting mother fuckers," I bitched.

Doc chuckled, "Why don't you tell me how you really feel?"

"No seriously, man. There's nothing to do in America. Being a warrior is the only thing that sets us apart. Most people live day to day doing the same things and the weeks blur together because nothing ever changes and they think they're better because they think they're standing on some moral high ground by refusing to fight. Well guess what mother fuckers, that's what human history is about. That's the only thing that's never changed. War is the way of man. And if we ever go to outer space and find aliens we'll probably fight them too. I just hate the fucking liberal pussy ass mindset that peace and love can solve everything. That hippy shit pisses me off. And the conservatives are just as bad."

"Oh yeah? Enlighten me."

"Well most of them talk like they're all high and mighty but the most hardcore thing they've ever done was go deer hunting. I don't hate them as much because they're not spitting their shit on the news. As far as I'm concerned, as long as they show up to fight they have my respect. Fuck, I respect the Taliban more than I respect most of our politicians. At least the Muj gets that if you want something you have to fight for it and not just send some other poor-ass cock sucker to do it for you."

"You think of it like that?" Doc asked.

"Not like that, like that. I mean, I'm not here because some asshole in Washington sent me, I didn't join the Marine Corps because I hated Iraqis or Afghans, I joined because there was a war going on, there was something to get got and I wanted to get some. I'm not a fucking bitch like the rest of this fucking generation is. I know I'm probably not going to make it far in life but I won't ever have to wonder if what I did in life mattered. I'm trying to avoid people asking me why I didn't do something. Like when I was in high school I had an anatomy teacher who gave us his little history of Mister Hoops' story and he said he was born in forty-eight. I asked him if he went to Vietnam and he said 'No.' I was about to call him out on being a fucking bitch but he said, 'I saw Vietnam on TV and went to join the army but they made me a medic and stationed me in Germany.' I can't hate on him for that, at least he fucking tried. That's what I'm doing, I'm fucking trying. I know we're all going to die someday anyway, but I'll be happy knowing I fucking did my part."

Doc looked over the desert. "I hear ya, man. You get it. It's just the way things are and no one in the States appreciates anything anymore. I mean, think of the kids you went to high school with. I remember one kid whose family was poor as shit and he wore the same thing to school every day because that's all he had. Then you had these rich kids who never wore the same thing twice and the emo kids. What the *fuck* did they have to be upset about? Oh my God your mom didn't buy you the new Phone. Fuck you, you fucking pussy. If you're going to appreciate life you have to struggle with it. Enlist in the military, not the fucking air force, but the military, and don't be an officer. Go eat dirt, live in filth, embrace the suck, and when you're done you're set for life. It's not like you're never going to have financial or personal issues after that, but you're for goddamned sure never going to take cold water or a fucking bed for granted again."

"I'm going to have to disagree with that," I said.

"Why?"

"Because there's only two branches in the military."

Doc raised an eyebrow. "How so?"

"The military is the Army and the Navy. The Air Force is a corporation and the Marine Corps is a fucking cult."

Doc laughed. "Okay I get that. But I'm fighting to fight, and to fight with my brothers. If I die, that's okay. Those faggots that say, 'I'm not joining because I don't want to go and die for ideas I don't believe in' are pussy ass do nothing faggot slots of wasted air space. Sure, admin and supply guys are fucking POGs…"

"I'm a POG," I interrupted.

"Yeah but you're a cool POG, you're out here."

"Okay."

"But admin and supply, they're doing their part, they're not holding up signs saying 'no blood for oil' or some other bullshit like that. What pisses me off is that the wars didn't even really affect anyone in the States, there hasn't been a fucking draft, what the fuck do those loudmouth pieces of shit have to lose, and what the fuck are they complaining about? If it doesn't affect you shut up and let the warriors war for whatever reason we want. It's an all-volunteer force and we joined to go fight the enemy. If we're bad people for it, then all I have to say is 'come at me, bro!'"

"I hear you, man. I just wish there was a better stance for us to argue from than pretending it's a crusade against Islam."

"Huh?"

"Think about it, Islam is the reason everything's fucked up, right?"

"Yeah?"

"Wrong! Indonesia has the largest Muslim population on the planet and they're not being a bunch of cunts, they're fighting terrorism. Know who's next?"

"Iran?"

"India has the second largest Muslim population and they're fucking up the Pakistanis. It's not a problem with Islam. And it's not even really a problem with Arabs. I know plenty of them that are great human beings, them and Pashtuns and Persians, and dammit if they don't kick some ass and their women aren't beautiful. The problem is when you combine the two. The problem with the world is Arab Muslims."

"Eh, that's debatable," Doc said.

"How?"

"Well think about it. Back in the day the Middle East was the center of the world as far as math, science, literature, medicine, and everything. Europe was in the dark ages and eating shit and fucking their sisters and Arabia was up high. Then they pissed off Genghis Kahn and he literally fucked this place so hard that they still haven't actually recovered. Did you know that Baghdad isn't the old Baghdad? When the Mongols destroyed it the locals rebuilt it across the river."

"I did not know that," I admitted.

"Yeah, so I don't know if it's really the Muslim's or Arab's problem, but they'd probably be more advanced than we are now if they didn't fuck with the Kahn."

"Either way… there's something rotten in the state of Denmark."

"What?" Doc asked confused.

"Never mind."

"Have you written to Kennedy yet?"

"No. I don't know what to say, man."

"I don't either, but you have to say something," Doc told me.

"Like what? 'Dear Kennedy, I finally met your family. I cut your dad open like he was a fucking thanksgiving turkey.'"

"I don't know if you have to go that far."

"Well, the fuck then?"

"I don't know. I've gotten a few letters from Reagan, she's all pissed off that I haven't been writing her. But it's like 'I'm sorry, I'm kind of fighting a fucking war.'"

"Yeah." The sting of tears grew behind my eyes. "I don't know what to do, man. I don't know if I could live with myself if I didn't tell her, but if I do there's no way she'd stay."

"She might, man."

I looked Doc in the eye and said, "Don't bullshit me, man."

"Yeah, you're fucked either way."

My eyes started to water.

Doc put his hand on my shoulder. "Hey man, it's not the worst thing that's ever happened to you. It's not like we were going to marry those strippers."

I forced a smile, but I could tell my eyes were bleeding.

I did what I normally do when life's just a little too much to handle, lit a Lucky's.

"I know shit sucks, man, but you have to tell her. If you don't you're going to live with it bottled up forever. Or worse, you'll marry her and cave in and tell her when you're fifty and just have to face it then and she'll leave with the kids and your bank account and you'll be alone with nothing but me and your jeep."

Doc was right. When we got off post the next morning I sat down, and because I couldn't find any paper wrote on a piece of cardboard:

Yasmina,

I'm sorry that I haven't written to you. I know you're worried and the news on TV can't be helping the situation. I'm alive, I haven't been seriously wounded, and for the most part I'm in alright spirit. I miss you, I miss you dearly. You're the only thing I think about and I dream of the time when again you're in my arms, I'm looking into your deep-sea eyes, and holding your long, beautiful black hair.

I don't know how to say this, I can't think of any way that I really can. Whatever I'm about to write, when I'm done, whatever you decide to do I'll understand, however much it may tear me apart, just remember that I am SO afraid of losing you.

We're in a city named Al Kut. We were clearing buildings during an assault and I killed an Iranian Officer. When we kill people we have to go through their pockets to see if there's anything that has intelligence value. This officer had a picture in his wallet of you and me and the same picture of you and your father that you have in your bedroom. His identification named him Amir Al Aziz Muhammad Kassandrazaden.

If this is what I think it is, for whatever it's worth I am sorry.

Hank Thomas Allensworth

9 BEANS, BULLETS, BANDAIDS, AND BAD GUYS

In the distance we could see the Marines of the other battalions pushing through the city. The Persians were in a pinch and starting to get desperate. There was no more 'No Man's Land' in Al Kut. We had a block of the city and Hajji had the buildings across the street.

Our trucks were peppered and dinged from enemy rounds. The ballistic glass windows were spider webbed and our tires were shot out. It slowed us down a little, but it didn't stop us. MRAPS could take a beating.

The battalion commander had issued the order to start pushing through.

We took heavy fire from a café across the street. Fonzie turned it into Swiss cheese. Our truck assaulted through the intersection. A burst of rounds raked the front of our vehicle and finally shattered the windshield. Fowler took a bullet in his arm. Our driver wasn't that lucky.

Our truck slowed to a halt. Fowler was grunting a form of curses. He turned back to us and said, "Pull him back!"

McBland and Kyle grabbed the driver and pulled him to the back of the truck. His face had been hollowed out.

"Goddamn it," Doc squeaked.

Fowler, covered in his own blood, maneuvered himself into the driver's seat. He hit the gas and turned the truck around.

Fonzie turned the turret to face back towards the enemy and kept delivering hate. "A T AND T MOTHER FUCKERS! REACH OUT AND TOUCH SOMEONE!"

Fowler put the truck in reverse and shot us full speed into the café. The Fonz ducked into the truck so he wouldn't get smashed. He saw the dead Marine laying on the floor. Fonzie's eyes turned to hate. He saw red. He hopped back into the turret and fired again. He screamed hateful words, but I don't speak Spanish so I couldn't tell you what he said.

"Let's go!" Fowler barked.

We jumped out of the truck to finish a few soldiers off, but everyone was either crushed by the MRAP or torn to shreds by Fonzie's fifty.

"McBland, driver's seat." Fowler looked at the rest of us. "You three, stairs. Let's go!"

Doc cut him off, "You should really let me take a look at that arm, man."

"Not now! Let's go!"

We filed up a stairway in the corner. Our rifles pointed in all directions. Bullets drilled holes into the wall above our heads. We shifted our muzzles and emptied our magazines into the Iranians on the deck.

With the hallway clear, we lined up close to the wall beside a door. Fowler lifted his leg and broke open the hatch. Kyle went in first, silhouettes appeared in his view and fired but missed. Kyle and I dodged out of the way and fired back. There were two of them hiding behind a desk they turned into a makeshift bunker. They should have kept firing instead of letting off a few rounds and ducking. Kyle and I unloaded into the desk. A hand rose over the pseudo bunker wielding a little metal ball that he let roll towards us.

"GRENADE!"

Kyle hurled himself on me forcing both of us to crash through the flimsy plaster wall.

BOOM!

Kyle rolled off of me. "You all right, dude?"

Before I could answer I looked up to see three stunned Persian soldiers. They raised their weapons at us. I rolled away, holes from their AK rounds followed me. Kyle lunged at one of them shoving his knife between the soldier's legs. Kyle swung around behind the soldier who was howling in pain and put him in a headlock. Kyle grabbed the soldier's weapon and fired it at the other two.

One of them fell dead and the other jumped to the ground and landed beside me. He looked me in the eye and I broke his nose with my helmet. I straddled him and started beating his face with my fist. He held his arm over his face trying to stop my assault and pulled out a knife and drove it into my leg. My body seized and he shoved me off. But before he could get up, Kyle ran over and stomped in his skull.

"DAMMIT!" blood started to pool around me.

The Iranians below the desk started shooting at us through the wall.

Kyle hit the deck and crawled to me. "Hold on, Kodak!"

I gnashed my teeth and wailed. I forced myself to stop gripping my leg. Shuddering violently I pulled the tourniquet off of my flak and tried to wrap it around my thigh.

Kyle flung my hands away and tightened it. I let out a scream and the blood stopped. Then he pulled off the dead Iranian's scarf and tied it around my leg to help soak up the blood.

"You're going to be alright, dude."

"You're a little close to my dick there," I moaned and shivered. "You could have got me dinner first."

175

"Ha," Kyle said unenthusiastically. Bullets still flung over our heads. "Sergeant!" Kyle screamed into the other room.

"Yeah? You guys alright?" Fowler called back.

"Kodak's hit! You got any frags left?"

"Just a Willy Pete!"

"Light 'em up!"

"Don't tell me what to do!" I heard Fowler bark through the wall. "Keep your heads down!"

"Roger!"

Fowler lobbed in the grenade, it popped, the two Iranian soldiers screamed. They tried to claw the fire off of their skin and fell, rolling in anguish.

Kyle helped me to my feet. "We're coming out!"

"Roger!" Fowler yelled back.

Kyle pulled my arm over his shoulder and helped me limp through the room. I stared at the Iranian soldiers who were still screaming to survive. The phosphorous turned their skin black.

Doc put bullets in their skulls.

We went downstairs and they laid me on the ground in front of the truck.

"You alright, Kodak?" Fonzie yelled down from the turret.

"Day in the park, man!" I gritted through the pain. Sweat and tears stung my eyes.

"Alright, this is going to fucking hurt." Doc ripped open my pants around where the knife was. "Guys, hold down his shoulders." Doc grabbed the Iranian dagger and yanked it out of my leg.

I tried to flail but Kyle, Fowler, and McBland kept me in place. Doc opened a pack of Quick Clot and poured it into the hole in my leg.

"MOTHER FUCKER THAT BURNS!"

"You're going to be okay, man." Doc wiped his hands on his trousers. "Alright Sergeant, you're next." Fowler turned so his wound was facing Doc. Doc ripped open Fowler's sleeve and inspected the wound. "Oh this ain't bad, you just got grazed." Doc wrapped gauze and elastic bandage around Fowler's arm.

I picked up the scarf and the Iranian dagger that had been lodged in my leg. It looked like an old Russian weapon. I hadn't seen any other Iranians with knives. Maybe I just failed to notice them. I slid the knife into the pocket in my flak jacket.

We loaded back in our battered and bruised MRAP. Doc wrapped a poncho over the dead Marine in the back. Fowler stuck his barrel out of what was left of the front window and McBland backed us out of the café. The truck rocked and stumbled because we were driving on the rims. Our tires were shreds.

The hobbled truck crawled to the command vehicle where the SirBot was standing on the roof behind his turret gunner calling in air support. When he saw us the SirBot climbed down. Fowler stepped out to greet him.

"Good afternoon, Sir."

"Oh yeah, it's fucking great. You look like shit," the SirBot spat. "Y'all alright?"

"Uh, no sir," Fowler said as he scratched his face. "We have a routine casualty."

"Fuck! Who?"

"My driver."

"Goddamn it. I'm sorry, Sergeant."

"Yeah…" Fowler paused then added, "Me and Kodak are hit. I'm not too bad, but he might need a ride out. We emptied out the café on the corner; I think we got about fifteen of 'em."

"Alright," the SirBot said sternly. He walked to the back of our truck and opened the hatch. He uncovered the Marine under the poncho. The SirBot didn't flinch when he saw the crimson cave where a young man's face used to be. "What's up, Kodak? You alright?"

"I got stabbed in the leg, Sir." I displayed the dagger. "But I think I'll be alright." I forced myself to say through the pain.

"You fucking sure? I don't need anyone slowing us down; if you think you can still fight you can stay, but if not I'll put you on a bird and get you down to Kuwait."

"I'm fine, Sir," I lied through the hellish anguish in my thigh.

The SirBot looked at Doc. "You look him over?"

"Yes, Sir."

"Alright, it's your call. Is Kodak going to be alright to keep going?"

"Are any of us?"

The SirBot stared at Doc, then nodded and said, "Semper Fi mother fuckers." He patted the Marine in the poncho. "Put him in my truck and I'll get him on a bird."

Al Kut was cleared within a few days. I spent most of it in the back of the truck handing up boxes of ammo to Fonzie. We took a few more casualties.

Once the city was cleared a logistics train resupplied us with MREs, water, ammo, mail, and hot chow. The cooks had set up shop in a blown-out building on a corner. The second floor was mostly intact. Only a couple of beams held up the ceiling. "I don't remember the last time I had hot chow," I said to Doc as we walked to the make-shift chow hall.

"Najaf," Doc said. "We haven't bathed since then either."

"Shit, I don't think anyone has taken off their uniforms since then," Fowler chimed in.

I don't think I had realized that. "We probably fucking stink, too." I laughed limping. "It's good to have our flaks off for a bit." We all were covered in dry blood, sweat stains, dirt, piss, and God knows what else.

"How's your leg, man?" Doc asked.

"I think I'll be skipping leg day for a while."

As we got to the chow hall, First Sergeant Kegal, from Echo Company, stopped us. "Aye Marines, where you think yer goin?"

"Get some chow, First Sergeant," Fowler responded.

"Look'n like that?" First Sergeant asked.

"Huh?" I raised an eyebrow.

"Ya heard me, Marine. When's da last time y'all shave?"

"uh…"

"Yer uniforms are torn up and ya ain't shaved in days. Y'all go clean up 'n get yerselves haircuts before y'all can eat."

"FUCK YOU!" Doc exploded. "You fucking pog ass piece of shit mother fucker!"

"Whatchew say? Marine?"

"I'm a fucking corpsman you bitch!" Doc tried to swing at him but Fonzie and Fowler held him back. "I'LL FUCKING KILL YOU! You fucking pussy bitch fuck with your clean uniform you haven't done anything in! How the fuck have you kept that thing so nice? You just hide and cry while your Marine's did all the fucking work?" Doc kept thrashing trying to get to the first sergeant.

"Sailor, you've got some fuck'n nerve…"

"What the fuck is going on?" Our battalion master gunnery

sergeant walked out from the building.

"Master Gunz, these Marines were about ta come in for chow look'n like a bag a ass. I told 'em to go clean up and this corpsman starts yell'n."

"Why the fuck were you turn'n them away?"

First Sergeant Kegel looked shocked. "Master Gunz, they ain't uphold'n the uniform standard."

"Standard? *Standard?*" The master gunnery sergeant looked us then the first sergeant over. "These Marines are the standard! It looks like they've been out kicking ass and you look like you're getting ready for prom. That corpsman's right. Why the fuck is your uniform so clean?"

"Uh… Master Gu…"

"Shut the fuck up!" The master gunnery sergeant pointed inside the building. "Y'all marines go get some chow."

We scurried into the building. I looked back to see the first sergeant standing at parade rest with the master gunnery sergeant barking at him like a rabid hyena. "I fucking love Master Guns Wentz. I don't care if he looks like he's six hundred years old."

"Yeah, real motivator," Fowler said. "Hey, isn't that first sergeant a weather balloon operator?"

"Yeah, that or an air traffic controller," said the Fonz. "Either way, they shouldn't have put him in a grunt battalion."

We got our field rations and sat down around a pile of bricks, there were no chairs.

My leg ached from not moving it for so long. "I'm okay with the cat poop sausage."

"I'm kinda glad they had breakfast and lunch food," Doc said while stirring his macaroni. "I mean, this shit's terrible, but after a couple weeks of MREs it's not bad."

"We're all going to shit our brains out in about fifteen minutes," Fowler said and laughed.

"I could use some real food," Kyle said. "But this works for now."

"Hey," Fonzie said. "You guys remember that time in Bala Baluk when we were ripping out with Three Eight?"

"When we got the interpreter to get us real food from out in the village?" Fowler said.

"Yeah!" Fonzie laughed. "And we'd been kicking ass and taking names for the last month and we were all lined up for chow…"

"And then we started getting mortared!" Fowler said with his mouth full. "And all the Three Eight guys started freaking out because they'd only been in country for a week and we all just moped to the trucks?"

"Yeah, man!" The Fonz waved his fork around. "Damn that foot bread was good!"

"Oh my God, yes!" I said. "I don't even care that they made it with their feet after walking around in goat shit in sandals all day. Fucking delicious!"

"Those were the good ol' days, man." Fonzie chewed on the processed military chemicals labeled as *food*. "No rules of engagement, no FET teams, and no bullshit."

"Fuck, those female engagement teams were fucking worthless," Doc spat. "When they showed up halfway through the '09 deployment…" Doc pretended to vomit, "BLEQ!"

"Stupid fucks showed up to the FOB and just started fucking everybody. They served no purpose, caused needless drama, and they all thought they were Billy-Badass because they went into places where there was no enemy," Kyle said. "I'm not saying all female Marines are worthless, but the ones on the FET teams are."

"Motor T and engineer chicks are pretty legit," I said. "Remember that blonde seven-ton driver?"

"You mean that girl that was always bench-pressing truck tires?" asked Fowler.

"Yeah, fuck'n Amazon!" I scratched my chin. "That chick was beast mode, I wouldn't fuck with her. Fuck it, if she can carry me out then she can come with."

Fowler raised an eyebrow to me and said, "So what you're saying is, as long as they lift they can ride?"

"Yup. And even then only the lesbians, because they don't cause drama and get everyone's head fucked up."

"And those female engagement sluts don't lift." Fonzie pointed his fork at us and smiled. "Hey, remember when Lohan tried to bang Amazon…"

"And she told him that she'd rather sew her twat shut!" Doc said, making everyone laugh.

"So, have these malaria pills been giving anyone else nightmares?" Fowler asked.

"Dude!" Kyle motioned his hands to simulate his brain exploding. "I used to have a bad dream every once in a while about Afghan, but these pills are fucking me up, and it's weird shit. The other night I had a dream I was in a trench in World War One, but World War One was on the Moon and the Germans were these little red devil-looking guys. But they didn't have guns they just threw pitchforks at everyone's ass."

"Yeah, that is pretty weird," Fowler said. "I've been dreaming about being in a hookah lounge with Vlad the Impaler and he keeps ripping people's hearts out and drinking their blood through a straw. Then he looks at me and says, 'Wake up.'"

"Huh." I rubbed the area around my leg where my knife wound was healing. "I keep having weird ass dreams about my ex."

"Kennedy?" Doc asked. "How do you know she's your ex

already?"

"No not her, man. This one chick I dated for a while up until right before my first deployment, Satin. I don't know why, but I just keep having weird ass dreams about her."

"Like what?"

"I had one where I was snow skiing through the hallway in her house and she was worried her parents were going to catch us then her dad, who was Bigfoot, chased me out with a collapsible chair. Then there was another one where we were in her basement and the floor turned to sand and started to swallow us. They haven't been particularly nightmarish, they just have an eerie feel to them. One of them though was really bad. We were in a mansion and the bottom floor was the beach and demons were stalking us. I was pulling her up the stairs, which were upside down, to a room in the middle of the ceiling, like the room hung from the ceiling. When we finally got through the maze and to the door, giant bats swarmed us. "

"You ever talk to her about that?"

"Fuck no! That bitch fucking hates my guts!" I laughed.

"Yeah but for good reason, right?" asked Fowler.

"Totally." I lit a cigarette. "So I heard the 82nd Airborne's been kicking some ass up in Karbala."

"That's kind of a no shit statement," Fonzie said. "Does anyone know what Fifth Marines is doing?"

"Probably telling the Iranians how cool they are because they went to France in 1918 instead of fighting in Latin America like Seventh did," Fowler replied. "Then choking Hajji out with their fourragères.

We finished eating and headed back to the trucks. We passed Éclair on the way. We just nodded at each other. He looked fucking beat, then again we all did. I was glad he wasn't hurt.

Since we had some down time we took showers and changed our

uniforms. They weren't real showers. Some Marines used baby wipes. I poked a hole in a water bottle and squirted it over myself. Nothing would replace a nice hot shower, but when it feels like the sun's eight feet away from you and the last time you cleaned yourself was almost a month ago, bottled water works. I scraped off as much of the caked sand that was on my skin as I could with my nails. There wasn't much hope for the dirt hiding between the hairs on my scalp, but I tried. I rolled up my dirty, blood soaked uniform and stuck it in the bottom of my main pack. It felt good to be in soft clothes again. They weren't stiff from blood and sweat, or torn to tatters. I took the scarf from the Iranian and tried to wash the blood out of it. When it dried I wrapped it around my neck. It may have originally been red, but it had faded to an obscure shade of orange.

Fowler's blouse was almost completely red. He borrowed a pair of surgical scissors from Doc and cut it to ribbons. He took down the Jolly Roger that had been flying from the truck and sewed the ribbons onto the flag to spell, "Cock-Strong Warrior Man-Gods 2/7 WPNS" then hoisted the colors back up.

We spent the next week in Al Kut eating hot chow, smoking cigarettes, and fixing our vehicles. We had almost pushed the Persians out of Iraq. The battalions were holding still and getting refit for the push into Iran.

Our battalion held a memorial service for the Marines we had lost thus far. It was held in a church—what denomination it belonged to, I didn't know. I was actually kind of shocked to see one at all. I knew there were Christians in the Middle East, but I hadn't ever seen one, Iraq or Afghanistan. The inside looked like it may have been Catholic, but none of the crosses had Jesus on them. Then again, the whole place was ransacked and crescent moons were spray painted over everything, probably courtesy of the Iranian Army. There was a battle cross in front of the altar with a decent amount of dog tags hanging from the M16.

Chaplain Taylor called us to attention and gave his invocation. He started by telling us that we should, "Fear no evil, for the Lord is with us." I wasn't really worried about evil; I was worried about going home a burn victim.

"Exodus 15:3 tells us 'The Lord is a Warrior...'" the Chaplain continued. I'm not going to lie; I really eat up the tribal warlord, blood, and guts parts of the Bible.

I really liked this chaplain. He was a prior Marine, and back in the day was a real heart breaking, blood spilling son of a bitch, before he found God. His sermons were more like religiously inspired war propaganda than what you'd normally hear in church. Considering his position though was to inspire Marines, I dug it.

"Behold, I give unto you power to tread on serpents and scorpions, and over all the power of the enemy: and nothing shall by any means hurt you..." The Chaplain wrapped up his motivational speech and geared towards the fallen Marines. It was short, but it put me on the verge of tears, not so much from the religious rhetoric, but I fucking hate even hearing about dead Marines. Especially when they were ones I knew.

Chaplain Taylor handed the floor to a visiting three-star general. I think he was one of the generals from the MEF, but I don't remember off the top of my head. This mother fucker though...

He gave this awesome heartfelt speech about the Marines that had fallen. Probably the same speech he'd given at every memorial ceremony he'd ever been to. Calling the fallen Marines his brothers and talking about how much they'd be missed. He spoke about how our brothers fell far from home and about how the values they stood for live still in our hearts. The tears were still held behind my eyes, but they turned from sorrow to hate. With every word that came out of that general's mouth my fists grew tighter. I turned my brain off until the ceremony was over.

I waited until we left the building to go off. I've never been much for morals, but I've never been kosher with swearing in a church. "Who the fuck was he calling 'Brother?'"

"What?" Doc asked.

"He didn't know these Marines' fucking names until about fifteen minutes ago. He hasn't been down here with us eating dirt. And thanks for the sentiment, you fucking faggot ass piece of shit, but who are you going to miss, your goddamned coffee boy!?"

185

"Hey, calm down, man, it's alright…"

"NO! It's *not* alright! That fucker doesn't know Lance Corporal Schmucatelli from his fucking asshole and he wants to talk about this fucking brotherhood he had with him!? Fuck him! I hate that shit! He wasn't here on the ground living this shit! It might as well just be a fucking movie to him! I didn't see him jump in any fox holes with anyone, he didn't go on patrol! He sure as hell ain't fucking General Mattis! If Mattis said that shit I'd be okay with it! Because he'd be down here slaying people with us, not hiding up at the fucking MEF!"

"I know, man, but…"

"But fucking nothing! Almost all of these goddamn fucking officers are like that! Fucking planning the fucking war but not being in the fight! Then they're going to go back home and be fucking okay with soaking up all the credit for the shit *we* did!" I bit my bottom lip to keep from crying and mumbled, "Fucking piece of shit cock sucker, he ain't pullin any triggers."

10 INTO THE LAND OF THE ARYANS

We spent the rest of our time in Al Kut smoking and playing spades.

The First Marine Division rode over the border into Iran; any heavy ground resistance we would have encountered was taken out by the Navy. More lines of dead Iranians and their equipment were left in lifeless pools of blood in the desert.

Our battalion's objective was a city called Dezful. The city's buildings ominously silhouetted the setting sun. The sky was hazy. F18s, Harriers, and Cobras had been blasting the city since before dawn. Through the fires and smoke I could make out what looked like medieval castles rising up from the horizon.

"Hank?"

"Yeah Doc?"

"You remember that castle in Lashkar Gah?"

"The one the Afghans said Alexander the Great built?"

"Yeah," Doc said and laughed nervously. "Remember how the ANA would take Taliban and have donkeys fuck 'em?"

"I don't think that's what's going to happen here, dude." I faked a smile.

Fowler yelled back from the commander's seat, "Yeah, it was just this much more satisfying than just shooting the fucks."

When we were about a mile away, the city erupted with fire from every window in every building. Our tires slipped in the sand. McBland, who was now driving, swore. Jets rained fire on the city, completely leveling the first few blocks.

When we reached the walls of rubble everyone besides the drivers and the turret gunners dismounted and took cover behind the debris. The crumbled buildings were a cursed blessing. Machinegun fire kept our heads down. The concrete chunks of the buildings blocked the roads, but their size provided cover enough to move around.

The SirBot surveyed our area. "Alright Marines, the trucks are going to climb forward over the rubble, we're going to crawl behind them." The vehicle commanders relayed the orders back to the trucks and slugged in behind them.

The trucks snaked over the concrete with the grace of a methed-up epileptic tortoise, bouncing and shaking, moving only inches at a time. It would probably be fun if we were doing that in the Rockies and if we weren't getting shot to all hell. Bullets pinged off of the vehicles and chipped away at the concrete surrounding us. All the trucks' guns fired at the cyclic rate.

We followed the trucks on our bellies using the rubble for cover; we didn't want to give Hajji an open target. Fox Company was spread between the vehicles, their Marines bounded taking turns firing.

The moment we hit the street, the Marines swarmed into the first line of buildings. CAAT 1 stayed with the trucks and posted up at nearby intersections where we could provide supporting fire. We had a squad from Fox held up with us. Éclair was among them.

The fire had turned sporadic in our section, but by no means silent. Jefferson's truck was next to ours behind the intersection. An RPG screamed down the street and Jefferson's truck exploded.

Éclair pointed to a building down the avenue and screamed, "HE'S OVER…" Before he could finish the sentence the building exploded. One of our trucks had fired a TOW missile leveling it.

Doc sprinted towards the burning vehicle. Fowler, Fonzie, Kyle, four Fox Marines, and I followed him. Fire spat from the windows. A Fox Marine ripped open the back door. Two Marines jumped out and rolled on the ground. They were burning and screaming in agony. One Marine pulled out the truck's fire extinguisher, but it had been punctured, rendering it useless. Another Marine had a poncho liner in his pack and tried to smother the flaming Marines.

Fowler and Kyle went for the front passenger, but he had been killed on impact. He looked like raw hamburger meat stuffed inside a flak jacket. I threw up.

I helped Doc pull the driver's door open. The driver was moaning in his seat. Dear Lord he looked terrible. He tried to worm out of the seat but his skin and uniform had melted to the chair. Doc and I tried to yank him, but he howled and didn't budge.

The ammunition in the truck started popping off due to the spreading flames. Doc muttered, "Fuck," and pulled out his KA-BAR.

"What are you doing, man?" I demanded nervously.

"It's the only way, dude." Doc started cutting the Marine's back skin off to release him from the chair. Fire crept up the seat. Blood pooled down Doc's arms and the driver whimpered. Tears started flowing down Doc's face as he sliced through the meat on the Marine's back. "It's okay, man, we're going to get you out of here."

I pointed my rifle down the road so I didn't have to look. I couldn't bear to watch. I was breathing too hard, I had an abhorrent feeling in my chest, and a queasy feeling in my gut. I could feel myself quiver. My eyes were so open I thought my eyelashes were going to scratch my brain. I could hear the knife cutting, Doc was slicing through a well-done steak. I couldn't imagine what Doc felt, much less the charbroiled Marine in the driver's seat.

"Hank, help me with him."

I turned back to Doc.

"Grab his legs!" Doc barked. He grabbed the Marine by the shoulders and we rushed him behind cover. The Marine's seared black skin was bubbling. Blood spewed from his entire backside. "SOMEBODY GET ME A FUCKING PONCHO LINER!"

One of the Fox Marines laid the poncho on the ground, and we positioned the driver face down. Doc ripped open his medical bag and spilled the contents next to the Marine. Doc's hands shook, and sweat beaded on his face.

Fowler had shown up next to us. Doc threw an IV at him and said, "Put this on him!" Doc slathered as much ointment as he could on the Marine and started wrapping him with bandages. When he was done, Doc packed his bag. "Alright, who else is hurt?" He panted a half sob.

"Our corpsman is taking care of the others," said a Marine from Fox Company.

Doc looked behind him to the other corpsman. "Yo!"

The other corpsman looked up at Doc and gave him a thumbs up. "They'll be alright if we can get them on a bird in the next half hour."

Doc stared at the driver on the ground.

Fowler put a hand on Doc's shoulder and said, "Come on, man, you don't need to be looking at this."

"Yeah." Doc bit his bottom lip, turned around and pulled out a cigarette.

Dezful took us longer to push through than the cities of Iraq. The Iranians fought bitterly and made us bleed for every block we took. By the fifth day we had lost almost all of our trucks. We lost ours to a mortar round. Doc hit his head pretty hard in the blast, but besides that we managed to save our weapons and ammo.

191

Our team was perched on top of a three-story brick building that overlooked the mouth of a small river that ran into a valley. Downstream trees grew out of the water. On either side of the river there were rows of buildings that blended in with the sand. A series of small waterfalls fed the bowl-shaped basin where the river started. I don't think it was the best position we could have ever been in, but it worked. Other teams were perched on the adjoining buildings.

The Fonz had set up the fifty caliber overlooking the river. It was a pain in the ass to haul all the ammunition up the narrow stairwells of the building.

"We've been up here for two fucking days," Kyle muttered.

"Two days too long." Fonzie kept his eyes on his field of fire.

"Why haven't we pushed any further? Why did we stop here?" Kyle asked.

"I don't know, but I'm about out of smokes." I dug one of my last packs of Lucky's out of my Alice pack. "I'm surprised they've lasted this fucking long."

"Especially with all the Morning Prayer they've been playing," said Doc.

"Don't even get me started on that." I lit my cigarette. "Iran sucks. I know it was shitty that they killed or displaced everyone in east Iraq, but shit, at least we didn't have to deal with civilians running around. It was like…" I raised my hands pretending I was holding my rifle. "There's a guy. BAM!" I lowered my hands. "Now I have to make sure the fucker has a weapon before I can wax 'em."

"Yeah," Fowler said. "Rules of engagements are for pussies. We should have a standing policy that if we invade you because you pissed off America for whatever reason we kill and destroy everything and don't fucking rebuild it. Old Testament style."

"Yup," Kyle said. "Sergeant, why the fuck was Iran trying to invade Iraq right after we fucking left the place?"

192

Before Fowler could answer Fonzie said, "I don't give a good Goddamn why they did it, I'm happy to send them all to hell." Fonzie pretended to knock on a door. "Knock knock mother fuckers, seventy-two virgins dating service."

"Yeah that's about how I feel." Fowler looked over the parapet. "And we're probably sitting around because the fucking POGs can't keep us supplied with water and ammo fast enough to keep us moving."

"Hey man, I'm a POG," I said half-sarcastically.

"Yeah, but you're a cool POG," Fowler said back. "I mean, you're a fag, but you're a cool fag, like Freddie Mercury."

We all chuckled a little.

"But seriously," Fowler continued, "two days is too fucking long to just sit here. I haven't seen Hajji since last night, and that fucker's up to something. Probably getting snipers and artillery ready."

The SirBot called for the team leaders over the radio. Fowler left the roof. We sat there for about an hour staring into the valley. The sun felt like it was only ten feet away, all of our bodies were slick with sweat. When Fowler returned he told us that we were moving out shortly after dusk. There was an airbase on the other side of the valley where the Iranian Army was holding out. Apparently the reason we had been holding the same location for so long was because we were waiting for the rest of the regiment to circle the enemy. We could knock out whatever unit was here and not have to deal with them again down the line. Fowler stood watch and made the rest of us sleep until it was time to get on the move. It didn't matter that it was a hundred fourteen degrees, we were all so exhausted that we passed right out.

I awoke in a dream. I was still on the roof, but I was alone. The desert sands were deep shades of blue and black, and the sky was red. I looked into the valley before the building. Marines scrambled along the riverbeds, but they had no flesh. They were only bones, uniforms, and weapons. I climbed down the face of the building to catch up with the Marines, but they were gone by the time I got to the water. I ran along the river until I arrived at a ziggurat. The walls of the giant step pyramid started to melt. I heard my name called from behind. I turned to see a woman walking out of the water. Her body was covered in long black robes. She held her hands in front of her face; they were wrapped with prayer beads. The woman pulled the black drapes from her head. It was Satin! Hell was in her eyes and she stank like sulfur. She stopped when the water was at her thighs. She pointed behind me. Slowly I turned back to the ziggurat. The melting walls combusted and spat molten rock. I drew my sword. An explosion rocked the top of the pyramid and a scaly, clawed arm punched through. A mighty dragon slithered through the hole in the hellish structure. It laid its eyes on me; they were but black spheres of hate.

I jolted back awake. My heart was trying to box its way out of my chest. I sat there panting.

Fowler gave me a disturbed look and said, "You okay, Kodak?"

"Malaria pills…" I rubbed my eyes with my palms.

"Gross."

"Tell me about it." I lit a cigarette. "When are we taking off?"

"About an hour. Wake up the other guys for me."

I woke up the Marines on the roof and scarfed down half of an MRE. Fonzie broke down the fifty caliber and threw the weapon over his shoulders. Kyle carried the tripod on his back. We headed down out of the building and linked up with the rest of CAAT 1.

Our platoon fell in behind Fox. We patrolled down the streets parallel to the river valley under the crescent moon. I kept thinking about my dream. *What did that mean? Did it mean anything? Was it just a side effect from all the fucking pills they were making us take?* I shook my head trying to get my mind back in the game. This wasn't the time to freak out. My leg was still sore where I had been stabbed and my chest was still tight from when I got shot. I needed all the mental power I could muster if I was going to survive, especially now that we were walking with all of our gear on our backs.

We came up to about fifty yards away from the gates of the airbase. We crept through the alleyways and brush so that the Iranians on the base wouldn't see us. The whole battalion circled around the post. The machine gunners set up their weapons and we waited for the order to push.

The SirBot whispered, "Danger close, keep your heads down."

There was a loud shriek. The roar of F18 engines shook the ground. They jetted over the airbase and left a string of five hundred pound gifts falling to the ground. The blasts were so close the heat rattled our teeth.

The lieutenant screamed, "OPEN FIRE!" The machine gunners sent a few hundred little friends to the buildings on the post.

"Let's go!" The SirBot took off at full speed towards the now-shattered gates of the airbase. We were all close behind him. Machine gun fire opened on us from the buildings and foxholes around the airstrip.

We sprinted to what looked like an old barracks and huddled against the wall for cover. An engineer with Fox Company produced a shotgun and blasted the hinges off the door. A squad rushed into the room. Gunfire briefly came from the room before we heard them call it clear. The Fox Marines started laying down suppressive fire from the building.

"What splendid women's quarters." The SirBot spit a large wad of tobacco into the dirt. "Team leaders! Get all the heavy machineguns we have left on the roof! Keep the 240s with us. Everyone else fix bayonets!"

"Fonzie that's you!" Fowler yelled over the fire.

"Aye, Sergeant." Fonzie and Kyle disappeared into the building.

Our machine guns decreased the intensity of the Iranian fire. The SirBot looked back to the team leaders. "Alright gents, on my command everyone with 203 rounds left hammer the foxholes in line in front of us. Immediately after that we'll charge the platoon. Don't let anything you're in that hole with live!"

The Marines who still had the forty millimeter grenade rounds left readied them. Our machinegun fire intensified. "FIRE!" The volley of grenades launched to the Iranian line with heavy thumps.

I lifted myself off the ground and sprinted with CAAT 1 across no man's land towards the enemy front. My rifle leveled in front of me with bayonet, the modern spear. The surviving Iranian soldiers hurled bullets toward us. We let out our war cries. I jumped over a small berm built in front of a foxhole and came down onto a soldier who tried to point his weapon at me. As I landed, I thrusted my bayonet into his neck and sank into the hole. Putting my boot on his face I pulled out my weapon, then I stabbed him six or eight more times to make sure he was dead. I raised just enough of myself out of the hole to point my rifle back at the enemy. I looked to my flanks to see if the other Marines had taken their positions. They had, so I put my eyes back toward where the enemy should have been.

Cobras and Hueys circled the battleground, intermittently sending down fire. We were only a couple dozen yards from the airstrip. There were burning aircraft on the tarmac, they looked like F14s, but I wasn't sure. I could see the control tower, machine gun nests surrounded it, and the helicopters were taking care of them. One of the Cobras strafed the tower, raining down steel and hate. A rocket led a column of fire towards the helicopter from the tower and slammed into its hull.

The Cobra's metal guts spilled to the ground, killing the Iranian soldiers under it. The bird started to spin and drift away from the tower. It hit the sand hard with its belly, its rotors dug into the dirt between the runway and us. It burned. Iranian bullets chewed holes in the bird. The canopy didn't open.

"MACHINE GUNNERS! SUPRESSING FIRE!" the SirBot ordered. "BRAVO SECTION COME WITH ME!" The SirBot jumped out of his foxhole and sprinted towards the burning Cobra; we hauled ass after him.

We jumped to the prone around the downed helicopter and shot at the enemy. Fowler broke open the canopy with a crow bar and pulled out the pilots. They were bruised up, but nothing terribly serious. Doc looked them over.

Gunfire intensified around us. The hail of bullets was getting too strong. One of the Marines screamed, "We've got to fucking get out of here!"

The SirBot, with his ever-present grimace and mouth full of tobacco, surveyed the area. "There's a trench right before the tarmac. We'll get shot to shit if we try back for the line."

"We running or crawling, Sir?" Fowler asked.

The SirBot grabbed his radio. "Alpha Section, CAAT 1 Actual, focus all fire on the pillboxes, fire on cyclic." The SirBot looked at the pilots and said, "Can you run?"

"I don't think they can, Sir," Doc answered him.

The SirBot grabbed one of the pilots and threw him over his shoulders. "One of you grab the other one." Then, with an injured Marine on his back and his rifle in his hand, the SirBot sprinted towards the Tarmac, firing one-handed along the way.

Doc lifted the other pilot and sprinted after the lieutenant. The rest of us ran a few feet around Doc with our weapons facing outwards firing at anything we saw.

About halfway to the trench I took a bullet to my right thigh and face planted on the ground. "GODDAMMIT!" I grabbed my leg and squirmed. "That was the good leg." I rolled over and tried to start crawling towards the trench. Two other Marines were lying on the ground. Bullets hit the dirt around me. I brought my weapon up and pointed towards the Iranians to our right and squeezed off a few rounds. Another sting of rounds impacted around me, and this time I caught two in my left shoulder. I screamed and slammed my head into the dirt.

I looked back up, my vision was getting blurry from the loss of blood, and I saw Doc dragging one of the other wounded Marines to the trench.

I rolled around and started crawling back towards the helicopter with one good arm and a bum leg. I was about back to the burning Cobra when another round shot through my left side, right below my armpit. I groaned and coughed up blood. I tried to swear but there wasn't enough strength in my chest. I tried crawling again and more rounds grazed my back. It would have been alright if I still had my plate in my flak jacket, but I switched it to the front when it got shattered in Iraq. Instead I had lines of meat carved out of my back. But somehow, by the grace of God, I made it to cover behind the helo.

I looked back and saw Doc carrying the other Marine back to the trench. The SirBot was firing his pistol at the enemy, he must have been out of ammo. A squad of Fox Company Marines was crawling towards me, but they were getting pinned down. Hajji wasn't fucking around anymore.

I tried to open my med kit but it was on my left side, and that arm wasn't cooperating. I leveled my weapon towards the enemy and laid facedown. I wasn't worth much anymore, but if those fuckers showed up I could probably take one or two out with me.

My vision started going dark, and things started to get cold. *I guess dying wouldn't be too bad,* I thought. *At least I won't have to shave anymore.*

Bullets ripped through the helicopter behind me. I tried to growl but it probably sounded more like muffled blubbing. I didn't want to die. I tried looking for something to motivate me to keep fighting for life. I drew blanks. I looked at the dirt under my face and there was a puddle of blood I had spat up. "Goddamned fucking Iranians…" I gnashed my teeth and scowled. I forced myself to crawl to the edge of the burning wreckage. *If I'm biting the dust I'm taking a few more of those fucks with me.* My vision was too bad to see anything more than muzzle flare, so I emptied my magazine at that. I reached for another mag with my bloodied malfunctioning arm. The sand in front of me spat up from impacting rounds, I tried to roll but I wasn't in the best state to do that. A line of bullets raked my left side putting more holes in my left arm, and new ones in my left leg and my guts. I tried to push myself up; I tried to roll; I tried to fucking do anything. All I managed was chattering my teeth, all I could do was bleed and hurt.

I didn't understand why my lips were dry because my mouth was full of blood. The game was over. *Fuck it, I'm out. I guess this is God's way of saying, 'You're fired!'*

Something grabbed the back of my flak jacket and turned me over. I looked up. "Doc…"

"Hold on buddy, I'm getting you out of here." Doc looked like shit. He too was covered in blood. His uniform was ripped to shreds, covered in soot and carbon.

I tried to ask him where the fuck he's been all my life, but we can effectively translate to whimpers and tears.

"I know, man." Doc hoisted me up over his shoulders and started sprinting to the Fox Company Marines behind us. Dirt, blood, and sand flew up from the ground around us. Doc's shoulders ground into my guts from the bounce of the run. I could feel more blood spilling out of my body. *Goddammit, Doc, I was okay with dying there, why'd you have to make me do more work.* I grabbed the pistol Doc had on his belt and fired it behind us. If I had the strength I would have been swearing enough to put the Fonz to shame.

BOOM!

There was a blast, then nothing but silence in the darkness...

11 CADUCEUS AND CADENCES

I stood alone in the darkness. It was hot. I could feel the sand beneath my boots shift. There was a light! Doc stood there with just enough fire coming from his flamethrower to illuminate the area around us.

I started to say something to him, but he motioned me to be quiet. He pointed behind me. Looking into the darkness I saw several sets of eyes watching us from the black. The eyes moved to the light. It was Kennedy and her father! More eyes came, about fifty Iranian soldiers and a few Taliban fighters. The last set of eyes came and they belonged to Satin Sheats.

The ground started to shake and we stumbled in the sand. A hoofed leg protruded from the ground, then another. Before us grew a giant freak of a thing. He looked like a bull, but with the head of a man and a long black beard. He raised one of his hoofed hands to us. It was holding a castle made of one gargantuan diamond.

Doc dropped the flamethrower, but the light stayed. The monster's eyes illuminated the space. Holes opened in the sand; long twisted arms seized everyone around us and dragged them underground. No one screamed, they just glared at us until they vanished below.

Doc grabbed his spear and hurled it at the bullman. I drew my sword. Flares from a mortar team exploded, lighting everything with a yellow hazy glow. A field of severed heads on pikes surrounded us. The monster disappeared and the sand turned to ankle-high water. The pikes transformed to wolfberry bushes…

Then I woke up.

It didn't register to me where I was, and quickly and violently I sat up. I felt rips and tears in my body and laid right back down. I pushed my eyes shut and grabbed the pain in my abdomen. I felt around. *Where's my flak?* I opened my eyes to look. No flak, no dirt, and no stench of burning flesh. The stench was rubbing alcohol. I was in a hospital room. *What are all these tubes?*

I was choking. I had a tube in my mouth. I pulled about a foot of thick plastic out of my throat, then an air tube from my nose. I looked around to see a row of hospital beds stretching in the darkness. *It was nighttime.* I rubbed my face and was surprised to find a decent amount of facial hair. I ran my hands over my body, my arms were terribly weak. I felt for my dick, *oh thank God it's still there. What's this fucking thing?* I pulled a catheter out of my shaft. I tried to sit up, but there was yet another pipe stuck up my ass. I yanked it out with a grunt. I pulled the last piece of plastic out of my arm.

Slowly, I sat up and swung my legs over the mattress. I looked down the row of beds. Everyone was lying straight on their back, I thought that was strange. No one sleeps on their back. *Holy shit, McBland's here.* He was laying still in the bed next to mine. He had weird burn marks on his arms, they almost looked like a chain-link fence. *What happened to him?* Keeping a grip on the bed frame I lowered my feet to the floor; it was cold. I let go of the bed and stood for a moment before the floor was so kind as to introduce itself to my face.

I laid there for a second with stars dancing behind my eyelids. I clawed back at the bed and pulled myself to my knees. Every muscle in my body was weak. I forced myself to my feet, keeping as firm of a grip on the bed as I could. I grabbed the IV stand, and used it to stabilize myself.

I walked to the end of the hall. My legs trembled from the weight and my arms shook from the strain. Who knows how long it's been since they'd moved last.

There was a small office at the end. A light shined through the window. A short blonde woman in scrubs was doing paperwork at the desk. Behind her hung an Army uniform. *Well at least I'm in a military hospital.* I knocked on the window. The woman's head jolted up at me, her eyes were wide. Her mouth gaped open. The woman jumped up and opened the door.

"What are you doing?" she demanded.

"Uh, I don't know, I just woke up."

She pointed down the hall and said, "In here?"

"Yeah…"

The woman took my arm. "Sit here, Sir." She sat me in a chair in her office. "Hold on a minute. I'll be right back!" She sprinted down the hallway.

"Well alright then." I sat in the chair naked, except for a hospital gown. I looked up at the uniform hanging on the wall, it had a captain's insignia on it. She looked a little young to be a captain but what the hell did I know.

After a few minutes she walked back with a Navy commander in a khaki uniform. "Good evening," my frail voice said. "Or morning. What time is it?"

"Who are you?" the commander asked.

I showed him my hospital bracelet. "Corporal Hank Thomas Allensworth. First Marine Division Combat Camera. I'm attached to Second Bat…"

"And you were in this hall?" the commander cut me off.

"Yes, Sir." I asked cautiously, "What's the big deal?"

The blonde captain handed the commander a file. "You're supposed to be brain dead."

"Well, my first sergeant thinks that too, but that doesn't keep me from eating crayons." I thought about what I said. "I mean, not… eating crayons." I scratched my temple and added, "I don't eat crayons."

The commander flipped through the file. "Okay Marine, well we're glad you're awake. We need to do a complete physical and a few other medical procedures."

"Well my arms shrank, can you get me my gains back? I look like I don't lift."

They both looked at me blankly. "Well at least you're in good spirit," the captain said. "We're going to move you down a few floors to another area."

"What's wrong with this place?"

"No one in this hall is ever expected to wake up again."

A sick feeling grew in my gut. "Oh." I took a deep breath and looked out the window. I couldn't see much besides snow. Last I remembered it was July or August. "Did I forget a bunch of shit or have I been out for a few months?"

"We'll explain everything to you in a little bit," the commander said. "But let's get you moved first."

"Well, can I get some pants at least so I don't have to walk around with my dong waving all over the place? I don't want to get court martialed for sexual assault for just bumping into the wrong person in the hallway."

"Yeah, we'll grab you something else to wear."

They led me down another hall to an elevator. I was moved to a different side of the building and shown to a room. They helped me along so I didn't have to stumble with my IV cane.

It was about half the size of a barracks room with white brick walls, a small bed with a green wool US-issue blanket, a metal desk, and a small television. There was an adjoining bathroom with a small shower and a toilet.

They left me alone for a few minutes. The captain came with a thin blue pair of pants and a shirt. "These should hold you off for a while."

"Thanks, Ma'am." I took the clothes. "What's your name again, Ma'am?"

"Captain Frame."

"Killer. When's breakfast around here?"

"At zero six, just down the hall here. I'm on shift right now. I'll come get you when it's time to eat, but if you're really hungry I can grab you something from the vending machine."

"What time it is now?"

"Zero four."

"I can wait, thank you though."

The captain left me alone in the room. I checked myself out in the mirror. I had a decent-sized beard and whatever happened to me didn't screw up my face. My tattoos were all where they were supposed to be but my body was almost completely withered away. I looked like I just got released from Auschwitz.

I found the remote to the TV and put on the new clothes. I turned on the tube looking for the news but there was an action movie on, it had been one of my favorites since I was a kid. It was about a Special Forces team in the jungle being hunted by an alien. I said to hell with the news and sat on the bed watching the movie.

When commercial breaks came, I didn't recognize any of the ads. That was usual, deploy for a while and the ads change, they could have made the ads more comical though. After a car insurance ad went off a man in a suit appeared on the screen. "Hello America, this is your president..."

What?

"We've been through a lot since the turn of the century, and I want you to know you can all count on me to..."

This guy's the president? I thought to myself. *How the fuck long have I been out? I don't even know who the hell that guy is. The election wasn't supposed to be until this year... if it's the winter I think it is anyway. It's at least two years from now. I've been out for at least two years!"* I scrambled to find a calendar with no luck. I grabbed the remote and turned the TV to a news channel to try to find the date. The anchor was talking about the disappearance of some pop singer. "Who the *fuck* cares about that!" I slapped the television. "Calm down, Hank," I said to myself. "Just ask the captain later, it'll be easier than trying to figure things out watching the fucking news."

I sat down and turned back to the channel with the movie, but I didn't pay attention.

Captain Frame came around a little before six and took me to the mess hall. I don't know how the food was. It tasted great to me, but I hadn't eaten anything in God knows how long. I scarfed it all down before the captain was halfway done with her meal.

"We're in Bethesda, right?"

"Yeah, how'd you guess?"

"The commercials on TV weren't AFN so we're not in Germany, and it's snowing so we're not in Balboa."

"Good reasoning. Was there anything good on?"

"Well, I saw the president. I've never even heard of him before. I must have been out for a while."

"Yeah, I guess there's been a lot of changes since you've been out."

"How long has it been?"

Captain Frame reached into a satchel and pulled out the file from earlier that morning. "Are you sure you want to talk about this right after you ate?"

"Yes, Ma'am."

She flipped the file open and set it down next to her plate. "Sixteen months ago…"

"That's it? I thought it had to be at least two or three years because of the president and all."

"No, he just took office."

"Okay, so it's *my* next January?"

"February," the captain continued. "Sixteen months ago you were wounded in combat in Shush, Iran. You were shot twenty-three times, you had over a hundred pieces of shrapnel in you, the bones in your limbs were shattered, almost all of your skin was covered in third-degree burns, and it's estimated you lost two thirds of your blood. You were pronounced dead on the evacuation helicopter. Navy medical personnel were about to load you into a coffin at a morgue in Kuwait when they noticed you were breathing. You were shipped to Germany until your wounds had healed enough to bring you to Maryland. Your body made a pretty fantastic recovery but readouts from tests on our medical equipment estimated that you would be brain dead for the rest of your life."

"Huh." I stared into the captain's eyes with a bewildered look on my face. "Do you know anything about what happened to Doc?"

"Who?"

"Sorry, Wilson Evans, he was my corpsman. The last thing I remember was that we were in a firefight. I kind of got separated and shot up and I was bleeding out. He came back for me and hauled me off. That's the last I remember." Images of Doc's pistol in my hand firing at the enemy found their way to my mind.

"I can look him up for you."

"I would appreciate that, Ma'am." I looked at my reflection in the napkin dispenser's metal side. "I don't have that bad of scars from all this. Why have I healed so well?"

"We don't know. Maybe God love's you, maybe you're a freak."

I chuckled. "So what else did I miss, besides the president?"

"A lot."

"A lot like we beat the Iranian military and now we're bogged down fighting another insurgency?"

"Actually no, more and less than that. It turned out that the Iranian people were tired of the government's crap and are working well to rebuild their nation. All the people who would have resisted us, the theory now is that we killed all of them when they came to fight us in Iraq and Afghanistan."

"Well alright." I leaned back. "So I probably won't be going back then."

"No, probably not." The captain took a sip of her coffee. "But before you go running around or watch too much television there's something you ought to know."

"Okay? What? Are we at war with China or Russia now?"

"No, and I personally don't think that'll be happening anytime soon."

"No?"

"I think this actually happened before you were wounded, but I can understand why you wouldn't know, I know how slow news moves when you're down range. But we made contact with extraterrestrials."

I laughed and said, "You're shitting me."

"I'm not."

I kept my smile. "Well cool. Are we speaking to them via Morse code or the Voyager find them out past Pluto?"

"Their ship showed up in orbit. After a couple of months several countries let in enclaves as refugees."

"Holy shit." I looked skeptically at Captain Frame. "Show me a picture."

The captain pulled out her phone and brought up a news article about the aliens. "Look for yourself." She handed me the phone.

"Whoa!"

"Right?"

"Is this an iPhone five?"

"Huh?"

"This thing is ancient! You can't afford a new one? How fucking bad is the economy?"

She snatched the phone back. "It's not that bad! I just don't see the point of getting a new one when this works just fine!"

I laughed.

"You're not worried about the aliens?"

"Why would I be? If they've been here this long and haven't killed us all yet or made us slaves, I doubt they will."

The captain smiled and said, "I guess that's a good way to look at it."

"Hey, Ma'am, you don't by chance have a cigarette do ya?"

She looked at me sternly. "A cigarette? You're in a hospital and by all accounts you shouldn't be alive, much less have limbs."

"Well I have arms, legs, and lungs."

"You know cigarettes will kill you, right?"

"Well apparently I can survive some tough shit, I think I can manage a cigarette."

"My shift's over and I'm leaving." She stared at me. "What brand do you want?"

"Lucky's would be nice, but if not I'll be okay with a Marb."

"Alright, I'll have something for you before I come in tonight."

Captain Frame went out for the day and I was left at the mercy of the physicians who poked and prodded me. I wasn't injured anymore. The doctors said it was miraculous that I healed as much as I did. I had some aches and pains, but apparently they were from moving too fast after such long inactivity.

During chow I sat with some other patients. They told me how the war was going, or should I say, how the rest of it went. Iran was taken a few weeks after I was knocked out. There had been pockets of insurgency but the people of Iran were fed up with their government and didn't want another similar regime, so they stomped out the insurgency fairly quick. There were a lot of people there that identified as Persians, not Arabs, and didn't like how the government oppressed their culture in the name of Islam. I was happy that Iran wasn't turning into another ten-year war.

When I was done being examined for the day I went back to the room and waited for Captain Frames to return to work. She finally showed up around seven with a pack of Lucky's. I asked her to come smoke with me outside.

Outside, I opened the pack of cigarettes and tinkered with the cheap lighter. "I wish I had my Zippo."

"Yeah, I can't be sure…" The captain started. "But I'd imagine your stuff is in a warehouse with your parent command."

"You're probably right." I inhaled the smoke. I closed my eyes and enjoyed the feeling. "Have you found out anything about my friend?"

"Evans?"

"Yes, Ma'am."

"He's at Balboa Naval Hospital."

"You know how he's doing?"

"Well apparently he's stationed there, he's not a patient."

"Yeah?" I smiled. "Good for him."

"I couldn't find too many details but they gave him a Navy Cross."

"Well... shit." I took another drag. "Fucking deserves it."

"Do you want to talk about it, Corporal?"

"Nope." I wrapped my arms around each other. It was still snowing.

"Have you gotten any sleep yet?"

"I've been asleep the better part of two years, I don't need sleep. I need some warmer clothes, my Jeep, and a bottle of rum."

"You should be able to go back to your command here in a few weeks. Or at least when your medical work comes back and you're cleared."

I looked at the cold concrete below us. "That'll be good."

"Pendleton, right?"

"Yeah, it'll be warm."

We stood there in silence for a minute. I lit another cigarette.

"Have you made any phone calls out yet?"

"I tried to call my girlfriend, but I think she changed her number. It's some Mexican family on the other end now."

I was still looking at the ground, but I could sense the captain frown. "Jody get her?"

I didn't want to tell the full story, not to anyone, especially some soldier I just met. "No. She was Iranian."

"Oh."

"Yeah. Thanks for the smokes, Ma'am."

I stayed in Bethesda until April. They wouldn't let me drink and it was a pain in the ass to get smokes. There were other veterans there, but I didn't want to talk to any of them. I kept to myself. The most interaction I got was when the doctors came to check on me. At night I would stare at the ceiling until I passed out alone with my thoughts.

They chopped my orders and sent me on a plane back to California. I didn't have anything besides a phone and a couple sets of uniforms. I was glad I didn't need to check a bag. I caught a shuttle from San Diego to Pendleton. After I checked in with the Officer of the Day I walked over to our building, 2665, First Marine Division Combat Camera.

When I walked in the door the PFC at the front desk gawked at the ribbons on my chest. "Good afternoon, Corporal. Can I help you with something?"

I walked right past him.

"Are you checking in, Corporal?"

Walking through the door to the back of the building I muttered, "Shut up, boot." No one stopped me on my way to Gunnery Sergeant Cantut's office. I paused before his door in the hall. Gunny was in there chewing someone's ass. After a moment I said, "Fuck it" and walked in.

First Gunny looked at me with anger, wondering who had the gumption to just walk in during an ass chewing, then shock. "Get the fuck out of my office!" he ordered the Marine in the room. As soon as he'd left, Gunny jumped up and squeezed me with his arms. "Allensworth you son of a bitch!" He grabbed my shoulders and shook me. "Where the hell? I thought you were supposed to be in a fucking coma until Christ came back!"

"The doctors got tired of me shitting my pants in my sleep. So they woke me up and kicked me out."

Gunny Cantut laughed. "Fuck me run'n. You just get back?"

"Yeah, like *just* just. I haven't even gotten a barracks room yet."

"So you came *right* back! They let you take leave or anything yet?"

"No. They packed me up and shipped me home. I'll put in a leave request tomorrow. I'm just going to check my shit in today and try to get my Jeep out of storage."

"Alright cool, man." Gunny rubbed his chin. "Write down your phone number for me in case we need you for whatever reason and come back Monday."

I left Gunny Cantut's office and walked to the smoke pit. I lit a cigarette and looked around to see what had changed. Our building was the first in a row of old Korean War-era squad bays. The smoke pit was between our building and the chemical warfare guys'. We had an old picnic table out there. It was battered and worn. The wood was falling apart. The whole thing would lean if you put any amount of pressure on it. It was painted black and had our platoon logo stenciled in with yellow paint in the center. Combat Camera Marines had been carving their names into it for about twenty years.

I finished my cigarette and went to the billeting office. They put me in back in the same barracks, colloquially known as Castle Grayskull. It was five stories of rough-cut cinder blocks on the face of a cliff in the Pendleton Mountains. Whoever designed it didn't have drunken Marines in mind. The Marine at the billeting office said I was going to be in a room with a lance corporal; on paper Marines were supposed to share rooms with someone of the same rank, but that goes out the window when the barracks reaches max capacity.

I walked into my new room, it was fairly empty besides the stock furniture. I unpacked what little I had and changed into a pair of jeans and plain black t-shirt I picked up in transit from Maryland.

I grabbed my cigarettes and started to walk out but the door opened. *Okay let's see who fuck they roomed me with.*

It was Éclair! He looked at me in utter shock.

"Hey man, what's up?"

"Uh, nothing much, just getting off work," he said confused.

"Cool, you wanna drive me to the liquor store and get fucked up?"

"I thought you were dead, man."

"So is that a no?"

"No, I'm down, man. I'm just a little freaked out now."

"Well I'm not a ghost."

"You sure?"

I pulled out my lighter and ignited the flame by Éclair's face.

He swatted my hand away. "Okay, okay." Éclair smiled. "Holy fucking shit, man."

Éclair drove me down to the Pendleton's liquor store. He had bought a '69 Camaro when he got back from Iran. I grabbed a bottle of rum, a two-liter of DP, and a carton of Luck's. They had a Zippo display by the counter so I got a new lighter, too.

We got back to the barracks and started drinking. Éclair got a twenty-four pack. I mixed my rum and DP and we blasted John Lee Hooker on the stereo.

"So you got that Camaro right when you got back?"

"Yeah. I got a pretty good deal on it too."

"When'd you get back?" I walked out to the catwalk to smoke.

"About six months ago. They kept us over there for a while." Éclair followed me.

"Well shit, man. How far did you guys make it?"

"Almost to Afghanistan." Éclair laughed. "That shit was fucked up."

"You're telling me, man. I did two pumps to Afghan without a scratch, unless you count food poisoning, prickly heat, or dog bites, then I go to Iran and get three fucking Purple Hearts."

"I don't know how you survived that, man."

"I don't really remember what happened."

"I saw it. I was in the building with Fox."

I took a long swig from my glass and lit another cigarette. "What happened?"

"You were behind that helicopter, everyone was shooting everything. That other Marine had grabbed four or five other dudes and drug them to a trench before he came to you."

"That was my corpsman, Doc Evans."

"Oh, my bad, dude. Anyway, he grabbed you and started running towards us. We were giving Hajji everything we had, trying to suppress their fire, and then we started taking artillery. One of the shells landed right on top of you guys."

"Fuck... Yeah, I don't remember that much."

"I'm surprised as fuck you're alive at all right now. And you have skin and your limbs. I thought *if* you lived you'd be like that poor fuck from One."

"Yeah, I'm not sure what the hell is going on." I took a deep drag. "The docs at Bethesda thought I was going to be a slug for the rest of my life. They said I was pronounced dead on the bird out."

"That's what they told us, that you guys were waxed."

"Yeah, I need to get ahold of Doc. I heard he was down in Balboa."

"I don't really know him, man."

"It's cool. So what's this bullshit I hear about aliens and shit?"

Éclair chuckled. "That shit?" He shook his head. "I don't know. They just showed up one day apparently, we were still in Iraq when they made first contact. I haven't ever talked to any of them, but they're all over San Diego."

"Really?" I raised an eyebrow. "Well if I could live anywhere in the world I'd probably stay in SoCal too."

"Well not all of them are there. They spread out all over the planet. They have little groups here and there. I think that's just where the government stuck them. But apparently they're mixing in with people and getting jobs and shit."

"So they're actually integrating and being productive members of society?"

"Yeah."

"Good for them."

I drank that night until I passed out. Éclair hit the rack a bit before I did. He had to go to work the next day.

Thank God for alcohol. It got me to sleep that night without having to lie there for three or four hours. I hated being alone with my thoughts at night. I would always find a way to think myself into a downward spiral and end up feeling like shit.

I woke up the next day around ten. I caught a ride up to the supply warehouse and checked out my Jeep and my personal effects. The Jeep was running a little sluggish, to be fair it had been sitting for about two years. I dropped it off at a mechanic out in Oceanside and walked towards the 101 Café. The sun felt good on my skin. It was warm but not blistering hot. There was a slight breeze and the air smelled like the ocean.

I walked into the restaurant, nothing had changed. The red and white walls, the shined metal accents, and the old photos on the walls. I ordered eggs, grits, bacon, and coffee. I never found out what brand it was, but that was the best damn coffee on the planet. Sue, the waitress told me that Rachel had gotten married and moved up north, her new husband did something with railroads. I caught up with Sue while I ate and when I was done I walked down to the beach. I sat in the sand in my jeans and Converse and stared at the ocean until the mechanic called me.

After the Jeep was fixed I drove back to the barracks and unloaded my stuff. I took the doors off and collapsed the soft top. I headed back out. I took Highway 76 east and drove until I hit San Marcos. I fueled up and drove up into the desert. I didn't have anywhere to go or anywhere to be. I just aimlessly drove around the desert until about midnight seeing nothing but what the headlights illuminated. I let the music do the thinking for me. I knew that if I got a hotel I wouldn't be able to sleep. I put *Appetite for Destruction* in my CD player, cranked the volume to eleven, and headed to San Diego.

I got breakfast at some diner outside of the city and rolled into Balboa Naval Hospital around eight.

I walked up to the counter and asked the woman on duty to see Hospitalman Third Class Wilson Evans. The woman asked me to take a seat and after a few minutes someone else grabbed me and led me through a series of hallways. We stopped at a door and the attendant knocked.

Doc opened the door.

"DUDE!"

Doc was surprised to see me. "Dude!" He pulled me into a hug. "How you doing, man?"

"Fucking alive, bro!"

The attendant left back down the hall.

"What the hell, man? I thought you were working here. What's with the patient room?"

"What made you think I was working here?"

"That's what they told me in Bethesda when I tried looking you up. They said you got a Navy Cross and now you're working here."

"Yeah, well I'm technically a patient, but since I'm a corpsman they've been letting me help out." Doc stepped out of the room and closed the door. "Let's go smoke, man."

We walked outside and across the street. You're not allowed to smoke on hospital property.

"So have you been here the whole time?" I asked.

"Yeah, man. You said you were in Bethesda?"

"Yeah. They said they thought I was brain dead and I shocked the shit out them when I woke up."

"Really? Brain dead?"

I laughed. "Yup. I told them my first sergeant would probably agree with them."

"They told me the same thing. When did you wake up?"

"February, why?"

"Me too."

"Weird. Has anyone told you what happened to us?"

"No? No one knows anything except *that* something happened to us. I barely remember it. I got shot to shit pulling those Marines out of fire. Then I remember running back towards the helicopter and finding you, but my vision was blurry and it was dark. I don't even know if I'm remembering that right."

"You remember Éclair?"

"Yeah, ComCam buddy in Fox?"

"Yeah. He saw the whole thing. Apparently we got hit with an artillery round."

Doc stared at me. "Then how the fuck are we alive? And how are we not charred to a crisp and limbless?"

I shrugged.

"Fuck, dude." Doc took a drag from his cigarette. "I guess we should be grateful."

"Odd question."

"What's that?"

"Your tattoos healed right?"

"Yeah, why?"

"Mine too."

"Huh. What do you think's up with that?"

"I don't know, man."

Doc glanced at his watch. "Hey man, I have to get going with some shit here. I should be back in Pendleton in a couple of weeks."

"Score, dude. Hit me the fuck up when you get back."

A month went by. I did very little besides drive around aimlessly, drink myself to sleep, and dick around with Éclair. I showed up to work, but I didn't really do anything. I hadn't stopped accumulating time in service points while I was knocked out and got promoted to sergeant. I abused my recent promotion to skate out of work.

The last Friday of the month the battalion commander decided he wanted to have a formation run with the whole unit. The colonel wanted to start running at zero eight, so the company commanders wanted us at the field around seven, which led to our individual section staff NCOs to have us there at about six. That may sound stupid, but that's about the way it works.

We were all standing around in formation, waiting for something to happen, when I saw Doc walk by. He was in his full uniform, not his PT uniform like us, and was wearing his flak and Kevlar. They must have made him the safety driver for the run. I wondered why the hell he didn't say anything to me when he got back to Pendleton.

One of the other Marines yelled out to him, "Hey, man! Why you get'n in the Humvee instead of run'n?"

Before Doc could answer that obviously stupid question I yelled out, "Because you're fucking fat, Doc!"

Doc looked over at me and raised his palms. "Really, dude?" Then he squinted to see who called him out. "Dude! What's up?"

"Freezing my balls off in green on green! When'd you get in?"

"Last night."

"Figured. Find me later, man!"

"Will do!"

We stood in formation in our green short-shorts until the colonel decided to grace us with his presence. We were called to attention and we ran towards the main side of base in a square made of people screaming our cadences.

Halfway up the first hill Éclair got called out of the formation to call cadence. Éclair started, "MY GIRLFRIEND IS A VEGETABLE!"

The formation repeated it.

She lives in a hospital
She's ain't got no arms or legs
All she's got is hooks and pegs
And I would do anything
To keep her alive
She's got her own TV
And it's called an EKG
One day I played a Joke
I pulled the plug and watched her choke!

The company first sergeant snatched up Éclair and threw him back in formation, telling him that his cadences were too insensitive. First Sergeant Charlie had a hard on for political correctness. That may be fine in the real world, but when your job is killing people, I think we rated a little slack. I think everyone resented having leadership that dodged the last decade and a half of continuous war by being a recruiter or a drill instructor instead of eating sand in the desert.

One of the other Marines jumped out to sing the calls.

Who can take your sister,

Tie her to a chair.
Fuck her with a broom while you cousin pulls her hair...
The SNM man!
Who can take a baby,
Nail it to a board.
Swing the runt around by its umbilical cord...
THE SNM MAN!

First Sergeant Charlie threw the Marine out of formation and screamed at us. "You Marines better start actin in line and quit jack'n around!" He ran us silently for a minute then called out the next motivator.

I jumped out of the formation.

First Sergeant First Sergeant I'm in pain,
First Sergeant First Sergeant I can't train.
I've got sand up in my clit,
Tell Doc to give me a light duty chit!

I switched out with another Marine before First Sergeant could find me to deliver an ass chewing. The cadences were somewhat tame for the next mile or two, mostly that 'C-130 roll'n down the strip...' and 'M-A-R-I-N-E-S...' cookie cutter bullshit. On the way back I found myself next to one of the company clerks, the guys who hang out with the brass all day, doing the bullshit paper work and fetching the officer's coffee. I asked him what the First Sergeant's daughter's name was then got back out to call cadence.

One Two Three and a Quarter!
I've got a date with the first sergeant's daughter.
One Two Three and a Dime,
I told him I'd have her home by nine.
Even though she looks like a child,
That bitch gets up and goes buck wild.
First Sergeant First Sergeant he's a sucker,
Doesn't he know how I'm gonna fuck her?
She's a pretty girl so we're in luck,
'Cause every time I see her she always wants to fuck.
Fuck First Sergeant's daughter Liana gang bang all day,
Who we gonna gang bang if his daughter Liana goes away?
Some girls work at gas stations some work at stores,
Liana works in a house with forty other whores.

LA Girls use KY and San Diego girls use lard,
Liana uses axle grease and fucks us twice as hard.
Some girls like it soft and slow and some hard and fast,
Liana likes it hammered deep inside her ass!

I disappeared back into the formation and another Marine took my spot calling another bland cadence.

First Sergeant Charlie screamed at us and demanded to know who was singing about butt fucking his fourteen-year-old daughter. No one directed the blame in any direction. He didn't put up with any more of our crap and he called cadence for the rest of the run.

When the run was over and the Battalion Commander dismissed everyone, First Sergeant Charlie held our company back and chewed our ass for about half an hour. He gave us the same bullshit rhetoric about professionalism, sexual harassment, being considerate of other's feelings, core values, and all that shit.

When we were finally released I walked with Éclair back to our building to shower.

"What a fucking dumbass," Éclair blurted out.

"I know, man. No deployment bitch ass fuck."

"I mean, it's like 'Hey First Sergeant, didn't you know there was a couple of wars going on?' Fucking fleet dodger. How the fuck did that guy make it to first sergeant anyway?"

"Because the Marine Corps doesn't care about experience or how good you are at your job, they only care about how many pull ups you can do, how fast you can run, and how you look in uniform."

"Dude, he should be fucking ashamed of himself for being that high up with as little as he's done. I no shit have twice as many awards as he does and I'm a fucking lance corporal."

"The Marine Corps doesn't actually respect veterans. I've heard a bunch of fucking morons site promoting boots and fucking POGs over combat vets saying shit like 'combat isn't a measure, it's an opportunity.'

And I'm like, well first off it's not that I can and he can't, it's that I *did* and he *didn't!* And after that the Marine Corps' *only* mission is to win America's battles, so if you haven't even been in a battle then how the fuck can you justify ever doing your job?"

"I hear you, Sergeant…"

"Quit fucking calling me 'Sergeant' when we're not at work."

"Sorry, but I know what you mean. There's all these twats saying, 'I just haven't had the opportunity.' Well, I ain't no infantryman. I'm a fucking camera guy, but I still found a way to go get some."

"Yup. And I'm not saying that you have to see combat to be a *real* Marine, but if I've done something you haven't then as far as I'm concerned you have no right to tell me *shit*."

We reached our building, Éclair went in first. I noticed something strange about his feet. "Éclair, where's you right sock?"

"Oh." Éclair chuckled. "I fell out of the formation to drop a deuce in the bushes. Sacrifices had to be made."

12 MUSTACHE PARTY

I had gotten orders to leave First Marine Division Combat Camera and report over to Camp Pendleton's base unit. The same things would happen work wise, except there'd be no deployments, no fieldwork, just mundane base exercises.

"I don't know what to think of it," I said to the boys. Éclair, Doc, and I were driving down to San Diego's Gas Lamp District for my unofficial going away party. "On one hand, I won't have to go on any deployments, but I didn't join the Marine Corps to sit around on my ass *not* doing anything."

"Plus, you're going to have to work with all those non-deploying faggot ass bitches," Éclair chimed in.

"They really that bad?" Doc asked.

"Think of it this way," I turned in my seat. "We're in the same MOS as the base guys, but we go out and do shit and don't get promoted because we've been deployed and didn't have a chance to run a good PFT or shoot on the range, while these base fucks get to go on boards and keep up on bullshit training that shouldn't matter, but does anyway. They're all sergeants before any of the Division Marines pick up corporal."

"And it's almost all chicks," added Éclair.

"No, they're *all* women." I flicked my cigarette out the window. "But it should be chill."

Doc's Mustang screamed down I-5. Éclair leaned forward so he wouldn't be forgotten in the conversation. "Have you guys been out in SD yet since you've been back?"

"Not really," I replied.

Doc said, "No."

"Dude, there's like a million aliens down here," Éclair stated.

"What? What's that about?" Doc asked.

"I don't know, man. That's just where they went."

"All of them?" I asked.

"Na, they spread out over the planet. Their mother ship or whatever is still floating around in orbit, but little colonies came down and planted themselves all over the place."

"And the government's cool with this?" Doc asked.

"Well, the government's cool with the aliens from Mexico," I muttered.

Éclair adjusted his hat. "I don't know. I saw something on the news about them trading technology for rent or some shit."

"Well what do they look like?" I asked. "I haven't even seen them on TV or anything yet except for pictures. They're just green right?"

"Yeah. They look like us, except they all have green skin," Éclair said.

I raised an eyebrow and said, "You know, I always thought that if there were going to be aliens out there that they'd look so different that they'd have to CGI them into movies instead of just painting a dude green. Are they at least midget-like and short like a Christmas elf?"

"No, they're about the same size as us."

Doc grimaced. "That's lame. You'd think God would be more creative than that."

Éclair laughed. "And what if I don't believe in God?"

Doc rolled his eyes. "Then I'd think that evolution would have diversified the dominant species of planets throughout the universe. And learn to take a joke."

"*I was* joking dude." Éclair patted Doc on the shoulder.

We drove through downtown San Diego. There were about as many green people walking around as there were regular people. They looked just like everyone else minus the skin. Their hair colors were more vibrant, but they were still shades of yellow, red, orange, brown, and black. They all had light color eyes and thick freckles.

"This is weird." Doc pulled into a parking garage down the street from the Padre's stadium.

"They're usually really nice though," Éclair added.

"Even if they *are* dicks, there's no place I'd rather be than California," I said as Doc parked the car. "I know Californians catch a lot of flack about being tools, but I haven't met *that* many of them."

Doc killed the engine and stepped out. "They're probably all up north." When we were all out Doc locked the car. "Hold on a minute guys." He walked to the front of the vehicle and squatted. "Damn it."

"What?" I asked.

"Jessica's pissing antifreeze all over the damn place."

"Will she be alright for the ride back?" Éclair asked.

"Yeah," Doc muttered, "but we're probably going to get too trashed to drive and have to get a hotel tonight anyway."

"True that!" I pulled out a Lucky's.

We walked down to a place called The Kilt. It was kind of like an Irish

Hooters, except the women were attractive and the food was good. We sat at the heavy black wood bar. Doc and I ordered stouts, Éclair got an IPA.

"So have you guys heard of that transvestite prostitute squatting in the old Motor T barracks?" Éclair asked.

"What?" Doc and I asked simultaneously.

"Yeah, apparently he… er uh, she… it? It was living in the barracks laundry room selling meth to some guys. The barracks duty caught him and called PMO."

"How the fuck did she get on base?" Doc asked.

"Yeah, especially all the way up to Margarita, that's like the middle of Pendleton. Did he walk?" I asked.

"I don't know, man. Fuck I don't even know what to call it." Éclair took a sip of his beer.

"Well," Doc said, "I think if they're pre-op and still have their schlong they're 'he' but I don't know."

"What if they've already got tits?" I asked.

The barmaid eyeballed us from the other end of the bar. She wore a skimpy Catholic schoolgirl short skirt uniform. Her cleavage protruded through a conveniently placed hole in her blouse. I pretended not to notice the look she was giving us, and made a mental note.

"Well, what do you call someone who has a sex change and then bangs people from their original gender?" Doc inquired.

"I don't know," Éclair chuckled. "Fucked up in the head?"

"Yeah but what if they're hot?" Doc laughed.

"Like if a chick turned her twat inside out and banged chicks with it? Or just grew her clit out to be eight inches long and made other chicks suck it?" Éclair asked.

"Maybe." Doc took a sip of his beer. "Or like if a dude swapped his schlong for a pussy and then had other dudes pound it."

"A fucking sailor would ask that question." I laughed.

"Fuuuuuuuck you," Doc said and finished his stout.

We joked about the tranny situation for a few minutes until the barmaid came to ask us if we needed more beer.

"I'll take another," Éclair said.

"What about you?" the barmaid asked me.

"Well actually I have a question."

"What's that?" She probably expected a question about what's on the menu.

"If a gay dude's watching porno, is he jacking off to the dude sucking dick or the guy getting his cock sucked?"

Without missing a beat she responded, "I don't know, ask your sailor buddy."

"What the fuck?" Doc laughed.

"I like you!" I handed her a twenty dollar bill. "We're going to say a lot of fucked up shit tonight, but we tip well so keep 'em coming."

The barmaid smiled and shoved the money into her bra. "Stout, right?"

"Yes, ma'am."

We drank and got rowdy at the The Kilt for a few hours before stumbling out to find another venue. We weren't super drunk, but we were beyond tipsy. Éclair was on the phone telling his girlfriend goodnight.

"Hey Doc," I said.

"Yeah, man?"

"You ever talk to Reagan anymore?"

"Not really. She won't answer my calls. She didn't block me on anything on the Internet, but she doesn't respond to my messages. You talk to Kennedy at all?"

"No. She changed her phone number, moved…" I punched myself in the chest and belched. "I don't know what the fuck's up. I mean, I know what the fuck's up with not wanting to talk to me, but I don't know where she went or anything. It's weird."

"What's weird?"

"Well after I put it together that Kennedy and I were through I didn't miss her."

"Yeah?"

"Yeah, I went right back to missing the chick I dated before that."

"Satin?"

"Yup."

"I know what you mean, man. I got a chick kind of like that."

"What's the story with that again?"

"There was this chick," Doc started. "Her name's Alice. I used to date her sister and then I ran around with her for a while. We never got into anything serious but it was love at first sight with her, she never paid me the time of day."

"There's a lot of chicks like that, man."

"Yeah but I think this chick's fucking with me. Like before every deployment I go on she tells me to write her, so I do, and send letters with my fucking return address on them, and she never so much as sends a postcard back."

"That's cold, man. You'd think she'd at least pretend to be your friend."

"Yeah, she'll want to hang out whenever I go home on leave. And If I bring home a girl that's got bigger tits than her, Alice gets all jealous about it. Then I'll look her up on Facebook or whatever and she's always dating some greasy fucking losers. I don't get it. It's like I'm sorry you couldn't fit time into your busy schedule to write me a letter."

"Man, fuck that bitch. If she don't wanna pay you attention our buddies Jameson and Guinness will!"

"That's why I like you, man. You're always looking at the brighter side of things."

"Women don't matter, they come and go… or they cum and you stab their dad in the fucking neck. But alcohol will always be there for you!"

We found our way to another Irish pub called The Field. It was a hike. Doc and I smoked a few cigarettes while Éclair finished his phone call.

"So this one time I banged this Air Force chick." I lit my Lucky. "I was at her place fuckin her on the couch. Her phone rings and she picks it up and says, 'Oh Brandon, what's up?' Then she rolled her eyes and said, 'No, I'm not cheating on you. I'm sorry you had a bad dream.'"

"No way." Doc smiled.

"Swear to God, man. Then when we were done there was a Rubik's Cube under the lamp that was like solved, right. I picked it up and rearranged all the colors. Then this chick grabs it and in like two moves fixes the thing."

Éclair put away his phone.

"How's your girlfriend, dude?" I asked.

"She's good."

"What's her name?" Doc asked.

"Virginia, but people call her Ginny."

"Cool."

We walked into The Field. It looked like inside of a medieval tavern.

Rumor had it that a barn from Ireland was brought over plank by plank. There was a bunch of aliens in the place. They were drinking and having a good time.

We ordered more beer and dinner. The Field had good corned-beef.

The evening went on and we found ourselves entertaining a bachelorette party. They were all wearing fake glue-on mustaches. I think we were invited in because we were the only other people at the bar with facial hair.

The bachelorette was an obese Mexican girl. She was cute and had gigantic tits, but I had a suspicion that if her bra was taken off they'd roll down over her beer gut and slap her shins. She was putting shot glasses between her breasts and people took turns taking the shots until it was just Doc doing it solo.

One of the bachelorette's friends wrangled me up. She was about six inches taller than I was, with long platinum blonde hair and a fake handlebar mustache. She looked like she could have been Hulk Hogan's sexy twin sister.

"So your friend really likes Samantha," the jolly blonde giant said.

"Is *that* her name? I thought it was Fu Manchu with that mustache."

She laughed. "What's your name again?"

"Hank, you?"

"Gloria."

"Well that fits, with the golden hair and all. Glorious."

Gloria smiled and moved her body closer to mine. "That's a nice thing to say."

I wrapped my arm around her waist. "Well I'm a nice kind of guy." I pulled her in so that our hips were touching. Well, her hips and my belly. Her white dress was soft and I liked the way it slid against my jeans.

We swayed back and forth to the rhythm of the music; she put her chin on my shoulder. It was kind of awkward doing the grind dance with a chick that was tall enough to be the big spoon.

I saw Doc and the balloon woman bachelorette disappear into the back of the bar. I kissed Gloria's clavicle.

She whispered, "I might actually like you, Hank," into my ear.

"Oh yea?" I said in my sly voice.

"You're sweet."

"Oh now we can't have that." I smiled.

"No? Are you going to get rough with me?"

"That all depends on how sturdy your dresser is."

"Well I just have to make sure Samantha gets home alive and then we can go see how you stack up."

"Yeah, she disappeared with Doc. They could be anywhere."

"Doc's an interesting name," Gloria said curiously.

"Well that's not his real name, he's a corpsman."

"A what?"

"He's like a medic, but with the Marines."

"Oh." Gloria pulled herself a few inches away. "You're military?"

"Yeah?"

"Are you enlisted or officer?"

"Enlisted."

Gloria broke contact with me. "I'm sorry but I can't be with someone who hasn't been to college. They're just not smart enough for me."

I smirked. "Oh, okay. Well I can't be with someone who's had more than three cocks shoved inside her at the same time, so I guess we're both off the list tonight."

Gloria shot me a look of hate, threw someone else's drink in my face, and stormed off. I turned around to the bar, grabbed a napkin, and wiped the beverage off of my brow. Guessing from the taste it was a White Russian. "That's going to smell good later."

"Woman trouble?" a green-skinned woman beside me inquired.

"Not really." I smiled at her. "Nothing's really trouble if it's taken in stride."

"That's a good way to look at it," she said. "I wouldn't worry about her. She seemed like a twat anyway."

I gave the green woman a smile. "Twat huh? Interesting."

"Why's that?"

"Because no one on this side of the lake uses that word like that. How'd you learn English?"

"When we were in space we picked up your planet's radio signals. A team of engineers was able to translate the signal into something we could understand and teams of linguists were able to translate your language. So most of us learned your language through your visual media. I learned English from James Bond and the Doctor."

"Well, I guess that kind of explains the accent, but you do sound more Scottish than English."

The woman shrugged and took a sip of her drink. "The name's Penelope."

"Hank." I extended my hand for her to shake. "That's a very Earth-like name to have for an ali... What are you people called?"

"Virescent. The name thing is kind of a long story."

"Well, would you mind telling it to me sometime? I have to go find my friends before they get us all arrested."

"I would be more than happy to." She smiled revealing extended canines. She wrote her number on a napkin and handed it to me. "It was nice to meet you, Hank."

"Hopefully it won't be the last." I turned around to look for Éclair and Doc. They were nowhere to be found. I looked back to Penelope and said, "Hey do you mind if I take a picture with you?"

"Okay."

"You're the first person like you I've ever talked to."

"So I'm a novelty?" she said with a smile.

I tried not to stare at the two fangs on the edges of her lips. "Strange and exotic." I opened the camera app on my phone. Penelope leaned into my shoulder and smiled at the camera. "Thanks."

"Good luck with your friends."

I disappeared back into the crowd and found Éclair outside smoking.

"You ain't seen Doc have ya?"

"He might be out back around the corner. How much have you had to drink?"

"Not enough, why?"

"Because you're accent's coming out."

"What accent?"

"You have a really strong southern accent when you drink."

"Yeah okay, dude." I lit a cigarette. "Let's go find Doc."

We walked around the block and down an alley between the bars. We found Doc eating out the bachelorette behind a dumpster. She was standing up with her legs spread. Doc was on his knees with his head shoved up her crotch. Her gut jiggled its way down below Doc's shoulders. One of her nipples was exposed. It resembled something halfway between a pancake and a tube sock with a baseball in it and hung well past her waist.

I was trying to think of something crude to say before we were noticed but Éclair pulled out his phone and started recording the event on video. "This is fucking ridiculous."

"Dude," I whispered over to Éclair. "Let's both hide and record what happens and then I'll edit the video later and we'll give it to Doc for his birthday or some shit."

Éclair nodded with a smile and hid behind some trash. I snuck around and found a spot to peeve from.

We were in for a show. Doc started really getting into it. The bachelorette's belly trembled over Doc's back. She couldn't reach Doc's head through her fat so she put one hand on her gut and the other on the tit that was still secured to garments.

Samantha, the bachelorette, moaned and her whole body shook. I guess you could call it a grunt, but the noise she made sounded like someone stuck a nightstick up a horse's ass.

Doc pushed himself out from under the beast and yelled, "YOU PISSED ALL OVER ME!" He tried to wipe the liquids off of his face.

"I'm sorry," said the bachelorette.

Doc leaned over and vomited on her shoes.

"UGH! These shoes are brand new, asshole!" Samantha slapped Doc on the back of his head.

"Bitch! You *pissed* in my mouth and you're pissed off about your fucking shoes?"

Samantha slapped Doc again. "Don't call me a bitch! I'm a lady!"

Gloria exploded from the back door of the bar and stumbled on top of Samantha and Doc. Gloria looked like she had been crying, mascara was running down her face and her hair was a mess.

I guess that gang bang joke really struck a nerve.

Gloria looked at the wet and dirty couple before her in bewilderment. She grabbed Samantha by the arm. "Come on, we're leaving." The women disappeared back into the bar.

I motioned to Éclair and we walked out to Doc. "Rough night, huh?"

"Fucking bitch!" He wiped his face with his shirt.

"Yeah, well what kind of principles do you want from a chick who's about to get married and fucks strangers in alleyways?"

"Eh." Doc grabbed the dumpster and pulled himself up. "Wanna get another beer?"

"Yeah, but I closed our tab here, and you smell like piss."

Éclair lit a cigarette. "I'm sure there's a dive bar around here somewhere that won't mind if we stink. The drinks'll probably be cheaper too."

We stumbled to some other bar, ordered a few drinks, and blacked out.

I came to again outside. I was howling at the moon. Doc was passed out face down in the pavement.

Éclair was pissing on the wall and singing his own lyrics to an old country song.

I fell on my back laughing. Éclair got me up and we dragged Doc through the city back to the Mustang. I dug the keys out of Doc's pocket and we dumped him in the trunk.

I started the engine and hauled ass up I-5. Éclair started calling people to see if there was a place to party or if we had to crash at the barracks. I blacked back out.

I was cold and my teeth hurt. My throat was dry. I opened my eyes to pavement. I didn't know where I was or how I got there. It was dark, but it was warm like it was the afternoon. I looked around. I was in someone's garage surrounded by beer cans and plastic cups. There was a table with pools of dried, spilled beer. I was wearing women's sunglasses, the top half of a ghillie suit, and someone else's shoes.

I pulled out my phone to call Éclair, he probably had a better idea of what was going on. I had fifty-seven missed calls and it was three in the afternoon. I opened the message app; all the missed calls were from Doc. I pressed 'Call Back.'

Before the first ring was over Doc picked up. "HANK!"

"What's going on, man?" I coughed. My voice was raspy.

"You gotta help me, man!"

"What's going on dude?" I said concerned.

"I'm locked in someone's trunk! I called the police, but they have no idea how to find me. I'm probably in Mexico. The fucking cartels are going to harvest my organs!"

"Doc…" I had a somewhat violent coughing fit. "Chill out, you're in your trunk."

"What?"

"You passed out last night and we didn't want to drive on base shit faced with a passed out guy in the back seat, so we dumped you in the trunk."

"You fucking dick! Come let me the fuck out!"

"I will when I find you. I don't know where I am."

"What do you fucking mean you don't know where you are?"

"I don't know, man. I just woke up. Give me a few minutes." I hung up the phone and called Éclair. He picked up. "Hey dude where are you?"

"I'm in the kitchen eating breakfast."

"Okay." I put the phone in my pocket and walked through the door in the garage. There were a bunch of Marines I recognized passed out on the floor. I walked over them to the kitchen and found Éclair eating cereal.

Éclair looked up at me. "Sup, dude."

Falafeller was in the kitchen. "What's up, dude?"

"Fuck if I know, man." I rubbed my eyes with the heels of my hands. "We at your place?"

"Yeah, you guys showed up around two last night plastered and we played beer pong until about five."

I squinted at Falafeller. "Mmmmm okay. I don't remember any of that."

"Yea, you guys were hammered. I don't know how the fuck you made it on base."

"It's cool. Did I have fun?"

"Oh yeah. Can't you tell? You're wearing the party outfit."

"Yeah." I pulled off the ghillie suit and the glasses. "Thanks for putting up with us."

"Anytime, dude."

"But hey man, Imma get rollin. My buddy's locked in a trunk."

Éclair's eyes were wide open. "Oh shit!" he laughed. "I forgot about Doc!"

"It's whatever, he'll live."

We walked outside to find the Mustang in the middle of the lawn. The grass was already starting to die where the antifreeze spilled out. We helped Doc out of the trunk and I drove us down to the 101 Café for chow. Thank God for twenty-four hour breakfasts.

I had been to that diner so often and gotten the same thing that they didn't even ask me what I wanted to eat, they'd just bring me my usual. I scarfed my food down and when we got back to the barracks I slept until Monday morning.

13 PURPLE CHURCHES AND GREEN WOMEN

Monday morning rolled around. I put on my Alphas and drove to base Combat Camera with my orders. There was a civilian working the front desk, Mrs. Hirkland. She directed me to the photo section.

As I was walking through the hall, a voice stopped me.

"Sergeant."

I turned to see a haggard gunnery sergeant. Her hair was the color of a moldy peach and her teeth were crooked. Her nametapes read, Chanceworth.

"Good morning, Gunnery Sergeant." I thumbed my orders.

"You checkin in, Sergeant?"

"Yes, Gunnery Sergeant." I extended my hand to shake. "I'm Sergeant Allensworth, I'm coming over from Division."

"Yeah, I know." She didn't shake my hand.

I brought my arm back down. *Bitch*. "Are you the Ops chief?"

"Yeah." Chanceworth eyeballed my face. "Are you video?"

"No, I'm photo."

"Alright. Staff Sergeant Bistro's your staff NCOIC."

"Awesome."

"Yeah. Hey, Allensworth? Is that right?"

"Yes, Gunnery Sergeant."

"I'm going to need you to shave that mustache."

Goddammit, not another one of these shitheads. "Yeah, I'm not going to do that, Gunnery Sergeant."

"What?" she spat.

"That's an unlawful order, MCO P1020.34I states…"

"I know what the order says, *Sergeant.* And I'm telling you to chop it off."

I took a deep breath. "If that's the way this is going to be Gunnery Sergeant, then I'm going to need you to help me request mast so you and I can sort this out with the Battalion Commander."

Chanceworth glared at me. "Go fucking check in, Marine." She disappeared back into her office.

Great first impression, bitch.

I introduced myself to Staff Sergeant Bistro. He was chill enough, but I didn't like his vibe. I was made the NCO in charge of the photo section and introduced to my new Marines. I had two corporals, four lance corporals, all female, and one PFC who was currently that rank for the third time. None of them had so much as been on a serious training exercise, much less a deployment—a whole section of fucking hardcore POGs.

I asked my new staff sergeant what I was supposed to do with them and what kind of things we covered. Apparently that unit existed for the sole purpose of promotion photos and covering change of command and retirement ceremonies. I didn't know if I was in luck or if I had been cursed.

I tried to spend time corralling the Marines, but they were tame. They were a strange kind of disgruntled. They were unsatisfied with their base unit careers and since they hadn't ever been anywhere or done anything they didn't get unruly. Because of the political nature of my new environment I couldn't beat the Marines when they did something stupid. Then again, they never did anything stupid enough that I think would warrant corporal punishment.

I spent most of my time smoking or complaining about boredom to my staff sergeant. The day to day at a base unit is Hell for a Marine who's *ever* done anything.

I was lounging around my barracks room after my first week at the base unit drinking rum. I had to keep it hidden when I wasn't drinking it. Although hard liquor was forbidden in Barracks Marine Corps-wide, it was usually overlooked at fleet units. I heard from the Marines around there that the commander would crucify people he caught with booze. I kept my rum in a two-quart canteen.

I was going to link up with Doc later that night and hit the Purple Church. In the meantime, I was still going through some things I hadn't unpacked yet. I had a box that I was half afraid to open, my personal gear recovered from Iran. I held it for a minute and decided against opening it. I had no idea what was in the box, it had a healthy weight, but I didn't want to open any doors that would take me somewhere dark at the beginning of the night.

I went down to the smoke deck and waited for Doc. That barracks was bullshit. Nobody could get away with anything. The old barracks I could smoke on the catwalks, this one I had to walk all the fucking way downstairs and then about a hundred more meters to the authorized smoking area before I could light up.

I was burning the fourth Lucky's when Doc's Mustang screamed into the parking lot. I opened the door and fell in. "Hola."

"How's that base life treating you, bro?" Doc punched the gas and we roared down the street.

"It's fucking stupid."

244

"Already?" Doc laughed. "You've only been there a week."

"Man, everyone there's a fucking boot and they all have this POG ass mentality towards everything. Like the goddamned platoon sergeant is this fucking idiot that's never been anywhere or done anything. Seriously, fucker has five ribbons, no deployments, and no personal awards. The only reason they put him in charge is because he picked up sergeant real fast and has been sitting there. I told the staff that I should be the platoon sergeant but this Kellington fuck has more time in rank than I do, so even though he has *no* experience they're still making him in charge of the Marines."

"That bad, huh?"

"Dude, this fuck walks around pretending to be a drill instructor all day, imitating the voice and calling marching cadence to himself and fucking everything. He's never even been to the fucking drill field, he just never got out of that boot fucking mentality because he's never done anything with his life."

"You'd think the staff would know better than that."

"Dude, it's the garrison side of the Marine Corps, they don't know dick. There are three staff sergeants and a gunnery sergeant and civilians running the place. Two of the staff sergeants think they're hot shit because they were in Okinawa…"

"But no Iraq or Afghan?" Doc cut me off.

"Nope!"

"Those dudes are fucking fags."

"Yeah. And the other staff sergeant went to Iraq one time in 2008, so the war was already over, he was just chilling out, and he thinks he's hot shit. Then the fucking place is run by civilians; I have a fucking civilian writing my fitness report!"

"HA!" Doc laughed. "You're officially a fucking POG!"

I pressed my hands to my forehead and screamed. "Then I got my fucking ass handed to me this morning."

"For what?"

"We were going on a cadence run for PT…"

"Oh God, what'd you say?"

"I stole Éclair's song."

"Which one?"

"Well, keep in mind that the platoon is seventy-five percent female. We were running down Vandergrift and I get out and say:

I can get pregnant like this
All the way to pregnant with just one kiss
And when I get pregnant Gunny's gonna say
How'd you get so pregnant in just one day?
And I replied with a bunch of motivation
Blood and guts and anal penetration!

Doc laughed. "All that in front of females?"

"Yeah, one of those bitches ratted me out to the gunnery sergeant and she threatened to fucking NJP me if I didn't clean up my act. She only let me go because we were in Charlies today and I have three stars on my purple heart."

"Your gunny is a chick?"

"Yeah, six ribbon, heinous excuse for a Marine. It pisses me off because it's like hey, I know you're a female and they won't *let* you go out with the grunts, but fuck you, I have. You don't rate to tell me shit, cunt!"

Doc chuckled and said, "Why don't you tell me how you *really* feel?"

"No, this bitch was chewing my ass about professionalism and shit and I wanted to go off on her. I mean, you can't tell me dick about professionalism when A: I am a professional and I've been doing the shit since I got off the yellow footprints and she hasn't done dick, and B: her fucking name is Condom Chanceworth!"

"You're shitting me!"

"Nope, her fucking name is Condom."

"Well, man," Doc started. "If there's going to be a place where the Marine Corps is all fucked up at least it's not a fleet unit so they can't actually ruin anything important."

"Doc, I agree with you. And they said they were sending me to base to give me a break from the constant rotations, but fuck! This isn't a break, I'd rather be in combat than dealing with these fucking idiots! Life was *so* much simpler when all I had to do was stay alive."

"I hear you bro, you'll be alright."

"Yeah, I just need some tits shoved in my face."

"Hell yeah, man." We finished our cigarettes and walked into the strip club. We ordered stouts and sat at the bar, first row by the stage.

"Shit," Doc said as the first girl walked out on the stage.

"What, dude, she ain't that bad." I sipped my beer.

"No man, I forgot to wear sweatpants."

"Ah."

A woman in a corset paraded about the stage. She whipped her dirty blonde hair in circles as she grinded on the pole. She thumbed her panties and released them with a snap. She touched her fingers to the hands of her reflection on the stage's back mirror.

I nodded in approval and put a dollar down on the bar. The woman dropped her corset leaving her wearing nothing but a G-string, tattoos and stretchmarks.

I took my dollar back.

Doc gave me a look. "Seriously?"

"There's nothing quite like stretch marks on a stripper, dude."

"Okay, man."

I patted Doc on the shoulder.

Another woman wearing fishnets and leather manifested behind us. "Either of you gentlemen want a lap dance?"

"I'm game. See ya, Doc." The fishnet woman led me to the chairs in the back. "So what's your name?"

The stripper smiled at me and said, "Molasses."

"That's an interesting stage name. Isn't Molasses supposed to be brown?"

"Well I'm half."

"You don't look it."

"You haven't seen my ass yet."

I smiled.

Molasses pushed me into the chair and waved her ass in my face. She did her best to entertain me, and she wasn't doing a bad job. She had a beautiful body, but the rules in California were stupid. We weren't allowed to touch the girls, and forget about a tug job. But hell, what the fuck else is there to do on a Friday night in Oceanside?

When the dance was done I slipped her a twenty and told her, "Thanks, Imma go smoke."

"That good huh?" She smiled.

"No, I'm just a nicotine addict."

"Maybe I'll see you out there, smart ass," she said with a smirk.

I sat down outside the front door and lit up a Lucky's. A few minutes passed, Molasses appeared in a robe and sat down beside me. "It's a nice night out."

"That it is," I said back.

"So no big plans for the weekend?" Molasses asked.

"Well, I got a date tomorrow, but nothing really besides that."

"And you're at a strip club the night before? Shame." she joked.

"I just wanted to look at some tits." I smiled.

"That works. Who's your date?"

"This chick I met in San Diego a week or two ago."

"Is she pretty?"

"I don't know, I've only seen her once and I was pretty hammered. I've just been texting her all week." I exhaled. "What's your story, Sugar Cane?"

"Nothing special." She flicked the ash from her cigarette. "My husband's a Motor T guy. I met him in Jacksonville a while back and we got here from Lejeune about a year ago."

"And he's okay with you giving lap dances to strangers for cash?"

"They're not really lap dances."

"No," I said and rolled my eyes. "They're not."

"It's no worse than a nude beach."

"At least here anyway. God knows what you'd have to put up with in another state." I laughed. "These clubs are kind of bull shit here."

"Pays the bills though. And if they're bullshit why are you spending your money on it?"

I looked Molasses dead in the eyes and smirked. "Because I wanted to see some boobs! What's wrong with that?"

"Nothing at all." She smiled and put out her cigarette. "Back to the grind. Have a good one if I don't see you."

"You too."

No one at the Purple Church that worked there a few years ago was still around. None of the girls or staff were familiar. I guess that makes sense though in a place with so many people moving through.

I found Doc and proceeded to get obliterated. When the night was over I stumbled back into my barracks room. I turned on the desk light and pulled out my canteen of rum. I got a glass of ice and sat down with my box of things from Iran.

I cut the brown packing tape away from the cardboard with my pocketknife. I pulled out the contents and piled them on the desk. My old computer was in there, I'd want to take the pictures and my music off of that later. There was a crushed pack of Lucky's. "These are probably stale as shit." The copy of *Fifty Shades Of Dave* that was floating around made its way to my box.

At the bottom of the box was the Iranian dagger and scarf. I guess whoever packed my stuff convinced the customs guys that these weren't war trophies. I rubbed the part of my leg that the knife was once in. It didn't hurt at all. The wound healed without any scar. Hell, I didn't have scars from the bullets or the fire and steel rain. *What the fuck is going on with this?* I felt like shit. The bottom of my eyes got heavy and my breaths short and choppy. I tightly rubbed my hands together in an effort to comfort myself.

I took a big gulp of the rum and a deep breath. I got up and went outside to smoke. I didn't bother walking down to the smoke deck; I lit up on the catwalk. If the duty had something to say then he could kiss my fucking ass. I chain smoked five or six cigarettes and didn't move an inch more than I had to.

When I had enough I went back into my room and grabbed the Iranian scarf and my sewing kit. In one of the corners I marked a rough circle about the size of my fist. Over the next hour I sewed an Eagle Globe and Anchor over the circle, then diagonally under it, "ALLENSWORTH" and "USMC."

Late the next morning I parked my Jeep in front of an apartment building in downtown San Diego. I unplugged my phone from the radio to stop the music and dialed Penelope.

"Hey, are you here?"

"Yes, ma'am, I am."

"Okay, I'll be right down." She hung up the phone.

Penelope agreed to give me the whole day as a date window. I told her to bring a pair of hiking boots and a swimsuit.

The Jeep didn't have doors or a back, just the bikini top. I perched myself up on the roll bar to keep an eye out for her. I was drunk when we met and only had one picture on my phone of her face. I didn't know what she'd be wearing. I didn't have a good idea of what her face looked like. I kept an eye out for green people, but there was a decent amount of them walking the streets.

"Hank?" the Scottish sounding voice came from behind. I turned to look. Penelope was wearing a khaki button-down shirt, sleeves haphazardly rolled. There was a rose garden tattooed over her left arm, all the way down to her hand. She had tricolor camouflage short-shorts and tan boots. She had the same style tattoos covering her left leg as she did her arm. Her bright orange hair was split in the middle and weaved into a braid that ended by her belt.

"Hey." I smiled. "How's it goin?"

"Not too bad." Penelope patted the Jeep. "This your animal?"

I wasn't a hundred percent sure if she didn't know words for automobile or if she was just joking. "That it is." I hopped to the ground. "Ready to rock?"

"I am."

"Well then let me get the door for you," I joked.

Penelope smiled and climbed into the passenger seat. The Jeep had a six-inch lift so I got a good view of Penelope's trunk. I nodded in approval and jumped into the driver's seat. "Any preference on music?"

"I'm partial to jazz but I'm still learning your music. Mind's open."

"Well, all the jazz I have is on a soundtrack for a TV show about cowboys in space."

"Clint Eastwood shot a movie in space?"

"No, the show was a cartoon. And we don't go to space to shoot movies."

"Why not?"

"Our technology's not that good yet. We can't just go to space for whatever reason. We went to the moon a few times but that's about it."

"Oh." She looked almost embarrassed. "I'm still learning."

"Na, it's cool. And Clint Eastwood doesn't play *all* of the cowboys." I chuckled.

"Well they fooled me."

"So what kind of movies do you guys have?"

"Mostly the same things, comedy, drama, and action. We just don't have cowboys, samurai, or the same holidays."

"How about dragon slayers and Vikings?"

"We have the same concepts, but our ancient warriors and beasts are different."

"That makes sense. So cartoon jazz or...?" I looked into the eyes of my reflection in her aviators for the answer.

"Put it on random and we'll see where it takes us."

"I like that idea." I started the engine and backed out of the parking lot.

"So where are we off to today?"

"This place called Cedar Creek Falls. It's a bit of a drive away, then it's a bit of a walk."

"Is that why I brought the boots?"

"Yeah."

"Okay." Penelope looked around the Jeep. The wind flung her braid. She tucked it into the seatbelt. "What are the horns for on your grill?"

"Those? A few years ago me and my buddy Doc were off-roading and we found this buffalo that had been eaten by coyotes. I buried the skull and kept the horns on the Jeep."

"Why's that?"

"I don't know. I thought it'd be fun."

"Huh."

"Yup. So you said that your name was a long story. What's that about?"

"Well, legally my name is Penelope Gina VanIthica. There's no direct translation between the names in our language and yours. We found spellings that we thought were as close as we could get our names to your language and used that. My name's spelled P E N E L O P E, it's pronounced a little different, but I don't mind being called Penelope. A name's a name."

"Well a rose by any other name smells so sweet."

"Did you come up with that yourself?"

"Sure," I lied.

"So what's your full name?"

"Hank Thomas Allensworth."

"Isn't Hank supposed to be short for something?"

"Maybe, but not me."

The Jeep rumbled and shook its way west to Ramona. Penelope held onto the backpack on her lap. I tried to sneak a few peeks of her breasts but her shirt was buttoned just one button too high to get a good look without making it obvious.

I drove the Jeep up a dusty dirt road on the side of a mountain and put it in park. "We gotta walk from here." I unlatched my Alice pack from the back of the Jeep and threw it on my back.

"It is beautiful out here." Penelope slid out of the Jeep. The sun brought out her freckles. "How far is where we're going?"

"A couple miles down into the valley on the other side of the mountain."

"On the other side?"

"It's too steep for a vehicle, and the trail's a narrow dirt path."

"Well then we'd better get to it." Penelope pulled a water bottle out of her pack for a sip.

The downward trail was steep. There was an occasional tree but most of the vegetation was knee-high grass, brown as it is in the California summer. Boulders stood from the sides of the mountain like monuments to old pagan gods.

"I like how many yellow and purple flowers there are here." Penelope swung her arms. "And the amount of sun you can get here is phenomenal."

"Yeah, the sun's never a bad thing. It's good for the skin." I looked at my arms, they weren't as brown as they used to be; I guess I had been spending too much time inside. I compared my skin to Penelope's. Her's was a bold emerald with little olive freckles, on her right anyway. Her left was rose tattoos.

"But not like me." She looked up to the sun.

"How so?"

"Well," Penelope kicked a rock down the trail and continued, "I have to eat real food, but I also *need* sunlight. It helps my body generate energy." She raised her forearm to my face. "These little spots…"

"Your freckles?"

"Yeah, they're not just little bots of pigment, they capture the sun for me."

"Huh. That's pretty cool."

"The sun feels so good. It's the main reason I left the ship."

"What ship?"

"The ship we came here on. There was no real light on it, just imitation, it doesn't do anything for my body, that's why I'm so short."

"Short?" I raised my eyebrow. "You're almost as tall as I am."

"If I got enough light when I was younger I'd be at least six inches taller."

"Okay. Did some people stay on the ship?"

"Yup. They're up there floating around right now. The ship was a home to me, I spent sixty years on it. Well sixty of your years. But being on it made me weak from lack of sunlight."

"Hold on, sixty years? How old are you?"

"Eighty-sevenish. In your time."

"Holy crap." I looked her over, toe to tip. "You could probably pass for eighteen here."

"Longer life span I guess." She shrugged it off as if it meant nothing to her.

"I guess." I took a sip of water. "Wait, so you guys were traveling for sixty years through space? Did y'all find a way to break the speed of light?"

"No." Penelope had an expression on her face that told me the gears were turning in her head. "I don't know how exactly it works, but because of how fast we were going our time slowed down and we were really traveling for however many amount of thousands of years, but to us it felt like it was only sixtyish years."

"I think I know what you're talking about. So why'd you guys leave?"

"I don't really want to talk about that right now."

"Alright." I snatched a stem of purple flowers and handed them to Penelope.

"Awe, for me? Thank you kind sir." She imitated a monarch.

We reached the bottom of the mountain. The trail snaked deeper into the valley under a row of trees about a hundred yards thick along a stream.

"So do you watch a lot of cowboy movies then?" I asked.

"I watch all sorts of films. But yes I have been viewing a lot of westerns recently."

"Anything specific?"

"Not terribly. I watched one called *Tombstone* the other night."

"That's an awesome movie."

"It was."

"How about *Two Mules for Sister Sarah*?"

"I don't think so, what was it about?" Penelope asked.

"Clint Eastwood is helping a Nun get across Mexico during the war with the French. It has a pretty interesting plot twist."

"I haven't seen a great deal of different movies until somewhat recently. On the ship we only could really watch TV as it came from the radio waves out in space. Even then people only started really watching it after we figured out how to translate English."

"So you've seen a lot of TV movies then."

"Yes." Penelope looked up to the trees we were walking under. A thin layer of sweat shined off her skin. "Shade feels nice."

"What happened to needing sunlight?" I joked.

"Just because I need the sun doesn't mean I don't get hot."

"Good to know." *Oh you're hot alright.*

"About me getting hot?" She looked me in the eye smiling.

"Yeah. But don't worry, there's a pool ahead."

The trees spread out as we reached the beginning of the stream we had been following. There was a massive rock formation around a lake that was about two hundred feet across. Up the face of a cliff that led straight up the mountain from the valley was a waterfall.

"Hank, oh my god this is wonderful." Penelope gazed at the awe-inspiring product of nature. "How deep's the water here?"

"It should be at least a few feet, I think."

Without a word Penelope stripped down to a red bikini and left her clothes lying on top of her backpack. She didn't bother folding them. She had the same tattoos on her side as she did her arm and leg. She took off in a sprint towards the water and jumped in feet first.

When she emerged she rubbed the water out of her face and waved. "Are you coming?"

"Yeah, sorry it takes me a minute longer to take off my clothes than that." I laughed. I left my things near hers and dove into the pool. The water was cool. It felt good on a hot day. We paddled in the neck-deep water.

"There's a rope on the tree over there to swing in off of."

"How do you mean?"

"Come on, I'll show ya. It's a little shallower over there by the edges." I led her to the other side of the pond near the base of the waterfall. I reached the other side first, Penelope wasn't as strong a swimmer as I. Without waiting for her I ran up the rocks, past the lonely tree under the waterfall, and quickly turning around as I grabbed the rope and swung over the water.

I let go of the rope and yelled, "CANNON BALL!" I splashed about two feet away from Penelope.

When I came back to the air Penelope called me a jerk and splashed water in my face.

"Come on, get your turn; it's fun."

We spent a few hours clowning around under the waterfall careless of the time. When we had had our fill we grabbed our things and perched up on a boulder over the pond. There was a good view of the waterfall. It was narrow but tall and the rushing stream almost hid behind the rocks it had been cutting into over the millenniums.

I rummaged through my pack. "You like turkey?" I offered her a sandwich.

"I do." When she reached out for the sandwich I finally got a good look at her breasts, they were substantial in size, but not so big to be grotesque, and perky. "I think this is a good idea. We didn't have this."

"No?"

"Well we had bread and meat and the like, but we didn't assemble them like such."

"What kind of food did you guys have?"

"On the ship it was mostly vegetables and bread, but back home we had animals and wine too."

"Wine, huh?"

"Oh yes." She smiled. "You'll have to try it sometime."

"Made from grapes?"

"The plants are close enough."

"Like your roses?"

"Yes actually. They're almost the same plant. And what about the tattoo on your chest?"

On the left of my chest over my heart I had the First Marine Division's emblem. The blue diamond with a big red one in the center surrounded by the stars of the Southern Cross. Inside the one, instead of reading "Guadalcanal" like it should, mine read "Afghanistan."

"It's my division's logo, I just put Afghan in there instead of what it's supposed to say."

"You're a soldier?"

"No, I'm a Marine."

She gave me a confused look. "So you're a sailor?"

"No, it's like in the middle. We get on ships and float around at sea then get off and fight the enemy from the beach."

"Okay, so you *are* a soldier?"

"No." *Bitch quit calling me that. I'm not a soldier, I'm a fucking Marine.*

"I don't see the difference. How aren't you a soldier?"

"Because soldiers are in the Army. Marines are supposed to be more like the Navy's ground forces or like the guys that would capture a ship from another ship."

"Okay." Penelope half-rolled her eyes. "Well anyway your tattoo. Why do you have *those* stars on it?"

"Because during a war a long time ago the division was fighting on a little island in the Pacific Ocean and this constellation was the most prominent one in the sky."

"I haven't seen that constellation yet from here."

"You can only see it from the southern hemisphere."

Penelope put a finger on one of the stars. "I'm from that star. That's one of the reasons a lot of us went to Australia."

"Why didn't you go?"

"I knew more about American culture and it seemed like I'd have an easier time assimilating."

"You didn't see, like anything, about our history did you?"

"Not too much, why?"

"Don't worry about it." *Coming to America with dark skin because you thought it would easy to assimilate. Good luck.* "You like pie?"

"I haven't had it yet."

"Well there's an awesome pie company up in Julian if you'd like to go."

"I'd love to."

"Good, all we have to do first is get back to the Jeep."

14 THE BLACK WINE OF HESPERIDES

"What is your obsession with PBR, Éclair?" I opened the refrigerator in the barracks room Éclair and I used to share.

"It's nice when I have too much month at the end of my money."

I grabbed one and tossed it to Éclair.

"Ginny said she's buying me dinner tonight."

I cracked open my beer. "Yeah? You're just going to party at the barracks with her and eat ramen? That's not fucked up."

"No, I'm going to pick her up in the Camaro and go find something to do. She said she wanted to buy dinner tonight."

"That's cool, I wish chicks would take *me* out on dates, pay for dinner and shit."

"Yeah, but you're dating a fucking alien, I don't know if you're even *allowed* to complain about women anymore."

I laughed. "Yeah, I guess you're right. But I haven't seen her in a few weeks."

"Why not?"

"Work," I said with a shrug.

"Gross. How's that retarded ass base unit treating you anyway?"

"Same stupid shit. I had one fucking lance corporal who was about to get discharged on some program that would have put her through the Naval Academy and the government would pay for it and all that, but she fucking backed out, dumped her boyfriend, and then married another female marine in another section."

"You're shitting me, right?"

"Nope, that all happened in a week. Then we had a health and comfort inspection because the fucking CO thought someone had drugs in the barracks and when they came through my room the fucking sergeant major found a bag I had full of protein powder and he thought it was cocaine. Fucker tasted it and everything and kept saying, 'This narcotics, Devil Dog?' I fucking hate being a POG."

"I hear you, man, I'd rather be in Iraq too."

"It's whatever."

"What's Doc up to tonight?"

"Uh, I think he's on a date with some island beaner."

"What is it with the sailors and Filipinos?"

"I don't know, man. I have a buddy that's been on like six MEUs and he says every port they go to the hookers are little Filipino girls, like even Saudi Arabia and Spain."

"That's probably just human trafficking at that point."

I pulled out my phone, it had been buzzing for a few minutes. "Hey I just got a bunch of text messages from Penelope. She got ahold of some of that Virescent Black Wine."

"Oh yeah?"

"Yeah, she wants to know if you and Ginny want to double date it up?"

"Uh yeah, let me text her."

"Cool, Imma go smoke."

I stepped out to the catwalk and lit up a Lucky's. Before I was halfway done with it Éclair came out. "Ginny said she's in."

"Sweet. When are y'all getting married again?"

"A couple of months. We were trying to figure out if it would be easier to take her whole family to Indiana or my whole family here, then we said fuck it we're going to do it in Vegas."

"That way *everyone* has to travel?"

"Yeah."

We stood there in silence smoking for a minute before Éclair said, "But I don't know, dude."

"About what? The wedding?"

"No, I mean I love Ginny and all…"

"Dude she's stupid hot."

"Yeah, but I don't think I've banged enough chicks to get married."

"Ah, I get that, man. You been out prowlin?"

"I set up a fucking thing on a dating site, but the chicks there are either fucking pricks or fucking losers."

"Why do you care, dude? If you're just gonna fuck 'em and chuck 'em, what does it matter what their personality is like?"

"Because I don't have the game to just show up and fuck, I have to talk to them for like fifteen minutes in person first, then buy them dinner or some shit, and I can't stand talking to them. There's a reason they have to find men online, they're such fucking weirdos that they can't find people in person. Sometimes I just troll the app for laughs. Here let me read you something." Éclair pulled out his phone and opened his dating app. "Ok, check this out." Éclair read, "Teacher, feminist, humanist, and loudmouth.

We are complicit in a white supremacist society and responsible for breaking it. If any of that sounds gross to you, peace! Swipe left for guns and douchbaggery. I'm generally more attached to oddballs, somewhere outside the mainstream, but I'm shallow and will right swipe anyone who is hot."

"So she'll fuck a stranger she met on the Internet but doesn't want to date a real man?"

"Yeah, no shit the skeezer has to meet people online." Éclair put his phone away. "She probably just got tired of the glory hole."

"I know what you mean, man. I tried that online shit, but it turned out that I just fucking hated everyone so much that I didn't even send people messages. It's like, hey I don't want to read your profile and I don't want to get to know you, I just want to punch your cervix with my dick."

"Yeah, where's the site for that?"

"I know right?" I laughed.

We stopped by my barracks so I could grab a nicer shirt. I grabbed a purple button down with vertical black stripes. We took Éclair's Camaro down to Encinitas to pick up Ginny.

She was waiting outside when we pulled into the parking lot. I climbed into the back. Cars from the sixties were made for midgets and there was no reason to make them that small.

Ginny's sunglasses held back her blonde hair like a tiara. "Helloooooo." She plopped into the passenger seat. Éclair and Ginny leaned into each other and pecked lips.

Éclair moved his head around in a circle. "Ginny Ginny Ginny Ginny!"

Don't get me wrong, I love my friends, but sometimes those two could get so cute it made me want to commit Japanese ritual suicide.

"And how are you, Allensworth?" Ginny turned around. She refused to ever call me by my first name.

"I'm doing well, how are you?"

"Not too bad. So your girlfriend scored hallucinogenic alien booze?"

"I don't know about all that. I thought it was just exotic wine from outer space."

"Some of the people I work with were talking about it, they said it's dangerous, in a good way."

"Hey dude," Éclair said back to me. "Where are we going?"

"This place called Spike's, it's a jazz club in SD. I think I know how to get there from the Gas Lamp."

We headed south on Highway 101 over the twists and turns along the shoreline. People waded in the Pacific's surf almost the whole ride from Pendleton to San Diego. Sometimes when I needed to relax, and I was sober enough, I would just drive up and down the 101 for kicks.

We drove around the block Spike's was on. Éclair kept his head on a swivel. "Parking here is ridiculous."

"We might have to just walk." Ginny stuck her head out the window looking for a place to leave the car.

We ended up having to park a few blocks away, but the lot was cheap and we'd be able to keep the car there all night if we needed to.

"I don't think I've met your girlfriend before, have I?" Ginny asked.

"No, I don't think so." I lit a cigarette on the walk. "Have you met any of these green people yet?"

"Yeah, I work with a few of them, they're great chefs. And I like how they all sound Scottish."

"Yeah apparently that's from watching *Doctor Who* and James Bond while they were flying through space."

"Yeah, that's what the guys at work said."

"I wonder," Éclair started. "If these guys found us from our radio waves, what if some other aliens that want to destroy us and take our resources find us that way too and come to kill us all?"

"Well dude, as long as they don't come to America they'll be okay. We have the First Marine Division, and all the communists in Hell couldn't overrun that, so aliens would be cake. That and Texas is a thing."

"I think aliens would be easier to fight than communists."

"How?"

"Well, aliens are from space and commies are from Hell."

"Yeah, and we'd probably be fighting them here, and at least that's better than fucking Iraq."

"Fact." I pointed my finger at Éclair like it was a gun. "And if we were fighting aliens they probably wouldn't be playing Morning Prayer at five the fuck o'clock in the morning every day."

"Dude you would get *so* pissed off about that!" Éclair laughed.

Ginny let out a disgruntled sigh. "You two better not just talk about Iraq all night."

"Don't worry, we won't," I lied.

Éclair threw his arm over Ginny's shoulders and said, "Na, we won't, we got Iran to talk about too."

"UGH!" Ginny rolled her eyes.

We walked into Spike's. There was a small band playing a bebop tune. The pianist, trumpeter, and the bassist were old black men. There was a Virescent playing something that looked like a saxophone, he was in a note for note duel with the trumpeter. When the jazz assault from the horns slowed, a haggard middle-aged white guy with short curly hair sang. His voice sounded like he hadn't ingested anything besides bourbon and cigarettes since 1923. The band all wore loose suits with loose ties.

The club was illuminated by a dim yellow light and smoke filled the air. Persian carpets covered the floor. The furniture was all black leather. The chairs wrapped around the seat like a big letter C and the tables were simple cylinders with red candles. The walls were all covered in ivy. There were pictures and lamps sticking out of the leaves.

Penelope was sitting at the bar talking to the man behind the counter wiping down glasses. She spotted me and waved us over. "Good evening!"

"Hey!" I wrapped my arm over Penelope's shoulder and she put hers around my back. "You've met Éclair before."

"Once or twice." Penelope smiled. "Hello," she greeted Éclair.

"And this is Ginny, Éclair's lady friend," I introduced her.

The girls smiled and shook hands.

"Hank," Penelope said and pointed her thumb to the bartender. "This is my brother Thom; he manages the bar."

"Oh hey." I stuck my hand over the bar. "Nice to meet you, dude."

Thom shook my hand. "As to you." He didn't seem to be too enthused.

I looked around the bar and said, "So this place is pretty hip. How is it cool to smoke in here? California isn't hammering you for this?"

Thom kept cleaning the tumblers. "The Virescent-Paul Act allows Virescent owned and operated establishments to conduct business in manners that will help them thrive in order for us *extraterrestrials* to be productive and not just a draining plight on society."

"Shit. I wish the fucking government treated Americans that good," Éclair commented.

Thom half shrugged.

"So can we order from here?" I asked

"You absolutely may," Thom replied.

Penelope tugged Thom's sleeve. "Would you be so kind as to grab those bottles I ordered?"

"Starting the night off like that huh?" Thom put down his rag. "Give me a few minutes. You all have a seat, I'll bring the wine."

We took a table towards the back. We were close enough to still clearly see the band, and we wouldn't have to worry about people walking all around us if it got too busy.

"I really like your dress," Ginny said to Penelope as we sat down. Penelope wore a shoulderless, jet black dress, a little shorter that knee length. I fantasized about rappelling down her cleavage. I felt a little underdressed in my purple button down and jeans.

"Thanks!" Penelope grinned. "I like your boots. We should get together and shop sometime."

Ginny had her tight khaki slacks tucked into knee-high, brown leather boots.

"Oh hey Éclair, check this out." I pointed to Penelope. "Their home planet is in the Southern Cross."

"What?" Éclair looked puzzled.

"The stars in the Blue Diamond, dude."

"Oh shit, *really?* That's pretty cool."

"So is that like a big thing then?" Penelope asked.

"Just to the Marines in our Division," I told her.

"Yeah, I have the emblem tattooed on my chest." Éclair patted his peck.

"Like Hanks does?" Penelope asked.

"Yeah same thing," Éclair bragged.

Thom reappeared with a black bottle. It had an emerald green label and gold trim. The bottle had glass rivets that circled the circumference. It looked more like a decanter a wizard would have in a fantasy movie than a bottle for wine in an alien jazz club. Thom poured our drinks into stemless wine glasses and placed the bottle in the middle of the table.

"Should I get you menus?"

We all shook our heads and Penelope placed her hand on Thom's arm. "Maybe later, but thank you."

"So what's this called?" Ginny asked taking a sip. "Oh, wow! This is really good!"

Penelope explained, "Hesperides. It's made from a fruit that looks similar to a grape except it's a heavy golden color instead of yellow or red or green. It's also a little bigger and has more seeds and grows on something similar to a rose bush."

"Huh." I took a sip. It was definitely interesting. It was sweet but it wasn't overbearing, and it was dry at the same time.

The four of us chitchatted and laughed drinking the black wine until well after the sun went down. More people started to flood the club. The band took their occasional break then hit the music back in full force.

The drummer beat his sticks taking off on a high beat rhythm, the bassist followed shortly behind him. The trumpeter and the guy with the sax quickly worked their way in with a synchronized tune. There was a quick stop in the music, half a second later when it came back the pianist and the front man started singing about catching mermaids on a warship south of Singapore.

Penelope grabbed my wrist and pulled me up. "Come on, Hank let's dance."

We hoofed it around the table and spun. There wasn't a dance floor. The tables were far enough apart though for people to do their business. Apparently that was the Virescent way of doing things.

Éclair grabbed Ginny and joined us.

Penelope wore me out. I didn't really know how to dance. My legs weren't really good for much besides hauling around heavy shit. Hell, I'd spent most of the last six years humping around the desert. I was surprised I kept up as much as I did. But Penelope was having fun, and that's what mattered. I played the game.

I pretended I was having fun, and to some degree I was. It wasn't that the night wasn't enjoyable. I was still in that post deployment funk where nothing was fun unless I was trashed, the music was too loud, and something was either being destroyed or on fire.

We danced until we were covered in sweat, I guess the heat didn't help.

A couple of waiters brought food to out table, along with another couple of bottles of the black wine.

"I'm not that drunk that I already forgot that we ordered food, am I?" I asked Penelope.

"No?" She looked over her shoulder at the table. "Oh, no. Thom said dinner was on the house tonight under the condition he arranged the meal."

"He's not going to poison me is he?" I joked.

Penelope showed me her vampire fangs through a menacing smile. "No, he's only done that once."

We sat back down. I chugged the rest of my wine, half of the glass of water, then poured myself another glass of the Hesperides.

The meal smelled phenomenal, especially for being in a room full of smoke; thick, juicy grilled chicken, asparagus, and chopped potatoes. I figured there'd be something more alien there, but I wasn't going to complain.

Ginny and Penelope yacked about God knows what kind of girly stuff. Éclair and I wolfed down our food and started drinking the rest of the wine.

"What's the alcohol percentage in this?" I asked lighting a cigarette.

"I don't know, man, but it's pretty high, especially for being wine."

"Well it's not *really* wine."

"Alien wine then."

"It was aliens!" I showed him the palms of my hands and rattled my head.

While we were all bullshitting, a woman with curly red hair pulled up a chair and sat next to Ginny.

When Ginny saw her, she hugged her. "Hey you!" Ginny turned back to the table and said, "Guys, this is Kelsey."

Kelsey waved. "Hey."

"Hey, Kelsey, what's up?" Éclair greeted her.

"Uh," Ginny started. "This is Hank and Penelope."

"Nice to meet you!" Kelsey hooted over the music. She had blue eyes, fair skin, and she was wearing a trendy, checkered collared shirt. "You mind if I join y'all?"

"No, the more the merrier." Penelope grabbed an extra glass from another table and poured Kelsey wine. "Join in."

I think we went through another three or four more bottles. The girls had their own conversations.

"So there was this guy in Al Kut," Éclair said as he ashed his cigarette. "He fired at us and started running back. I sight in on him and fire nine fucking times and the fucker kept running. So I think, 'Fuck, I can't shoot for shit! Who the hell let me in the Corps?' Then when we get down the street the guy's laying there bleeding out and he's got nine holes in him.

He was all there shaking and shit. I'm pretty sure he was already dead. So I stick my finger in one of the holes to feel for a pulse…"

"That's not how that works, dude." I chuckled. "Plus, you probably have AIDS now."

"Na."

"Well dude this one time in Afghanistan we rolled up out to the middle of nowhere and we come across this compound up in the hills outside of Herat. This old timer comes out and says, 'I haven't seen you guys in a while.' And we're all like, 'The fuck are you talking about? We just got here.' And the old guy says, 'Y'all are Russians right?'"

"No!"

"Yeah! And we're like, 'Dude that fucking war ended like twenty fucking years ago, man. Have you ever left this fucking farm?'"

Ginny let out a disgruntled sigh.

"What?" Penelope asked her perplexed. The girl's eyes were glazed from the booze.

"When those two get drunk all they do is sit around and talk about how awesome the Marine Corps is and Iraq, Iran, and Afghanistan."

"What's Iraq, Iran, and Afghanistan?" Penelope asked. "I haven't really been paying attention to them."

"How do you not know what that is?" Kelsey blurted out.

"Because I've only been on your planet for about two years," Penelope retorted sharply. "I'm sorry I don't know fucking everything yet."

"Sorry," Kelsey apologized. "Didn't mean to offend."

"They're countries," Ginny answered.

"So what's the deal with drinking and talking about them? Did you both spend a deal of time there?" she asked us.

"We fought a fucking war there!" Éclair exclaimed.

"Fuck yeah!" I put my fist up and Éclair punched it.

Penelope looked at me with a motherly concern. "You were in a war?"

"I was in one," Éclair said proudly. "He was in two."

I raised my glass as if to toast.

"Why didn't you ever tell me that, Hank?"

"I dunno. Ain't never came up."

Penelope looked at me silently with anxiety and awe. She blinked a couple of times, visually inebriated. "Alright." She took another sip of her wine and turned back to Ginny and Kelsey to continue their conversation. I put a cigarette in my mouth. Before I could light it Penelope spun back around. "Have you ever killed anybody?"

Éclair and I busted out laughing, we slapped each other on our backs with a cackling roar.

I slapped Éclair's chest with the back of my hand. "Have I ever killed anybody?"

"No no no." Tears were rolling down our cheeks. Éclair put his hand on his forehead. "No we just send a lot of assholes to go meet their virgins."

Penelope was confused. "Um… I'm not following."

I put my hand on Penelope's thigh. "Babe, this is a conversation we'll have when we're sober."

"Alright. It just doesn't seem like there was a war here recently."

"Eh…" I lit my cigarette. "No one here really cared. The only people it really affected was the military. They didn't even really talk about it in the news."

"Yeah, the media just fucking ignored it because it wasn't popular," Éclair added. "And the fucking government's shitting on the veterans." Éclair burped. "Fuckers."

"Fuck it dude." I grabbed my glass. "I got smokes, booze, and boobs, there's not much to complain about right now."

Ginny shook her head with a vexed face.

Kelsey excused herself to the bathroom, Ginny and Penelope followed.

I waited until they were out of sight. "So what's up with that Kelsey chick?"

"She went to high school with Ginny, apparently they've been best friends since they were fifteen."

"That's cool."

"Yeah but she's a skeezer."

"What?" I laughed.

"Filth pig."

"Fuck me for quarters type?"

"Oh yeah. Dirty slut fucked her way through One Five before her husband in One One found out about it and divorced her. Bitch owes me two hundred bucks, too."

"You bang her?"

"Ugh. God no. I don't want my dick to shrivel up and fall off."

"Just wear a condom, man, you'll be alright. Get Ginny in on it and you'll have a grand old time."

"No thanks dude."

"Come on man, Ginny can wear a strap on and you two can double team her."

"I ain't all about that, man."

"What happened to auguring out chicks you met on the Internet? It's like the same thing."

"I don't know, man. I think that gig's about up."

"You can always just microwave a watermelon and fuck that."

The girls came back. We drank and talked for about another hour. We stumbled out the front door and smoked another cigarette under the red glow of Spike's sign.

"I'm too fucked up to drive," Éclair bumbled to Ginny.

"We can get a hotel," she answered.

I had my arm over Penelope's shoulders. I looked over to her and said, "They're my ride."

"Oh, good, I was planning on taking you home anyway." She clawed my shirt.

Kelsey disappeared into the shadows with a stranger she met about fifteen minutes prior.

15 HANGOVER FUEL

Monday morning rolled around and I sat on the smoke deck behind the building at work. All the smoke pit had was a decaying pine picnic table and an ammo can for butts. I cradled my face in my arms on the table. I had Coke, coffee, and a breakfast burrito, none of which were very well consumed. I felt like God slugged me in the head with a baseball bat and Satan was fucking my stomach. My cigarette was half burned despite me only taking two drags.

"You alright, Sergeant?" a voice said from the other side of the table.

I looked up to see Lance Corporal Glædwine. She was a cute blonde with a bob cut. I don't think I'd ever define her as beautiful, but definitely cute. Her uniform looked like a tent on her. She had to eat an immense amount of junk food to stay at the minimum weight for the Marine Corps' standards. Sometimes I was afraid the wind would blow her away if it caught her at the right angle. I liked looking at her, but I didn't want my eyes open at anything at all right then.

"Hangover from hell." I put my head back down.

I heard her light a cigarette. "You know cigarettes will kill you too, Sergeant."

"They said the same thing about Chechen snipers, Al Qaeda, and the Taliban," I grumbled.

279

"Rough night then, Sergeant?"

"Rough Friday night."

"Holy shit. What were you drinking?"

"Fucking alien bullshit wine liquor."

"Is it that bad?"

"Oh no, it was fucking delicious. It just kicked my ass."

"So you ended your weekend on Friday night?"

"My girlfriend made me soup and rubbed my stomach, but yeah, besides that I was about dead."

"If it helps my weekend was quiet too. I just fed the cats and banged my husband."

"Glædwine, that's way to much information." I lifted my head enough to take a drag. My chin was planted on my forearm. Glædwine had a book with her about four times as thick as a King James Bible. "Light reading material?"

"Yeah, it's commentary on the socioeconomic struggle and resource development of…"

"Neeeeeerd…"

"I take it you don't read much, Sergeant?"

"Oh no, I read all the time. I was just making fun of you."

"What do you read, Sergeant?"

"Science fiction or comic books, for the most part."

"And I'm the nerd?"

"Yup." I lifted my head up enough to pull my arm from under it and rubbed my eyes. "It's usually Heinlein or Asimov, those fuckers wrote so many books it'll take forever and a day to read them all."

"That sounds about right." Glædwine put out her cigarette. "Well Sergeant, I have to go back to pretending to work."

"Well at least you're honest about it."

I killed my cigarette and went back up to my section. My desk was in the back of the room overlooking the other Marines' workstations. I felt like a fucking POG for having a desk. I nibbled my burrito and watched my Marines.

Lance Corporal Cana, who suffered from chronic bitch face, was editing a video for a change of command ceremony. I never understood why those were recorded. They were a waste of everyone's time. I guess shooting one was better than standing in formation for sixteen trillion hours trying not to pass out. Either way you had to listen to some dumb shit officer thank everyone for being there. *Why do people feel the need to thank you for something they forced you to do? Is that just salt in the wound?*

I had zoned out watching Cana and didn't notice when she turned around.

"Sergeant, I have a question."

I answered, "What?" in a tone that could have been translated into, *What the fuck do you want? What the fuck are we doing here? Why the fuck does this unit exist?* "Is it about your haircut? Because your haircut's fucking stupid."

"I think your mustache is stupid."

I wanted to slap her but I had a policy against retaliating against a good come back. "What's your question, Cana?"

"There's a shoot next week on Ospreys. What do I have to do to get on that?"

"You're exited about that?" I asked judgmentally.

"We're at a base unit, Sergeant, that's about as exciting as it gets."

"I'll talk to Staff Sergeant about it."

Instead of eating lunch that day I took a nap in the Jeep. When I woke up I dredged back inside. Glædwine was manning the front desk. "Sergeant, Gunny Chanceworth is looking for you."

I grunted and made my way to the Gunnery Sergeant's office. "I was told you were looking for me, Gunnery Sergeant."

Gunny Chanceworth looked up from her computer. Her snaggletooth mouth said, "Come in, shut the door."

I did as she said and stood in front of her desk.

She looked at me with malice. "Marine are you drunk?"

"No, I'm just a little hungover."

"Hungover huh? Do you think that's acceptable?"

"Gunnery Sergeant, I'm not drunk. If you want I'll go over to the SACO and…"

"That's not what I asked."

Goddamn it this bitch is not *trying to chew my ass.* I just stared at her.

"Well?"

Well what, fuck pig? "I don't know what you want me to say, Gunnery Sergeant."

"Coming in on duty, either it be hungover or still drunk is extremely unprofessional!"

Yeah, you know what that means because your worthless ass has ever *done anything professional.* "Aye, Gunnery Sergeant."

"You're setting a bad example for the junior Marines…"

A bad example huh? I guess with three combat deployments and killing more people than you've fucked, I'm the perfect bad example. "Aye, Gunnery Sergeant."

"You're shedding a bad light on the Marine Corps coming in like that…"

God forfuckingbid the Marine Corps wanting Marines who actually got dirty and did shit over shiny boots in a pressed uniform who've never been more than half a mile away from Pendleton. "Aye, Gunnery Sergeant."

"I know you *think* you're a badass because you've been on deployment…"

Don't go there bitch…

"I've been to Iraq, I know what it's about! And there's no excuse for acting like an unprofessional child!"

No you didn't go to Iraq, you went to Al Assad in 2008, when that war was already the fuck over and slept in a trailer and ate hot chow and ice cream whenever you wanted. You had fucking USO shows and watched movies. You had Internet access and a phone and talked to your friends and family every fucking day. Camp Cupcake does NOT count as a deployment, you worthless ass shouldn't have even gotten the deployment ribbon! You never took fire; you never even went on patrol! Fuck, I'd bet my left nut you never so much as even loaded your goddamned magazines! You sat on your pussy all day instead of hiking an eighty-pound pack around the desert. You fucking flirted with the male Marines while your husband was back here with a job, and IF you even touched your camera it was to take photos of visiting generals and celebrities! How DARE you compare experiences you fucking cunt! You want to call me unprofessional? Yeah I'm a cameraman but I still went out there with the grunts. I ain't no oh three eleven, but I sure as shit did a hell of a lot more that you ever will! How many of your friends got killed? How many times did you get shot at? WHAT THE FUCK DID YOU ACTUALLY DO!? How dare you even think you rate to talk to me like that. If there's even ONE professional in this unit, it's fucking me! I'm the only one here who's ever actually even done the fucking job! Fuck you! Fuck everyone like you!

"Aye, Gunnery Sergeant."

"Since we're at it, *Sergeant…*"

YOU WORTHLESS FUCKING WHORE! DO NOT USE MY RANK LIKE THAT!

"You need to fix your mustache and your haircut."

You dense bitch, your mustache is thicker than mine is! It's obvious that you have nothing to do with your time you swine! "Aye, Gunnery Sergeant."

She told me to get out of her office and I stormed to the smoke pit. I was so infuriated I didn't even pull out a cigarette. I just glared at the mountain behind the building with my hands on my hips.

Glædwine was resting on the metal railing around the pit. "Sergeant, has anyone ever told you that you always look like you want to kill someone?"

"Nope!"

"You alright, Sergeant?"

"NOPE!"

"You wanna talk about it?"

"NOPE!"

"Alright." Glædwine put out her cigarette. "Gunny Chanceworth?"

"YUP!"

She started to walk back inside. "Don't let her get to you, Sergeant."

I skipped dinner that night in favor of rum. I brewed in the barracks room, filled to the brim with hate and discontent. I didn't turn on music or the television, I just drank.

Around ten o'clock I called up Doc. "DOC!"

"Hey man what's up?"

"Hey dude, did you know the Japanese Commander of Tarawa said it would take a million men a thousand years to take the island then the Second Marine Division took the fucking rock in less than seventy-two hours?"

"Hank, how much have you had to drink?"

"A lot, why?"

"Because you get fucking retard motivated when you drink too much."

"Fucking so?"

"So nothing. I'm just looking out for you, man."

"Yeah, no. My cunt slutbitch fuckpog faggot… bull dyke shithead fucking cumslut gunnery sergeant pissed me off."

"You think you used enough fucking swear words there, bro?"

"*NOOOO!* That bitch is a *biiiiitch!* She doesn't know shit about fuck!"

"Shit about fuck, huh? What'd she say?"

"Bitch was mad I was hungover at work and was telling me that fucking getting fat on Al Assad was the same thing as being with a grunt unit."

"Oh dude, yeah, fuck her, dude."

"Fucking bitch." I stumbled outside and tried to dig for my cigarettes. "What the fuck has she ever done? Get a bronze medal in a cum eating contest?"

"You can't let those assholes get to you, man."

I pulled the pack out of my pocket and immediately dropped them off the balcony. "FUCK!"

"What?"

"I dropped my goddamned cigarettes off the fucking… Goddamned… The thing."

"You dropped your cigarettes off the thing?"

"The fucking metal thing outside the rooms!"

"The railing?"

"YEAH! THE FUCKING RAILING!"

"HEY!" a voice screamed from another deck. "SHUT THE FUCK UP DEVIL DOG!"

"HEY! FUCK YOU POG!" I screamed back. "COME DOWN HERE AND SAY THAT SHIT! I'LL CUT YOUR FUCKING DICK OFF AND FUCK YOUR GRANDMA'S CUNT WITH IT FAGGOT!"

"Hank," Doc said trying to get my attention back.

"Hold on a minute Doc, I have to go stretch some bitch's dick hole over their fucking face."

"WELL BITCH?" I screamed back into the night.

"YO FUCK YOU!" the voice called back.

"NO, FUCK YOU YA FUCKING PUSSY BITCH!"

"I'M CALLING THE OOD!"

"CALL THE OOD! HE CAN'T UNFUCK YOUR MOTHER'S ROTTEN CUNT WITH MY RUSTY KA-BAR!"

"HANK!" Doc barked into the phone. "Walk down to the seven day store and I'll be there in five minutes."

"No, I'm going to fucking…"

"HANK! STORE!"

"FINE DOC!"

I stumbled across the street to the PX grabbing my cigarettes on the way. I leaned against the bricks and lit up. A few minutes later I saw the barracks duty and the officer of the day patrol barrack's catwalks. "That fucking pussy piece of shit. It's not even late yet."

Doc pulled up in the Mustang, killed the engine, and stood beside me. "You look *fucked* up."

"Well maybe I *am fucked up.*"

"We're all a little fucked up, man."

"Meh," I scowled. "I'm fucking tired of working with all these pussy minded shit fucks."

"I know man, they just don't have the same mindset people who actually did shit do."

"Shit was *so* much fucking easier when all I had to do was *not* fucking die."

"Yeah, I'd rather be in Iraq right now too."

"Doc."

"Yeah man?"

"What was that place?"

"In Al Hillah?"

"Yeah. What the fuck was that?"

"I don't know bro."

"You think it had something to do with why we didn't get waxed on that airfield?"

Doc paused for a second. "No. No man that's crazy talk. There was nothing down there but some fucking ancient booby trap bullshit."

"Then why are we alive, man?"

"I don't know, man. I really don't. I just know that we're alive now and I don't ever, *ever,* want to get blown up again."

I whispered, "Ka boom…"

"Come on man, let's get you to bed. You're all drunk and stabby."

The next morning at work I printed out the after action reports for my combat experiences and copies of my Purple Heart citations and stuck them on the read board next to my desk. I wasn't quite as hungover as I was the previous day, but I was probably still going to get it from Gunny Chanceworth.

Staff Sergeant Bistro moseyed out of his office. The new papers on the board sparked his curiosity. He pulled them down and read them over. When he was about a third of the way through he started taking turns staring at me and the papers. He left the room papers in hand.

My plan was in motion. I cracked half of a sly smile and headed down to the smoke deck.

The little blonde girl was already down there.

"Glædwine, do you do anything besides smoke?"

"Sergeant, every time you see me smoke you're down here too."

"Smart ass." I lit my own.

"Feeling better today, Sergeant?"

"Yeah, that alien shit fucked me up something fierce."

"What's it like?"

"It's kind of like wine, but it's sweet and dry at the same time. It's all the good stuff from red and white wines, with none of the bad. And it's black, like jet black."

"So black you can't see light through it?"

"Yeah, but it looks like it'd be syrupy, but it's the same consistency as a regular wine, and there's a ridiculous amount of alcohol in it."

"Well that sounds like a good time."

"It was. What do you think about the whole alien thing?"

"I think it's interesting. I think it's funny how it's nothing like it ever is in the movies. We find extraterrestrial life in the movies and the entire earth bands together, we cast aside our petty differences and the world becomes a utopia. But here we are, there are still wars, drugs, crimes, suffering, starvation, hunger, and disease. There isn't any inkling of the forming of a One World Government under Novus Ordo Seclurom, no Annuit Cœptis. I find it particularly entertaining how it's shaking people's faiths. For some reason a lot of people seem to believe the idea of extraterrestrials and God don't correlate. I personally don't see a problem with that."

"Well there's two ways to think about that." I said, "A: There's a God, or B: There's no God. If there isn't a God then it's mathematically impossible for something else not to be out there in the universe. If there is a God then it's both ignorant and arrogant to think we're the only things He ever made."

"I agree. What do you think about the whole alien situation, Sergeant?"

"Personally or politically?"

"How about politically?"

"They're assimilating and not being a plight on society, they have jobs, and put money into the economy. What's not to like about them?"

"Well Sergeant, what do you think about their technology and what new stuff they're bringing to the earth?"

"I had cigarettes, booze, and my Jeep before they came. If there's anything else they bring, cool, but if not I already have the material things."

"What do you think about them personally?"

"Well I'm dating one of them, so there's that."

Glædwine looked surprised. "Really? How's that work?"

"Their anatomy is stupid similar to ours, like to the point where it made me think God wasn't really that creative. My girlfriend's told me about it all, but the only thing I've really noticed, besides the skin pigment, is their hair is a lot softer and their pussies taste like honey."

"Too much information, Sergeant!"

"Sorry."

"It's alright."

I finished my cigarette and walked back into the office. Staff Sergeant Bistro told me to stay away from Gunny Chanceworth the rest of the day. She wouldn't be hunting me down, but I should still avoid her.

16 BARRACKS RAT

I drove over to Camp Margarita after work on Wednesday. Doc was tinkering with the Mustang's motor from under the jacks.

Éclair watched Doc through neon green sunglasses under one of the scraggly trees in the parking lot with a cooler of beer and a lawn chair.

"What are you doing, Éclair?" I asked walking up from behind.

"Getting my tan on, man."

"Not going to help poor old Doc?"

"No one's crawling up Jessica's skirt but me!" Doc yelled from under the hood.

His toolbox was scattered into a million pieces across the pavement. His legs, black with grease, were the only visible part of his body.

Éclair handed me a beer. "Doc told me you found about sixteen new ways to use the word cunt."

"Did he?" I popped the tab on the can. "Maybe I should start writing poetry."

"Ha, yeah. To cunt, or not to cunt, that is the cunstion!"

"Pretty much. Have you had any luck on your find-a-cunt-dot-com thing?"

"Na man, I told you, they're all a bunch of fucking brain dead, antisocial dunces. It was kind of just for fun though. I don't know if I was actually going to do anything with anyone. How could I?" Éclair pulled out his phone and read a woman's profile aloud. "*Hello, fellow sojourner in the search of truth. I'm smooth and sexy.* Her photo says otherwise. *Swipe left if you're a republican. Looking for a partner in crime, I keep it real. Must love all things Italian, looking to meet new people, but no hook ups.* Why is she here then? *No time for games.* Because dating sites aren't arenas. *My kids are my life. Single mom.* Maybe if any of her kids were the same color someone might take her seriously. *I love to travel and dance the night away...* Blah, blah, blah. Nothing but losers on this fucking app."

Doc rolled out from under the car and hopped into the driver's seat. The hood was still up. The starter whined and there was a loud grinding, then a pop and the engine died. Doc screamed obscenities, Éclair jumped up, and we all leaned in over the steaming engine.

"What the fuck happened?" Doc screamed, putting his eyes on every nook, cranny, and bolt in the engine bay.

"Doc," I pointed to the discrepancy. "Your fan jumped up and ripped a hole in your radiator." There was a long rounded gash in the metal of the back of the radiator and the fan blades had chunks ripped out of them.

"Mother fucker!"

"Looks like she's down for the count," Éclair said.

"No," Doc said and pulled out a cigarette "She's just twice as fucked up as she was earlier."

"What was wrong with it?" I asked.

"I cleaned the carburetor and I decided that while I was down there I should tighten some things up. I don't know how the fuck that happened. One of you mind taking me to the auto store?"

"I gotcha, man," I said.

Doc packed up his tools and we rode out to Oceanside. We pulled around the Crazy Chicken Shop and turned into the shared parking lot.

"Hey man, remember the last time we were here getting shit for the Mustang?" Doc asked me.

"Yeah man, that was fucked up. Let's not do that again." We both laughed. I shut down the engine and we hopped out.

Doc got the parts he needed and I got a Coke. When we got back to the barracks Ginny and Kelsey were sitting with Éclair by the Mustang. Doc and I waved our hellos. Éclair introduced Doc to Kelsey, then Doc grabbed his tools and crawled back under the Mustang.

"So Penelope's nice," Ginny noted.

"Yeah I think so. I may keep her around for a while."

"Yeah, so what's up with her anyway?" Kelsey asked.

"I don't know," I shrugged. "She's green and knows how to work my shaft."

"Yeah? How do you think she got to be good at *that?*" Kelsey asked, trying to get under my skin.

"Well she's almost ninety, I'd hope she'd know how to suck a dick by now."

"What? No. She's like twenty at the *most.*" Kelsey didn't believe it.

"No, they live to be pretty old," Ginny backed me up.

"Weird."

"Yup. I haven't really looked into how they age yet, but I think they can go on for centuries." I lit a cigarette.

"Yeah that's what one of the Virescents at work was telling me," Ginny said.

"Well then what's she doing with you?" Kelsey tried to provoke me. "If things work out between you two aren't you going to die when she's pretty much twenty-five?"

I didn't let her get to me. "Yeah. But she likes the way I grease her gears. And I'm okay with it if I end up being ninety and have a chick that looks like she's twenty."

"That seems like a win-win to me." Éclair crushed his beer can and grabbed another.

"Yup," I said. "Hey Kelsey, you fuck any alien guys yet?"

"That's a little forward," she retorted indignantly.

"I just want to know if all the hype the movies used to have about little green men from Mars coming and probing people was accurate."

"Well, you would know better than I would."

"You know the whole alien probing thing, maybe that's just their version of S & M."

"Well this conversation's getting dark." Ginny grabbed Éclair's arm and continued, "Can we go talk about something?"

"Sure." The couple disappeared into the barracks.

Kelsey slid her head back and forth. "Bow Chicka Wow Wow."

"Yeah, that sounds about right." I offered Kelsey a cigarette. She waved no. "So what's up with you?"

"Not a whole lot. I didn't have much to do today so I was hanging out with Ginny."

"Yeah, it seems like y'all are attached at the hip."

"We've been friends for a long time."

"Yeah that happens. I'm like that with Doc."

Doc was still under the car swearing at parts.

I looked at Kelsey's eyes. They were piercing blue. "So what do you do?"

"I'm still going to school, trying to be a lawyer."

"Oh that's the top of the good chain."

"Huh?"

"On the list of evil," I said and smirked.

Kelsey half-smiled. "Is that so?"

"Yeah. Lawyers are the worst. Then it's social workers, congress, Satan, Al Qaeda, communists, and the Nazis."

Kelsey chuckled. "Politicians aren't on there?"

"I said congress. But you can't just jumble *all* politicians together. I mean, Teddy Roosevelt and Joseph Stalin were both politicians."

"Good point, good point." Kelsey looked around the parking lot. "Where can I use the bathroom around here?"

I pointed to the dumpsters.

"Ha ha," she sneered.

I hollered, "Doc!"

"What's up, man?" came from under the hood.

"Can this chick use your pisser?"

"Sure bro, door's unlocked."

I looked back to Kelsey and said, "Room five thirty-one."

"Thanks." She waved bye and headed in.

I sat outside drinking beer and handing Doc tools.

"Hey Hank," Doc said and grabbed a wrench.

"Yeah?"

"You still have fucked up nightmares all the time?"

"No. I specifically get shit faced every night so I can avoid that. If I get enough booze in me I don't dream a fucking thing, I just pass the hell out. What about you?"

"Not since I woke up. But that probably has something to do with not taking malaria pills."

"God those were bad. It's like, 'What? Regular nightmares aren't *good* enough for you!?'" I imitated what I thought was a wealthy Englishman, "Here chap, take these hallucinogens! They're *great* for your liver too!"

Doc laughed. "Yeah, I'm still waiting for the commercials they're going to have on TV in twenty years saying, 'Were you in Iraqistan? Were you exposed to Mefloquine or Doxycycline? If so call one eight hundred fuck me right!' Fuckers." Doc rolled his eyes.

"What do you think that hole we were in was? With all the gold and the traps?"

"I don't know man, I try not to think about that one. It was probably an old temple, or a dungeon, or fucking gateway to Hell. Fuck, for all I know it was Poseidon's whorehouse."

"Why Poseidon?" I laughed.

"Because I don't know who the Greek God of constellations was."

"Yeah, but we were in Iraq."

"Okay, then it was a fuck chamber Saddam Hussein built after watching *Indiana Jones* one too many times."

"Dude, I miss Saddam Hussein."

"What?"

"He was a really good bad guy. Like a real life Bond villain."

Doc raised his eyebrows. "He did write that Koran in his own blood."

"And that's some dark shit," I said and smiled. "They should make a movie out of that! Think about it. Saddam Hussein writes a book in his own blood, but instead of the Koran it's like a..." I spun my fingers trying to think. "Like a whatever the Muslim version of the Satanic Bible would be."

"And what would he do with that?"

"I don't know, be a bad guy?" I pulled out a cigarette and watched the flame from my lighter burn the end of the Luck's in my mouth. "He'd start a gang of Persian Gulf Pirates!"

"I dig it."

"Then they'd go around raping and pillaging, and I mean graphic raping and pillaging scenes with thousands of dollars spent on fake blood and semen."

"Who's going to be the good guy in that?"

"King Tut." I shrugged.

"Nobody knows a damn thing about King Tut."

"Exactly! I make up whatever I wanted to and get away with it!"

"Because Saddam Hussein as a pirate wasn't already made up enough?"

"Yeah, but King Tut'll still be a mummy, zombie, demon, monster thing, risen from the grave to get revenge on Saddam because Saddam fucked a hooker in King Tut's tomb and snorted all the cocaine he was buried with."

"I can see that." Doc nodded.

"Then we make the hooker Jewish because the Egyptians and the

Iraqis both hate Jews."

"No!" Doc interrupted. "The Jewish chick wasn't a hooker, she was one of Tut's concubines that was buried with him and Saddam is a necrophiliac who busted into the tomb with his buccaneers and fucked all the mummies!"

"YES!"

"And King Tut is like a total badass."

"Yeah man." I opened another beer. Éclair had left his cooler under the tree. "You ever get back ahold of Reagan?"

"No man, I haven't. You heard from Kennedy?"

"Nope, and I felt it best not to try to hunt her down."

"I feel ya, man."

"Yeah, well you know what's funny about it all is when I accepted that the whole Kennedy thing was over I went right back to missing the chick before that."

"Yeah, that's fucked up how that works. But shit, we're starting to get to the point where we're talking about this in years, not weeks or months."

"Well I was fucking in a coma for most of that."

"Yeah. So tell me about Penelope, I think I've only met her like twice."

"Well, I don't think she owns underwear that aren't lacey and black, and unless she's wearing pants she's always wearing thigh highs. Real classy. Her vampire fangs are kind of a let down. I think they're hot, but they don't inject poison *or* suck blood."

"I was asking about personality, but I guess that works too." Doc rolled his eyes.

"She's sweet, but she can snap and be a real bitch. She hasn't flipped a switch on me yet, but when she goes off on other people I think it's hot. I'm trying to get her into a fist fight just to see how much ass she can kick."

"She didn't seem like that kind of chick when I met her."

"*Most* of the time she acts like a civilized human being. But I don't know, she makes me happy, and for some fucking reason I can't stand that. Like, I'm addicted to chaos and I'm not happy unless I'm living in squalor."

"Yeah, that sounds about right."

"Shut up, Doc."

"Don't tell me to shut up!"

"Shut up." I half-smiled.

Doc pulled himself out from under the car and looked at me vexed.

Maintaining eye contact we both lit cigarettes and after one puff we both put the burning end of the smokes into our left forearms. We glared each other down with half a smile.

"Keanu Reeves is a better actor than Brad Pitt." Doc didn't flinch.

"Brad Pitt would kick his ass in real life." My face was stone.

"Reeves would fuck Pitt's wife and adopt Brad as a step kid." Doc's eye started to twitch.

"Reeves would take the red pill and wake up as Brad Pitt."

Doc pulled the cigarette off his skin. "Damnit alright, you win."

I slapped Doc on the back and we laughed. "You about done with the car?"

"No, but it's getting dark. I'll just walk to work tomorrow." We packed up Doc's stuff, grabbed Éclair's cooler, and hauled it to Doc's room. Doc pulled out his key and opened the door. "WHAT THE

FUCK?" Doc cried walking into his room.

"What?" I said as I stuck my head in the door.

Kelsey and Scott were on Doc's bed scrambling to cover themselves.

"Sorry sorry sorry!" Kelsey fumbled for her clothes.

Doc looked at Scott and raised his hands palm up. "The fuck man? You couldn't take her back to your room?"

"Sorry Doc, I don't even know what this chick's name is," he said nonchalantly as he pulled on his pants.

"Oh, thanks asshole!" Kelsey bitched at Scott.

"Don't get mad at me about that. I didn't even meet you half an hour ago."

"Both of you get the fuck out of here!" Doc barked.

"I know, I know, sorry." Kelsey was still scrambling for her clothes.

"You know, you've got a nice set of tits. You should be a stripper," I taunted her.

"Fuck off, Hank."

I shrugged. "Or at least trim that bush. I'm half expecting a platoon of Viet Kong to jump out and ambush us."

Kelsey shot me rage as she pulled up her panties.

"You're taking too long." Doc snatched up both of their clothes and threw them off the balcony. Before either Kelsey or her fling could grab anything with which to cover themselves, Doc and I grabbed both of them and pushed them out of the room still mostly naked.

Kelsey swore at us through the door. I could hear Scott laughing and running off. Kelsey ran after him yelling, "Wait for me!"

Doc growled, "Fucking cum dumpster. Now I have to burn my sheets."

"Did they leave a condom anywhere?"

"I hope he was at least wearing one."

"It's not his fault, he was just try'n to get some ass."

"I'm just glad they weren't doing some German porn shit. Can you imagine what it would be like to clean up?"

I laughed and said, "Yeah, now that would be fucked up. I'm going to use your pisser." I walked into the bathroom and started peeing. I looked in the shower, there was an ass sticking out of the wall. I leaned over to get a better look at it, being careful not to piss on Doc's floor. It was like a sex doll, but it was only the butt cheeks, anus, and vagina. There were toothbrushes and razors stuck in the orifices.

"Doc!"

"What's up dude, need me to hold it for you?"

"What's this fuck doll ass in here?"

"It's my toothbrush holder."

"You couldn't use a cup or a wire?"

"Eh. Sometimes I like to get my nut off when I shave and brush my teeth, and my hands are busy."

"You're fucked up, you know that?"

17 FIFTY SHADES OF DAVE

Friday afternoon I sat on the smoke deck at work. I tried to justify going back inside and pretending to work, but I couldn't even justify that unit's existence. The only thing that place was good for was taking promotion photos. It wasn't like I really wanted to work, but shit, the Marine Corps could have at least put me somewhere where I had something to do.

"Good afternoon, Sergeant." Glædwine lit a cigarette as she leaned onto the railing.

"Why am I still at work, Glædwine?" I whined.

"I don't know, Sergeant. They don't trust that information to lance corporals."

"Ugh! We're just filthy enlisted swine."

"Yeah…"

"This is bullshit." I flicked my cigarette into the parking lot instead of putting it out in the can and lit another. I didn't really want to smoke, I just enjoyed Glædwine's company and I didn't want it to look like I was only out there for the sake of talking to her alone.

"Well it's a garrison unit, Sergeant."

"Which is bullshit! There's no reason to even have this place. The

Marine Corps has *no* mission on this side of the lake. And everyone here thinks garrison shit is a means to its own end, and it's not. Your boots aren't laced a certain way just for the sake of it, they're laced that way so that you get used to doing all manners of things in a regiment and build muscle memory habits so you have a better chance of surviving in combat. But this unit doesn't go to combat, this unit doesn't leave the fucking base!"

"Yeah, I have no argument against that."

"I didn't join the Marine Corps to sit on my ass not doing anything, if I wanted to do that I would have kept mowing lawns."

"Well at least you *got* to go do things, Sergeant. Most of us spend our whole enlistment here never doing anything."

I looked at her from under my eyebrows. Glædwine didn't spend that much time on her hair that morning. It was stormy and wild. She looked like one of Santa's elves that just worked a double shift in the toy line. I thought, *I bet that hair is still silky smooth*, and then I imagined being in Vegas playing roulette and gambling with people's hair instead of chips. *Martinis and wigs for everyone!* I entertained the thought of jumping in my car with Glædwine and running away from life.

"It's still a fucking stupid problem to have. There's a million things going on here but not *one* of them is a thing that actually matters. Every time another one of these stupid things comes up I make a comment or try to fix it, quick and in a hurry, and I keep getting told, 'Allensworth, you *can't* do that.' And I'm like, 'I just did!' Then I get a talking to by the fucking civilians here that don't understand that we're fucking Marines and trying to do a job, however unentertaining it may be."

"Sergeant, you probably shouldn't be saying that to a junior Marine. I think they call that spreading dissent."

"I'm not planning a mutiny."

"I know." Glædwine smiled, then being the smartass she was said, "In the Uniform Code of Military Justice, Under Article…"

"NERD!"

"Sergeant, I heard through lance corporal underground that you put on a cape, watch Dracula movies, and drink wine pretending that it's blood and go around pretending to be a vampire."

"That happened *one* time."

"Just say'n."

"Just say'n what?"

"Just saying that. I also know about the Black Beard incident."

"Fucking OPSEC violators!"

Glædwine laughed. "Are you going to stop calling me nerd or do I have to keep going?"

"Eh, I'll stop for now. You have any plans for the weekend?"

"I volunteer at the SPCA in Carlsbad, so that. And I'm reading *War and Peace*."

"That's a good chunk of book there."

"Yeah, I used to be a history teacher."

"Well then, now I have proof you're an idiot."

"How so?"

"You've got a degree and you're enlisted. Instead of bullshitting out here on the smoke deck you should be drinking coffee with bars on your collar."

"Well my dad was in Vietnam, and he told me that all that non infantry officers did was sit around and do paperwork. I didn't want to risk that."

I pointed to the building and said, "That seemed to work out well."

"It's not the worst that could have happened." She exhaled through her nostrils. "What are you doing with your weekend, Sergeant?"

"My buddy's girlfriend is out of town seeing her aunt or grandpa or someone, so I'm going to go get shit-housed tomorrow. I think I'm going to spend tonight with my girlfriend."

"Ah, the Virescent girl. Have you met her family yet?"

"Just her brother. He runs a jazz club in SD."

"I was actually reading an article about them the other day."

"Anything fun?"

"Just that the Westboro Baptist Church thinks they're an abomination."

"Yeah the 'God Hates Fags' fags are fags. That's my analysis on that."

"What I think's funny about it is that they think that we were here first. Obviously humans were on the planet first, however, even though the Virescent only perceived traveling in space for about six decades, they left their planet before the pyramids were built."

"You're not thinking about it right. The fag hater fags think we've only been here for five thousand years."

"What I think's funny about the young earth argument is that everyone thinks evolution is a *why* and not a *how*. I mean, in the Bible there was nothing, then space, then light, then earth, then mountains, then water, then plants, then fish, then animals, then people. Science says there was nothing, then space, then light, then earth, then mountains, then water, then plants, then fish, then animals, then people. You have to put the Bible in perspective. If you were an all powerful, omnipresent, omnipotent being and you wanted to tell your story but all you could talk to were dirt farming shepherds, you'd have to find a good way to explain it. Shit, have you ever tried explaining the concept of a week to a four-year-old?"

"Something similar, yes."

"Now go find someone that thinks mixing water and clay to make bricks for a house is wizardry and try to explain to him the concept of evolution over the course of forty billion years. Personally I think both sides of the evolution versus creation arguments are manned by zealots and

I think there's better things to do than sitting around and arguing about it on TV. I believe there's a God, but he must *love* stupid people because he won't stop making them."

"Even from that perspective though, the only thing I don't really understand about it all is that if God made everything and he wanted people to know about it so we could either worship him or be his friends, whatever the reason for making us was. Why is it that he waited so long to say hello to anyone?"

"What do you mean?"

"Well, there was Adam and Eve and Noah and a few people He talked to, but going off of the biblical timeline as it compares to real world events, when God revealed himself to Abraham people had long already been practicing Buddhism. One would thing that the creator of the universe would have the oldest religion. That idea doesn't shake my faith, and I'm not denouncing anything, but that's a question I'd like to have answered. You know what else I want answered?"

"What's that, Sergeant?"

"Why haven't they called fucking liberty yet?"

I spent that night at Penelope's apartment. I had one glass of Hesperides with dinner then switched to rum. We didn't have anything too special. I grilled up some fish and Penelope steamed vegetables and baked.

I sat on Penelope's dark purple loveseat. The leather was pillowed and the buttons on the back were deep enough to stick a finger into. We had kettle corn on the wooden coffee table and candles dimly illuminated the forest green wall.

Penelope had her head in my lap with her feet hanging off the sofa's arm. She would occasionally reach for a handful of popcorn and eat half a kernel at a time. I thought the way she ate was weird, then I reminded myself I was dating someone that wasn't even my species and probably didn't have the right to think anyone was a weirdo anymore.

Her hair was parted in the middle with a set of thick bangs over her forehead. The hair growing out of the top of her head stopped at her shoulders. The layers underneath went almost to her waist. I twisted strands of her orange locks around my fingers as we watched the TV.

We had rented the movie they made out of *Fifty Shades of Dave*. It followed what I had read of the book pretty closely.

Dave rolled open the sliding glass door and walked over to Claudia. She spread her legs apart further and pulled the blunt out of Dave's mouth. Dave didn't bother to kiss Claudia. He ran his long pale fingers down Claudia's beautiful sun bronzed skin and started to lick the yogurt off of Claudia's vagina.

"So you guys will put anything in movies, won't you?" Penelope nibbled on the kettle corn.

"Yeah pretty much. But there's worse. There's a lot worse."

Claudia moaned with pleasure. With one hand she smoked the rest of the weed Dave had brought. The other hand held Dave's head in her crotch. Claudia wrapped her legs over Dave's shoulders.

In her thick Salvadorian accent Claudia told Dave to, "Lick my other hole." Dave's head shifted and Claudia's beautiful body shivered.

"People do that?" Penelope asked puzzled.

"Yup. Welcome to Earth."

"Is it that common?"

"I really don't know. People only really talk about it joking around. I don't think I've ever actually heard anyone talk about it seriously."

"Hmm. I've legitimately never even heard of anyone doing that before. I don't know if it sounds terrible or exciting."

"Well, I'll have my head down that way later tonight. I'll stick my tongue in your butt and you can let me know how it is."

She smiled up at me nervously as if to say, *You're shitting me right?*

Dave picked up Claudia and carried her to the kitchen table. Claudia stuck her tongue down Dave's throat and unbuttoned his pants.

"I think it's hilarious how they've managed to be this dirty and not even show a nipple yet," I said groping Penelope's breast.

The movie cut to a shot of the outside of the house. We could still hear Claudia's moans and Dave's panting. The sun flew across the sky and darkness fell over the landscape. The full moon slowly rose.

The scene cut back to Claudia's face shoved in a pillow. She was covered in sweat, her thick black hair clung to her skin, soaking wet. It zoomed out to reveal Dave's hand holding Claudia's head down. She was screaming, "Tear me apart!" Her ass was up in the air and Dave was pummeling her rear side.

The camera angel changed to over the back of Dave's shoulder. He gripped Claudia's hair and pulled back her head. Through the window the moon came into full view. A close up showed Dave's mouth growing more and more open, spit and saliva seeped from his lips. The camera panned up to his eyes, they were bulging out of his head. The little red veins in his eyes pulsed and stretched. His nose arched and hair grew from all over his skin. His back arched forward and he let out a terrible howl. Dave had transformed into a wolf in the moonlight!

"What?" I laughed.

"I don't understand," Penelope cried confused.

"You guy's don't have werewolves?"

"No. What is it?"

"It's like an old myth of a cursed person that transforms into a wolf on nights when there's a full moon."

She rolled her head to look up at me. "You people are weird."

I just shrugged.

Claudia looked back, her ecstasy turned to horror. She screamed in terror and tried to claw away. The wolf on her back held her down and continued to thrust. Claudia began to wail, tears poured from her eyes as she screamed for help and demanded the wolf to get off of her.

The wolf flipped Claudia over and reinserted himself. Claudia started punching the wolf and screamed, "STOP FUCKING ME!" Claudia went to strike the wolf in the face. He caught her hand with his fangs and bit it clean off. Claudia screamed in agony and gripped her bloody stump with her other hand.

"Hank, don't let me pick movies any more."

"What? This is awesome! What are you talking about?"

Claudia's hand reached for something. She found a spoon and drove it into the wolf's front leg. The wolf yowled then sunk his teeth in Claudia's throat. Claudia's breaths became weak and blood spewed from her mouth. Her body went limp; the cold glowless glaze of death crept over her eyes as the wolf kept shoving himself into her.

The screen faded black and came back with Dave sleeping naked under the table. He sniffed and opened his eyes with a look of curiosity and disgust. He stood up and looked at the mutilated corpse on the table. Horror filled his eyes. "NO! NOT AGAIN!"

""Wow! And I thought this movie was going to suck!" I laughed.

"You're enjoying this?" Penelope asked judgmentally.

"Trust me babe, there's a lot worse out there. And how the hell is this only rated PG-13?"

"There's something wrong with you."

"Yeah maybe. But you're fucking me so what does that say about you?"

Penelope rolled her eyes, reached up, and lightly scratched the skin behind my ear.

Dave started to freak out. "I can't believe I forgot!" He took Claudia's lifeless corpse and chucked it in his pool-cleaning van, cautious to make sure no one saw him. He went back and grabbed his cleaning equipment and Claudia's spare body parts. He drove downtown into an alley. He stopped the van just over a manhole. Dave lifted the cover and dumped Claudia's body in the sewer.

The movie skipped five years into the future. Dave smoked a cigarette outside a bar overlooking the San Francisco skyline. He was shaking. The clouds separated in the night revealing the full moon. He began to transform. He pulled something out of his pocket and put it to his nose. The transformation stopped. Dave put the small bag of white powder back into his pocket.

"What was that? A drug?" Penelope asked.

"Yup."

"In San Francisco?"

"Yeah, have you been there yet?"

"I actually haven't been terribly far from San Diego."

"Hmm. We should go on a road trip sometime."

"I would very much like that."

Imitating Penelope's accent I said, "Do you know what I would very much like?"

She smiled at my gesture. "What's that, Hank?"

I shot both of my hands to her rib cage and dug in my fingers. She started writhing and blurting out laughs. "Stop it!"

"Well then stop laughing!" I continued.

"No fair!" She started tickling me back and we fell to the floor. She landed on top of me and I let her pin my hands down. "I've got you now," said her low lustful voice.

"You had me 'Twat.'"

She laughed, "Good."

I unbuttoned her jeans and she wiggled as I slid them off.

Penelope rubbed the bottom of her panties on my cock through my jeans and started kissing my neck just under the ear.

I freed my hands and ran them down her back. I slid one hand into the back of her underwear and squeezed her ass cheek. Her skin was softer than her silk-like hair.

Penelope reached down and freed my dick from its jean prison. She glided the head of my penis inside her panties and rubbed it on her clit. "Tell me you want me," she whispered in my ear.

"Oh don't you worry about that, sunshine."

She lightly licked the inside of my ear. "Tell me you want my tight little pussy wrapped around your big strong cock." She started running the tip back and forth between her lips. The warm juices from inside of her seeped down my shaft.

"Baby I want all of you." I sent my unoccupied hand under her shirt to unlatch her bra.

Penelope put her hand on the back of my head and ran her bottom lip on my top one. I licked under her bottom lip and she scratched mine with her teeth. She spun the head of my penis inside her lips around the opening of her vagina.

She came down just enough to get the head in. When I thrusted my hips up she rose too. "Not yet." She smiled almost sinisterly.

She slowly slid a finger inside of herself then put that finger in my mouth. Instead of being salty like every earth girl, her fluid was sweet like honey. Penelope pulled off my shirt and held my shoulders down. Maintaining eye contact she played with my nipple with her tongue then kissed her way down to just above my penis. She paused for a few seconds, smiling at me with sexual appetite, gazing with her cobalt eyes. She wrapped her hand around my shaft and ran her tongue from the base to the tip. She extended her tongue and rubbed the head down it. She went to do it again, only this time halfway down the tongue she wrapped her lips around it and slid them halfway down and back up. I started to breathe heavier as she stroked my cock. Penelope started her grip loose and tightened it as she got closer to the top.

I gripped a handful of her hair and guided her head. With me in her mouth she stuck her tongue out and licked the parts under her lips. She drove her head down until her bottom lip was resting on my balls, then licked them. She twisted her head to and fro then slowly back up. Penelope cupped my balls, gently squeezing them.

Penelope stood up and said, "Give me a minute, and don't have any clothes on when I come back."

I stood up and took the rest of my clothes off. Before I could decide if I should stay up or lay down Penelope came back with a bottle of Hesperides, she had dropped the rest of her clothes and put on black thigh highs. She took a long drink and offered me the bottle. I took the wine and she dropped to her knees.

I took a swig of the black wine and Penelope tried to get the head of my penis into her stomach. I kept drinking and she kept sucking. Shaft in mouth, Penelope circled the base of the head with the end of her tongue.

I put the bottle down on the coffee table. I moved my hips back, pulled out of Penelope's mouth, grabbed my cock, and rubbed it on her face. She chased it with her mouth. Penelope pushed me back into the loveseat and straddled me. She grabbed my dick and ran her teeth over my neck. I winced a little from her fangs. She pulled my cock to her pussy, sat down and whimpered, "Hank."

Penelope started gyrating her hips. I put my hands on her thighs. She put her hands on the back of my head and pulled me into her breasts. She started slamming herself onto me. I wrapped my hands under Penelope's legs, lifted us off the sofa, and pinned her to the wall. I had the back of Penelope's knees by my shoulders and drilled my cock in. I loved the way she'd scream, "Fuck me!"

I lowered Penelope's legs. When her feet touched the floor I turned her around and stuck my cock back in. I gripped her pussy hair with one hand and her arm with the other. I held her against the wall as I hammered in. She took my hand and wrapped it around her throat. "Give me that cock, Hank." She dropped her head; her long orange hair swayed with the rhythm. Penelope's breath grew shorter, sharper, and faster. She almost sounded like she was about to break into tears when she told me, "Give me your cum Hank, give it to me." I moved one of my hands to her hips, choked her with the other, and started pushing her out to where she was almost off my dick and slamming her back on me. Her arms quivered and she collapsed into the wall. I grabbed her arms above the elbow and held them back while continuing to punch her cervix with the head of my dick. Her screams of, "Give me your cum," turned to pleads of, "Cum in me."

Our bodies were drenched with sweat. I felt the hard pressure build up inside my shaft. Penelope had already came. "You want my cum?"

She panted, "I want your cum, baby."

"You want it?"

"I want it."

"Where?"

"I want it in me."

I pushed my dick as far as I could into her, pressing her into the wall. Penelope moaned and I shot my load in her pussy like Lee Harvey Oswald shot his load into JFK.

I pulled back and Penelope started to fall. I grabbed her and laid us both on the sofa. I pulled the blanket off the back of the loveseat over us. Penelope laid on top of me. Keeping her eyes closed she smiled and rubbed her head into my chest in a way that reminded me of a cat or a dog patting down grass before they went to sleep.

The lights were already out, and I figured the candles would be okay. I grabbed the remote off the coffee table and I looked at the TV. The credits were rolling for *Fifty Shades of Dave*. "Damn, I missed most of the movie."

"You can watch it again sometime," Penelope whispered.

"Eh."

"Just no more tickling."

"Why not? It seemed to turn out pretty good for me."

Penelope reached up and patted my cheek.

18 LET THE BODYPARTS HIT THE FLOOR

The next morning I sat in a booth at a diner in with Penelope. We sat in the same seat to be closer to each other. I ordered four eggs. I had worked up a pretty decent appetite earlier that morning. Penelope woke up first and I guess she decided that since we were both already naked we might as well start the day off with sausage and tang.

Penelope sipped her coffee and cut her waffle. "We don't have anything like coffee or tea."

"Yeah?" I drowned my eggs in hot sauce.

"Nothing like it at all."

I looked over at Penelope. "Babe."

"Yes?" She looked back with passion in her eyes.

I drew my face in close to hers. She opened her lips to kiss me. "You have cum in your eyelash."

"Damn *it*, really?" She grabbed a napkin and started pulling at her eyelashes. "Is it noticeable?"

"Not unless you're up close, and even then people might think it's an eye booger. It's just a little speck."

She kept wiping her eye. "Did I get it out?"

I took a look. "Yeah, you're good." I chuckled.

"It's not funny."

"Then why are you smiling?"

"I'm not." She was.

"Okay babe."

"Maybe it's because I like you too much."

"Can you like someone *too* much?"

"Yes." She smiled over at me. "You know, I've been thinking." She drank her coffee. "You know that place you took me for our first date? The waterfall."

"Yup."

"That would be a good place to go during a zombie apocalypse. You know, if one happened like in the movies."

"Yeah I can see that, fresh water and it's far enough away from populated areas that zombies probably wouldn't find you."

"That's what I was thinking, yes."

"What about an alien invasion?"

"Haven't you already had one of those?" Penelope asked farcing confusion.

"Yeah but I ended up probing the alien."

Penelope nudged her shoulder into my arm. "Smart ass."

"For real though, we could get invaded again. If you guys were out there someone else has to be out there too."

"I don't think a hostile invasion is something to really worry about. The galaxy takes too much time to navigate. The invaders would be on a one way trip just to plunder a planet for whatever reason. They'd never get to go home to their loved ones, even if they did, thousands of years would have passed. Everyone they plundered for would be long dead," Penelope said.

"Do you think they'd get paid in their relative time or the time that they'd been away relative from their planet?"

"That's a good question. But if you're going to be in outer space for that long there's a good chance you're never coming home. Unless you managed to figure out hyperspace or worm holes or how to travel faster than light."

"Well you guys took a risk coming out on your own not really knowing where you were going. You found us by radio waves after you'd been floating around for a while, right?" I asked.

"Yes, but it's also not like we were the only ship. There were twelve and we all set out in different directions from Virescent."

"Interesting."

"Actually, no. I was mistaken. There was one race that developed hyper drive that we knew of, anyway. But they were almost like a legend and I'm afraid I don't really know anything about them except for a few stories. The last we saw them was thousands of years ago. It would be feasible for *them* to invade you if they had a reason."

"So what about why you guys left your planet in the first place? If you had twelve ships that big and sent them out all over the galaxy there must have been something pretty bad going on."

"Yeah, I really don't want to talk about that."

Penelope hadn't brushed her hair that morning. She had only ran her fingers through to pull out the knots. She braided her hair as we waited for the check. She didn't do it eloquently, just enough to hold it together and keep it out of her way.

"So you and Éclair are getting together tonight?"

"Yeah, Ginny's out of town so we're going to raise some hell. You can expect drunk texts and maybe a phone call. But I plan on getting so drunk I forget how to speak English, so we'll see."

I kissed Penelope goodbye when I dropped her off at her apartment and headed back to Pendleton. I showered, put on my GNR shirt, and picked up a bottle of rum and a thirty rack on the way over to Margarita.

Doc was sitting on the Mustang's trunk with a cigarette and a beer. I parked next to him and pulled a beer out of the back.

"Sup bro?" Doc asked.

"Not too much. Got back from San Diego a couple of hours ago. Gonna get fucked up tonight!"

"Yeah, what are we doing?"

"I don't know, I'm still waiting on Éclair to call."

"I figured you'd be hanging out with your chick. You're leaving her all alone on Saturday night." Doc shook his head. "Shame."

"She'll be alright. And I could use getting drunk and bull shitting with you guys. I mean, I like Penelope and all, but I can talk to you guys. Know what I mean?"

"Yeah I get ya, man."

"I mean, I don't think I *could* talk to her about a lot of stuff, and if I did she wouldn't understand."

"I feel ya. It's like, how the hell do you tell your chick that you just watched some guys burn to death and didn't do anything to help them?"

"Doc, didn't you shoot those dudes?"

"Oh yeah," he said and laughed.

"Dude, dude! You remember that time Fonzie went to throw smoke and we got hit with an RPG and he dropped the grenade into the truck and smoked us out?"

"Yeah man! It looked we all got gang fucked by Grimace!"

"And why the fuck was he trying to throw purple smoke anyway?" I smiled at the mountain behind Camp Margarita and drank my beer. "Those were the good old days, man."

"Yeah, but one day we're going to look back and think *these* were the good days. You know how the military is. We're going to get out and go home then we're never going to see each other again but for once a decade."

I knew Doc was right. I didn't say anything, I just lit another cigarette.

"So I told you I'm dating this chick, right?" Doc said.

"Filipino?"

"I already told you?"

"No, but I think I've only seen you with one chick that wasn't a little island person."

"So I've been stereotyped?"

"I'm not saying anything's wrong with it. Whatever floats your boat, man. I'm just waiting for you to come out of the closet."

"Why would you think I'm gay?"

"Because you're in the navy."

"HA HA!" Doc said sarcastically. "So I'm out with this chick Kristy a couple of nights ago…"

"Dodging out of field day?"

"Yeah." Doc laughed. "So we're hanging out in Vista and…"

"Hold on a minute Doc." My phone was buzzing in my pocket. "Hey it's Éclair." I pressed the answer button. "What's up dude?"

"Dude where are you?" Éclair sounded scared.

"I'm out in the parking lot with Doc. You alright, man?"

"No dude, I need you to come to my room."

"What's the matter, man?"

"Just come down, man, and bring Doc, I fucked up real bad."

"Alright dude hold on." I put the phone back in my pocket.

"What up?" Doc asked concerned.

"I don't know man, he's freaking out."

We walked down and knocked on Éclair's door. He yanked open the door and pulled us in.

"What's going on, man?" Doc asked.

"Okay..." Éclair was visibly nervous, he was shaking and stuttering, his clothes were put on sloppy, and his room was trashed. "So you know how I had that dating profile on the Internet?"

"Yeah?" I answered. "So what?"

"Did you accidentally get herpes from a tranny?" Doc joked.

"No." Éclair looked at the floor. His eyes were bulging out of his head and he started to shake more violently. "I stopped using it because the chicks were retarded and I figured Ginny would be enough."

Doc and I looked at each other confused then back at Éclair. "Okay?"

"Well Kelsey fucking found me on there."

"I wouldn't worry about that," Doc said and smirked. "I mean, so what if Ginny leaves you, there's other chicks out there."

"Awe man that sucks!" I laughed. "Is she going to tell Ginny about it?"

"Kelsey said she wouldn't tell Ginny if I fucked her."

"Okay," I cheered. "Isn't that kind of what you were going for anyway?"

Éclair's eyes turned red and tears rolled down his eyes. "She came over…" He stopped, his heavy breath was getting in the way of speech.

"Damn dude, it couldn't have been that bad," I said heartlessly. "What'd she throw on a dildo and butt fuck you with it?"

Doc looked over at me and said, "Na dude, he probably just feels really ashamed of himself for cheating on his fiancé and he's trying to talk to us about it and you're being a dick." Doc put his hand on Éclair's shoulder. "If you need to let it out man, let it out. What happened next?"

"Kelsey. She came over and we started making out, then we got naked and started bangin. Then I started choking her…"

"Sounds like a good time to me dude. That chick had some big ol' titties!"

Doc shot me a dirty look. "Okay, well I mean, so you had freaky sex with your fiancé's best friend, it's not the end of the world."

Éclair looked Doc in the eye, reached behind him, and ripped the sheets off the bed. Kelsey laid there, her face was contorted, her eyes lopsided, and she was completely motionless.

Doc and I stared at her in horror.

"Dude, is she…"

"Yeah," Éclair answered before I could say, "…dead?"

"HOLY SHIT DUDE!" Doc screamed.

"Doc! Keep it down!" I grabbed the bed sheet and threw it back over Kelsey's corpse.

"I don't know what to do," Éclair cried, not looking back at the body.

"Well you obviously knew to make us accomplices!" I barked at him.

Éclair glared at me.

"I'm sorry, dude."

"Well, we can cut her up and feed her to coyotes," Doc said and scratched his head.

"Really Doc?" I said judgmentally. "That's the first thing that comes to mind?"

"Well, let's hear your ideas jack ass."

I suggested, "Dump her in the sewer?"

"Did you just watch *Fifty Shades of Dave?*"

"Yeah. I missed the ending though."

"Awe dude, that's the best part. Dave goes and…"

"DUDES!" Éclair cut us off. "I got a dead bitch in my room!"

We stood there silently for a few moments before Doc suggested, "How about we bury her on an impact range?"

"Huh?" Éclair croaked.

"Think about it—put her in an impact area. People don't go through there a lot because artillery's always blasting the place and if we bury her shallow enough coyotes will dig her up and tear her apart and a triple seven will blow her into tiny little pieces."

"Okay, good idea," I started, "but how do we know they're not shooting right now? I don't want to get blown into hamburger meat trying to get rid of a dead chick."

"Well, to be fair it wouldn't be the first time you got hit with an artillery round," Éclair tried to cheer himself up.

Doc and I mean-mugged him. "You're funny, dude," I bit.

"And to be fair this isn't the first time you've killed anyone," Doc shot at Éclair.

"Yeah but that was different," Éclair defended himself.

"Okay so we put in her an impact range," I started. "How do we get her out of the barracks?" I thought for a second. "We could stuff her in a sea bag."

"I don't think she'll fit in a sea bag," Doc noted.

"Okay we cut her up and put her in two sea bags." I looked at Éclair. "You got any?"

"Just one," he said.

"Okay Éclair, you go to the PX and buy a few sea bags and bleach. Just hang out in your car for a few minutes first to pull yourself together. Doc and I'll stuff her into garbage bags."

Éclair nodded his head and started out the door.

"And use cash."

With Éclair gone I turned to Doc. "You cool, man?"

"Yeaaa," he forced himself to say.

"Yeah, me either," I mumbled. "Go get your KA-BAR real quick and some trash bags. I'll stand post."

Doc ran up to his room and I sat with my back to the door. "Goddamn it," I sighed. I leaned over, opened Éclair's nightstand, and pulled out his KA-BAR. Doc returned and I locked the door. I went to the bed and put my arms under Kelsey's shoulders, Doc grabbed her feet. We hauled her to the bathroom and placed her in the shower.

The bathrooms in the barracks had a decent-sized shower. They were about as long as a bath tub but just a flat faux porcelain floor.

"How you wanna do this, man?" Doc asked.

"I kinda wanna fuck her first."

326

"Really, dude?" Doc shouted.

"I'm kidding."

"I *know* you're kidding! But seriously!"

"Well I didn't fucking choke her out."

"That just makes this more fucked up!"

"Well, shit! How do we even know she's dead? Maybe she's just unconscious."

Doc leaned into the shower and grabbed Kelsey's face. He felt for a pulse and did something else with her eyes and mouth. "No, she's fucking dead, man."

"Well we should probably cut her at the joints."

"Why not just in half?"

"Because then we're going to have to deal with all the guts. You know when you're skinning a buck and there's that sack all the organs are in?"

"I'm pretty sure the internal organs of a deer and that of a human fucking being are just a *little* bit different."

"But guts," I argued.

"Okay, okay, we'll get her at the joints."

"Cool, I'll get the arms."

"The fuck you will! I'm not cutting the legs off with her pussy that close. It already smells bad enough!"

"You're a needy bitch, you know that, Doc?"

"Fuck you, dude!"

"You're the medical professional! You should be doing *all* of this!"

"I'm a corpsman not a fucking surgeon! And you have more

experience cutting people up than I do!"

"Doc, if you don't start cutting legs off I'm going to start fucking her!"

"I'll cut off *one* leg." He raised a finger. "One! And an arm. You get the other side. Fair?"

Doc and I each grabbed an arm and started sawing into Kelsey's shoulders.

"Why the fuck are *we* doing this anyway?" Doc bitched.

"Because we don't want Éclair to go to jail, and he would do it for us."

Blood started to pool in the shower. I had cut about halfway through the shoulder. "Doc, you ever listen to Slayer?"

"Shut the *fuck* up, Hank!"

I started to sing 'Spill the Blood.'

Doc chopped through the rest of Kelsey's arm and slapped me in the face with her hand.

I looked back at Doc and said, "Really? And you're saying I'm the one who's screwed up."

"You *are* the one who's screwed up! Talking about fucking her and shit."

"I'm still down for that!" I joked. "Her pussy's still intact." I picked up Kelsey's other arm and rubbed her clit in a circular motion with her fingers. "Huh? *HUUUUUH?*"

Doc kept a vexed look on his face, gritted his teeth, and started slicing away at Kelsey's leg. "You're going to *fucking* Hell, dude."

"I'm just fucking around, dude." I started cutting away at the other leg.

"Yeah, and that's fucked up."

"Alright, alright."

We finished cutting off Kelsey's limbs and wrapped them tightly inside of garbage bags. We placed them by the toilet and turned on the water in the shower. I think we did a pretty good job about not leaving much blood, we didn't even get more than a few splatters on our clothes.

We walked out to the catwalk and lit cigarettes. Doc had a blank stare. "You know, I always thought the most fucked up thing I'd ever do was something in Iraq."

"And what was that?"

"I don't know, just *something*. I really never saw myself doing this."

"Yeah but it's for a friend, and he'd legitimately, probably do it for us."

Doc sighed and said, "Yeah…"

"Hey Doc?"

"Yeah man?"

"Do you think there's enough time before Éclair comes back to cut off her face, wear it like a mask, and jump out and scare him?"

"Dude, you seriously need to see a psychiatrist."

"Come *on,* Doc." I tickled his arm with my index finger.

Doc smiled a little bit.

"Would you fuck me? I'd fuck me! I'd fuck me *so* hard!"

Doc chuckled with a slight hint of insanity and ran his hand over his head. "We're fucking going to Hell. We're going straight to Hell, we're not passing 'Go' and we're not collecting two hundred dollars."

I'm sure Doc was convinced I was a psychopath, but if I hadn't found a way to laugh I probably would have had to kill myself out of disgust. I had the feeling that I needed to take a shower, but knew no mater how much I scrubbed, whatever I was trying to get rid of wouldn't wash off. Water can only clean so much, comedy blankets the internal wounds.

The Camaro rolled into the parking lot and Éclair came back carrying sea bags. We stuffed Kelsey's trash bag clothed body parts into the olive green bags and carried them to my Jeep.

"So where are we taking these?" Doc asked.

"I'm thinking Case Springs." I jumped in the driver's seat.

Doc rode shotgun and Éclair got in the back with the bags. We took off towards the Pendleton Mountains as the sun set over the hills behind us. We pulled off Basilone Road and I put the Jeep in four-wheel drive. I stopped when we were deep in the mountain range surrounded by craters.

I pulled out the shovel I kept in the back for camping and we took turns digging. It was my turn to dig. I lifted the earth from the ground and put it in a nice little pile next to the hole.

"What are we going to do now?" Doc asked himself.

"Well, we could either run away to Mexico or join the mafia. My vote's for Mexico, the chicks are hotter." I flung out more dirt.

"I'm probably going to drink myself to death," Éclair murmured.

"No seriously, what the *fuck* are we going to do now?" Doc shouted.

"Get seriously fucked up." I eyeballed the hole and crawled out. "I think this is good enough." I handed Éclair the shovel and Doc and I kicked in the bags.

A couple hours later the Jeep was parked at the peak of Mount Margarita, or Recon Hill, or the Dragon's Back, depending on who you ask. It was a pain in the ass to get the Jeep up there, even in four-wheel drive. The path was almost vertical and not very wide.

Éclair, Doc, and I each had a bottle of something strong. We drank and smoked sitting in the dirt a few feet from the Jeep looking over Camp Margarita. We just drank in silence staring at the buildings below.

"Okay, so I've been thinking," Doc started. "We can't tell anyone about this."

"No shit, really?" Éclair barked back.

"Well people always get caught and go to prison because they tell other people," Doc continued.

"Yeah but we all did *something*," I grumbled.

"But we can't tell anyone *else*." Doc had probably lit eight cigarettes and only taken a combined total of ten puffs the entire time we were on the mountain. His current one was burning into the filter.

Éclair looked over at Doc. "Dude, I'm about to marry a girl and I can't even really talk to her about the war. Who the fuck am I going to tell?"

"We at least have each other to talk to about it." I put out my cigarette. "Shit, we already only really talk about Iraq with people who were fucking there. Just treat this like that. If we just talk to each other about it, it probably won't drive us insane."

"There's already something seriously fucking wrong with you, dude," Doc barked.

I rolled my eyes. "And I take it you're fine?"

"No I'm not fine! I just cut up Éclair's fuck buddy!"

"She wasn't my fuck buddy. That bitch was blackmailing me!" Éclair shouted.

"Then why are we so upset?" I asked. "I mean, obviously there was something wrong with that bitch, she was blackmailing people and I don't think I've spent more than an hour with her and not seen her go find some random dick to suck. Shit, we probably all got syphilis from dealing with her. Fuck her, dude. Fuck her right in the pussy. She was a fucking asshole. I'm not saying that she deserved to get chopped up and thrown in a shallow grave, but are we *really* missing anything from her not being around?"

"Ehh, I guess," Doc mumbled and turned his head to Éclair. "You should probably burn your sheets and delete your online dating profiles."

"Ginny's gonna freak out." Éclair shook his head.

"No she's not. How the fuck would she even know?" I lit another cigarette. "Just pretend you haven't seen her."

"And what, just remember that sometimes you have to chain smoke your problems away?"

"That's the spirit." I patted Éclair's back.

I drove us back down the mountain at about two miles an hour. The terrain was rough and I was plastered, I didn't want to roll the Jeep down a cliff and get killed. I parked the Jeep next to the Mustang and racked out in Doc's room that night.

In the morning Doc and I went to make sure Éclair was alright. We peered through the window and he was passed out on what used to be my rack. I smoked a cigarette with Doc and drove to the 101 Café for breakfast.

19 GLÆDWINE'S GULF WAR

I got to a new level of fucked up every day of the next few weeks. I made sure to avoid Gunny Chanceworth's hangover witch hunting at work. I spent most of my time hiding out in Staff Sergeant Bistro's office or on the smoke deck.

"So are you doing alright, Allensworth?" Bistro asked.

"Yeah Staff Sergeant, things have just been a little rough."

"You've come in to work reeking of alcohol every day this week." Bistro didn't say that in a judgmental tone, but a concerned one.

"Yeah, well I've been getting hammered every night."

"Any specific reason?"

"Na, just drink'n for the sake of it," I lied.

"Do you think you might want to see the substance abuse officers about it?"

"Oh hell no, Staff Sergeant. With the way the Marine Corps is kicking people out nowadays? They'd Ad Sep me in a week."

"They're not kicking people out for that kind of thing."

"Staff Sergeant, they're kicking people out for anything they can. It's like this every time a war ends. 'Thanks for your service, but we don't want the problems we made for you, now get the fuck out.' Then the Corps is too small when the next war comes along. Fuckers."

"I think you'd be alright."

"I don't. There was a guy at my old unit, he was thinking about killing himself. He didn't do anything stupid, he went to try to get help. He talked to the chaplain and the psyches and all. They decided he was a lost cause and separated him without putting him through any kind of therapy. The fucking officers are always talking about how we need to help each other and if we have a problem to tell someone. All that really does is identifying ourselves as targets for separation. The fucking Marine Corps is making people into monsters and then refusing to take responsibility for it. So if that kid ever takes himself out, it will be okay because it won't be on the Marine Corps' books and the commandant won't have to answer to congress about it."

"That is kind of fucked up."

"That's why good Marines are getting chewed up. We have problems because we're fucking human beings and we've done some pretty inhuman shit and it messes with our fucking head, but if we try to get professional help, Uncle Sam will say, 'Oh, okay. Look, we'll help you!' They'll help us alright. They'll help us get the fuck off the numbers so we're not their problem anymore. Cock suckers. Marines are going to continue down the path they were going, it's not like the government is actually helping any of them."

"Alright. I know Gunny gets pissed about people being hungover, but as long as you're not drunk I don't really care. But would you at least find a way to quit smelling like alcohol at work?"

"I'll figure something out, Staff Sergeant."

Chow time rolled around and I went to the PX to grab a sandwich and a Coke. When I came back to the building I drove around the back to see if Glædwine was on the smoke deck. I'd started to develop a small crush on her. I felt a little bad about it because I had Penelope, but I figured I couldn't help feelings and as long as I didn't act on it, it was okay. Besides that, Glædwine was married and a junior Marine, so doing *anything* with her would kill my career and my personal life and I'd probably go to the brig. At the very least I'd lose a few stripes. I'd never say anything to her about it, but that didn't mean I couldn't enjoy her company during smoke breaks.

There was a group of five or six Marines on the smoke deck. I parked behind and walked up with my chow.

"Good afternoon, Sergeant," they said between their jokes.

Sergeant Rainer, Corporals Neilson, Arnold, and Gint, and Lance Corporals Glædwine and Schrub all sat at the rickety picnic table smoking and joking.

"So anyway," Schrub continued a story which I missed the beginning of, "We were on the firing line at Parris Island, it's freezing cold out and everybody's huddled together. This kid, a few ammo cans down from me, kept a round from when he was firing. He loaded it straight into the chamber without a magazine and put the barrel in his mouth and pulled the trigger. The guy's Kevlar flew off his head. And one of the drill instructors started running to the kid. It looked like he was running in slow motion screaming, 'NOOOO!' When the DI gets to the kid he immediately starts giving him CPR. We were all just staring at him; I wanted to tell the DI that the kid was missing half his head and CPR wasn't going to work out for him, but we got pulled off the line and just sat in the squad bay the rest of the night staring at the wall."

"You know what my favorite part of boot camp is?" Rainer asked. "Not being such a boot that all my stories come from Parris Island."

They all laughed.

I started eating my sandwich.

"But anyway," Rainer continued. "When I was in Afghanistan there was a hit on a Taliban compound way out towards Herat. The Air Force sent a C-130 to go annihilate this place, I mean like a biblical amount of destruction. The platoon I was with goes to do a BDA the next day and the villagers all come up to us saying that we had to save them from the dragon. We were like, 'What dragon? The fuck are you talking about?' Then the villagers tell us that a dragon came out of the mountain the day before and burnt down half their village."

"What a bunch of dumb asses," Corporal Gint said and laughed.

"Na, that makes sense," I butted in. "I mean, if the most advanced thing you've seen in your life, besides and AK47 or a cell phone, was a bicycle, and a big giant black thing comes to your village from behind a mountain and destroys the countryside with fire, you'd probably think it was a dragon too."

"I guess," Gint agreed.

"People outside of the developed world don't live anything like we do," Glædwine added. "When I was in Jordan the people were still living in clay huts. They had their cell phones, but besides that and some metal pots and pans, it was just rugs and dirt. People managed, but it's not luxurious like it is here. Impoverished Americans live like royalty compared to a lot of other places in the world."

"What were you doing in Jordan?" I asked.

"I was there with my dad for his work," she replied. "Everyone there did everything they could to sell people trinkets."

I chuckled a little. "When I was in Kuwait, on the way home from my second deployment, there was this kid that came up to me and said, 'Mista, mista, buy something!' He had a hand full of bracelets and beads and shit. I didn't want to spend anything, so I told him, 'Sorry, I don't have any cash.' This little shit laughs at me and said, 'Ha, ha, you don't have any money!' So I pointed at him and said, 'HA, HA, YOU LIVE IN A THIRD-WORLD COUNTRY!' He got *so* pissed off. It was great."

Half of them laughed, the others looked at me like I had a dick growing out of my forehead.

"Kuwait's not really a third-world country," Glædwine said. "They actually have a lot of money there."

"Yeah, but when it's reasonable to assume that pretty much everyone there has had sex with a goat there's something wrong with the place," I said.

"Sergeant, you've obviously never been to Kentucky," she said back.

"HEY!" Schrub shouted in protest.

"Yeah, Glædwine!" Rainer snorted. "Kentucky folks fuck pigs; it's different!"

Glædwine shrugged and took a drag off her smoke.

"Well either way, we beat them back to the Stone Age," Rainer said and smirked.

"Erroneous there, Devil Dog," I jested sarcastically. "Bombing someone back to the Stone Age implied that they left it."

"Alright I'll give you that," Rainer ceded.

"Yeah, but we didn't really win," stated Glædwine.

"Excuse me?" I put down my sandwich.

"A super power hasn't won a war against an insurgency since the Peloponnesian War," she continued.

"What?" Rainer looked confused. "That's bull shit. What about the Banana Wars?"

"Those wars are actually still being fought, only it's the DEA not the military fighting them. Same people and ideals."

"What about the French Underground? The Nazi's were kicking the shit out of them," Rainer added.

"Nazi's lost."

"Yeah but not to the French. I'm pretty sure the Russians were the ones storming Berlin."

"Nazis still didn't win the war," Glædwine shrugged.

"Alright, well how didn't we win Iraq or Afghanistan?" I inquired.

"Afghanistan has been in near constant combat since Alexander of Macedonia left. And Iraq when?"

"We were winning when I left." I lit a cigarette.

"Yeah but the war's not over, we just quit fighting it."

"That doesn't mean we lost. The government lost. The Army and the Marines kicked the shit out of everything there. Fuck, the battalion on my first deployment killed almost twelve hundred Taliban and we lost less than thirty Marines. I mean, there were a lot more casualties than that, but only twenty-six of them went home in a box."

"Well if you go by that argument, Sergeant, we also won Vietnam."

"We *did* win Vietnam!" I growled.

"Could you defend your argument, Sergeant?"

"Yeah, within six months of the Tet Offensive we completely destroyed the Viet Cong, but during the actual fight Walter Cronkite got on TV and said we lost the war back in 1968. That killed morale for the US population and congress wouldn't let the fucking military win. It was the same shit in Afghanistan. Fucking Afghan could have been over and done with in six months if the god damned government would keep their fucking dirty fingers out of the military and let us do our fucking job! How the fuck are they going to send us over there and tell us to win a fucking war then tell us that there are fucking rules? Fuck them! A fucking war is supposed to be so fucking brutal that the other side says, 'Fuck it. I'm out.' But we're not doing that. We're shooting people and breaking shit then rebuilding the fuckers' villages to be better than when we came in, and giving people medical treatment and food, and it's like, 'No fuckers! This is war!' The last person that fought a war the right fucking way was Genghis Kahn! Tell people to quit being stupid and if they keep it up kill *everyone* and burn *everything*! And you only have to do that once or twice then other people stop fucking with you."

"Well you can't kill *everyone*," Rainer interjected.

"The *fuck* we can't! No quarter, no prisoners. If they want to live they better find another place to hide and if they fuck with us from there, then we fucking go there and fucking kill everyone the fuck there too!"

"Sergeant," Glædwine started. "What about situations like Germany and Japan where the governments declared war against the will of the people?"

"I would have killed the fuck out of those fucks too if I were in charge. If they didn't want to feel our wrath then they would have revolted, hung their leaders, and said, 'Hey America, we killed the people responsible, we're sorry, don't kill us.' But if we got to them first then I'd have lakes of blood. Japan would be West Hawaii and Germany would be East Pennsylvania. Then there wouldn't be a North Korea or a fucking China, and Afghanistan would be Texas Two."

Glædwine half smiled and said, "Sergeant, as a Texan I take offense to that."

I rolled my eyes at her.

"What about Vietnam, Iraq, and Iran?" she asked.

"Vietnam never did anything to us, nor did Iraq, so we wouldn't have fucking gone in the first place. Then *if* we did the Iraq thing properly we probably wouldn't have done Iran."

"But Korea would have still happened?"

I grunted, "EH," and pulled out a cigarette.

"So you believe in total war, but don't think we should go unless it's warranted?"

"Yup, and I don't think Iraq was warranted."

"Well the Gulf War was about breaking up OPEC. Saddam Hussein never did anything to us," Glædwine stated.

"And Iraq the second time was about making sure Saddam didn't change the oil trade currency to the Euro and thus destroy the US economy. Bush told that fucker not to fuck with him then Saddam was like, 'I'm going to trade oil in *not* dollars.' And then Bush dismantled the Iraqi government and executed Hussein on TV to give the rest of the Middle East a warning about what would happen. America's the new empire. I just wish that we'd own up to it and really start imperializing shit instead of pussy footing around trying not to hurt people's feelings."

"That sounds like an elaborate conspiracy theory, Sergeant."

"Whichever it was, the reason America is starting to lose wars is because the fucking media twists the facts to make people think what they want and then the people and congress bitch out even after the military kicks whoever's ass it is. I mean shit, in the early two thousands when we invaded Iraq the news kept talking about the terrible death toll the war was taking and more people were dying from gang violence in Detroit than in the fucking war! Fuck, I don't remember anyone complaining about fighting the Germans. They didn't fucking bomb Pearl Harbor. North Korea never attacked us, neither did Vietnam, all three of those wars were started by Democrats and the media didn't protest. Clinton started bombing Bosnia without the UNs approval and nobody complained about it, *but as soon as a Republican does it* everybody loses their shit! The fucking news was complaining about how long the fucking war took but it took more fucking time for Ted Kennedy to call the police after he crashed his Oldsmobile into a fucking river and killed that chick than it did for the First Marine Division and the Army's Third Infantry Division to kill Saddam's Republican Guard! That shit pisses me the fuck off! Fuck! I have to get permits and shit to buy and keep a fucking gun that the Second Amendment guarantees my right to, but any fuck with a microphone can just abuse the shit out of the First Amendment with no fucking consequence! God fucking dammit!"

"Sergeant," Glædwine snuffed her cigarette. "You say 'fuck' more that anyone else on the planet."

"Fucking so?"

"Just pointing it out Sergeant." Glædwine smiled.

20 INEBRIANCE

Wednesday night I went to go check on Éclair—make sure he didn't off himself or anything stupid like that. I was still jolted from the Kelsey thing, so he couldn't have been feeling good. When I rolled up to the barracks he was by his Camaro smoking a cigarette.

"Sup, dude?" Éclair stared at the pavement below.

"Not much man, just gettin off work." I stepped out of the Jeep next to Éclair and lit a Lucky's. "How ya doin?"

"I'm still a little messed up, but I'm doing better than I thought I'd be."

"That's good."

"Yeah. I'm going over to Ginny's tonight. She hasn't said anything about Kelsey yet. She said she's been talking to Penelope a lot, they're trying to do something this weekend."

"Yeah, Penelope said something about that."

"I'm just wondering when people are going to notice she's missing and what if they come looking my way for her?"

"I don't know, man. She had her own apartment right? I don't know how much she talked to her parents so that they'd be wondering, or her school or work or anything."

"I guess we'll see, man."

"Just act normal around Ginny and if she says anything about Kelsey just shrug it off."

"And if something triggers insanity I'll just blame the war, man." Éclair smiled.

"That is such a cop out. But I like it. I'm going to use that."

"My moral compass is spinning on all this, man."

"My moral compass is in the Bermuda Triangle."

About a month went without incident. It was late August and Thom threw a party at Spike's for Penelope's birthday. Ginny and Éclair came, Doc brought his new squeeze, Kristy. Instead of just a nice shirt, Éclair, Doc, and I wore suits. They weren't extravagant, but it was better than jeans. The band was playing a song about shenanigans in Chicago.

Penelope had most of her friends there, she was short in comparison. I hadn't met a majority of them before. Penelope was five ten or eleven, and most of her Virescent friends were over six three.

I was sitting on a stool, resting my back on the bar. My tie was loosened and I was sipping on a rum and Coke. Doc and Kristy were still in their cute and flirty phase of their relationship.

Éclair flung himself onto the barstool next to me. "Sup brother!"

"Not much man, how's it hangin?" I took a swig of my drink.

"Eh. Fucking Ginny's pissed off because I'm 'too drunk already.'"

"She'll be alright, man."

"Eh," Éclair huffed. "Is that Doc's new chick?"

"Yeah, Kristy, I think. I've had like one conversation with her."

"She's cute."

"I guess. I'm not really into Asians."

"Filipinos are Pacific Islanders, man."

"Okay, well either way it's too close to Thailand and I'm not attracted to chicks with dicks."

"What about that time…"

"Let's not go there, man. I bailed out in time."

Éclair laughed. "Sure."

"Dick."

"Hey!" Éclair leaned over me to Doc and Kristy. "I'm Éclair." He extended his hand.

"That's a weird name." Kristy stuck her hand out to shake.

"No one calls him by his first name besides his girlfriend," Doc said between them.

"What's your first name?" Kristy asked with a curious look.

"Richard." Éclair took his hand back and grabbed his drink.

"Okay Dick, I can see why." Kristy laughed.

"Hey Doc," I said and chuckled. "She's cool. She can hang out."

Ginny walked past us. If she did notice us she was pretending not to. Éclair grabbed her wrist, pulled her in, and wrapped his hands around her waist.

"Ginny Ginny Ginny Ginny."

Ginny was obviously annoyed. "Richard! You're drunk."

"So are you," Éclair protested.

"I'm not *that* drunk."

Éclair incoherently flapped his lips and rubbed them on Ginny's shoulder over her dress.

Ginny tried not to laugh. "Fine, fine." She kissed him on the temple and demanded, "Buy me a drink."

Éclair ordered two White Russians. When the bartender delivered the drinks Ginny said, "I like how they dress like they're in an old western." The bartender uniform was black slacks, a white collared shirt, and armbands with clamps. They all had their hair slicked back and most of them had thick mustaches. "Kelsey said she hooked up with one of these guys a while back."

"Yeah?" Éclair asked nervously. "What's she been up to recently? I haven't seen her around."

"I don't know." Ginny sipped her drink. "I haven't seen her either. Last time I heard from her she said she was going to hang out with you and that there was something she said she wanted to talk to me about later that night."

"Dude, that was a crazy night," I butted in. Éclair glared at me.

"Oh yeah?"

"Yeah, she came down to the barracks and we were all playing beer pong on the smoke deck. Kelsey got super fucked up and started to give this dude a hand job then she walked off with him," I lied through my rum.

"That sounds like her." Ginny smiled.

"Yeah, she seemed like she had some serious daddy issues."

"Maybe. But it's been a while since I've talked to her. I should probably call her tomorrow, see what she's been up to."

"She probably took up a room on third deck at the barracks and pays her rent in pussy," I joked.

Éclair downed his White Russian in one gulp and waved down the bartender.

"Oh! Allensworth," Ginny started. "Did I tell you about my boss yet?"

"No?"

"I think you and Richard would like to meet him sometime. He's this old Vietnam vet."

"Okay?"

"He usually runs in the morning and showers at work. I saw him the other day in the back on accident without a shirt…"

"He didn't have a shirt or you didn't have a shirt on?" I asked.

"*He* didn't have a shirt. Anyway, he has the same Marine tattoo you and Richard have, the diamond on your chest. Except his 'one' is filled in red."

"That's pretty neat," Éclair said in a break between sucking down drinks. "Does he have a palm tree and a seven like I do too?"

"No, he has a bunch of skulls there. He says each skull was from a confirmed kill in 'Nam' and he always talks about 'Killing Fucking Charlie' and 'Slaying poon.'"

"Now that's a man after my heart!" I put down my drink and searched my pockets for my cigarettes.

"What's *really* weird though," Ginny turned to Éclair. "Is that he looks *just* like your dad."

"Maybe he's his long lost brother," Éclair responded.

"Well his name's Erick LaClare."

Éclair gave Ginny a funny look.

"Yeah, Richard Éclair, Erick LaClare… weird right?"

"Sounds like a ghost story to me," Kristy interrupted from behind.

"I don't think we met. I'm Ginny." She extended her hand.

"Kristy." She looked back to Doc and said, "I'm just meeting all your friends tonight, huh?"

"But anyway," Ginny continued. "I'm pretty sure his favorite words are gook, nigger, muj, and fucknut."

"That's kind of weird that a Vietnam guy uses the word muj," I observed.

"Yeah, but he's usually pretty nice to me and the other girls that work there so he can say whatever he wants. You guys should come in sometime and meet him."

"Sounds good. I'll be back." I left an empty glass on the bar and found the men's room. When I walked back out to the main area Penelope waved me down. She was sitting with a group of Virescents I hadn't seen before. I dragged over an empty chair and sat down.

"Hank this is Fay, Amel, Rohn, Frince, and Junde." She introduced the others at the table.

We exchanged hellos and they poured me a glass of Hesperides.

Fay had straight shoulder length hair that covered the right quarter of her face. It was so black that light didn't reflect from it. I couldn't make out where one clump of hair ended and another started. I wondered if it was that way in the sunlight too, or if that was because the lights were so low. It couldn't have been that, Doc had black hair and I could make out strands in his. Fay had a black vest over a white blouse and was relaxing into Frince's shoulder.

"So Penelope tells me you're a soldier," Fay tried to start a conversation in her thick accent.

"Did she?" I turned to Penelope. "Soldier, huh?"

Penelope smiled over a shrug drinking her wine.

I wanted to tell her, 'Believe it or not I *do* like it when you're being a bitch, but there *is* a limit,' but I settled for a dirty look.

"Is that not right?" Fay asked inquisitively.

"I'm not a soldier, I'm a Marine."

"What's the difference?"

I started to wonder if Fay was being sincere or if Penelope put her up to this for her amusement.

"Soldiers parachute in and fight, Marines come in from the water."

"So you're a sea soldier?"

Penelope sported a shit eating grin and put her hand on my thigh. Now I knew she was screwing with me.

"If anything we're more like sailors."

"Oh?" Frince smirked. "How so?"

"Yeah, you know, travel the world…" I reached for my Lucky's. "Meet all kinds of new and interesting people…"

Fay and Frince nodded their heads.

I pulled a cigarette out. "Fuck the women raw in all their holes…"

Their smug smirks turned to grimaces.

I flicked open my lighter and said, "Then hit the beach, stomp on people's throats, and stab them in the fucking neck for a paycheck." I lit the cigarette.

The table was silent. Penelope leaned in and with an embarrassed voice said, "I'm sorry, Hank's dru…"

I slammed the table with my fist and roared laughing. "COME ON GUYS! I'M FUCKING WITH YOU! IT'S A PARTY! LAUGH!"

They looked at each other and burst into nervous laughter, except

Penelope who looked at me unsettled.

"That was good, Hank!" Frince chuckled. "You really had us going!"

"Yeah man, it was funny. Pour me another glass of this wine." I handed him my glass and leaned into Penelope's ear. "Don't *ever* have your friends do that again. Quit calling me 'soldier.' I'm a *fucking* Marine."

"Hank, it was a joke," she apologized.

"I didn't think it was fucking funny."

"It's just a *word,* Hank."

"No it's not." I looked around the table, everyone went back to having their own conversations. "I'm going to go make sure Doc and Éclair are staying out of trouble."

I stood up and said, "Excuse me." I buttoned my jacket and walked towards Doc and Éclair. I could feel Penelope staring at me from behind. I heard her start saying something to her friends about Iraq.

I leaned on the bar behind Ginny and Éclair and looked over at the barkeeper. "Hey, Thom."

"Hank."

"Mind pouring me a shot of Jager and a glass of whiskey?"

"No problem." Thom started mixing my drinks.

"Hey, so how'd you get into this?"

"Bartending?"

"Yeah."

"It's fun. I did it while we were on the ship and it seemed easy to get into when we got to Earth."

Thom handed me my tumbler of whiskey. I swallowed it in one

gulp and spun my finger for another one. "Please."

Thom placed a bottle on the bar. "Already one of those nights?"

"Every night's one of those nights."

"Would you like to talk about it?"

"Sure, Thom. Why the fuck not."

"What's on your mind?" Thom poured the whiskey in my glass straight.

"Just shit. People don't get shit. I'm not like, fucking trying to force things on people, but, it's like 'fuck dude.' Ya know?"

"No. Absolutely nothing about what you said was coherent."

I stared at Thom through my bloodshot eyes as I downed my whiskey. As he refilled the glass I said, "You're a waiter, right?"

"No, I'm a bartender, there's a difference," he stated calmly.

"Exactly. You sister keeps calling me a fucking waiter."

Thom shrugged with one shoulder. "You don't have to get angry about it."

"If I could help that Thom, we wouldn't be having this conversation. Now would we?"

"I suppose not."

I raised my eyebrows.

"But warriors are always proud, even when they're humble."

I grabbed the shot of Jager that had been sitting there. "Thom." I took the shot. "You're alright."

"Thank you."

"Hey, what do you guys do for birthdays anyway? Break piñatas and eat cake?"

"We have dinner and there's a toast to age. Sometimes there are games. It's usually just a big party."

"How do your years work, like with aligning with ours and all?"

"I don't know what exactly the math is, but a year on our old planet is six or eight of your years. It's becoming customary for us to wait until our birthday on our calendar and adopt whatever day it first falls onto *your* calendar as our new birthdate."

"That makes sense. What do you do for gifts? You guys have some weird thing you wrap presents in?"

"We don't do gifts."

"Really?" I queried.

"Really."

"What about on Christmas?"

"We were introduced to *that* concept in the last year."

"Ah, yeah. So no presents at all?"

"It's not our tradition."

"Well, alright."

"Would you like any thing else?"

"Na." I lit a cigarette and said, "Just leave me the booze."

Thom attended the other patrons. I drank the whiskey and smoked my Lucky's. I sat there angry at the world. I pulled out my phone and flipped though pictures I had on it of Iraq, Iran, and Afghanistan. I stopped on a photo of Doc, Kyle, Fowler, the Fonz, and me standing on top of our truck with our platoon's flag flying on the antenna. "Life was so much easier when all I had to do was not get killed."

Éclair turned around. He was sweaty, red, and his eyes were bloodshot. "You alright, man?"

"Yeah." I put my phone away and lit another cigarette. "Did you know Smedley Butler had an EGA tattoo from his collar bone to his hips?"

"Uh, no? But okay..."

"When he got his first Medal of Honor, the South America part of the tat was blown off trying to save his company commander's life."

"That's legit."

"When he got his second one he sent it back to congress and told them he didn't rate it."

"Okay that's bad ass."

"Then when he was a Lieutenant General they tried to court martial him for publically calling a foreign head of state a tyrant."

"I can see that."

"It was Mussolini."

Éclair squinted. "Well the big green weenie fucks everyone."

"Did you know that the Japanese commander at Tarawa said it would take a million men a thousand years to take the island and one Marine Division took it in less than seventy-two hours?"

Someone placed a hand on my shoulder. I turned to see Penelope.

"Heyyyyyyyyy." I leaned back onto the bar.

"Hey. Are you alright?" she asked.

"I'm alright." I took a drag.

"He's *fucking* drunk," Éclair butted in.

"I'm not *that* drunk," I protested.

353

"Well how drunk's *that* drunk?" Penelope asked.

"He's been over here blabbering about the Marine Corps for the last half hour. He's *fucking* drunk," Éclair said with a chuckle.

"How much *have* you had to drink?" Penelope asked.

From behind me Thom said, "A bottle of rum, a fifth of gin, eight shots of Jäger, a bottle of whiskey, plus whatever he had before he sat down."

"Narc."

"Christ, Hank! How high is your tolerance?" Penelope cried.

I rolled my eyes and shrugged.

"Well, can you walk?"

"Sure."

"Can we talk for a moment?"

"Sure."

I followed Penelope outside the club. It was warm out and the breeze felt nice on my skin.

"Hank," Penelope started. "I'm sorry about earlier."

"It's alright," I grumbled.

"No, I offended you." Penelope stared at the ground. She grabbed my hand and started rubbing my fingers. "And if I'm to be your lady then that's not right of me to do. I thought it was in good fun and misjudged." Her voice was heavy with shame.

I held an unsympathetic look on my face and stayed silent.

"I shan't do it again."

I pulled my hands away from hers and stuck them in my pockets.

Penelope started to sniffle. "It was only a joke, Hank," her trembling voice whispered.

I was wobbling in my attempt to stand up straight. I pulled out my lighter and smokes and set flame to one of the little white sticks.

Penelope crossed her arms and looked to the street, tears rolled down her face.

I reached into my coat pocket and pulled out a thin rectangular black box and extended my hand towards her.

"What's that?"

"Take it."

Her slender green fingers wrapped around the box. She removed the cover and looked inside. There was a rose pendant inside about the size of a quarter. The pedals were carved out of a ruby and the leaves from emerald. The rose hung on a silver chain.

Penelope wiped her eyes with the wrist of her free hand. "What's this?" she sobbed.

"It's your birthday present."

"What?" she asked confused.

"Don't tell me with all the TV you watch you don't know what a birthday present is."

"I'm sorry but I'm lost."

"It's something I got for you. For you to keep."

"It's mine?"

"From me."

"Like Christmas?"

"Yes."

"I don't have anything for you."

"Your birthday present is like Christmas just for you."

Penelope took a step into me and placed her head on my shoulder. I put a hand on her waist and wrapped my other arm over the back of her neck.

"Are you angry still?" she asked.

"I'm always angry."

Penelope half-snickered through a sob. "At me, you twat."

"Na." The hand around her shoulder held my cigarette. I pulled it to my face to puff. "You're one of the few people I don't want to hit in the face with a brick."

"I like you too, Hank. And I promise not to have my friends make fun of you again."

"Yeah."

"And the necklace is beautiful. No one's ever given me anything before."

I stroked her bright orange hair over her head and stopped at the back of her neck. I put my forehead on hers and said, "Let's go home, babe."

"My dad's inside. He said he wanted to meet you."

"Can it wait for another time?"

"And have us just disappear?"

"Why not?"

Penelope paused a moment. "Okay."

We grabbed a taxi and made our way to Penelope's apartment. We walked into her bedroom without bothering to turn on the light. She still held the little black box. I slid it from her hand. I swiped her hair from the back of her neck and latched on the silver chained rose necklace. Penelope rubbed it with her fingers and turned her head to mine, connecting our lips.

Penelope broke contact and kissed my neck. She pulled my jacket down to my elbows and undid the rest of my tie. I felt the blood start to build up in my loins. She ripped open my shirt and kissed her way south. Penelope unbuckled my belt and unbuttoned my trousers. My throbbing cock popped out; Penelope jerked her head back to dodge it. She wrapped her fingers around my shaft and looked up. Her left eye had begun to drift, it happened when she had been drinking too much.

She smiled and said, "You've been waiting for me!" and wrapped her lips around the head of my penis.

I put my hands behind Penelope's ears and bit my bottom lip. She milked my cock like an Amish butter churner. I pulled her head to my crotch and stuck my cock down her throat.

Penelope gagged and yanked her head back, but before she could pull my dick all of the way out of her mouth she vomited, violently. The hot ooze covered everything below my hips.

She turned her head up and with a pathetic sounding voice said, "I'm…"

Before she could say, "Sorry," the stench of her stomach fluid mixing with my inebriated state made me eject hot vomit full force in her face causing her to vomit again, all over my balls. I flailed down on top of her and started puking uncontrollably.

She did the same.

We laid there for a few minutes, unable to do anything except spew out the hot contents of our stomachs. We squirmed in a pool of our collective bile. It was hell—it was fucking hell. Penelope hurled and her whole body contorted, she accidentally kicked me in the torso, repeatedly.

I staggered to my knees and tried to lock my elbow into Penelope's arm. Our skin was too slick from the filth and I slipped. Penelope's head hit the floor and she let out a loud grunt. I grabbed her again, this time putting both arms under her armpits and locking my fingers together. I started dragging her to the bathroom. Penelope was groaning and still spewing up chunky liquid onto herself. The pressure and nausea grew in my belly again, I tried to puke to the side, but most of it went into Penelope's hair, baptizing her in my bile.

When we reached the bathroom I turned on the shower and stripped us of the rest of our clothes. I pulled Penelope into the tub and wrapped my arm around beside her. I tried to get the thick brown slime and chunks of undigested food off her body. Every time I about got her clean she puked again on me, causing me to vomit on her.

I wiped the spittle and slobber from Penelope's sobbing face. "Hank…"

"Shh. Don't talk. I'll take care of you." I rubbed her forehead. I hated to see her in so much pain, even though I was in just as much. I felt like I was going to fucking die. In my mind I was begging God for any mercy… or death. Either would have worked.

"Hank," she murmured meekly.

"Yeah?" I whispered softly in return.

"I love you, Hank."

Laying naked in a shower in San Diego with an alien, covered in each other's vomit, begging God for mercy or death, whichever was faster, and now she want's to tell me she loves me. How fucking romantic.

"I love you too, babe."

21 EVERY BOOK HAS A BAD CHAPTER

I woke up the next morning on the couch under Penelope and a thin blanket. I guess sometime in the night we moved and deemed the bedroom off limits, for good reason.

I slid out from under Penelope and tucked her back under the blanket. I had no idea what time it was. I stumbled to the balcony door and pulled back the curtain. The sun punched me in the face. If a curtain could be slammed, I did it. I rubbed my eyes and grimaced.

I made my way to the bathroom. There was a river of chunky, damp ooze snaking from Penelope's bed to the shower. The smell made me shudder. I bore through it long enough to piss and get back to the kitchen. I cooked up some eggs, bacon, and toast, and woke Penelope.

She wrapped the blanket around herself and sat up on the sofa. I had placed a plate for her on the coffee table. She half-smiled at me and started to eat. "Did you get much rest last night?" she asked.

"Yeah, but cooking bacon naked probably wasn't the best idea."

Penelope's left eyelid didn't fully open. It wouldn't until she either got up and started moving or drank something with caffeine.

"Hank, about last night."

"Don't worry, it wasn't the first time I've been covered in someone else's bodily fluids."

Penelope gave me a queer look. "Um…"

"Don't ask."

She chewed a bit of toast. "Hank, I was serious when I told you I loved you."

"I was serious when I said it back."

"I haven't said that to anyone in a while."

The queasy nausea in my stomach started to work itself back up. "Well, no one's told me that in a while."

Penelope smiled and elbowed my arm playfully. "Is that why you're such a prick to everybody?"

Really, bitch? I wanted to slap her and storm out, but I didn't. "I'm not a prick to everyone," I calmly defended myself.

"Well you're not really all that nice to anyone either."

"I'm nice to you."

"Most of the time." She smiled.

Just let it go Hank.

"So who was the last person that said she loved you?"

I burped up a vomit-reeking belch. "This chick, Kennedy."

"What happened to her?"

"We had a disagreement about the Marine Corps."

"How so?"

"Well, her family was from Iran and she didn't really dig the whole me going over there to kill Iranians thing."

"Ah. Still talk to her?"

"Nope, haven't heard from her in a little more than two years now."

Penelope pushed away the rest of her food and nested her head on my shoulder. "Who loved you before that?"

"A chick named Satin."

"Satan?"

"*Satin.* I went to school with her."

"What happened to her? Was she from Afghanistan and didn't like you killing her tribe?"

"No." I gave her a dirty look. "Afghans are actually some of the nicest people on the earth."

She gave me a doubtful look.

"When they're not trying to kill you. But Satin was before that. She and I started off with a passionate summer playing guitar on the beach and ended as a storybook romance, only I ended up being the bad guy and a shiny white knight swooped her away."

"You were the bad guy?"

I shrugged and said, "Eh." The nauseous feeling in my gut was growing stronger.

"Well if they ever make you into a movie you'd better hope they don't use that chapter."

"I don't know. I think I'd make a good bad guy. I could *really* get the audience to hate me."

"Now Hank, that's dreary."

"Eh."

"So do you still play guitar then?"

"Yeah, usually when I'm drinking alone at the barracks."

"Do you know how often you do that?"

"Yeah."

"Well you should play your guitar for me sometime."

"I think we can arrange that."

"Good."

"What about you, Miss Eighty Eight? What's your romantic background?"

"Ah well, you know, there've been a few guys. It was hard to date on the ship. Even with as little people as there were, rumors spread around fast and even going on one date got you labeled a strumpet."

I raised an eyebrow. "Strumpet?"

"What about it?"

"We need to teach you better English."

Penelope pinched my arm. "Ass."

I jerked away and wrapped my arm over her shoulder. "What kind of dating can you do on a ship?"

"There isn't much. Mainly just eat or go to social events together."

"Like a movie night?"

"Yeah. More or less. And when there are that many people that close together everybody knows everybody and getting to know someone new isn't really that fun. Then if you decide you don't like them it's impossible to get away. There's nowhere to go, you're on a ship. But you're my first alien."

"Wait, what? I'm the alien?"

"Aye."

"You're on *my* planet."

"Meh."

I told Penelope I'd help with the mess and suggested renting a steam cleaner. However, she was out of coffee and killing the hangover was the first priority. My clothes from the night before we ruined far beyond anything dry cleaning would ever be able to fix. Luckily I had left an Iron Maiden shirt at her place. Unluckily, a pair of yoga pants was the only thing Penelope had that would fit me.

We hunted down a donut shop for coffee. I wasn't a terrible snob when it came to the stuff, but Penelope was. We sat at Happy Time Donuts drinking coffee. People were giving me strange looks, it was almost like they'd never seen a guy in yoga pants before.

"So do you guys have anything like tea? I remember you saying no coffee."

"They're making something similar now using a plant from Virescent, but it's a new thing."

"Yeah?" I looked over Penelope's shoulder to the TV on the back wall. It wasn't loud enough to hear, but beside the anchor's head was a picture of Kelsey and 'MISSING' in big red letters.

SHIT!

I had to keep Penelope's attention from the TV. I didn't know what she knew about the situation, but I didn't want it to get worse or to get bogged down in conversation about it.

"So what kind of trees are they? Like how big are the leaves?"

"The trees aren't really all that tall and the leaves are more like the little scales on a pine cone than a leaf."

GET OFF THE TV! My mind screamed. "Dunk'm in water the same way?"

"And drink it hot, yes."

FUCK, THEY'RE SHOWING THE BARRACKS! "You guys ever add sugar or something sweet and drink it cold?"

"Ewe," Penelope scoffed. "Do you do that with tea?"

Oh great, Pendleton's front fucking gate! "Yeah, you haven't had it? We do it in the South."

"I don't know if I'd like that."

Thank God. The channel cut to another story. "I'll find us a way to try it sometime. But hey, let's go get that steam cleaner, that's probably going to take all day to clean your apartment."

After about seven hours of steam cleaning Penelope's apartment, and a greased lightning ride back to Pendleton, I busted into Éclair's room. "DUDE!"

"I know, man!" Éclair's room was trashed, he was shoveling clothes into a sea bag.

"Wait, what are you doing?"

"I'm going to fucking Mexico!" He was distraught. "Doc's packing his shit too, man! We gotta get the fuck out of here."

"You can't go to fucking Mexico, man!"

"Yeah but I'd have to take leave to get enough time to get to Canada before anyone got suspicious, and if I take leave the command will start to think and... WE'RE FUCKED!"

"Dude, if you go to Mexico they'll *know* it was you!"

"*Me?* You fucking cut her up!"

"Covering for *YOU!*"

"Fuck, man!" Éclair kept shoving things into his bag. "Shit I have to call Ginny. Wait no, I can't... Man, fuck, fuck it! Ginny will figure it out, and there's chicks in TJ. There ain't no chicks in prison, Hank! I'D BE THE CHICK! I ain't taking no dick!"

365

Doc kicked open the door and shot into the room. "DUDES!"

"Hi." I pulled out a cigarette. "If you're going to Mexico I'm smoking in here."

"Dude you gotta come too, man!" Éclair shouted. "You stay here and they're going to fucking burn you!"

"No, hold on, man!" Doc panted, fumbling with Éclair's TV.

"What? Do they have a live feed of them coming to get us?" Éclair panicked.

"No, hold on, man." Doc flipped through the channels.

I lit my cigarette and ran my fingers through my hair.

An anchorman appeared on the tube. He was standing in the barracks' smoke pit and the sun was shining. It had to be at least a few hours old.

Éclair, Doc, and I huddled around the television.

The anchorman spoke into the camera, "The young woman was last seen at this building. We don't know with whom the last person Kelsey was with, however…"

"Who the fuck let these fucks on base?" I demanded of the television.

"Shut up!" Éclair and Doc said in unison.

A Marine with a five o'clock shadow in green sweatpants and a giant Eagle Globe and Anchor tattooed on his chest wandered into the frame.

"Excuse me, Sir." The Anchorman rushed to the Marine.

"Don't call me, Sir, man, I work for a living." The Marine lit a cigarette.

"I'm John Longson with WKGB."

"Cool." The Marine smiled, obviously drunk.

John Longson presented the Marine a small piece of paper. "Have you seen this woman?"

The Marine examined the photo for a few seconds and scratched his belly. "Yeah man." He poked the paper repeatedly with his finger. "Totally dude. Her name's Alyssa, or Kaleesi, or Melissa, or something."

"Kelsey Lovechalk."

"Yeah!" The Marine's smile grew bigger. "Yeah man, that's it!"

"You've seen her?"

"Yeah dude, like me and fifteen of the other guys in my company fucked the shit out of her a few weeks ago!"

The anchor looked like he wanted to say, *You can't say that on TV,* but he let the Marine continue.

"She was wandering around the barracks look'n to party and we snatched her up, played some beer pong with her, and then stuffed her like a turkey!"

"This was four weeks ago, Sir?"

"You ain't gotta call me Sir, dude."

"I'm a journalist."

"It's cool, man. But yeah four weeks ago sounds right. Shit, we fucked her in my room. I still might have her panties somewhere." The Marine laughed. "Wanna go check?"

"Absolutely!"

The cameraman and the anchor followed the Marine to his room. There were five or six other Marines in the room drinking or passed out. The Marine in the green sweatpants looked at the anchor and said, "Hold on man, I gotta find'm." The Marine opened a drawer and started flinging things out. Condoms, empty packs of cigarettes, knives, beer bottles, porno DVDs, duct tape, a ski mask, rope, KY jelly, not one thing that could even be construed as innocent.

I looked back and forth between Doc and Éclair. "I think we're off the hook."

"Yeah," Doc whispered. "You didn't call Ginny yet did you Éclair?"

"No." Éclair looked over at me. "I don't think we're going to have to go to Mexico."

I took a deep drag off my cigarette.

"And First Sergeant's going to flip shit when he smells smoke in my room." Éclair eyeballed my cigarette.

"Ah, shit. Sorry man." I flicked the butt outside.

We turned back to the TV, the Marine was brandishing a neon pink G-string and a smile. I muted the TV. "I don't know if we're golden, but we're definitely bronze."

Éclair's phone started buzzing. "Shit."

"Ginny?" Doc asked.

"Yeah."

"Good luck bro." Doc showed me his cigarettes. I nodded, walked outside, and lit up on the catwalk.

"Ginny Ginny Ginny," Éclair answered his phone.

Doc laughed with a mentally deranged look on his face. "Close one right?"

"Doc?"

"Yeah man?"

I put my finger over my mouth. "Shh."

"Oops." Doc chuckled.

We smoked our cigarettes in silence. After a few minutes Éclair walked out putting on a jacket. "I gotta go clear shit up with Ginny. She's all pissed about me letting Kelsey '*Indiscriminately fuck everyone at the barracks.*'"

"It's not your fault she was a dumpster slut," I shrugged.

"Yeah, but you know how women are." Éclair rolled his eyes.

"I don't know how women are," Doc said. "They keep changing shit, scares the fuck out of me. Fuck, Hank left women all together. Fuck'n aliens 'n shit."

"Meh."

"But I ain't going to prison." Éclair walked to his Camaro and burnt off into the night.

"Alright Doc, lets go drown our sins in stout."

Monday morning I sat at the smoke pit's picnic table, drinking my coffee and burning a cigarette. It was the first day in weeks I didn't have a hangover at work. It may have been months. The wind was blowing east and I could smell the ocean from over the mountains. I was shooting the shit with Rainer. He was trying to tell me about *Fifty Shades of Dave*. I told him I hadn't seen the ending of it and not to ruin it for me.

"Good morning gentlemen," Glædwine said sitting down.

"Hey dude what up?" Rainer casually returned the greeting.

"I'm not a dude, Sergeant."

"Eh, same same."

Glædwine lit a smoke.

"Hey, Glædwine," Rainer pointed to me. "This guy hasn't seen *Fifty Shades of Dave* yet."

"What?" She was shocked. "That's probably the greatest film of the decade."

"I've seen half of it," I defended myself.

"What the hell drug you away from that masterpiece?" Glædwine asked.

"I decided to tongue punch my girlfriend's fart box instead."

"Sergeant," she laughed. "We've had this conversation and have established that that is way too much information to be sharing with lance corporals."

"Tongue punch her fart box?" Rainer chuckled. "I like that, Imma use that."

"Well, in the spirit of not losing a stripe because Gunny Chanceworth may be listening, my husband's getting a new job."

"Oh yeah, what's that?" I asked.

"You guys know he's a computer engineer, right?"

"Yeah."

"He got a job working on this new project. The focus is to integrate US and Virescent technologies."

"That's pretty cool." I lit another cigarette, giving me an excuse to stay outside longer.

"So what are they going to like put together F-18s and some weird alien space robot to make super weapons to fight Al-Quesadilla?" Rainer joked.

"Actually it's more along the lines of making a computer code that recognized Windows, Mac, Linux, and Virescent software so the communication between scientists and engineers can flow more fluidly."

"That's actually a really good idea." I ashed my Lucky's.

"God, can you imagine what it'd be like without that?" Rainer started. "There'd be some poor bastard with two computers open just typing out on one what's on the other."

"Yeah fuck that."

"Apparently there's a lot of really interesting technologies that are supposed to come out of it once we can openly communicate with the Virescent systems. My husband, Jerry, has been telling me little tidbits here and there. He doesn't know too much about the individual programs, but it's not his job to, so he hasn't looked too deep into them."

"Well what kind of programs?" Rainer asked. "Is the porn industry going to steal alien probing devices for better S & M videos?"

"Uh, no." Glædwine flicked the ash off her cigarette. "But there is a program for a fighter-plane-type plane or ship that works in space. Another thing, Jerry didn't remember what it was called, but it's pretty much a giant Japanese robot, only it's used like a tank."

"That's neat. I'd go over to the air wing to get to tinker with that." Rainer nodded.

"Yeah. Jerry said there's also a long-term plan for a hyperspace program."

"It'd be cool if they figured that out." I burned though my cigarette.

"There's also at least blueprints for space colonies."

"That sounds like a logistical nightmare."

"Well Sergeant, the ship the Virescents came on is sixteen times the size of a Nimitz Class Aircraft Carrier."

"Jesus," Rainer shouted.

"And there's plans for terraforming other planets in the solar system. Apparently they found a way to do it that doesn't take anywhere near as long as we thought it would."

"Wait, if they could do that, why'd they come all the way here?" I asked out of confusion.

"I think their sun expanded and swallowed all the planets in the solar system, so they had to go somewhere."

"I guess that makes sense."

"Why hasn't your girlfriend told you that? She's an alien, right?" Rainer asked.

"I don't know, she doesn't want to talk about it."

"How's all that going, by the way?" Glædwine asked.

"Not too bad. We kind of had a rough weekend, but it's whatever."

"Did she call you fat, Sergeant?"

"No, Glædwine, she did not call me fat."

"Did you call *her* fat?"

"It's going to be too much information, Glædwine."

"Ah, got it."

My phone rang. "Hey give me a minute." I put the phone to my head. "Hello."

"DUDE!" It was Éclair.

"What's up, man?"

"You are not going to believe what's going on right now!"

"You finally got your period?"

"No man, half of fucking Truck Company is in handcuffs laying facedown in the parking lot at the barracks."

"What?"

"Yeah dude, the MPs are swarming the place and there are officers fucking everywhere. Like the goddamned Commanding General is fucking here, dude."

"Well what the hell are you doing there? Why aren't you at work?"

"They came in and started kicking in doors and getting everyone outside at about zero four and I just now got back to my phone."

"Holy fuck, dude."

"Yeah that John Longson guy's here recording it and everything."

I laughed. "Man, the fucking Commandant is probably even going to go down for this shit!"

Éclair chuckled. "Yeah man, especially after that dumbshit on TV said half of fucking Motor T gang fucked her that night."

"Yeah, on TV. Plus all that shit he had in his room. I mean, we *all* have all of that shit for legitimate reasons, but that's not what you show a reporter when they're looking for a missing chick you said you fucked the night she disappeared."

"Seriously bro, what a dumbass."

"Hey man, has the First Sergeant there had a brain aneurism and fucking fell dead on the sidewalk yet?"

"No, but he looks like he might. But hey bro, I gotta get dressed and get to work n' shit."

"Alright man, see ya."

Glædwine and Rainer stared at me during the phone call. "That was your old barracks?" Glædwine asked.

"Yeah, you guys picked up on that?"

"It's all over the fucking news, man!" Rainer laughed. "Shit, I'll be surprised if they don't do cavity searches on everyone on post at some point today."

"And you're right, Sergeant," Glædwine said. "That guy on TV was a fucking dumbass." She put out her cigarette. "Gentlemen." She bid Rainer and I farewell and walked back into the building.

I leaned onto the table and smirked at Rainer.

"I wonder what they did with her." Rainer lit another cigarette.

"I don't know, man," I lied. "They probably just drug her up the mountain and fed her to coyotes."

"Do you know that dude that was on TV?"

"Yeah. Hey so what do you think about Glædwine?" I tried to change the subject.

"I think she has horse teeth."

"I don't think they're that bad."

"Yeah but you also have a thing for her."

"No I don't," I lied again.

"Dude you are always out here bullshitting with her about nothing and I've seen you look out here to see if she's here or not before you decided to smoke."

"Okay, first off I don't need a reason to smoke. Second, so what if I like talking to her, she's smart. At least more so than the other knuckle dragging mongoloids around here."

"Then why'd you ask me about her?"

In a very satirical tone I said, "Because I cut up that missing chick on TV and stashed her in a sea bag and wanted to change the subject."

"Shut up Allensworth, that's bull shit. You dug yourself in a hole about Glædwine and now you're trying to get out of it."

"Eh." I waved Rainer off and flicked my cigarette over the rails.

Because it was so close everyone at work kept talking about Kelsey. I tried to avoid the conversations. I didn't order anyone not to talk about it, I thought that would raise suspicions. I also didn't really think anyone thought I had anything to do with it, but when you think you're guilty you also think that everyone knows it was you, they're all just trying to get you to admit it. I told myself to quit being paranoid.

22 WALTZING MATILDA

A few months went by relatively quiet. It was the tenth of November and Marine Corps Base Camp Pendleton's Headquarters Battalion was holding the Marine Corps Ball. Penelope and I were drinking at the Casino, waiting for the ballroom doors to open. People meandered about drowning the sorrows for the fortunes they lost. The Marines, already in their blues, began making fools of themselves before the party even started. I liked the place because I could smoke inside, a rarity in California.

Penelope wore a shoulderless black gown. The dress had a thick red stripe filled with small black sewn roses on her right from her chest to the bottom seam of the skirt near her feet. She had her hair smoothed down and tucked behind her left ear, loose curls covered the right side of her face. She had a thick rhinestone bracelet on the hand holding her martini and her rose necklace was around her neck.

"So this ball is for the Marine Corps' birthday?" Penelope asked me.

"Yup. Almost two and a half centuries of helping America's enemies die for their country."

"Well it seems like a good time."

"Yeah, I don't know how it's going to go."

"How so?"

"Because the other balls I've been to were all with Victor Units and they had their own traditions and had done things to actually be proud of. Since this is a base unit that hasn't, and won't ever actually do anything worthy of calling themselves Marines, they're probably going to talk about the Marine Corps in general instead of the actual unit history."

"I'm not sure if I'm following."

"Very few of the people here have been overseas but they're going to pretend like they're a bunch of badasses."

"Ah."

Rainer appeared out of the crowd with a beer. "Hey man."

"What's up, dude?" We shook hands. "Rainer, this is Penelope. Penelope, this is Jarrod, right?"

"Yeah, Jarrod." Rainer and Penelope shook hands and Rainer introduced his wife, Kelly.

"You ready for this shit show?" Rainer asked.

"Yeah I was actually just telling *her* about that."

Penelope gave me a look as if to ask for an explanation.

"Rainer's the only person at work I don't feel a compelling urge to stab in the face."

"Oh." Penelope, smiled at Rainer. "So you're not one of the uh… What do you call them, Hank? Fucking POGs?"

Rainer laughed. "Yeah, I think we're the only guys that have been to Iraqistan."

"Eh. Some of the staff has but all they did was sit around with their thumbs up their cunt. So it doesn't count."

"How doesn't it count?" Kelly asked.

Rainer leaned into her and said, "Because they didn't leave base. They just sat around all day on the Internet eating cake."

By the time they opened the doors to the ballroom I had drank enough to get a good buzz going. We found ourselves on the seating chart and hunted down our table. There was a formal dinner setting over a red table cloth.

Penelope picked up the nameplate on her glass. "Sergeant Allensworth Guest. I feel fancy."

"Give it an hour." Rainer sat down next to me.

"What happens in an hour?" Kelly asked.

"I'm going to get shit housed and ruin the party."

A few minutes later Corporal Gint and his girlfriend, whose name I don't remember, and the recently promoted Corporal Glædwine, and her husband Jerry, filled in the seats of the table.

When Glædwine sat down Rainer elbowed me and smiled with an eyebrow raised. "You gonna liquor her up and take her home?" he joked.

"Yeah, ha ha," I said satirically. Turning back to Penelope, I introduced her to the rest of the table.

"It's nice to meet you." Glædwine shook Penelope's hand. "Your boyfriend's said a lot about you."

"Really? Hopefully nothing good." Penelope smiled.

"Sometimes it's a little too much information. But it's fun."

"What was your name again? Glædwine?"

"You can call me, Lovis."

"That's an interesting name, I don't think I've heard that one before."

"It's Danish."

"Are you from there then?"

"Just the family."

"Ah."

"Yes, Ma'am. I've been reading a lot about the Virescents. Jerry actually got a job working to integrate our technologies together."

"Oh really? Well he's going to have a good time with that. I don't believe that we brought a lot with us though, besides people."

"Maybe not physically, but your technology's light years ahead of ours."

"Maybe space travel is, but we didn't have jazz or coffee."

"Well how the hell did you survive without that?" Glædwine laughed.

Penelope shrugged and took a sip of her drink.

"Ladies and gentlemen," the announcer spoke over the speaker system. "If you would please take your seats the ceremony will commence shortly." The ballroom silenced. "Ladies and gentlemen, please raise for the invocation by the chaplain."

Everyone in the ballroom stood on their feet.

"Let us pray..."

We bowed our heads. Penelope looked around confused. I tapped her wrist and motioned my head down.

The chaplain asked God for a good night and to bless our bountiful harvest. He said nothing motivating or worthy of being asked by barbaric, child-eating, blood-spilling Marines. There was no prayer or lament for the fallen or requests for bestowing victory in battle over our enemies. The chaplain's words, or his omission of certain ones, angered me. I had my own silent conversation with God asking for people to not pretend to be badasses and ride off the valor of the Marines who actually did something with their career so I wouldn't have to start breaking in their faces because they chose bitch jobs instead of ones that would have gotten them into combat in any of the three wars that happened that decade.

"...Amen."

"Ladies and gentlemen, please be seated."

The lights dimmed almost to black and a screen dropped from the ceiling. An image of a giant spinning Eagle Globe and Anchor appeared, then the commandant and the sergeant major of the Marine Corps both spoke. They wished us a happy birthday and reminded us of our illustrious lineage. They talked about what had happened in Iraq and Iran and how proud they were to be part of the organization that exhibited so much valor and made our enemy bleed. I zoned out while the commandant talked. Every word was gibberish to me. He was selected from the air wing. He had never seen any form of combat and they put him in charge of a bunch of bloodthirsty killers. I don't think there was one Marine in The Corps that honestly respected him. The sergeant major wasn't much better. He was a sniper, but as soon as he got to his current position he either covered up his old sniper tattoos or removed them and proceeded to shit on the Marine Corps' sniper community. I remember wondering why James Mattis and Bradley Kastle couldn't ever lead the Marine Corps. I figured congress was too afraid that Mattis would march the First Marine Division down Pennsylvania Avenue and execute everyone in the government for destroying the Constitution. The commandant finally shut his trap and the lights came back on.

The battalion commander came to the podium and called us to attention. A piece of cake was given to the oldest and the youngest Marines in the battalion. The oldest Marine was a decrepit looking master sergeant and the youngest Marine was actually a set of twin brothers.

The ceremony ended and the waiters started bringing us our meals. I looked over at Penelope and said, "Hey, I'm going to get another drink. You want anything?"

"Another martini please."

I patted her on the shoulder and walked to the back of the ballroom to the bar. I tried to dig my wallet out of my front pocket. Dress blues were a pain in the dick to get anything out of the pockets. Everything is thick, custom tailored, skintight wool.

While I waited for the barkeep to make my drinks I tried to ignore the jabbering of a female lance corporal at the bar next to me. She had her blues and no medals that meant anything. I remembered before I joined the

Marines I thought every medal was for doing something heroic, but nowadays everyone got one for joining while a war was happening regardless of whether or not they actually went to said conflict; and another one for just being in the department of defense during the Global War on Terrorism. This lance had those two, and that was it.

"So yeah, Marine Company's purty awesome," the lance blabbered to another Marine at the bar.

Yeah, because you would fucking know anything about being an actual Marine.

"Day after 'Don't Ask Don't Tell' got repealed, wife and me flew to Maryland and got hitched."

I looked over to reconfirm that her face was as troll-like as I thought it was. *Where the fuck did a lance corporal get the money to just hop a flight to Maryland?*

"And don't even get me goin on the house! It's totes awesome! We're only renting the top flo, but it looks right over the beach!"

I legitimately have more stars on my purple heart than you have ribbons and they're giving you enough money to live on the beach as a lance corporal and I have to live in the barracks. I tapped my fingers on the bar and stared down the bartender.

"So anyway, me and ma wife were at the beach the other day…"

I imagined the disgusting thing standing beside me in a bikini and shuddered in horror. *I at least hope her wife's hot, because if there's two things of that caliber walking half-naked down the beach someone's dick is never going to be able to work again. Then again, I've seen some pretty hot chicks sucking face with monsters. But this chick looks like the fat kid from the "Sandlot." Fucking pasty bitch.*

The bartended finally gave me my drinks. I tossed him a twenty and started off.

Before I could take a step I heard the ugly Cabbage Patch-looking troll say "…and I'm all like hate and discontent yo!" and laugh.

I glanced at her over my shoulder, apparently my look was disturbing enough to get her attention.

She gave me an indignant look. "Yeah?"

"What do you have to be hateful *or* discontent about?" I said without turning my whole body towards her.

She cracked a smart-assed smile and opened her hands. "'Cause, Sarn't, I am! Lance Coolie everyone's always tryin to kick aroun. I ain't gettin no respect from none of the higher ups. I live off hate. And you know what it's like, you a Marine just like me!"

I turned to face her. Her eyes got big when she saw my medals. "Listen you truffle shuffle lookin fuck. I am *not* a Marine like you, you are not a Marine like me. It fucking sickens me that I'm competing for space in the same organization with pug face, good for nothing, shriveled dick dwarfs like you."

"Sarn't, I'm a Marine too."

"It's pronounced 'Sar-gent' not 'Sarn't' and you're not a Marine, you're a fucking flight attendant. Don't believe me? Look at your uniform." The female dress uniform did look like something a flight attendant would wear. "Go do something with your career before you go blabbering about it. And I'm just guessing this one, but no one probably respects you because you're fat and you can't speak English."

"Sarn't..."

"'Sarge-ent' and I don't care about your comebacks or excuses, boot." Both the troll and the Marine next to her had terror in their eyes. I turned around, walked back to my table, and fell back into my seat with a grimace.

"You alright, Sergeant?" Glædwine asked.

"Yup!" I said in a hostile voice and downed half of my rum. Our food was already at the table. I looked at the chicken and vegetables and wondered to myself why the chow hall couldn't make food that good. Then I guessed that it was my fault for having to eat at the chow hall since I was responsible and didn't marry a stranger when I was nineteen.

Trying to eat in dress blues was a pain in the ass. The collar was so high that whoever was wearing it couldn't bend their neck. You had to either risk dropping the food on your chest or bend your whole body.

"This is nice." Penelope looked around the room. "I was expecting wine at the table, or perhaps not having to pay for it, seeing as how this is supposed to be a ball and all."

"Yeah, it's not really like it is in the movies, babe," I told her. "But we can still get pretty liquored up. These aren't as classy as they're made out to be."

"I still get to play dress up." Penelope smiled.

"Some of you do," Glædwine butted in. "We still have to wear this." She pointed at her uniform.

"You don't seem to really want to be here," Penelope pointed out.

"Our presence is mandatory, and it costs us about three hundred bucks every time we do this," Glædwine stated.

"Gross," Penelope sneered.

"And I would rather be Waltzing Matilda," I said.

"I'm sorry, what's that mean?"

"Never mind." I patted Penelope on the thigh and finished my drink.

"So Ginny tells me that they're postponing the wedding in the wake of all these Kelsey happenings," Penelope said after a few moments.

"Uh yeah." I wished I had more rum. "I think they're pushing it until the spring."

"That whole ordeal is really quite sad. That was Ginny's best friend."

"Wait, so you knew that girl?" Jerry broke his silence.

"Well, I met her a few times."

"Fuck her on non-payday weekends back when you were back at the old barracks?" Rainer joked.

"No, she was actually one of my buddy's wife's friends, and she probably fucked all but twelve dudes in that barracks," I tried to joke.

"Well how well did you know her?" Glædwine asked.

"I met her a few times, she *may* have come out drinking with us a once or twice." I pretended not to know my glass was empty and grabbed it to take a drink. "I'm going to go grab another drink. Anyone want anything?"

I bounced to the bar before anyone could roger up. I told the barkeep to make my rum and Coke a double.

"Sergeant Allensworth," a cold and evil voice behind me hissed.

I turned around to confirm my fears. "Gunnery Sergeant Chanceworth." *Damn it.* "Happy birthday."

"Yeah." She didn't have an ounce of amusement in her face. But she did look like she had had plenty to drink. "What's this I heard you said to a lance corporal earlier?"

"Uh…" The bartender put my drink down. I reached for it slowly. "If memory serves correctly, I called her a fat, truffle shuffle looking, mother fucker."

"Do you think that's professional, Marine?"

I sighed and gestured a shrug with my hands.

"What's your original MOS?"

I had had just enough to drink to stop giving a shit about this bitch. "Thirteen sixty-nine."

Gunny pulled her head back in confusion. "I thought you were a photographer, what's a thirteen sixty-nine?"

"Unlucky cocksucker."

Hate grew in her eyes and her mouth pulled back over her teeth. "You are one of the most unprofessional Marine's I've ever met. How the hell'd you make it to sergeant? You're from Division right?"

"Yes, I am."

"You damn troglodyte Division Marines. You think you're so much better than everyone else just because you deploy and go out with the grunts. And you… you walk around like you're God's gift to the Marine Corps!"

"You think he's not, Gunny?" Glædwine interrupted from the bar.

"Stay out of this, Corporal!" Chanceworth barked at Glædwine. She stuck her finger in my chest and growled, "You're flying too close to the sun, Devil Dog!"

"Well then it's probably a good thing I used lambskin condoms instead of wax for my wings."

Gunny Chanceworth saw red. "That's it! Monday morning, you and I are going to the First Sergeant's office! I'm taking your damn stripes and then we'll see who the badass is!"

"That's not happening, Gunny."

"Yeah? And why the hell not?"

"Because if you don't drop this, right now, I'm walking right the fuck over to the CO to tell him about how you grabbed my dick."

"What? No I didn't…" She paused and shook her head thinking. "He's not going to believe that! And the CO is going to take my word over yours!"

"It's not my word. My girlfriend saw it too. So did Glædwine."

Glædwine shrugged at Gunny Chanceworth. "My husband saw it too."

"This is mutiny!" Chanceworth barked.

"Gunnery Sergeant, how much have you had to drink tonight?"

She glared at me.

"Maybe you should go back to your table and sit down."

She squinted and said, "I'll get you," and turned away.

"Happy birthday, Gunnery Sergeant." I looked over at Glædwine and stuck my fist at her. "Thanks for the backup, dude."

Glædwine punched my fist. "No problem Sergeant, she's a fucking bitch."

"Whatcha drinkin?"

"Irish whiskey."

"Is that your go to?"

"Usually." Glædwine raised her glass, I tapped it with mine.

"Happy birthday."

"You too."

We downed our drinks and ordered another round.

"Sergeant, do you know from where toasting came?"

"I do not believe I do."

"In the middle ages people would all pour each other's wine into each other's goblets mixing everyone's drink together. That way if someone tried to kill someone with poison they had to drink it too."

"Interesting."

"Around the same time is where the handshake originated."

"How'd that come about?"

"A firm handshake was to make sure you didn't have a dagger

hidden in your sleeve."

"What if I had it strapped down? Like I was a ninja assassin?"

"Couldn't tell ya."

The bartender brought us our next round. Glædwine took a sip of her whiskey. Her eyes were already starting to turn red around the edges. She had that crooked tipsy smile. "So I take it you're not really too fond of this new peacetime Marine Corps."

"I don't think there's really such a thing as a peacetime Marine Corps."

"No?"

"No, there's just nothing that Uncle Sam really wants right now. As far as America goes war is a racket and we're gangsters for capitalism. We're just waiting for the next ass to kick. If the Marine Corps was at peace we wouldn't be training and people wouldn't be deployed 'keeping peace' anywhere."

"I've heard that somewhere before."

"Smedley Butler wrote a book about it."

"That's right."

"I mean, you join on apple pie and 'Murica' but you kind of end up fighting for whatever monetary gains the government's going to make. Ultimately you're fighting to keep the guys to your left and right alive but it's kind of shitty to think about your buddies getting killed so someone's stock can go up."

"So then why do you do it?"

"Glædwine, you watch football at all, or play it in your backyard?"

"Yeah."

"Well do you do it because you hate the Steelers or because you like the way the ball feels in your hands?"

"I see your point." She finished her drink and ordered another.

"Then I reenlisted because I got to do a lot in my first enlistment and thought I could get another go at it. Instead they sent me to this fucking base unit."

"Yeah, you can tell that you don't really belong here."

"Oh yeah?"

"You're out of place. Everyone else except a few Marines are walking around with two, maybe five medals and ribbons and your rack goes up to your damn shoulder."

"Eh." I shrugged and finished my rum. I put it on the bar and tapped for the bartender's attention.

"And all the Marines at the shop admire you because of the things you've gotten to do. You did all the things that we joined to do. You got to run around with a camera and a rifle and legitimately got paid to kill people and take photos of it. I think that's fucking badass."

"Oh... Thanks?"

"That and I've had some truly life-changing conversations with you on the smoke deck, thank *you* for that."

"Glædwine..." I leaned into her.

"Yes?" She leaned back into me, looking me straight in the eye.

"We should..." *We should what, Hank?*

"We should what?" She smiled.

Find a quiet place to be alone? Go back to the table? Go up to my room? Get another drink? What are we asking her Hank? "We should go out and smoke a cigarette."

"I'd like that."

We walked outside of the ballroom where smoking wasn't authorized

388

back into the casino. I lit my Lucky's. Glædwine put a cigarette in her mouth and fumbled for her lighter. I put the flame of mine to the tip of her smoke.

"I went to Iraq when I was a kid with my parents for their work." Glædwine inhaled.

"Yeah? How'd you like it?"

"I enjoyed it. Not as much as Jordan or Egypt, but it was better than I thought it would be."

"Well you seem like you're pretty open minded about immersing yourself into culture."

"Yeah. I've always wanted to go to some place like Nepal or India or Tibet, somewhere with the giant Buddhist and Hindu temples. The pictures and stories about those places make them seem like they'd be amazing."

"Yeah apparently there used to be Buddhas all around Afghanistan before the Taliban rolled in and tore them all down for their fucking Jihad. That's when we *should* have started killing those fucks."

"I haven't been there. What's Afghanistan like?"

"It's actually very beautiful, and the people are really nice when they're not trying to kill you."

"You know, you have an interesting perspective on things. I'd love to read a book you wrote on your experiences over there."

"Well, I am the sensitive, creative type…"

"Who kills people for a living?"

"Yeah, but I don't know about writing a book."

"Why not?"

"I don't know. It just seems like everyone and their brother that went over there's writing a fucking book about it. I don't want to get clumped in with those tools. It's like, 'I get it you're cool.' That and I haven't really done anything impressive, I don't want to bore people with stories about burning shit in a fifty-five gallon barrel and trading MREs to locals for knickknacks."

"I'd still read it."

"Why? Are you trying to swim around in my mind?"

"Maybe." Glædwine took a step closer to me and lit another cigarette with the cherry from the previous one. I followed suit.

"So you know those Buddhist temples…"

"Yeah?"

"Have you ever seen the pictures of the one somewhere in India that's just covered with statues of people getting it on?"

"Yeah?" Glædwine laughed. "What about it?"

"Do you think the statues are divided up by genre? Like there's a threesome statue room, and a gangbang one, or a room in the back that had a fountain that's just a bunch of dude statues doing bukkake on a chick statue's face?"

Glædwine laughed. "Probably not, but I'm pretty sure there's some horse and ox sex."

I shook my head. "What's the deal with chicks and horses anyway?"

"Most girls had their first orgasm horseback riding, so there's that connection."

"Ah, that's kind of why I love socks so much!"

Glædwine slapped my arm and laughed. "Gross."

"What? You started it!"

"I did not!"

"Did too." I leaned my face in towards Glædwine's.

She smiled back at me. The look in her eyes told me she was okay with whatever was about to happen.

I leaned in to kiss her. *This is it,* I thought. *I'm going to put my lips on the rose pedals of your face.* I could smell her through the smoke. I felt the heat of her body. *We're going to jump in the Jeep, hit the gas, and never look back. We'll run away together and... Wait. WAIT!!! This is a cocktail of bad decisions. You're not going to be okay with this when you sober up. Shit, you're married too. If we do this Lovis, it's going to fuck your shit up.*

I stopped my lips less than an inch away from hers. The heat from her body was driving me mad. *And I've got Penelope to think about. FUCK! I HAVE PENELOPE TO THINK ABOUT! I have a woman I care enough about not to screw around on in the other room and a woman I can't help but want to run away with here in my face. FUCK! This is bad. Why is this happening like this, dammit? This is royally fucking my shit up!*

"Glædwine, do you ever think God's fucking with you?" My mouth was an inch away from hers.

"All the time."

"Like when there's a steak and a lobster on your plate and you're starving, but you know one of the two is poisoned and will kill you?"

She let out a quivering sigh. "Yeah." She bit her bottom lip.

I ran my hand through my hair. "I don't believe in reincarnation."

"I don't either." She didn't understand what I meant.

"If we're wrong about that..."

"Yeah?"

"Find me in the next life."

"Okay." Glædwine half-smiled. She put her palm on my face. "You're right. We should probably get back in there."

We ordered eight shots and a few beers for the table so we didn't raise suspicions, I don't know if we were guilty of anything, but we felt like it. We put the drinks on the table. At some point Penelope took Rainer's chair to chat with his wife and Rainer had moved to talk to Jerry. Glædwine and I plopped into the open two chairs in the middle.

"Here's a round to the Marine Corps!" I raised a shot glass.

Everyone else grabbed a glass and held it to the ceiling.

"May the bottom of your glass never see the moon!" We all downed the liquor.

When the glasses landed back on the table Penelope turned to me. "So Hank, what's the point of this whole thing again?"

"The ball?"

"Yes. I mean, I'm having fun, but this is a yearly thing?"

"Yeah, it's pretty much just an excuse to get drunk and revel in how badass the Marine Corps is. Even though most of these fuckers don't really appreciate it."

"What do you mean they don't appreciate it?" A cold voice spoke from behind me like a fog creeps over a cemetery when Death raps his fingers over a tombstone in the snow.

I turned around to Gunny Chanceworth. *Goddammit bitch leave me alone.* "Well Gunnery Sergeant, most of the Marines here just see this as a party, they're not here to honor the fallen or remember the battles the Marines have fought, they're not here because they feel like they're part of the Marine Corps and honestly feel like they've earned a part in history, they're here because they want to play dress up and get drunk."

"What the hell are you talking about leatherneck?" the inebriated gunnery sergeant asked, wobbling like a drunken top.

"Gunnery Sergeant..." I turned around in my chair, "My first deployment was with Second Battalion Seventh Marines in 2008 in Helmand, Afghanistan. Our battalion held down what was later held down by almost an entire division, and we didn't have so much as air support. All

these stories people have about flying over Afghanistan, I did in a Humvee
with a CAAT platoon. When we were sent there we were supposed to be
there for five months and train the police and then leave because everyone
thought that Afghanistan was over. When we showed up and put little more
than a platoon in places like Now Zad, Sangin, and Balabaluk, instead of
training the police, we immediately get bogged down in killing Taliban. Out
of 800 Sailors and Marines, over twenty of us got sent to guard the gates of
heaven and almost 300 more were wounded so badly they were sent home,
most of them missing a few limbs. Granted we killed the shit out of Hajji.
When we showed up there were no IEDs because the muj thought he could
fight us toe to toe because they'd been used to fighting the Afghan National
Police and they'd been getting away with just using AKs and RPGs, and
they were damn good with them. People think the Taliban was a bunch of
poorly trained dirt farmers, but they will royally fuck shit up. In the end we
sent a hell of a lot more of them to meet Allah then they did us. Most of
our guys that got killed died because they bled out waiting for helicopters
that would never come. We were left the fuck behind, alone and unafraid in
a war we didn't think was still happening. Our five-month training mission
turned into a nine-month fight for life and we never lost our nerve. We
waited for the Pentagon to get their shit together and train up someone to
relieve us. When they finally did it was an entire Special Purpose MAGTAF.
Then the guys who got out of the Corps, about a platoon's worth of them,
fucking killed themselves! Even after another pump the next year and then
an entire other war in Iraq and Iran, there's not a day that goes by that I
don't think of the warriors of Two Seven and things we did. Now I want
you to look me in the eye, Gunnery Sergeant, and tell me that you honesty
think that these base unit Marines have the same sized chunk of their hearts
sworn to the Marine Corps. Try to tell me that their souls swell and scream
for the love of the United States Marines the same way someone who lived
as a Marine and had a full career's worth of experiences before they even
picked up corporal. Even if that lance corporal was fed up, disgusted, pissed
off and leaves, if he was over there being what it means to be a Marine, he
will always remember and revere the time he spent eating dirt with the
finest fucking fighting force the world has ever fucking seen."

Gunny Chanceworth glared at me. "You don't have to be a dick about
it."

"Gunny, on my last deployment me and my corpsman were hit with a fucking artillery round and pronounced dead on the bird and were somehow resuscitated and spent almost two years in a coma. If I want to be a dick about it I'm going to be a fucking dick about it!"

She stared with her drunken, glazed red eyes.

"Gunny, do you need another drink? Where's your husband at?"

"He's somewhere." She staggered back into the crowd.

"That's the most I've ever heard you say about any of that." Penelope looked shaken.

"Hey, I'm drunk and want that bitch to leave me alone."

"So, were you scared?" Penelope asked.

"Huh?"

"In Afghanistan."

"Hell yeah I was fucking scared! Before we went over there we heard stories about the Taliban grabbing dudes off of patrols when they'd get lost in fields and cutting their fucking heads off. Then it turned out Hajji could fight. And I don't care what anyone says, at the very least your first firefight is *fucking terrifying*. And I don't mean terrifying like 'I think I'm about to crash my car.' I mean terrifying like your brain can't process anything besides the words 'shit' and 'fuck.' That's why training until everything's muscle memory is so important. Now eventually instead of sheer terror you just start getting pissed off when you're in contact, but you're never *really* not scared anymore."

"I see." Penelope grabbed her drink and tried to change the conversation, obviously uncomfortable. "So if this is a ball, shouldn't we have champagne and dancing?"

I pointed to the dance floor behind Penelope. "That's all you're getting for dancing, but I can get you some champagne."

She turned to look at the people dancing, if you could call it that. The

DJ was blaring that year's pop and hip-hop. The Marines on the floor with their girlfriends and wives were twerking and grinding under the disco ball.

"Hank, when you said 'ball' I thought you meant something a little more classy. Maybe tango or even merengue, there's nothing elegant about this at all."

"Well I'd rather be Waltzing Matilda too, but this is where society has left us."

"That's the second time you've said that and I still don't know what that means."

"It means he'd rather be humping a pack through the desert," Rainer translated.

I shrugged and sipped my drink.

"Fay has a word for this," Penelope thought aloud.

"Yeah what's that?" I asked, but the feelings I had toward Fay prevented me from actually being interested in anything that she could have said.

"Give me a moment to think." Penelope put her hand over her mouth.

I looked at her with my eyebrows raised, then Rainer and Glædwine. They both shrugged at me.

I looked back at Penelope who said, "All niggered up? I think is how she would describe it."

"Yeah...You can't say that."

"Why not? That's what it is, right?"

"No 'nigger,'" Rainer said. "You can't say nigger."

"Why's that?" Penelope asked.

"Because it's racist," Glædwine informed her.

"Really?" Penelope had a confused look on her face. "For a word you can't say it really is used a lot."

"You're only allowed to say it if you're black." I rolled my eyes.

"Well that hardly sounds fair."

"Yeah," Rainer sighed. "That's what whitey used to call black people when they were slaves."

"White people used to be black people's slaves?" Penelope asked.

"No, black people used to be while people's slaves," I corrected her.

"Well to be fair, everyone used to be white people's slaves," Glædwine smirked.

"Yeah! Fucking white ass mother fuckers," Rainer joked.

"Shut up Rainer, you're white."

"No I'm not. I'm a Newyoricanmexiwindian. One big cocktail of everybody fuckin!"

"I have no idea what that is." Penelope shook her head.

"New York, Puerto Rican, Mexican, White, and Indian."

"All right then." Penelope took a sip of her drink. "But seriously, slaves? No wonder aliens never contacted you before we *had* to."

I squinted at her indignantly.

"But seriously though, how is this a ball if there's no dancing?" Penelope continued.

"I don't know man, it doesn't make much sense to me either," I grumbled.

"So you're not going to go up there and pretend you're Miley Cyrus?" Penelope laughed.

"No. I'm not going to disrespect my uniform like that," I said. "And how the hell do you know who Miley Cyrus is but didn't know we had slaves?"

"It's not my fault what they put on the idiot box."

I rubbed my forehead. "Okay babe. I'm going to go smoke a cigarette. Rainer, wanna go?"

"Yeah sure."

We stepped outside the ballroom doors and lit up by the ashtray towers.

"Glædwine was eyeballing the fuck out of you when you were telling off Chanceworth."

"Yeah?"

"Yeah! Then she watched us walk out here."

"Well, that's great..." *God dammit.*

"You should bang her, dude."

"I can't do that, man."

"Why the hell not? You ain't married."

"I know." I took a deep drag from my Lucky. "But I respect Glædwine too much, I feel bad for just thinking about her the way I do. Plus, I have the green one. It's all mixed up, man."

"Just keep it on the down low, man. You'll be alright."

"Na man. She seems happy with her husband and is probably only really into me right now because she's drunk. She'd probably be all fucked in the head when she sobered up. I don't want to do that to her. It'd be different if she wasn't happy with her husband and I didn't care about Penelope."

"Too much of a one woman man?"

"You know, not usually." I put out my cigarette. "Penelope's probably only the second chick I haven't ran around on."

"Well, alright man."

We got a few more drinks and sat back down. The table's attention was on Jerry. He was explaining the intricacies of the project at his job. "…but we're not the only one's doing it. There's a multinational conglomeration working on the project—China, Russia, Germany, Japan, Britain—there are a lot of people with their fingers in this. I think it'll do well. Hell, if we're lucky enough, we'll unfold some advanced technology that could stop war."

"Well we've kind of already stopped wars on some levels," Rainer's wife, Kelly, nudged in.

"How do you mean?" Jerry asked.

"If you think about it, the technology you're talking about could be related to nuclear weapons and democracy. Nuclear powers don't go to war against each other, nor do democracies. Sure there's saber rattling, but all the bomb did was make sure first-world countries don't engage each other in direct contact. Any new technology wouldn't do much more for peace then nukes did. Think about it, if there was no such thing as a nuclear weapon, or something equally destructive, America and the Soviet Union probably would have gone to war directly with each other in either Vietnam or Afghanistan. There would have been more Soviet involvement in Korea and Cuba would have become a state or a territory in the sixties. But no one wanted to risk nuclear annihilation, therefore none of those conflicts were deemed worth it by the other side to fight it all out."

"I see your point." Jerry nodded.

I turned to Rainer and said, "Dude, what the fuck is your wife's job?"

Rainer shrugged. "Fuck if I know, man."

"But maybe," Jerry started again. "Maybe with the Virescent terraforming technology we can get humanity into space and start fresh. If we do that then we should only have a few nations up there and if every country is a nuclear power then no one will want to fight with anyone at all."

"Aren't India and Pakistan both nuclear powers?" I butted in.

"Yes, but although they've had skirmishes they've never really been to war against each other."

"Okay." I sipped my drink. *I'm too drunk for this level of brain talk.*

We all sat around the table and talked for another hour. The conversation bounced back and forth between serious philosophical debate and complete nonsense. I kept sneaking my eyes over to Glædwine, when my eyes met hers she'd quickly look away. I did the same to her.

At the end of the night I laid in the hotel bed upstairs with Penelope. The room was nice, but the world was spinning from the rum and I just wanted to sleep. I had Penelope tucked inside my arm, her body was spooned up to me.

"Hey, Penelope."

"Yes, Hank."

"I want you to know that I love you."

"I love you too, Hank."

"No, I mean it. I really, *really* love you, like for real."

"Do you mean to say you didn't before?"

"No, that's not what I mean. I just want you to know that you've got a serious chunk of my heart."

"Do you love me as much as you love the Marine Corps?"

"That's different."

"How?"

"Because it was here first and hopefully you'll be around long after the

Marines are done with me."

"I can deal with that."

"Good."

"What if there's another war?"

"What about it?"

"Will you go?"

"If they let me."

"Not if they *make* you?"

"No, it's if they let me. I didn't join the Marines *not* to go to war."

"What if the war's really long and we have kids?"

"Then wait until our son has a beard and if I'm not back by then and you haven't heard from me then move on."

"Hmm."

"And what do you mean kids?"

"If we get married we have to have children."

"Who said anything about marriage?"

"You said you love me didn't you? Why wouldn't you marry me?"

Good job working me into a corner Penelope. "Have kids with your next husband."

"Why would I have a next husband?"

"Because I'm going to die sometime in the next ninety years, at best. If you have kids with me they're probably going to die before you do too. After I bite the dust marry some Virescent guy so you won't have to watch your kids get old and die before you do."

"That's dark, Hank."

"Am I wrong?"

"Eh. Well say you do die a millennium before I do, maybe I want a souvenir."

"Yeah, but then you're going to have a bunch of other kids from different dads and people will think you're a hooch."

Penelope patted my arm. "Well we can talk about it later, babe."

23 THE GOAT

Éclair and I drank beer on the back of my Jeep. Doc tinkered away on the Mustang a few spots away.

"I don't think he's ever going to get that done," Éclair observed.

"Well he keeps adding shit to it instead of making it drivable."

"It's drivable, it's just down for a few days a week." Doc banged something on the car and swore at it.

I lit a cigarette. "So how's everything with Ginny?" I asked Éclair.

"I don't know, man. She's still pissed off about Kelsey. She's not freaking the fuck out anymore, but things aren't good yet."

"You didn't tell her it was you, did ya?"

"*Fuck* no. I ain't going to prison. I might, *maybe* tell her on my deathbed. Plus, those Truck Company guys are getting pinned with it. We're off the hook."

"You know, I don't feel bad about that at all."

"I don't know man, it fucked me up pretty hard there for about a month. I don't think I was sober for more than fifteen minutes a week."

"No, I mean Motor T taking the fall."

"Oh. Yeah fuck those guys. Those assholes had the MPs at the barracks every weekend anyway. Things have actually been pretty quiet since that asshole was on TV. They're not even allowed to drink at the barracks anymore."

"That's fucked up."

"Yeah but their CO thinks they killed a chick after they gangbanged her."

"I'll give you that. So Penelope told me Ginny wanted to reset the wedding to next spring."

"Yeah that's the plan right now. But I don't know man, I might have to break up with her."

"Why?"

"Because I don't feel right about the whole thing. I mean, I'm the reason she's been so sad recently."

"Yeah, but she doesn't know you did it and if you deuced out on her that'd make it worse for her. Like she might kill herself if you leave, man. How would you feel losing your best friend and your future spouse in the same year?"

"I guess."

"Plus she's sweet. She makes me food when I go over there."

"Eh."

"Dude if you don't marry her I will."

"No you won't."

"Okay, well if there's another war and you get waxed, Ginny can live in the apartment above my garage and she can bake instead of pay rent."

Éclair laughed and said, "Okay man. So what's going on with Penelope?"

"All kinds of shit. I think I have to marry her."

"Why's that?"

"Well, long story short, you know that little blonde chick that works with me?"

"The ugly one with the horse teeth?"

"She's not ugly."

"Well she ain't hot."

"She's cute."

"She's cute for someone with horse teeth."

"Anyway, I was drinking with her at the ball and I had her outside the ballroom and I was about to try to take her upstairs and I couldn't do it."

"So you're at the point in the relationship where you can't get drunk and bang other chicks?"

"Yeah pretty much."

Éclair exhaled a plum of thick grey smoke. "I guess that's a pretty good sign. When you gonna propose?"

"I don't know, man. I don't really want to just jump into it. And like I don't know if I give her a ring if she'll even know what the hell it means."

"Huh?"

"Because she's an alien."

"Ah."

"Yeah dude, like she seems smart but she doesn't have culture down all the way yet. Like she said the ball was 'niggered up.'"

Éclair laughed. "Dude that's ridiculous."

"Yeah, so I don't know how she'll react if I get her a ring."

"Well Virescents get married."

"Yeah but do I get her a ring or two horses and a goat?"

"Eh."

"And like I bought her a birthday present and she about died. They don't have much of a concept of gift giving, man. I think they're starting to adopt Christmas, but that's about it."

"Well then dress up like Santa Claus and ask her," Doc yelled from under the Mustang.

"And put the ring around my dick?" I hollered back.

"Yeah that's a good idea," Éclair joked. "Just put a diamond on a cock ring and go wave it around at her."

"Yeah." I cracked open another beer and lit a cigarette. "Christmas is only a few weeks away. You guys got plans?"

Doc crawled out from under his car and joined the conversation. "I don't know, maybe hang out with Kristy." Doc wiped the grease from his hands.

"I think I'm going over to Ginny's folks' place. What about you?" Éclair said.

"I don't know. I don't really feel like going home. I fucking hate flying," I admitted.

"You probably should."

"Yeah," Doc added. "When was the last time you saw your family? Two or four years?"

"Yeah but it doesn't seem like that long."

"Yeah well you were in a coma for a year and half of it, right?" Éclair asked.

"Eh." I shrugged. Then thought about what Éclair said about the coma. "You know I haven't spent any of my deployment money yet."

"Really?" they both asked.

"Yeah."

"Dude you should spot me a grand," Doc joked.

"No. I have a better idea." I scratched my neck.

"Get married and buy a house?" Éclair asked.

"Something like that."

I told Doc and Éclair to meet me in the parking lot at the barracks on the next Saturday. I saw them before they spotted me. They were probably looking for my Jeep, but I wasn't in it.

I sped through the parking lot and made a dead stop right in front of them in a flat black 1968 Pontiac GTO. "Get in losers!"

"Whoa dude! The fuck is this?" Doc yelled.

"It's what I spent my deployment money on! Now get in!"

Éclair slid in what was technically a backseat and Doc fell in shotgun.

"Dude this shit's nice." Éclair fingered the leather seats.

"Right?" I put her in first gear and stomped down on the gas. We roared off Pendleton burning a trail east into the desert where the cops didn't care how the hell fast you went.

"This have the original motor in it?" Doc asked.

"No dude, guy I got it from put an LS1 in it." I lit a cigarette and put on my aviators. "Well actually home dude built the car and died and his wife sold it to me."

"Nice. How fast does she go?" Doc asked.

"We'll find out here soon! But hey Doc, you're in about the same financial situation as me, why don't you use the money to fix the Mustang?"

"Because I don't really want to drive her, I just want to play around under her skirt."

"Okay."

Éclair leaned up from the back. "So what happened to getting Penelope that ring?"

I stuck my hand in the inner pocket of my patch jacket, pulled out a little black box, and tossed it back to Éclair.

He opened the box and saw a gold band with a red diamond cut to look like a rose. "Dude, how much fucking money *do* you have?"

"About two years of corporal pay and a year of sergeant's."

"Fuck, man. That almost sounds worth missing a year." Éclair laughed and handed the box to Doc.

"Yeah this is good, dude." Doc inspected the ring. "So are you getting rid of the Jeep?"

"No," I said indignantly. "I'm just going to hog two spots at the barracks."

"Dick move, bro." Doc laughed.

"Eh. But the way I figure it is that people want things, and when they get married they can't ever get them because their wives tell them no. Penelope can't tell me not to buy the things I want if I already have them. I have a Jeep, a good guitar, a badass hot rod, and a set of tits to bounce around in the passenger seat. I'm set for life, man!"

We drove out towards the Salton Sea. The sun beamed in through the windows. It was early December, but it wasn't ever really cold in California. We played Guns N' Roses and Whitesnake as we sped over the desert.

"So I think my hair stopped falling out after Iraq," Doc said after a silence.

"What?" Éclair shouted over the blaring speakers.

I turned the music down. "You said your hair stopped falling out?"

"Yeah, I haven't lost any more of it since we got back from Iraq. It's still thin up there and what was already gone isn't growing back. It's just growing in this weird thin fucking way."

"How does that work?" Éclair asked.

"You think it was the malaria pills?" I joked.

"I don't know, bro. But there was a lot of weird shit that happened during that deployment," Doc said. "Like you still have all your tattoos, right?"

"Yeah. I thought that was weird too." I kept an eye out for the exit.

"Wait, what?" Éclair asked confused. "It's already a fucking miracle you're even the fuck alive. Like I'm surprised you guys don't look like Darth Vader, but your tattoos weren't burnt off?"

"Nope." I looked at him in the rearview mirror.

"I've had some pretty bad cuts and scratches since then from working on the car, and I haven't scarred up at all," Doc added.

Éclair squinted at us. "Yeah, that's fucking weird."

"Those malaria pills, man. That's gotta be it," I said again.

"Well I've been reading this book," Éclair started, "And it's about the fucking technology the aliens are bringing down. They're doing trials right now with like, uh…" Éclair opened and closed his fingers in and out of a fist. "Like prosthetic robot limbs and shit."

"Didn't we already have that?" I asked.

"Yeah but they're bulky and like only five people have them," Doc enlightened us.

"No but this book I'm reading's talking about how they don't need external power sources and only need maintenance like once every five years," Éclair continued.

"Well that's pretty neat. Where'd you find this book?" I turned the radio down a little more.

"I stole it from dental. It's really technical and I only understand about half of it. Whoever wrote it made it for doctors to read so every word has sixteen syllables and they use the proper medical term for fucking everything."

"Yeah, that'd be a pain in the dick. You should get Doc to translate it for you."

Doc looked at me and responded, "I'm not that kind of medical professional, bro."

I pulled the GTO off the highway onto a dirt road and we traveled a few miles into the desert. I stopped my new Pontiac along the side of the road and listened to the engine purring under the hood for a moment before I turned her off.

We got out and I opened the trunk. I grabbed a thirty rack and handed it to Éclair. "That's for you." I then pulled out a green can of ammunition and handed it to Doc. "And that's for you." Finally I took a long olive green canvas bag out and closed the trunk.

"Whatcha got in there, bro?" Doc asked.

"A rifle my dad gave me. I figured we'd hike out a little bit and shoot some cans."

"Mexi*cans*?" Éclair joked. "Or Afri*cans*?"

I patted Éclair on the shoulder and said, "You know you're the only white guy here, right?" I laughed.

"Yeah okay, dude." Éclair laughed back.

"No seriously, Doc and I are only half white."

"What's the other half?"

"Native American," Doc answered.

"I can see Doc, but why do you have blue eyes and facial hair?"

"Can't help the position my parents fucked in." I started to walk into the desert.

"That's gross," Éclair laughed. "So what's this gun?"

"The M14 my granddad brought back from Vietnam. He gave it to my dad and my dad gave it to me."

"That's sick."

Doc took the three empty beer cans and set them up about fifty yards away. We took turns shooting at the cans with the old wood-stocked rifle. When we'd finished a few beers we'd take a break and set them up with the other twisted tin shells of the others, and then fire at them, too.

Éclair took a drag off his cigarette and chambered another round. "So Hank, you ever finish watching *Fifty Shades of Dave*?"

"Yeah dude, what the fuck was up with the ending?"

Doc laughed and said, "What was wrong with the ending? You're not into wolf porn?"

"I mean, I get that he lost his job because he killed his boss and had to go on the run, but he ends up homeless and fucks other animals at the zoo? Come on!" I chugged the rest of my beer.

"Yeah, wolf porn." Doc watched Éclair blow holes in the cans.

"Yeah, but he was fucking monkeys and giraffes and shit. Why didn't he go around killing drug dealers and stealing their coke?" I crushed my beer can.

"Because that wouldn't have been as funny." Éclair pulled the trigger and a can flew into the air after a bang.

"The rest of the movie wasn't supposed to be funny," I protested.

"Yeah, but it *was* hilarious," Doc chuckled. "And his girlfriend at the end was hot. It kind of looked like they wanted to get Emma Stone to play the chick at the end but couldn't afford her and just got her stunt double."

"Yeah that chick really looked like my ex." Éclair fired again.

"Oh yeah? You been stalking her?" I joked.

"If cyber stalking counts." Éclair fired another round.

"That's healthy," Doc said sarcastically.

"Na dude, think of it like this. I keep tabs on my ex on the Internet, you know, study the relationship she's having with Jodie, and then I make sure to do better for Ginny than my ex is getting from her new guy; that way I win. I get to show myself that I can do better for someone than some bitch that rejected me is getting for herself." Éclair pulled the bolt back on the rifle, it was out of rounds. He handed it to Doc. "Know what I'm saying?"

Doc took the rifle and started loading rounds into a magazine. "I would get that if you didn't kill your fiancé's best friend then hack her up and dump her on an impact range."

Éclair grabbed a beer and pointed it at Doc. "You mother fuckers cut her up, I just squeezed a little too hard."

"No," I objected. "Doc didn't want to do it, I had to threaten him. But at the end of the day you're the only one of us that's had their dick in a dead chick."

Éclair shook his head in disgust. "Blech. I'm glad I don't believe in God or I'd be freaked out about going to Hell."

"Bro," Doc laughed. "Even *if* there isn't a God we're all still probably going to Hell."

"Probably," Éclair chuckled.

"Yeah, and besides, dead pussy's still pussy, right?" I pulled out another cigarette.

Éclair squinted at me. "Ha, ha. I didn't even wanna fuck the bitch. But If I didn't she was going to rat me out."

"She was probably going to rat you out anyway." Doc fired at the cans.

"Maybe, I don't know. But I'm not married, what's wrong with trying to get laid?" Éclair asked.

"Well if you didn't fuck Kelsey to death you'd probably be married right now." I lit the cigarette. "But I know what you mean. Who you have to watch out for are all those bleeding heart liberal feminists that are shitting on people talking about how banging someone you don't love is just masturbating into a woman's body."

"What's wrong with that?" Doc asked.

I shrugged, "That's what I'm say'n."

"That's fucking stupid," Éclair sighed. "First off, those are two different things, that's why they're different fucking words. And B…"

"Second," I corrected him.

"Yeah, Dad thanks. But second, if a chick says that, they're just pissed off that no one wants to fuck them and they're trying to ruin everyone's fun, and if a guy says that, he's just pissed I get more pussy than he does, it's like, 'Quit trying to ruin the party, fags!' Seriously though, I've *never* heard either a beautiful woman or anyone that counts as a lady complain about sexism. It's only ugly bitches with ugly souls."

Doc and I shrugged.

"Am I wrong?"

"No, that's about how it works."

Doc finished firing his rounds and handed me the rifle. "You know I've always hated calling my rifle a weapon."

"Why's that, Doc?" I took the gun.

"Think about it, a hammer doesn't drive nails. I drive nails with the hammer. A rifle doesn't kill people, I kill people with a rifle. The rifle's a tool; I'm the weapon."

"Doc, you're not a weapon. A BAND-AID, sure, but not a weapon." I loaded the rounds into the magazine.

"Yeah, but you get what I'm saying."

"I'm picking up what you're putting down." I pulled the bolt back and placed the butt into my shoulder. I aligned the sights on the first 'e' of "beer" and put a slow, steady squeeze on the trigger. The rifle shot back into my arms and the beer can flew away.

Éclair lit another cigarette. "So have you guys heard of this Moon Colony stuff?"

"I know they're building something up there." I sighted back in.

"Well they're taking volunteers for the thing they're building. Like a Marine Security Guard-type deal."

"Really?" Doc asked.

"Yeah, the whole thing sounds pretty sick," Éclair observed. "They need or want Marines to be the security forces up there."

"Wait." I raised the muzzle to the sky. "You're telling me there's going to be Space Marines?"

"Yeah, dude."

"Dude, that's fucking awesome!"

"The only shit part about it is that because of how much it's going to cost to send people up there it's a ten-year obligation," Éclair said.

"Well shit, I'm sure the pay's fucking ridiculous and you could retire anywhere you wanted to after that."

Doc asked Éclair, "Are they taking corpsmen?"

"I don't know man, I just heard something about volunteers."

I fired another round and a can went bouncing through the desert. "Yeah, I'm thinking I might get out."

"Really?" they both asked in shock.

"Well, the Marine Corps is getting too fucking political. It's at the point where I can put a dick in my mouth but I can't put my hands in my pockets."

"Yeah, well nothing's perfect." Éclair finished his beer.

"But I don't know," I continued. "We'll see what it's like next time I reenlist. I still love Marines, but I'm really starting to hate the Corps."

We finished drinking the beer, expended all but one box of the ammo, and headed back to the car. I put the rifle in the trunk and Éclair asked, "You guys wanna go sing karaoke tonight?"

"Yeah that'd be cool," Doc said. "Are we inviting the girls?"

"Why wouldn't we?" I closed the trunk.

"I dunno."

"If that's the case we should probably go grab Penelope because we're closer to San Diego than Vista." I looked to Éclair and said, "You're talking about Smitty's, right?"

"Yeah."

I texted Penelope to be outside in an hour and that we were going out, and she should dress casual because we were going to go cause some trouble. I turned the key and the engine turned over. The GTO vibrated and we screamed down the highway like a rocket blaring Whitesnake.

24 I JUST DIED IN YOUR ARMS
IN THE STILL OF THE NIGHT

We pulled into Penelope's apartment's parking lot. I dialed her up and told her we were downstairs. We all hopped out of the Pontiac and lit up by the entrance.

Penelope came out and almost passed us. She had to look twice to notice the three of us standing there. She was wearing jeans and a black sweater with a collar like on a button down. She had on Converse and was still almost as tall as I was. "Almost didn't see you there," she said in her Scottish sounding accent.

I pulled her in with my arm and kissed her on the cheek. "We're super ninja today."

"I guess so." Penelope sniffed my clothes. "Have you started drinking without me?"

"Yeah but not much."

"Hmm. What are we getting into tonight?" she inquired.

"Ginny and Kristy are going to meet us up north at a karaoke bar in Vista."

"Karaoke huh? I don't think I've done that yet."

"Well then it'll be a good time."

"I don't know, I might be too shy."

"Well you don't do it sober." I laughed.

"Okay." Penelope looked around the parking lot. "Who drove down? You didn't all fit in the Jeep."

"I did."

"In what?"

"Don't worry about it."

Penelope gave me a confused look.

I smacked her ass and smiled at her. We walked over to the GTO and I opened the passenger side door for her.

Penelope's eyes widened. "No fuckin way!"

"Yeah fuckin way!" I gestured my hand at the seat for her.

She sat down and ran her hand across the dashboard. "I love the interior. When did you get her?"

"This week."

"What prompted it?"

"Because I could. Put your feet in, babe."

"Oh right," Penelope said as if she wasn't paying attention to me. I closed the door. Doc and Éclair crammed into the backseat from the driver's side.

Penelope put on her seatbelt and said, "I like the wood in the dash, I don't believe I've seen that in a car yet."

I turned the key and the engine howled.

Penelope smiled over at me.

I put her in gear and we raced up I-5. We stopped Whitesnake in favor of Molly Hatchet. We dropped Doc and Éclair off at the barracks, they were going to go pick up their girlfriends and meet us at the bar later on. My green woman and I made our way to Vista.

"Why didn't you tell me you got a new car?" Penelope asked, still smiling.

"I wanted to surprise you."

"It's pretty awesome."

"Yeah it is."

"Is it newer? I don't recognize 'Pontiac.'"

"Well, Pontiac went out of business a few years ago, but this car's from the sixties."

"Really? It looks brand new."

"The guy I got it from did a lot of work on it. Like the interior's been redone, the engine's newer, that kind of stuff."

"Well it doesn't sound like there's a motor as much as it does a demon under the hood."

I smiled at her and replied, "Yeah, that's cool huh? It's not like putting around in the Jeep."

"How *is* the Jeep? You didn't get rid of it did you?"

"No, that thing's gonna be a lawn ornament one day."

We snagged dinner at a small sushi place beside the theater in Vista and made our way to Smitty's. It was a small hole-in-the-wall dive bar. It wasn't very big, but there was a stage, karaoke, and the drinks weren't bad. We got cocktails and waited for the others to show up. After a couple of drinks we stepped outside to smoke a cigarette and watch the sunset over the mountains.

Doc and Kristy rolled up as Penelope and I were about to go back inside.

"Heyo!" Kristy waved.

"Hey." We waved back.

We went back in and ordered a couple of shots and beer. Ginny and Éclair showed up in the middle of one of the first karaoke performances. An extremely inebriated, skinny white kid bounced around the stage to "Baby Got Back." The kid was shouting at the top of his lungs in to the microphone. It was awful. Éclair's first words in the bar were, "No amount of alcohol is going to remedy this guy's voice."

"Yeah." I looked over at him. "But at least it'll get tolerable."

Éclair laughed and patted my shoulder. "Imma go get a drink. Need anything?"

I shook my head no and brandished him my beer.

Ginny sat down next to Penelope and they started chatting. They'd been hanging out recently when us guys weren't around for one reason or another, but I don't think they've seen each other in a couple of weeks.

"How's it going, girl?" Kristy asked Ginny while sitting down.

"Not too bad, just re-planning wedding stuff."

"How's that going?" Penelope asked.

"Eh." Ginny shrugged. "It's not as much of a pain in the ass as it was the first time. I already know who to call for what. Most people were okay with just pushing the date."

"It's good that they're not giving you the run around," Kristy pointed out.

"Yeah. So what have you two been up to?"

"Not too much, just work," Kristy admitted.

"About the same with me," Penelope continued. "Although I went to the ball with Hank a while back."

"Oh yeah?" Ginny asked. "How'd you like that? I went with Richard."

"I was expecting more class. But you know the prayer they do at the beginning?"

"Yeah."

"Well that got me a little curious. I went out and bought a Bible and I'm about halfway through it."

"Really? Whaddaya think about it?" Kristy asked.

"I don't think that most of the stories are about what you're calling 'God.' They seem more like extraterrestrials to me."

Ginny looked at Penelope suspiciously. "Okay?"

"Well I mean think about it, half the time 'God' comes down to Earth to talk to people he's got a full entourage and he comes in some kind of vehicle like a chariot or a wheel. Why would the creator of the entire universe need bodyguards and a car?"

"I guess that's a good point." Kristy took a sip of her drink.

"And that whole bit about the flying cloud of fire leading the Hebrews through the desert that dispersed food, maybe it's just because I'm reading it with an outsider's perspective, but that also seems like advanced technology of some sort. But maybe that's just me. I just can't quite figure out why aliens would want to help helpless little earthlings running around the wilderness, either."

"Yeah I don't know." Ginny didn't really seem to care about the subject.

Éclair sat down with a couple of White Russians. We drank into the night watching people make fools of themselves on stage. Some people would mumble into the microphone, most others would sing off key, making the room miserable. My favorites were the people that were too drunk to sing and just got on stage and laughed with their friends.

During a lull in the performances, Ginny and Penelope went back to

421

chatting and the other four of us went outside for a cigarette. I walked out first and bumped into a woman on accident.

"Excuse me I'm..." Before I could say 'sorry,' I recognized the woman. "Reagan?"

"Hank?" She looked at me as if she'd seen a ghost.

Éclair, Doc, and Kristy fell out of the door.

Reagan looked around me. "Wilson?"

Doc gawked at her in horror.

"Hi." Reagan forced a meek smile.

They stood silent. Éclair moved his eyes from them to me and back with a dumbfounded look on his face. He had put a cigarette in his mouth but hesitated to light it when he realized something was wrong with the situation.

Doc and Reagan stared at each other. The cool winter wind blew Reagan's hair. They probably would have stood there until they turned to stone and eroded away if Kristy hadn't broken their gaze. Kristy put her head between the two and said, "Hi."

"Uh... hi," Reagan responded robotically.

Kristy, knowing something was rotten, tried to mark her territory. "I'm Kristy." She extended her hand to Reagan to shake.

Reagan ignored her. "I don't really know what to say."

"How about, 'I'm sorry?'"

"For what?" Kristy interjected. They ignored her.

Éclair eyeballed the situation as if he were a gunslinger in an old western Mexican stand off, unlit cigarette in his mouth and an itchy lighter finger, waiting for someone to pull the trigger.

"Where'd you go?" Doc begged.

"Nowhere. I stayed here, you left," Reagan retorted.

"Yeah, but I didn't leave you, and you knew I was coming back." Doc put his hands in his pockets.

"Will one of you explain to me what the hell is going on?" Kristy looked back and forth between the two old lovers.

"I didn't know that, Wilson. Things were bad here waiting for you and after what happened with Kennedy, I decided to move on."

"Whoa!" I shot in. "What happened to Kennedy?"

"She never told me Hank, but whatever it was it hurt her, and it hurt her bad."

I frowned wordlessly.

Reagan looked at me. "Whatever happened between you two was so terrible that she didn't even pack her things, she just got on a bus to Chicago and started a new life with nothing but the clothes on her back and a carton of cigarettes."

I didn't have words to say. I didn't even know where to look to find them.

Kristy's face grew the kind of scared people only get when their lover leaves them alone in the rain with nothing to keep them warm.

"So you left me because Hank hurt Kennedy?" Doc accused her.

"There were other reasons."

"What, Reagan? What other reasons could there possibly have been?" Doc demanded.

"It was nice seeing you, Wilson." Reagan paused. "I have to go."

We watched her walk into the night without looking back. Before she was more than two blocks away Kristy showed her anger. "Who the *fuck* was that?"

"Somebody that I used to know," Doc said and watched Reagan disappear.

"Well you obviously still know each other!" Kristy yelled.

Doc looked into Kristy's eyes and very calmly pleaded, "Babe, not now."

"Not now? Why the fuck not? Some random skank shows up and you just ignore me for a conversation!"

"Sorry."

"You're *sorry*?" she kept yelling. "I thought I meant more than that to you!"

"You do, babe."

"Obviously I don't!"

"Can we not do this right now?"

"No! We're doing this *right* now!"

I sat down on the curb, pulled out a Lucky, and played with it in my fingers. Éclair was still in his stand off, posed awkwardly, watching mommy and daddy fight.

"Kristy, I'm not doing this right now. I got a lot going through my head."

"Fuck you, Wilson. That's all I get from you? 'Not right now, babe.' 'I've got a lot to think about, babe.' I'm tired of this shit! Drive me home."

"What?" Doc snapped. "Drive *yourself* the fuck home!" Doc came and sat down next to me on the curb.

"Asshole!" Kristy stormed back into the bar.

Doc looked back to watch the door slam. "You alright, Éclair?"

"Uh… I have no idea what's going on and I'm really uncomfortable."

"It's alright man, come sit down," Doc told him.

Éclair plopped down next to us and finally lit his cigarette. I guess he felt the pressure in the air. Neither Doc nor I spoke. Éclair either didn't want to ask or was too afraid to know the answers. I didn't smoke, I just rubbed the cigarette between my fingers. There was a demon in my chest, he was clawing and pushing and it didn't feel like he was going to let go anytime soon.

After about three cigarettes worth of time, in which I didn't smoke, the girls came out of the bar. Kristy stayed by the door. Penelope kneeled down and put her hands on my shoulders. "Hank, can we drive Kristy home? She doesn't want to talk to Doc."

"I can't drive right now." I tried to hand her my keys. "But you can if you want."

"I can't drive stick." Penelope put her chin on my neck. "Are you alright, babe?"

"No."

Doc held up his keys. "You can take the Mustang, just bring her back in one piece."

Penelope took the keys. "Anything special I need to know about your old rust bucket?"

"Babe," I said.

"Yes?"

"Now's not the time for banter."

She squeezed my shoulders. "Do you need anything, Hank?"

"No. I'll be alright."

"Hank, how long have you been playing with that cigarette and not smoking it?"

"Since we came out."

After a few moments Penelope kissed the back of my neck and walked Kristy to Doc's Mustang. "You two look after Hank, I'll be back soon."

Kristy avoided looking at Doc as the two girls rolled out of the parking lot.

Ginny sat next to Éclair and wrapped her arm around his. "You guys alright?"

"I feel really awkward and have no idea what's going on," Éclair said to her.

"Has Hank seriously been out here this whole time *not* smoking?" Ginny asked.

"Yup." I put the Lucky in my mouth.

"What happened?"

"We ran into the girl that left me while we were in Iran," Doc confessed.

"Oh."

"I kind of figured something like that was up. When I looked at Hank and he didn't light up I knew something was wrong." Éclair looked at Ginny. "They were talking and everyone was ignoring Kristy and I guess that's what pissed her off."

"She went on a rant in there." Ginny tightened her grip around Éclair's arm.

"Yeah, she'll be alright." Doc ashed his smoke. "She gets pissed off every once in a while and runs home."

"Okay. Well then what's wrong with you, Hank?" Ginny asked sympathetically.

I took a long drag off of my cigarette. "The girl we ran into out here left Doc because my girlfriend left me."

"Um, okay?"

426

"She left me because of some shit that happened in Iran."

"Damn. What'd you do that was so bad that it made other people break up with their boyfriends?"

"I don't want to talk about it."

"Well," Ginny looked around. "I think I've known you guys long enough to know that you don't have any problems that can't be solved with tobacco and alcohol. What do you say we go back inside and start drinking?"

We crept back into the bar and started doing shots of vodka, gin, bourbon, and Jäger. After the four of us got good and liquored up we started joining in the terrible ensemble of drunken carolers. We sang, "Long Haired Country Boy" by Charlie Daniels, and "Nightrain" by Guns N' Roses. We knew the words by heart, but I can't imagine that we pulled it off well, even if the alcohol said we did.

When we got done Ginny and Éclair got up and started singing "Separate Ways" by Journey. As soon as the music started playing I looked at Doc. "Really? Those assholes are going to play this?"

Doc shrugged, took a shot of whiskey, and ordered another round. The drunken crowd started singing along with our friends, not one of them hit a note anywhere near where it was supposed to be.

"You know man," Doc started. "Life was fucking easier when all you had to do was fucking stay alive."

"Dude!" I slapped his shoulder. "I've been saying that!"

"But no, bro. That bitch never even said goodbye, she just started ignoring me."

"Yeah, but…" I shrugged and drank the shot in front of me on the bar and continued, "bitches ain't shit but hoes and tricks."

Doc gave me a dirty look.

I pointed at him and smiled. "George Washington said that."

427

"No Gandhi said that. And that was in a movie, not real life. Quit plagiarizing shit."

"I'll plagiarize your face, fucker." I petted Doc's face like a child would pet a small animal.

Doc smacked my hand away. "This whole thing's your fault anyway."

"How is it my fault?"

"For telling Kennedy what happened."

"I wasn't *going* to tell her! *You* talked me into it!" I lit a cigarette and stuck the burning cherry into my forearm.

Éclair and Ginny finished their song and rejoined us.

"Don't blame me for that shit, blame the fucking war." Doc followed suit with the skin burning. The bartender stared at us, not knowing what to do.

"Oh God," Ginny moaned. "Are you seriously talking about the war again? Are there any of you fucking people that do anything besides drink and bitch about the Marine Corps?"

I looked over at Ginny. "No… Fuck no." I leaned over the bar. "Hey barkeep! Can we get eight shots of spiced rum? Make it quick and I'll tip ya a twenty!"

The bartender said he'd do it if we put the cigarettes out.

"And we're not bitching about the Marine Corps," Éclair defended. "We're reminiscing about the best years of our lives and remembering our fallen brothers."

"You're not the only person who's lost people, Richard."

"Well I can't help that Kelsey was a soulless whore who fucked every swinging dick that fell in front of her and spread genital warts for charity."

Ginny put her index finger in Éclair's face. "That's *fucked* up, Richard!"

Éclair rolled his eyes at her.

"You're a fucking dick!"

Éclair raised his hands and mocked being scared. "Oooo." He backed off towards the restroom.

The bartender brought us our shots and I kept my promise about the tip. Ginny grabbed a shot glass and downed it before the barkeeper was done putting them all down.

"You know to be fair, she wasn't all bad," I tried to comfort Ginny.

"Yeah, thanks."

"I mean, genital warts are nature's way of making a dick ribbed for her pleasure, so Kelsey was actually providing a service."

"Fuck you too, Hank." Ginny grabbed another shot.

I put my hand on her shoulder. "Come on, I'm kidding."

"It's not funny."

"Kelsey would think it was funny."

Ginny mean-mugged me.

"You know she would, there wasn't anything that she wouldn't crack a joke about. Remember that time she wore that three-foot-long strap on under her pants and had the shaft sticking out the crotch hole?"

Ginny's eyes started to water and she tried to hide a little bit of a smile.

"Then she put peanut butter on the head and had dogs come up and lick it."

"Yeah," came from somewhere between a laugh and a sob.

"You'll be alright, things will work out. It's kind of been a weird night. I'm sure Éclair will calm down and you two can go home and do whatever weird shit you two are in to."

"Has he said anything about that?"

"I remember something about giraffes," I joked.

"SHOT IN MY HEART AND YOU'RE TOO LATE..." came screaming through the karaoke speakers.

"Ugh," Ginny groaned. "I fucking *hate* Bon Jovi."

"WHOA! What's wrong with Bon Jovi?" Doc yelled.

"Who the hell's playing this?" Ginny turned around to see Éclair on stage with the microphone.

Éclair pointed straight at Ginny, screaming the rest of the lyrics.

Ginny put a stern look on her face and downed another shot. "I'm out." She calmly walked out the door.

I looked back at Doc and laughed. "Oops!"

Éclair finished his song and rejoined us at the bar. "Where'd Ginny go?"

Doc told him, "She bounced, dude."

"Yeah I think you pissed her off," I laughed.

"Fuck it." Éclair grabbed two of the remaining shots and downed them back to back.

I looked at the glasses on the bar. "There's three left, gents." We each took a shot glass and knocked them down together. "Okay, Imma go smoke."

We stumbled out of the bar and lit our cigarettes.

"So'd she really just fucking leave?"

"Yeah man." Doc laughed. "She said 'Fuck you' and got out of here."

"Goddammit." Éclair fumbled his phone to his ear.

I smoked my cigarette and watched. It was cool out, but not nipply. Booze, hate, and my jean jacket kept me warm. People would eyeball me when I wore it, it was home to about seventy patches. The denim could hardly be seen. The three of us wobbled trying to stand straight.

A flirtatious college-aged couple came outside and lit up a few feet away from us.

Éclair dialed Ginny's number five or six times to no avail. "Fuck it." He put the phone away. "And fuck her, too."

Doc and I looked at him. "Wait, so that's cool?"

Éclair shot us the bird. "No, it's a fucking figure of speech dude." Éclair lit a new cigarette with the end of the old one and cast it aside. "It's whatever. All I need is the Corps."

"I hear ya, bro," Doc sighed.

"Dude you're in the navy," I bantered.

"Shut up asshole."

"But yeah man." I turned back to Éclair and said, "I want to call you a motard, but I get what you're saying. What is it that's so alluring about this gun club?"

Éclair shook his head. "I don't know man, there's just something about fucking shooting people in the face…"

The young college couple beside us stopped their flirting and stared at us disturbed.

I waved at them and said, "It's okay, we're Marines."

That didn't help. They crushed their cigarettes and scurried back inside. The three of us looked at each other and laughed. Éclair chuckled and said, "Well I don't think we should stay here, but I don't want to quit drinking yet."

"Where y'all wanna go?" I asked.

"I can call my chief and see if he can come grab us. He's always fucking out partying." Doc pulled out his phone.

"Okay."

Doc put the phone to his head. "Hey Chief! Yeah it's Evans... No, no we got stuck at this bar in Vista... Yeah? That's cool... No we didn't, my buddy pissed off our driver and she left us here... Yeah it was his girlfriend... HA! Yeah, women right? Yeah, I appreciate that, but we don't really have a ride and we were hoping you could help us out with that... Really? Well fuck probably, shouldn't use our arrive alive card for that then huh? Okay... Well we'll see what we can do..." Doc hung up the phone.

"What'd he say, man?" Éclair asked.

"Yeah we're welcome over there, but he's coked out right now and he's not going to drive."

"Wait, so he's got coke?" Éclair's intrigue piqued.

"Yeah dude, that fucker's got some Afghan shit."

"How far away does he live?"

"Not too far, I think a little bit towards San Marcos."

"Fuck it." Éclair pulled out his keys. "We got the Camaro."

We piled into Éclair's car and lit more smokes. He started the engine.

We took off east towards Doc's chief's place. Doc gave Éclair directions from the passenger seat. We avoided busy roads in an effort to stay away from the police. We were rolling through the streets outside of the small cities that populate southern California, the places where the rolling desert hills meet the suburbs. I was staring at the little yellow lines in the road, watching them weave between the headlights and disappear under the hood as if the car was eating them.

A cougar ran into the road and stopped in the middle of the street. This fucker was huge. He was eye level with us, and not backing down. We all screamed "SHIT!" and the Camaro speared through the mountain lion.

The cat's giant body exploded, covering the car in blood. The car spun sideways and flipped over. We screamed as the car flipped and rolled down the side of a hill. Then things went black.

I vaguely remember looking down, watching my feet drag away from the burning wreckage, then nothing until something hit my face and woke me. My head was pounding and my whole body ached. Doc had my shirt in his fist, slapping me. "Hank! Wake the fuck up!" He slapped me again.

I punched him in the face. "Quit hitting me, fucker."

Doc pulled me up so I was sitting and started trying to wake up Éclair. I held my head in my hands and tried to rub off the pounding in my skull. I looked at the fire then at Doc and Éclair.

Doc finally got Éclair to wake up. Éclair looked at the burning hulk that used to be his '69 Camaro and rubbed his face. "Goddamn it."

"Hey, we gotta get the fuck out of here!" Doc tried to get us to move.

Misery took Éclair's mind as he watched his precious car burn. He didn't say anything coherent. He pointed at the twisted wreckage and muttered halves of syllables. The flickering of the flames illuminated us. The skin under Éclair's eyes turned dark and a slow stream of blood flowed from his nose.

Doc limped up a small hill with his phone to the sky.

"What are you doing, Doc?" I called to him.

"Don't be calling the police, man," Éclair forced himself to say.

"I'm not, don't worry. I'm gonna call Penelope to come pick us up, she still has my car."

"Fuck. I forgot she was out with us." I took my hand off of my head and slowly inventoried my pockets for anything I may have lost.

"Yeah, good luck winning that argument," Éclair mumbled.

433

"You're fucking one to talk." I pulled out my lighter and tried to light it. The flint was out and the wheel wouldn't spin. I grabbed my cigarette and hobbled to the Camaro. I stuck the end of my Lucky's into the flames coming from what was once the bottom of the car.

"Man," Éclair protested. "Have some respect for the thing."

I scowled over my shoulder, "Well does your fucking lighter work?"

"I don't fucking know, man."

I crossed myself over the flames. "She was a good strong car, we rode through the Valley of Death, gasoline is neither patient nor kind, and she is now in the great big garage in the sky with her '72 Volkswagens. Fare winds and following seas." I turned back to Éclair. "Fucking happy?"

Éclair buried his face in his palms. "Goddamn it. What the fuck am I going to do?"

Doc returned from the hill. "You're going to get in my car when Penelope gets here with it, then we're going to go away, and tomorrow you're going to call the cops and report it stolen. But you have to wait until tomorrow so the cops don't get suspicious."

We sat at the edge of the flame's light until we heard the hum of the Mustang's engine, and climbed up the hill.

Penelope parked on the side of the road and stepped out of the driver's seat. "Need a ride?" She looked at us and noticed our limping. "What happened to you guys? And how'd you get out here?" I pointed my thumb over the hill. Penelope looked down at the burning Camaro. "Oh my God! Are you okay? What happened? Doc just said you needed a ride!"

"We hit a mountain lion," Éclair grimaced.

Penelope looked at us toe to tip and took a sniff. "How drunk are you?"

"We're up there, babe."

"And you were driving?" Her voice grew angry.

"Well…" I started.

Penelope backhanded me. "How fucking stupid are you?"

I grabbed my head, her hand didn't help the gremlins ripping apart my brains. "Goddamn it woman! That fucking hurt!"

"Well then maybe you stupid twats shouldn't be drinking and driving!"

"Hey, he wasn't driving, it wasn't his fault," Éclair defended me. Penelope bitch slapped him next.

"Get in the fucking car!" she ordered. Doc opened his mouth to say something but my jolly green giant punched the words from his mouth. "NOW!" She pointed at the idling Mustang.

We plummeted into the car and screamed to San Diego, silently. We journeyed to the west, the winds didn't shake the windows, no one smoked, we were silent in fear of Penelope's fist on our aching bodies, and there wasn't so much as quiet talk radio. The only sounds were the rumble of the engine and the tires on the pavement.

We stopped at her apartment building and Penelope took us upstairs. "You can all stay here tonight." She opened the door. "Find space where you can, there's blankets on the couch." When we were all inside she turned on the light. It burned straight into the three of our souls. Penelope glanced at us. "Make sure to take a shower first, I don't want my things bloodied and soiled." She disappeared into her room.

Doc grabbed Éclair by the temples.

"What are you doing, man?" Éclair protested.

"Be quiet. Open your eyes and look into the light."

Éclair complied and Doc inspected him. Doc then felt Éclair's pulse and checked behind his ears for bruises. He patted Éclair on the shoulder and told him he was okay to rack out and that he didn't really need a hospital, just water, Motrin, and ice. Doc gave me the once over and declared us all good. "We're all a little rattled up but no one needs stitches or a run to the ER, so I guess that's good."

"Fantastic," I mumbled. "I'll see y'all in the a.m." I stripped and turned on the water in the shower. I looked at myself in the mirror while I was waiting for the shower to warm up. Both my eyes were already deep purple and my arms and chest were bruised. I had dirt and soot ground into my skin.

The hot water felt good on the back of my neck. In all the excitement I'd started to sober up, but not a lot. I stood there for a few minutes doing nothing more than enjoying the hot water.

When I was clean, or as close to it as I could be, I wrapped a towel around my waist and stumbled to Penelope's room. The lights were out, but the cracked blinds let in blue and yellow streaks from the city's lights and the moon. Penelope sat on her bed still clothed, arms crossed. Her eyes slowly slid a sword across my throat. I dropped my clothes on the floor by her feet and fell face first onto her bed.

"You think you're sleeping in here tonight?" Her frozen voice chilled the room.

"I wasn't driving, babe," I meekly defended myself.

"You got in the car with them, and you were obviously pissed."

"Baby, when you've been through as much shit as I have with those guys drinking and driving isn't a big deal."

"Not a big deal, huh?"

"Penelope, I was literally facedown in Iranian sand bleeding so much from bullet holes that I was about to drown in my own blood and Doc ran three hundred meters through open terrain while Hajji tried to gun him down, to grab me and try to pull me to safety."

Penelope took in a deep, angry breath.

That's right Hank, blame the war. She can't win that argument.

Penelope's voice turned to heavy concern as she said, "Hank, I don't *understand* you. You're so damn proud of being a Marine, yet I haven't heard you actually say one good thing about your experiences. It's all blood and guts, and it seems like half the time the blood is yours."

"And?" I closed my eyes and tried to fall asleep before she could keep talking.

"Is that what they're calling PTSD?"

"PTSD? You mean the best years of my life?"

"That. I don't get the duality of it all, Hank."

"I think I just drank too much of the Kool Aid."

"What does that mean?"

"Never mind."

Penelope picked up my jean jacket and looked at the patches on its back in the dim blue moon light. She ran her fingers over the patch under the back collar. It was a blue diamond with a KA-BAR sticking through. "Ready for all... Yielding to none. That sounds like a good way to describe you." She kept looking at the patch. "Second Battalion Seventh Marines." Penelope sighed again. "I wonder how you would have turned out if you were never a Marine."

"Huh?"

"I wonder sometimes if we crossed paths and you were just a regular human being how things may have been."

I glared at her over my shoulder. She looked back at me. There was sorrow in her eyes. "What do you mean *regular* human being?"

"I don't know, Hank."

"I'm not taking this shit." I had nowhere to go and was too hurt and drunk to stand up and walk. I grabbed the edge of a blanket and rolled off the bed. I hit the floor with a heavy thud. My body cracked, I groaned in pain. It wasn't the brightest idea I've ever had.

Penelope stood up and pulled the blanket over me, tucking me in. I couldn't put my thoughts into words but I was angry with her. She ran her fingers over my hair and sat back down on the bed. Penelope picked my jacket back up and took her time inspecting the patched denim garment.

I was floating in that gloom filled watery place between sleep and awake when Penelope nudged me back awake with her foot. I pretended I didn't feel it and kept my eyes closed. *Bitch, let me sleep.*

"Hank," she whispered. She nudged me harder. "Hank."

"What?" I cried pathetically.

"What's this?"

I looked up at her silhouette. I had to squint to see what was in her hands. "It's a ring." I buried my head back under the blanket.

"Is it supposed to be for me?"

"It's supposed to be."

A few seconds passed and Penelope laid down on my back. Her breasts pushed into my shoulder blades as she wrapped her arm around mine. *Goddammit, I hate being the small spoon.*

"I know what rings like this are for, Hank," she whispered into my ear.

"But not birthday presents?"

"Hank, I worry about you."

"Thanks." *Let me sleep, woman.*

She held the ring in her open hand then slid it onto her finger. "Hank…"

"Penelope." *Go to bed, let me go to sleep. Hell, let me die, just leave me in peace.*

"If we're going to do this, you're going to have to start opening up to

438

me about things instead of bottling them up. I don't know if it's that you don't trust me or if it's that you don't think I'll understand, but I will always be here for you, and I want you to know that you can tell me anything."

My anger *slightly* subsided. "Yeah."

"Hank."

"Uh huh?"

"Who was that girl this evening? She obviously struck a chord."

"She's Doc's ex girlfriend."

"So why were you so upset?"

"You know that girl I told you about that left me while I was in Iran?"

"Yes."

"They were best friends. And there's more to that story than I've been honest with you about."

"How so?"

"Remember how I said that she disagreed with me being in the war at all and couldn't take it?"

"Something to that effect, yes."

"She didn't care about the war, she just wanted me home safe. Things looked like they might have worked out if I made it back home alive. Then we were in a firefight and I stabbed this *guy* to death. And I really dug into him. I cut out his intestines and sawed off his head. Afterwards I went through his wallet and he had the same picture my girlfriend had on her nightstand of her and her father."

"Wait, what?"

"I gutted her father like a deer."

"Oh…"

"I still have to drink myself to sleep to keep from having nightmares about that kind of shit."

Penelope was silent for a few moments. I figured she was trying to find a way to close what she thought might have been Pandora's Box. "It was just really weird seeing you sad. You're usually so angry about things that it's become the norm. You being sad was almost surreal."

"Can you see why?"

"Yes."

"So do you still want to keep that ring?"

"I do."

I rolled over and brought Penelope under the blanket. We spent the night on the floor.

25 GILGAMESH AND ENKIDU

"SERGEANT!"

Goddammit bitch, what do you want? "Yes, Gunnery Sergeant?"

"What happened to your face?"

It was six forty-five on Monday morning. The platoon had just gotten back from a run, which is not fun when your whole body ached from a car crash and was painted yellow, purple, and black.

"I lost a fight with a mountain lion."

"What?" Gunny Chanceworth rattled her head in disbelief.

"I was out in the desert with a couple of my bros and we had to jump down this cliff to get away from a cougar."

"Have you gone to medical yet?" Chanceworth actually showed a tone of concern. It caught me off guard. She was normally one of the most despicable human beings I've ever met.

"I had a corpsman look me over. They put me on a heavy regiment of changing my socks."

"Did they at least give you Motrin?"

"Yes, Gunnery Sergeant."

"Alright." Chanceworth looked around for a second as if she was trying to remember something important. "Oh, uh, don't forget the company has annual training today at the base theater."

"I'll have my Marines there, Gunny."

I showered, grabbed chow, and corralled the Marines across base to the theater. They all gave me funny looks, but I guess I couldn't blame them. Pendleton's base theater was a grand ol' theatre back in the fifties. It hadn't had an ounce of upkeep since then. My brain was still a bag of scrambled eggs, so situational awareness wasn't at its peak. I threw myself into a seat next to Rainer, so if anything, I could joke about how stupid the training was going to be. Glædwine sat in the seat next to me. We hadn't exactly been avoiding each other since the ball, but we were at a bit of a standoff. I guess we found ourselves guilty. I missed our conversations on the smoke deck.

Glædwine leaned over to me. "Sergeant, what's the point of these?"

"They want to make sure that you know how not to beat your wife and rape people."

"I don't have a wife," Glædwine said and smiled.

"Okay, well then they want to make sure you know how not to rape your husband."

"Ah." Glædwine looked around the room. "So, you were attacked by a mountain lion?"

"Something like that. Lots of blood, fire, twisted metal, alcohol, and pain."

"Sounds like a party."

"Yeah." I laughed then wheezed and coughed and grabbed my chest. It still hurt to laugh.

The theater was called to attention and sat back to rest. The company commander introduced the brief. He told us that we were all about to receive good training that day and we should pay attention because these things weren't something to gaff off.

The CO left, a random staff sergeant climbed the stage. He started off the bit like every presenter does in these briefs. "Good morning Marines, I'm Staff Sergeant Davis and I will be giving you the next period of instruction. These briefs are designed to be interactive, so the more you participate the quicker things will go. I'm going to start off with a question. Why is it that Marines will die for each other in combat but leave each other behind when we get home? There's a series of videos we're going to watch, then we're going to have a discussion about them. Before we start, do we have any questions?"

I wanted to say, *Yeah, how the fuck did the Marine Corps devolve to the point where we're sat down and shown videos like fucking twelve-year-olds instead of put through realistic training?* But I didn't want an ass chewing, so I kept quiet.

The lights went out and the theater's screen lit up. *The Marines in civilian attire were drinking at a bar. A basketball game was on the TV and they called each other "Devil Dog" and "Leatherneck." They watched a blonde woman in a skimpy dress come in and sit at a table with a fat bald guy in his forties with a Hawaiian button down, a gold chain necklace, and a goatee. The Marines made comments to each other, mostly about the blonde woman's breasts, and kept drinking. The blonde woman excused herself to the bathroom. While she was gone her bald goateed date slips something into her drink. The three Marines saw what happened and comment to each other how messed up that situation was. The woman comes back, drinks the drink, and starts feeling woozy. Her overweight bald date offers to take her home and they leave.*

The lights in the theater came back and Staff Sergeant Davis hopped on the stage. "Okay, let's talk about what we just saw." He pointed to random Marines around the room and they gave him the cookie cutter good boy responses.

"The Marines shouldn't have been bystanders."

"The Marines should have told the girl or the bartender."

"They didn't protect someone they could see was about to get harmed."

Then one Marine stood up and said, "Staff Sergeant, it's the woman's fault."

The theater went silent. "How so, Marine?" Davis asked.

"The guy she was on a date with looked like a convicted child molester. There's no way a woman that hot would be on a date with a douchebag-looking tool like that."

The theater erupted in laughter and was quickly halted by someone screaming, "Why's that funny?" I looked back to find a short, hairy, double chinned, female captain from the S3 with Elmer's Glue for skin and a face that would disgust Satan. She stood with her arms crossed hating the Marines. "Well?"

Staff Sergeant Davis shook his head. "Well, the captain's right. Why's that funny?"

The crowd murmured. The ass kissers offered their brainwashed opinions.

Rainer whispered to me, "Why is it there's always some fucking POG bitch trying to ruin everyone's fun? We're joking around, dude. We're not actually going to go pillage a village. Just because your uncle came in your ass doesn't mean you have to ruin everyone else's fun."

"It makes the victim look like it's their fault," one of the Marines volunteered.

"I still don't think a chick that attractive should have been in the room with a creep like that," I said to Rainer. "Glædwine, what do you think?"

"I'd rather cauterize my vagina shut with a curling iron."

The Staff Sergeant quieted us down and played the next video.

A Gunnery Sergeant and a Sergeant walked into an office at a supply warehouse. The Sergeant was a highly motivated young female who was excited to deploy with the unit soon. The two of them stood in front of their company commander, who also just so happens to have the face of a date rapist. The Captain welcomed the Sergeant to the unit and undressed her with his eyes. Over the next few days the Captain said a few things to the Sergeant that could either be taken as legitimate comments or blatant advances, depending on how you interpreted them. Eventually the Captain comes up to the Sergeant and proposed that the two of them go to a movie that night that he'd already bought tickets for. The Sergeant was crept-out and denied the offer. As the Captain walked away the Gunnery Sergeant asked him what had just happened. The Captain tells the Gunny that they were just talking about last minute predeployment issues that needed to be taken care of. A few more unintelligent scenes go by and the Captain corners the Sergeant and demands that she come to his house that night and discuss predeployment things. The Sergeant said no and the Captain reminded her that he was an officer and that was an order. The scene changes to the Captain in his house drinking. The door opens and the Sergeant is standing there. The Captain grabbed her and started raping.

"Alright." The staff sergeant stopped the video. "What happened here?"

"And no bullshit answers!" the troll of an excuse for an officer screamed from the back.

"That captain is a disgusting fucking *thing*," I complained to Rainer.

"I know, man."

One of the supply Marines stood and said, "She was just trying to work some overtime, Rah. That's what we signed up to do."

"He didn't sign up to do shit, fucking faggot box kicker," I griped.

Another Marine stood up. "Staff Sergeant, what happened was the Sergeant was approached by her CO and fell victim to him while her Staff NCOs just watched."

"So the moral of the story is not to be a bystander?" The staff Sergeant fished for an answer.

Glædwine stood up. "Staff Sergeant, this video is offensive towards women."

"How's that, Corporal?"

"Because if the Sergeant in that video had half of a brain she would have sought help from her Staff NCOs, she wouldn't have gone to the Captain's house, and she was obviously weak, because she was over powered by someone who was extremely inebriated. That video told me that the Marine Corps thinks all females, regardless of rank, are stupid, don't work out, or know how to defend themselves, and don't know how to take care of themselves in the working environment. What the Sergeant should have done was shot the Captain. However, since this video was made by people who look down on women, she didn't have a concealed weapons permit. While it wasn't initially her fault, she did *nothing* to take herself out of a bad situation."

"So Corporal, you think it's acceptable to shoot your CO?"

"Staff Sergeant, if my CO was trying to rape me I would put a bullet in his face."

"Hmm. Okay, well we have one more video and we'll take a break." Staff Sergeant Davis dimmed the lights.

I gave Glædwine the thumbs up and nodded, she smiled back at me.

The rest of the videos were just as ridiculous. People killed themselves after showing every sign of trouble and no one helped. Marines got home from Iraq and beat their wives, they stole money, and did drugs. Every video illustrated that the higher ups of the Marine Corps obviously had no idea what was happening at the lower levels. They were a knee-jerk reaction to the public accusing the Corps of these problems, which *did* exist, and now the Marine Generals could say, 'Look we're fixing the problem instead of reconnecting with the Marines and actually doing any work worth note.'

The training ended and we left the theater. The Marines had carpooled on the way over. The few of us that drove alone offered our seats to people to make the rides back less crowded. I took Rainer and Glædwine.

"When'd you get this, dude?" Rainer asked about the GTO.

"Last week." I started the engine.

"This is really nice, Sergeant." Glædwine climbed into the back.

"Thanks."

"What'd you do with the Jeep, dude?" Rainer inquired.

447

"I still have it."

"Are you just taking up two spots at the barracks?" Glædwine asked.

"Not really. I'm letting my buddy borrow the Jeep. He crashed his car and didn't have another ride."

"Ah." Rainer looked over the wood paneling on the dash. "So how stupid was that training?"

"Right? It's like, 'Hey, I know how to not do drugs, beat my wife, and kill myself.'" I pulled onto Vandergrift. "You guys need anything from the PX before we head back?"

"No." Glædwine shook her head. "But training like this is pointless. Rapists and murderers aren't going to stop doing what they're doing because they were all of a sudden informed what they were doing is wrong."

"Yeah, they should just cut rapists' dicks off and be done with it," Rainer said while rolling his eyes.

"And I *hate* that, 'What she's wearing isn't an excuse' argument." I lit a cigarette. "Saying that implies that I'm just a fucking animal and can't help myself from fucking something shiny that catches my eye. Rapist assholes are rapist assholes, no brief is going to stop that. So why the fuck do I have to waste half a day sitting through this bullshit?"

Rainer looked over at me and said, "Because *you're* not allowed to rape anyone but that big green digital weenie is lubed up and ready to penetrate. What I think is funny is that the Staff Sergeant dude was talking about fraternization, and I've seen that guy in the chow hall eating alone with a female lance corporal. Fucking douchebag."

"Well that's the thing," Glædwine started. "Fraternization happens. Most of the time it's consensual and a relationship forms, then it becomes sexual assault when the junior Marine, usually female, decided she wants out and thinks that if she calls rape she won't look like a harlot. And the Marine Corps blindly takes the woman's side of it and only prosecutes the male when *both* of them should have been court martialed. There was a Marine here a few years ago, her dad was the sergeant major at one of the other units on Pendleton. She showed up as a lance corporal right out of the schoolhouse. She starts having sex with one of the sergeants and after they got caught the sergeant gets demoted to lance corporal. A few weeks later she gets meritoriously promoted to corporal. She wasn't even there for a year before they made her a sergeant."

"Eh. I don't know," Rainer grimaced. "I think that's probably because daddy was the sergeant major, not because she's a chick."

"Wait, was that Garcia?" I asked.

"Oh, so you know," Glædwine cheered.

"I know the chick. Her fucking dad was the most fucked up Sergeant Major I've ever had. He would always tell us that it was the lance corporals' fault that the battalion was all fucked up. And I thought that if the battalion is fucked up it's probably the higher ups' fault because they're the ones that could do something about it. But yeah that fuck brought his asshole daughter over to ComCam and made us do a fucking dog and pony show for her before she even graduated high school. Then he works his fucking slimy Sergeant Major fingers and gets the bitch in the MOS. Now there's another useless fucking turd running around pretending they're hot shit. I don't fucking understand how people get that fucking self-entitled. It's like, 'Hey bitch, I've seen you in your chucks. I would be fucking embarrassed to be a corporal or a sergeant with that little experience.' I don't give a fuck if they end up having a good attitude about it and just try to learn instead of being a fucking dick head, there's been three fucking wars in the last fifteen years, why the *fuck* are you promoting someone who hasn't been there when you have ten other guys the same rank who just got back from their second deployment?"

"Why don't you tell me how you really feel?" Rainer joked.

"No dude, it's bullshit. I mean, I made it to sergeant, I'm over the hump. But I was a fucking lance corporal for four fucking years and I watched all these fucking retards get put on boards and get promoted because they either kissed ass or sucked someone's dick." I flicked my cigarette out the window. "That's another thing that pisses me off. If these

449

fucking females want us to stop accusing them of fucking the master sergeant for a promotion then they should probably stop fucking the master sergeant. There was this *worthless, fucking WORTHLESS* fucking bitch when I was a lance back at Division between deployments. If a male Marine went to the master sergeant for something he'd yell at us for not using the chain of command, but a female could walk right up to him and it was okay. And this cunt, Slater, would be in his office for hours at a time with the fucking door closed. That fuck got to division right when I got back from my fist pump and we were both lances. I go back to Afghanistan and she goes to Iraq. I'm running around trying not to get my ass shot off and to not lose my fucking legs because I stepped on the wrong fucking rock. Slater fucking goes to Al Assad, sits on her pussy, and doesn't do shit besides sit by the master sergeant and take photos of generals. Eight months later when I come home she's the mother fucking platoon sergeant! What the fuck is that about?"

"Sergeant?" Glædwine leaned forward between the GTO's bucket seats.

"Yeah?"

"You were ranting and missed the turn."

"Mother fucker!"

"But yeah, that shit's fucked up, dude." Rainer rolled up his window.

"I fucking wish I had a fat set of tits and could just fuck my way to the top. I'm fucking jealous!"

"Well if it helps, we're not all like that, but the women who aren't fucking the staff hate the ones who are more than you do," Glædwine informed me.

"Yeah, because the one or two sluts doing it make you all look like whores because y'all get grouped together."

"No seriously Sergeant, there's more than a few doing it. And it's fucking deplorable. I know that they're really just embarrassing themselves, but when you're one of the people that has to deal with the consequences it's fucking frustrating."

"It's just like those videos." Rainer laughed.

"No it is not." I pointed at him. "In the videos the man is the bad guy when in reality both of them need to be put in front of a fucking firing squad. And in the videos all the dudes were date rapists, not 'fuck me for rank' dudes. And I don't understand date rape guy. It's like, 'You're going to see these people at work tomorrow. How do you plan on getting away with that?'"

"I thought it was funny that all that bad shit happened to POGS and boots," Rainer joked.

"Well then there was the other one where the dude took the chick home and was banging her then halfway through she decided she didn't want any more and told him to stop and the guy ended up going to jail. That's fucked up. How are you going to dress like a slut, grind on a dude all night, get drunk as fuck with him, go home with him, *put his dick in your mouth,* then the next day say that you didn't mean to do it and call what he did rape? It's not rape if you were sucking his dick, you fucking slut. That was bad decision making."

"I feel the same way, Sergeant," Glædwine sighed. "I honestly hate female Marines."

"I know and don't get me wrong, I fucking love the Marine Corps. I just want better for it than the corrupted, immoral prostitutes that are filling the ranks. And this annual training pissed me the fuck off. None of that helps us survive in combat and we shouldn't be fucking doing it. It's a waste of time that could be spent on *actual* training and there are people that are going to die in a ditch in a faraway land because they spent their days learning about sexual assault instead of assaulting the enemy."

"True that, man," Rainer agreed.

I pulled the GTO into the parking lot, killed the engine, stepped out, and lit a cigarette. Rainer took off. Glædwine pulled out a smoke.

"There's so much fucked up shit in the Marine Corps…" I continued my rant. "But no one's ever going to fix it because the problems don't affect the people with the power to fix shit. Then those same assholes make stupid fucking decisions and don't have to deal with the consequences."

"That's not the Marine Corps, that's America."

"It's fucked up how much we fight for America when no one fights for us. The people in charge keep telling us they're taking care of us then they feed us to fucking wolves if they don't fucking eat us themselves. I'm not saying that I'm the most virtuous person that ever lived, but *fuck* dude, someone's gotta do something about the Corps."

"You're not this contemptible bastard you make yourself out to be."

"Eh." I took a drag off my cigarette. The smoke warmed my lungs in the cool winter morning. "I've done a lot of really fucked up shit Glædwine, and I know I'm calling the kettle black, but this shit just pissed me off."

"You're a good person, Sergeant. If you were as bad as you're always telling everyone you are then the ball would have gone differently and we'd both be in the brig."

I chuckled a little bit. "Ain't that fucked up? You can bang your master sergeant for rank but you can't bang a married chick."

"Well I don't know if I would have actually done anything. Yes, I was drunk, but I don't think I was willing to sacrifice my marriage for that. Although what you said about the next life, I do want you to know that I do…" Glædwine cut herself off at the sound of footsteps.

Rainer came back to the car. "You guys see my keys?"

"They in the car, man?"

Rainer opened the door and snooped around.

"Yeah, so have you ever read *A Thousand and One Arabian Nights*?" I said disguising our conversation.

"Uh, yeah."

"How do you pronounce the chick's name?"

"Shara...Sharons...Sharaz?"

"Sharazaidaboomshakalakalaka!" I laughed.

"Yeah that was it. Aren't books just dreams you hold in your hand?"

"That's about right. I did like though that the stories in there are completely different than they're interpreted now. Like how Aladdin is Chinese."

"There's a lot of them in there. Although I think the whole thing was inspired by the Epic of Gilgamesh."

"I don't think I've read that one."

Rainer mumbled something and walked back off.

"It's pretty interesting. Actually it's the oldest known story, the Sumerians carved it into stones before people were even walking around in Egypt."

"Yeah? Tell me about it."

"Gilgamesh is the king of Uruk and goes around having sex with everything with tits and a pulse."

"I already like him."

"The people call to the gods for help and the gods don't like him either, so they make a monster-man named Enkidu to kill Gilgamesh and curse him with terrible nightmares until he dies. Enkidu shows up to fight Gilgamesh and instead of killing each other they bro out and become best friends, but they still play pranks on each other and go on great adventures killing monsters so they'll have fame."

"Go on..."

"When the gods see that Enkidu didn't kill Gilgamesh they curse Enkidu to death, he falls very ill, and Gilgamesh swears to find a way to save his friend. He knew this old legend about Utnapishtim, who for all intents and purposes was Noah, after the ark and the flood the gods granted immortal life. So Gilgamesh goes to try to find who I'm going to call Noah because I can't pronounce 'Utnapishtim' correctly. Gilgamesh journeys to the end of the earth where there's two mountains that no one's ever crossed to a tunnel that no one's ever entered. The tunnel was guarded by giant scorpion-men that gave Gilgamesh puzzles that he had to solve to pass. He gets through and goes through this tunnel and there's a beautiful garden underground full of all kinds of trees and jewels and gold." Glædwine looked at me and then my hand. "Are you alright, Sergeant?"

"Huh?"

"You're shaking and you're about to burn yourself."

I looked at my hand. My cigarette had burned down to my fingers. I dropped it without bothering to smolder it out. "Keep going with the story."

"Sergeant you're white."

"Keep going."

"Well there's a waterway Gilgamesh had to cross to get to Noah and at the mouth there were two stone giants guarding the passageway. Gilgamesh destroys the giants who the ferryman later told him were the only creatures that could cross the Waters of Death. Gilgamesh then goes and cuts down a hundred twenty trees to lie across the water and get to the island where Noah lives. When he gets there they have an argument and Noah eventually tells him his story. The gods didn't like their creation and flooded the earth, but they liked Noah so they made him build an ark and spared him and his family. Noah gives Gilgamesh some challenges and he fails all of them. So when Gilgamesh goes to leave, Noah's wife persuades him to tell Gilgamesh a way to immortality. There's a plant that looks like a wolfberry bush and its berries make the eater immortal, but it only grows under water. Gilgamesh finds this plant and uses a rock to get deep enough to grab the berries off of the plant. He doesn't eat them though, he tries to go straight back to Enkidu and give them to him so he won't die from being sick. It's a long journey back and while Gilgamesh is taking a bath in a river a snake comes and eats the berries and Gilgamesh weeps because he's lost his chances of immortality and was now going to lose his friend. And that's pretty much the end. It doesn't have a great ending, but it's a good read."

Glædwine lit another cigarette. "Sergeant?" She waved her hand in front of my face. "Hey are you okay?" She pushed a finger into my shoulder.

I shook my head violently. "Yeah! Sorry. I…uh. I have to sit down." I put my back against the rear wheel of the Pontiac.

"You alright?"

"No." I tried to stop myself from shaking.

"What's wrong?"

"Iraq."

"Iraq?"

"Memories… Sorry." I stared at her for a minute. "I can get that like at a book store, right?"

"Yeah… Sergeant I'm not trying to be a bitch but did that story give you Iraq flashbacks?"

"Yeah." I had every second of what happened in that cave in Al Hillah running through my head at the same time.

"Do you want me to leave?" She recognized the awkwardness of the situation.

I was sitting with my legs crossed. I took off my cover and stared at the ground under me. I was scratching the crown of my head through my hair. I really didn't want her to go. "Just don't tell anyone."

"Alright. Let me know if you need anything." She touched my head and walked into the building.

I wanted to leave right then and bolt to a book store, but it was only fourteen hundred and at the very least I'd get some pretty bad paperwork if I left before we were released. I wished life could be simple like it was in movies and I could just leave and do what I needed to do without negative consequences.

I composed myself over half a pack of cigarettes. My hands wouldn't stop shaking. When my throat was too coarse to keep from coughing I forced myself inside to get water. I found a corner where I could be alone, pulled out my phone, and looked up the Epic of Gilgamesh. The basic synopsis was what Glædwine had said, and what had been in the cave.

When we were finally released from work, half an hour late because Gunny Chanceworth felt like being a bitch that afternoon, I changed over and tried to race to the book store in Carlsbad. It took me a fucking hour to get off base because of construction and about another hour to get to where I was going. I'm surprised I made it to the store instead of getting out of my car and beating shithead drivers in front of me to death. I found the book and after purchasing it sat down at the café they had and read it cover to cover in almost no time at all. I thought, *Doc has to see this*.

The trip back to base was a hell of a lot faster. But the thoughts of the similarities between the book and what happened in Iraq were too close. I was still shaking when I kicked in Doc's barracks room door.

He looked at me like I was crazy. I grabbed his phone and told the person on the other line, "He'll call you back," and I hung up. It immediately started buzzing.

"Fuck dude, I'm still in *deep* shit with her!"

I shoved the book in Doc's chest and said, "Read this."

He squinted at me. "The fuck, dude? You can't just…"

"FUCKING READ IT!"

"Fine dude, fuck. But you're going to have to deal with Kristy."

I let the phone keep buzzing and watched Doc read. He was already in a bad mood from his situation with Kristy and I wasn't helping the situation by holding him hostage. His eyes slowly went from anger to intense fear. As he neared the end he look up to me, "What the fuck?"

To which I replied, "Keep reading."

When he was done he held the book open and stared at me. "It's just like that fucking place in Al Hillah. The tunnel, the scorpions, the puzzles, the trees, the waters of death, and…"

"And I killed the snake that tried to take the berries, then we ate them."

We stared wide eyed at each other long enough for the sun to go down.

"Well what the fuck does this mean?"

"It means we know why we didn't die in Iran…"

To Be Continued…

Thank you for reading Smokepit Fairytales. If you enjoyed it, please leave it
a review on Amazon.
Come follow me on Instagram @trippainsworth
or on Twitter @trippsmokepit.
Visit Smokepitfairytales.com

Fonzie and his bag of dicks

Hank and Penelope after a bad night of drinking

The Sirbot

Richard Éclair

Virginia "Ginny" Éclair

Kennedy dancing behind the blinds

Kennedy and Reagan on Doc's car

Penelope in the GOAT

Penelope

Best Respect the Éclair

About the Author

Tripp, who sexually identifies as an American twin-engine attack helicopter, was genetically engineered in a laboratory in Florida. He cut himself from the womb with a rotary blade so he could put veteran's day on his birth certificate and forever have the day off work. He then ran away to be raised by badgers at the gates of Tartarus. Living by the mantra "If it bleeds, we can kill it," he watched the Battle of Fallujah on TV and promptly joined the Marine Corps as a combat cameraman so he could steal the souls of those killed by the Marines he was with. He deployed to Afghanistan with 2/7 and ¾ in '08, and '09-'10 respectively, then went on a couple of MEUs so he could drink on the ocean and anger sailors by calling their ship a "boat." Tripp spent his decade in the Corps drinking rum, crushing the hopes and dreams of mortals, and chain smoking. He has multiple awards for books he hasn't even written, once deadlifted a battleship, outwitted a sphinx, knows Vicky's secret (it's that she has a penis), is an award winning photographer, and at all times has been the best guitar player in the barracks. Did I mention he's handsome and has a glorious mustache? He's a great storyteller, specializing in fairytales and bullshit. About the only thing he doesn't have is a TV show based on his books (looking at *you* Netflix.) He hopes that you enjoyed this book, but if you didn't it doesn't matter. He already has your money and is currently spending it on strippers, cigarettes, and alcohol.

Made in United States
North Haven, CT
01 May 2023

36134547R00286